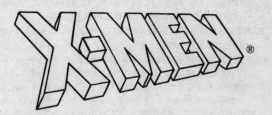

SMOKE AND MIRRORS

X-MEN ®

SMOKE AND MIRRORS

ELUKI BES SHAHAR

ILLUSTRATIONS BY ROGER CRUZ

BYRON PREISS MULTIMEDIA COMPANY, INC.
New York

BOULEVARD BOOKS
New York

Special thanks to Ginjer Buchanan, Steve Roman, Stacy Gittelman, Will Conrad, Ursula Ward, Mike Thomas, Steve Behling, John Conroy, and Carol D. Page.

X-MEN: SMOKE AND MIRRORS

A Boulevard Book
A Byron Preiss Multimedia Company, Inc. Book

PRINTING HISTORY
Boulevard edition / September 1997

All rights reserved.
Copyright © 1997 Marvel Characters, Inc.
Edited by Keith R.A. DeCandido.
Cover art by Greg & Tim Hildebrandt.
Cover and interior design by Claude Goodwin.
This book may not be reproduced in whole or in part,
by mimeograph or any other means, without permission.
For information address: Byron Preiss Multimedia Company, Inc.,
24 West 25th Street, New York, New York 10010.

The Putnam Berkley World Wide Web site address is
http://www.berkley.com

Check out the Byron Preiss Multimedia Co., Inc. site on the World Wide Web:
http://www.byronpreiss.com

Make sure to check out PB Plug, the science fiction/fantasy newsletter, at
http://www.pbplug.com

ISBN 1-57297-291-2

BOULEVARD
Boulevard Books are published by The Berkley Publishing Group,
200 Madison Avenue, New York, New York 10016,
a member of Penguin Putnam Inc.
BOULEVARD and its logo
are trademarks belonging to Berkley Publishing Corporation.

PRINTED IN THE UNITED STATES OF AMERICA

10 9 8 7 6 5 4 3 2 1

AUTHOR'S NOTE

This novel takes place three-and-a-half months after the events chronicled in the short story "It's a Wonderful Life" in the anthology *The Ultimate X-Men*.

CHAPTER 1

Forty miles north of New York City, in the northernmost tip of Westchester County, lies the small town of Salem Center, New York. It is the kind of place that driven Manhattan professionals like to escape *to*: Salem Center is surrounded by riding academies and private schools, all the grace notes of a life of wealth and privilege. It is a community of people who value privacy, where secrets are jealously guarded.

Some secrets, of course, are bigger than others.

On Greymalkin Lane the houses are set far back from the road. Their existence is proclaimed only by the pillars flanking the iron gates of the widely spaced driveways. On one gate in particular, as if identification of what lies within is particularly important, there is a small brass plaque: THE XAVIER INSTITUTE FOR HIGHER LEARNING.

Inside the Institute was a room like any other that you would find in one of the local high-ticket houses: A family room, the heart of the home, one wall filled with futuristic-looking home entertainment electronics fresh from Circuit City, its comfortable couches and tables strewn with half-read books, piles of magazines, and all the other litter of everyday living.

At the moment, the television was on, its channels changing to the rhythm of a restless surfer. Before its unseeing glass eye two people sat on the low comfortable couch (where they could argue about what to watch).

But unlike the house, the room, and the consumer toys, these two people were unlike any in the surrounding houses. Unlike any others in Westchester County, for that matter. These two were unique.

They were mutants.

The young woman scowling indignantly as she pointed the remote control box at the television had the brash prettiness of an all-American prime-time TV heartbreaker. The muscles that moved beneath the kelly-green workout suit she wore suggested professional tennis, or even something more athletic, though she was far too tall and robust to make any Olympic gymnastics team. She had a long white streak running through her unruly chestnut curls, and her Scarlett O'Hara-green eyes narrowed as she blipped from channel to channel almost too fast for the eye to follow—assessing, evaluating, the control box held in her yellow-gloved hands becoming an extension of her will, as if she pointed a weapon.

The man beside her seemed less interested in the programming grid than in his companion. He was tall and rangy, with disheveled brown hair. He had the lived-in face of someone who'd slept rough and lived hard, and mostly by his wits. He was several days late for a shave, and several weeks late for a haircut. He wore a sleeveless denim jacket over a T-shirt and a pair of battered Levi 501's that were gone at the knees. As he watched his companion channel surf, he patted himself down, searching for a pack of cigarettes. He wore fingerless gloves, thin leather that molded to the hand like a second skin.

"Prof don't want you t'smoke in the house, Remy." Rogue's voice was thick with the sound of moonlight and magnolias, but this southern belle was a steel magnolia, raised by the enigmatic Raven Darkhölme—Mystique—and, despite her youth, the veteran already of a lifetime of battles on both sides of the angels.

"*Le bon Charles* don't wan' me to smoke at all, *ma p'tite*," her companion corrected, giving up on the cigarettes and producing a deck of cards instead. He pronounced the name "Sharl," but despite the almost French lilt of his whiskey-and-molasses voice, he came from much the same part of the country Rogue did—only in Gambit's case, it was the bayous of Louisiana, particularly the streets of New Orleans, that the Cajun X-Man called home.

Not that he was likely to see it again any time soon. He'd been barred from returning both by the Thieves Guild he'd struggled so hard to join, and by his duties with the X-Men, where the roving outlaw had at last made an uneasy home for himself.

"Well, you shouldn't. It's nasty," Rogue said crossly.

"Ah, *p'tite,* I am a man wit' so few bad habits, you allow me dis one, *neh*?" He smiled at her, the red glow deep in his eyes kindling to sudden brightness.

"No," Rogue said implacably. "And don't you go tryin' to sweet-talk me, neither, Remy LeBeau. Here we are, with a big-screen color television hooked up to an antenna that can bring in talk shows from the Skrull Galaxy—two million channels, and there ain't a blessed thing to watch on any of 'em." She flounced back into the cushions, tossing the remote onto a table.

"You should broaden your horizons, *chere*. Perhaps de Home Shopping Channel?" Gambit said.

He smiled, turning toward her. Flirting with Rogue was a bittersweet business at best. To touch skin to skin for even the briefest instant meant oblivion—and not the sort a man could like, either—as well the transfer of his mutant power—and even his memories—to Rogue until he awakened, as Gambit already knew from bitter experience. Accidentally prolonging the contact would mean that Gambit's body would live on only as a drained husk, and Gambit himself would be a ghost—his powers, his memories, and all that he was trapped deep inside his lady love's mind.

It made romance a challenge.

Still, Gambit *liked* a challenge.

He'd planned to brush her hair away from her cheek—that much was safe for both of them—when Rogue sat forward again with a squeak and Gambit hastily retreated.

"—hear me? I can see you."

"We see you, Beast—and hear you, too," Rogue said excitedly.

In a small square at the lower right hand corner of the television screen, the fanged, blue-furred visage of Henry P. McCoy—sometimes known as the Beast—glowered worriedly at them.

"Turn to C-SPAN12 right now," Hank said.

"Why?" Rogue said blankly. "Yer callin' me up from the lab t'tell me t'improve my *mind*?"

Ignoring the byplay, Gambit pounced on the television remote and began punching buttons. In a few moments, all of the screen not filled with the inset transmission from Hank's lab was occupied with a high-up view of an auditorium. Both Rogue and Gambit stared at it without comprehension. There didn't seem to be anything here to warrant Hank's urgent tone. The man at the podium was the usual sort of scientist-type: pale and not particularly imposing.

"Looks peaceful," Gambit finally offered.

"You're watching the World Conference on Genetic Research, currently going on in Berne," Hank said. "I had it on for background while I was running a series on the sequencing computer."

"Sort of like MTV for eggheads, *neh*?" Gambit said, looking at the screen. The caption at the bottom of the picture identified the speaker as Dr. Arnold Bocklin of the Center for Genetic Improvement. He was reading from a sheaf of papers, his voice dry and unemotional.

"Hank, sugar, you *know* all this technobabble just goes right over my poor little ol' head," Rogue cooed.

"An' it isn't as if someone shootin' at us, *mon brave*.

How much trouble can dis *homme* make wid his *petite papier, hahn?*''

"Just about this much," the Beast said grimly. "According to Bocklin, he's discovered the chromosome pair which governs somatic morphology in humans, and worse, he believes it to be self-actualizing in nature."

"And that means?" Rogue prompted, after a dead pause.

Hank sighed and tried again.

"What Bocklin says, is that he has not only discovered and mapped one *single* chromosome pair site for human mutation, it is also his opinion that the mutants themselves determine the form their particular mutation will take—and he's devised a treatment protocol. Come on, we've got to alert the Professor."

"But . . . I don't get it," Rogue said. "What does this have to do with the X-Men?"

"How far do I have to spell it out?" Hank snapped in frustration. "If Bocklin's right, he not only knows how mutation is *caused*, but how to reverse it—whether somebody wants it reversed or not."

CHAPTER 2

To the inhabitants of most of the Midwest, Cleveland is where the East begins. Elliot Ness died here, the Cleveland Torso Killer (never captured) racked up a body count here unequalled until Carnage hit the scene, and the mighty Cuyahoga which flows through it has the distinction of being the only American river to ever catch fire. Cleveland is the New American City, the home of the Rock and Roll Hall of Fame, a place where old-fashioned values still (probably) hold sway.

And like every American city, it has some mean streets.

The warehouse district was not a good place to be, even at high noon. Bordered by old houses—more abandoned than condemned—and junk cars on the street, its warehouses and factories stood idle and empty, victims of a recession whose end had somehow never made things here go back to the way they'd been before. The young man walking past all this—the nearest bus stop was blocks away—ignored all of it with the ease of familiarity. That was why they'd picked this place—because it was isolated, because they could all get together without anyone seeing them.

And besides, if anyone down here tried to mug him, Jason Gerber had the power to punch their lights out.

Jason Gerber was a mutant.

Which didn't mean, he reflected, that he wanted to put his mutant power to the test any time soon. It was one thing to find out you were *different*—that for you the First Law of Thermodynamics was just a suggestion—and another thing to do something about it. He wasn't popular and outspoken like Adam—football hero, honors list, all-American jock. Jason was a grind, and a shy grind at that. At seventeen, he didn't even have his learner's permit yet. That was why he'd had to take the bus to get here.

Oh, God, what if his parents found out about this? He'd told them he was going out to study; they trusted him to be home by eleven-thirty at the latest. They wouldn't even check up on him.

Which building was it? He'd been here twice; he ought to remember. It was about seven o'clock Monday night, the week before Thanksgiving—River Street looked too deserted and not deserted enough.

There. Jason found the door—still open a crack—and slipped in.

The place where they met was an old factory. The equipment to do whatever the place had done had been taken out a long time ago, leaving an enormous open space. There'd been an office set up in one corner of the shop floor, shielded by partitions that were now gone, but most of the furniture was still there. That was where the others had gathered—three out of five of them, anyway. Lloyd, the only one of them who hadn't settled on a mutant code name, was late. Well, later than Jason, anyway.

Jason wasn't sure what impulse had prompted the five of them to meet in such secrecy, although they'd done it almost out of instinct. One thing they knew without having to discuss it: if anyone else found out what they were, there'd be trouble. Jason wasn't sure how much trouble, but you heard things, even if you were a kid. Things about the genejokes—the mutants.

Only he'd never liked calling them names just because they were different—enough people called *him* names, and he knew how much it hurt—and he liked calling them names even less now that he knew they weren't "them."

They were "us."

There was no power in the warehouse, of course, but

Adam had brought a battery-powered camping lantern from home, and it was on the desk, casting a surprising amount of light. Adam—no, Jason was supposed to call him Pipe-dream, that was what they'd all agreed on—was sitting on the edge of the desk, paging through a magazine he'd found inside.

Jason (no, it was Slapshot, not Jason) had envied Pipe-dream his blond all-American good looks from the day they'd first met. Nobody ever called *him* names when adults couldn't hear, just as if he weren't as American as they were. Jason had come to the Gerber household from Viet-nam when he'd been six weeks old—he didn't even *speak* Vietnamese—but there were times he thought that nothing, not straight A's, not cool sneaks, not even his own home-page on the World Wide Web, were ever going to make him feel like he had a right to be here. And sometimes he resented Pipedream for that, even though it wasn't Adam's fault.

"Yo, Jase," Pipedream said, setting down the magazine.

"That's Slapshot to you, *Pipedream*," the blonde ice-princess in the biker jacket said. "You're the one who kept saying it'd be, like, so totally awesome if we got these stupid hacker handles. Like, hang out a sign that says 'spir-itually abuse me.' "

"Give it a rest, Rewind," Pipedream said. The girl snorted and ostentatiously turned her back on both of them, her long blonde ponytail swinging like the pendulum of a clock, brushing the back of her black leather biker jacket. She wore a flippy little skirt, black fishnet stockings, and silver Doc Martens, and looked like a renegade from the Ice Capades in Hell—a look only rich WASP princesses could pull off.

And Peyton Conway was all of that.

There was no point in sighing after her, Slapshot told himself once again. Blonde attitude cases only fell for poor-but-honest grinds in bad fiction, even if you didn't play the race card. Peyton Conway belonged to guys like Adam Kirby—her natural prey. Adam and Peyton were the king and the queen of Kirtland High School; the jock and the head of the cheerleading squad. It was almost preordained.

Just like Romeo and Juliet.

"Is, um—Lloyd here yet?" Slapshot asked.

" 'The Dog With No Name'?" Charade asked. "Probably out baying at the moon."

None of them—including Lloyd—were really sure what he could do, although they were all aware of his augmented senses. Lloyd used to joke that he'd been bitten by a radioactive dog, and that was as good a template for his abilities as any. Only . . . what *were* the super powers of a dog, anyway?

Davetta Mantlo—Charade—hung back in the shadows, doing her Spider-Man imitation, Slapshot supposed. She had the lithe compact body of a gymnast—no surprise; she was on the gymnastics team—and her hair was elaborately beaded, the silver, gold, pink, and purple beads giving her the effect of wearing a jewelled helmet. Charade was the only one of them who seemed to think that *mutant superhero* was an entry in the Dictionary of Occupations. In honor of tonight's meeting Charade wore gold crush-boots and a skintight purple and black bodysuit. The only thing spoiling the effect was the fluffy pink fake-fur bomber jacket she wore over everything: it was *cold* here in the warehouse.

She was the youngest of the group—she'd been skipped two grades and got to high school early—and she could be ungodly convincing. In fact, Charade could convince *anyone* of anything, no matter how ridiculous, at least until they had time to think it over. It was the kind of mutant power that made for lynch mobs, something all of them knew and none of them had mentioned.

Jason turned up the collar of his jacket and stuffed his hands deep into his pockets. "You wouldn't try to goof me, would you, *Charade?*'' he asked warily.

''I swear!'' she protested. ''I would *never* use my powers on another member of the Ohio Mutant Conspiracy. I swore.'' Davetta giggled, spoiling the effect of her solemnity.

''That's right,'' Pipedream said. ''We can't risk turning on each other. We've got to stick together.''

''Yeah, well, it'd be a lot easier to stick together if 'No, No, Bad Dog' ever *got* here,'' Rewind snapped.

Rewind, Slapshot reflected, also had a particularly scary power as well as a really cool codename. She could make time skip backwards—if you knocked over a glass full of water, Rewind could set it upright again, full. It was true she couldn't turn time back *far*, but none of them were that old. Maybe their mutant powers would get stronger with age.

Yeah, like having a driver's license and going to college could affect something like a guy's ability to change the trajectory of any moving object.

''Look, maybe we could start without him and fill him in. Lloyd isn't exactly the, um, most proactive guy in the world,'' Pipedream said reluctantly.

''You're the boss, Adam—sorry—Pipedream,'' Slapshot said.

If they'd been going strictly by age, Lloyd Englehart was nineteen and should have been it, but Lloyd had only transferred to Kirtland at the beginning of the year. He was quiet (which Slapshot respected) and had made it clear that while he was in, he'd much rather follow than lead.

So Pipedream had been elected their leader, nearly by default. Slapshot was too shy, Rewind wasn't interested, and nobody in their right mind would trust Charade with the leadership of *anything*.

''*Ada-a-m*, you are seriously mistaking me for somebody who gives a care, you know?'' Rewind said. ''And maybe when we're done with the yippie-dippy Teen Titans part of

the evening we can go get a pizza or something *normal*?
Anybody else want some coffee? I brought a thermos.'' She
dragged her purse out from under the table and pulled out
a big silver thermos and some cups.

Jason suspected she smoked. He'd have to ask Lloyd—
he'd know.

"If my dad gets home and finds out I'm gone, he'll
ground me *forever*," Charade said. "I vote let's get
started."

"Don't worry, Charade, I can run you home after. I've
got my brother's car," Pipedream said. He pulled the collar
of his Airex merino-lined bomber jacket up, just as Slapshot
had done. "Let's do it, and set the time for the next meeting, and get out."

"Yeah," Rewind said, "and could it be, like, someplace
suburban next time? I don't want you guys coming to my
house, right, but could it at least be some place with *heat*?
I mean, the Avengers've got this Manhattan mansion, the
Fantastic Four have a whole *skyscraper*—"

"And we're mutants, and if anybody finds that out
there's going to be a padded cell waiting for each of us,"
Pipedream said. "And for you, *Rewind*, some place in the
CIA's basement."

He didn't look like he wanted to deal with this any more
than Jason did—than any of them did—but they knew that
they had to plan their futures carefully. It had taken them
a long time to realize that each of them was *different*, and
now that they'd managed to find each other, none of them
was really sure what came next.

"So—" Rewind said, drawing out the word in her most
irritating tone. She sipped at her coffee as she sat on the
edge of the desk, swinging one silver Doc Marten back and
forth. "What's next on *Lifestyles of the Mutated and Famous*? I've got cheerleading squad in the morning, so could
we snap this up here? Never mind reading the minutes,

Pipedream: we were all here, remember? So, do we get cool costumes and fight crime?''

''In Cleveland?'' Slapshot asked, bewildered.

"Run away from home?" Rewind persisted.

"Start a superhero group!" Charade cried.

Her voice echoed spookily in the enormous room; the sound seemed to overlay other sounds, hiding them.

Rewind was just opening her mouth to say something cutting, when there were several loud scuffling, banging sounds, and Lloyd Englehart appeared.

"Run!" Lloyd yelled. "There's guys—all over the place—outside—"

He skidded to a stop halfway across the room, his flannel shirt flapping open to reveal the usual "Lila Cheney and the Nazgul" T-shirt.

"Run!" Lloyd yelled again. He had a red gimme cap turned backward on his head, and beneath it his pale face was strained and scared.

The other four stared at him. Rewind set down her coffee. Charade half-raised her hand, as if she couldn't decide whether to wave hello or not.

Lloyd made shooing motions at the others with his hands. Ineffectual, silly—and somehow all the more frightening for that, as if they'd suddenly been drafted into the world's first reality-programming spatter sitcom.

Still they didn't move. Slapshot realized that he could hear an engine—a big one—idling outside.

He was turning toward Pipedream—slowly, everything seemed to move so slowly—when the wall of brick that passed for windows blew in behind them.

It didn't so much shatter as vaporize. The whole wall broke inward like the water from a smashed fish tank, the fragments glittering like thrown diamonds in the spotlights shining on them from outside.

Rewind screamed, sounding more angry than frightened. As if the sound had been a signal, the four of them finally began moving, crossing the floor toward the door.

Too little, too late. Men in black Kevlar came in through every opening in the building, all carrying guns and wearing visors similar to full-coverage Bell motorcycle helmets. One of them had already grabbed Lloyd.

Lloyd Englehart was stronger than any ordinary teenager, and far faster. But he'd never tried to hurt anyone before—a failing that had gotten him dropped from junior varsity in his freshman year back home in Atlanta. Now it cost him. He struggled for a moment with his faceless attacker.

"Leave him alone!"

Slapshot didn't know why he did it—he was already terrified, and the others had scattered. He grabbed the nearest heavy thing he could find—an ashtray made out of a cast steel fitting—and threw it.

It didn't matter what direction he picked to toss it in; as soon as it was an object in motion, it was his to command. Slapshot grabbed the ashtray with his mutant power, and the moment he did, it fell *up*.

Up again, in a different direction. Up again, for speed. Then sideways—then a right-angle turn—then down.

The ashtray struck the man holding Lloyd squarely between the shoulder blades. He let go of Lloyd, but it did no good—Lloyd ran directly into a blast of yellow gas. Jason heard him howl in agony. He could smell it from here. Tear gas. And if you had an animal's enhanced senses. . . .

But Jason had spent too much time attacking someone else's enemy. Suddenly light and sound were cut off as a hood was thrown over his head. And, as he struggled against the hands holding it tight about his throat, he realized that the air was cut off as well. The hood sealed itself against his face like wet linen, and he could feel his heart lugging in his chest as the noise of the gunshots suddenly seemed unimportant and far, far away . . .

• • •

Rewind heard fabric tear, and thought she heard Lloyd growl. *Way to go, homeboy.* There were gunshots and other noises—engines, shouting, the slow *whup-whup-whup* of a helicopter—and the dimness of the old factory was a chiaroscuro crazy-quilt of black and bright, dazzling and deceptive. Rewind ran, away from the noise and the invaders, looking for another way out.

The fire door at the end of the room was unlocked—she went through it, and realized that was a mistake. It provided no access to the outside, only a closed staircase leading up. But the door had locked behind her. There was no going back.

At least, not for anyone human.

Reality twisted like slow smoke, and Rewind shoved at the door a second before it closed. She shoved it open just in time to see somebody club Charade—giggly, silly Davetta—in the back with a rifle butt.

Nope. Can't go out there, a tiny part of her mind said with terrified reasonableness. Her heart was hammering with the effort of forcing time backward only a few seconds; there was no way she could shove time far back enough to make a space for them all to escape in.

The door was wrenched out of her hands.

"Adam!"

He shoved past her as if he didn't see her, then turned back, snatching the door to slam it again.

"Come on," he gasped, panting. "I tried putting a dream on them, but there's too many of them."

He started up the stairs.

"You can't go that way! There isn't anything there— just the roof!" Rewind cried.

Pipedream turned to look at her. His eyes were wide and scared. "You want to go back out there?" he demanded. "Listen, Pey—this is real. Those are Federal Marshals out there—not a dream, not a hoax, not an imaginary tale: this time our hero really dies. Now come *on*.'' He started up the stairs.

The building shook, and a flare of light shone through the small glass square window in the fire door. Rewind swore under her breath, staring at the door. She couldn't get the door open again—her rewind power wouldn't reach far enough back in time. She glanced up the stairs. Pipedream stood on the landing, looking down at her.

"Come on," he whispered desperately. Rewind started up the stairs after him.

She'd thought he was heading for the roof, but the fire stairs also opened onto the second floor: overhanging balconies in a short horseshoe shape around the short end of the building. The five of them had propped both of this level's interior fire doors open when they'd first explored the warehouse, and this one was still open. Pipedream eased the door open. Nobody here. He started forward, and froze.

No, wait. One man. There was one of them up here— Pipedream could see the white stencil with the words U.S. MARSHAL across his back. Why were the U.S. Marshals after the five of them—for trespassing?

Maybe it was all a mistake. Maybe they thought they were drug smugglers, or Hydra, or—

"Peek-a-boo, Hansel and Gretel. Time to say goodnight," the man said. As he spoke he turned toward them, moving with a spooky grace, as if he were some kind of Terminator, until the faceless black helmet was turned toward them, and Pipedream could see his reflection in it.

His heart hammered painfully—he couldn't even ask Rewind to undo this, because she'd just used her power. It usually took her a while to recharge. It was up to him. He reached out, praying—this time more than ever—that it would work, that it would *still* work, that a mutant power that often seemed like half-understood magic even to him would do what he hoped and save both of their lives.

"No tricks, prep boy," the masked marauder said.

Pipedream felt himself cast it—like a delicate pull all over the surface of his skin.

The barrel of the Marshal's gun swung toward them . . . and then away, the muzzle pointing toward the ground as the man, whoever he was, went off into a pipedream.

"Come on," Pipedream said in a shaky voice, pulling Rewind after him out onto the catwalk. The offices on the second floor were all cubicles built around the edges. He pulled open the door of the first one. He didn't know how much longer he could stay on his feet—he'd hit the man with everything he had, and the effort left him weak.

"How long?" Rewind said. Pipedream shook his head wordlessly. He had no idea how long the man's pipedream would last—not long, with all the distracting noise around them.

Some kind of leader he turned out to be. He'd run out on his teammates without a single thought. But there had been so much noise. It had all happened so fast. He hadn't been able to think of anything else to do.

This office, too, still had most of its furniture, as if it hadn't been worth taking when the warehouse closed. The windows had been blown in—what had crumbled the brick had powdered the window glass, and it lay in drifts over everything like sugar. Something in the street was shining a bright light directly in through the window, making the powdered glass sparkle like fallen snow and cast long black shadows across the street.

"Now what?" Rewind demanded. Tears of anger and fear glittered in her eyes. "If we go out that window they'll see us."

"Hide," Pipedream said simply.

Rewind was small and supple—Pipedream helped her crawl into the credenza and shut the door on her. Then he crawled under the desk, wedged himself into the footwell, and prayed—that the light would stay on, so nobody could get a good look at their footprints in the dust and powdered glass on the floor; that the man he'd hit with a pipedream would forget he'd ever seen them; that with all the noise they were making, the Marshals didn't have time for a thorough search.

But they were the *U.S. Marshals*, for God's sake! They were the law! They could take all the time they wanted. *This was such a stupid idea*, the leader of the Ohio Mutant Conspiracy thought. There had to be a better one.

But before he could think of it, he heard voices on the catwalk outside—shouts, and running feet.

No one came in.

The light outside went off. The darkness was like a blow. More shouts—these coming from outside—and then the idling engine moved away.

Darkness. Silence.

Before he could stop her, Rewind squirmed out of the credenza and ran for the door.

"No—wait!" Pipedream yelled. It took him several seconds to untangle himself from the desk and follow her, but she hadn't gone far. She was standing right outside the door, leaning over the catwalk, looking down at the floor below.

The camping lantern had been smashed, but with the brick pulverized, the streetlights provided enough illumination to see. The sharp tang of tear gas still hung in the air, but most of it was coiled near the floor in a white mist, already dissipating in the open air. Where the floor could be seen, it sparkled with broken glass.

Except for the two of them, the warehouse was empty.

"What happened to them?" Rewind demanded, as if he should know. "What did they do with our friends?"

CHAPTER 3

Putnam County, New York. North of Westchester the terrain changes, becoming a verdant panorama that seems unaltered from that which the first Dutch explorers saw almost four centuries before. Here the mighty Hudson River—broad and slow and almost clean—rolls slowly south, through dramatic gorges and rolling emerald hills. There's talk about making the river corridor into a greenway but, like similar bills before legislatures the country over, it looks like all the greenway's going to be for the foreseeable future *is* talk.

Meanwhile, Hudson Valley New Yorkers heading back to Nature get by with the region's many parks and wilderness areas—and, of course, the river itself, renowned as a pleasure boater's paradise.

Case in point: Bear Mountain State Park, just south of West Point Military Academy, on a bright sunny November day, sharp and cool but not yet settled into cold, grey winter.

Most of the surrounding hillsides were already brown, but here and there a lingering red-and-gold tree stood out like a rare jewel against the evergreens, maples, oaks, and birch. Midweek, the river had little pleasure traffic—most people had put up their sailboats and cabin cruisers already, waiting for spring—though the colliers and barges that plied the river from Canada to the Atlantic still went on about their workaday business.

There was one pleasure craft, however, which had not yet knuckled under to approaching winter. Anchored out of the path of the commercial traffic, a small white powerboat rocked gently to and fro.

A young woman was at the wheel, her flowing red hair as bright as the remaining fall foliage. She wore white jeans and a light blue sweater, her only concession to the season a down vest in a darker shade of blue.

She turned toward her companion, who was concentrating on something at the back of the boat.

"Scott?"

No reply.

"Scott? Husband? Darling? Lover?"

Silence. The man continued intent upon what he was doing. Sunlight gleamed down on his brown hair and glinted off the nearly opaque redness of the heavy light-blocking glasses he wore. He was dressed, as was his companion, in clothing suitable for a late autumn riparian outing—down jacket and a rugby shirt, khakis, deck shoes—but the wiry intensity of the man suggested he'd be more at home in a dark suit and a trenchcoat, maybe with a gun.

That guess would not be quite correct. While it was true that today's outfit was far from his usual garb, the man in the sunglasses didn't need a gun to wreak destruction on a scale undreamed of until the first H-bombs.

"Darling, the boat is sinking," the woman said.

"In a minute," Scott said, distractedly.

Jean Grey smiled with wry exasperation. She should have known that the moment she let Scott turn on that laptop, his attention would be absolutely elsewhere.

So, she smiled wickedly to herself, *why don't we just see how far elsewhere?*

With a simple mental command, Jean—the X-Man known sometimes as Phoenix—telekinetically lifted Scott Summers thirty feet into the air, holding him suspended above the river.

"Hey!" Scott protested, looking up.

"Ah, you noticed," Jean called up. "You know, this was supposed to be a day off for us—*together*—not me talking to myself while you surf the net on an atomic powered laptop with a satellite uplink."

"I promised Hank I'd check this out for him under field conditions," Scott pointed out. "You should be grateful; most husbands would be checking out football scores on a battery-operated TV."

"Field conditions, eh?" Jean said. Scott rose a few feet higher into the air above the river. "Give me one good reason, husband mine, that you and that box shouldn't check out field conditions at the bottom of the river?"

"Because without me you haven't the ghost of a chance of winning the Scully and Mulder Lookalike Couples Contest?" Scott suggested meekly.

Despite his tone, his lips curved in a rare smile, and Jean was pleased to see that he'd set aside, even for this brief moment, the enormous burden of responsibility that every X-Man lived under—Scott most of all.

Scott had been the first X-Man that Professor Charles Xavier recruited, and for years had been their only field leader. When X-Men—and even their sworn enemies—had died, it was Scott who felt he bore the accountability for their deaths, striving against chance, fate, and the X-Men's own treacherous luck to bring off victory in the face of insurmountable opposition and to gain success against the most overwhelming odds.

"So you think—" Jean began, and stopped. She was talking to herself again. Something on the screen had nailed Scott's attention, even thirty feet up.

Better go see what it is. With the briefest of thoughts, Jean willed herself into the air, as gracefully as if the air were an ocean she could navigate at will. In a moment she was hovering just behind her husband, looking over his shoulder at the screen.

"Well?" she prompted, leaning an elbow against his

shoulder. Scott was what he was; there was no point in trying to change him. She'd come to terms with that years ago.

"It's . . . odd," Scott said slowly. There was a sort of reluctance in his voice, as if to speak his disquiet aloud would somehow make it more real. "One of my usual newsgroups—alt.mutant.discuss—is carrying a lot of posts about a new bill before Congress."

"And?" Jean prompted. He'd worried her, but she tried not to let it show in her voice. She and Scott had faced the assembled might of the Shi'ar Imperial Guard, the government-sponsored Sentinels, even the unleashed fury of their deadliest foe, Magneto, together. It took a lot to upset a man like Scott Summers.

"HR-485—the Emergency Intervention Bill—is coming up for a final vote in about ten days. If it becomes law, it would make refusing treatment for a correctable medical condition a federal offense—which seats it in the bizarre, not threatening, section. I guess."

"Bizarre is right," Jean said, ruffling his hair in her relief. "But not a threat to world peace, right? And not a job for the X-Men. Besides, it'll never get out of committee."

"You're probably right," Scott said, but not as if he were convinced. "But it's gotten this far." He looked up from the screen, only now seeming to remember where he was. He closed the laptop and offered it to his wife.

"If I promise not to open it for the rest of the day?" he said meekly.

Jean smiled. "Well, okay. If you promise to be good . . ."

The two of them began drifting downward, toward the powerboat. Scott smiled.

"Lady, I have it on the best authority that I'm—"

Scott! Jean! The contact was never less than unsettling for all its familiarity. It was the telepathic voice of Professor Charles Xavier, founder of the X-Men.

"Yes, Professor, we hear you," Jean said calmly.

She spoke aloud so that Scott could hear her, and because there was no one nearby. Nothing that any of the X-Men did could ever be allowed to endanger Charles Xavier's most precious secret—that he himself was a mutant, born at a time when their numbers were still few. It was his dream that the X-Men followed, a dream of a world in which mutant and human could live together in trust and harmony. As often as the world had attacked his dream, Xavier had stood firm, rekindling the dream from the ashes of its numerous defeats, until his followers had begun to believe that the flame he kindled might truly be eternal.

I'm sorry to interrupt your holiday. But I need you back at the Institute. Please return as soon as possible. The contact was broken, and Scott and Jean looked at each other.

"I wonder what . . . ?" Jean said.

"If it were vital that we know immediately, he'd have told us," Scott said, sliding in behind the wheel of the speedboat and reaching for the ignition.

"Which is why we aren't flying back immediately," Jean finished for him, completing the thought. "But there's no reason for us to dawdle, either."

She set the laptop down on the seat and concentrated. A haze of ionized air appeared around her body, sparkling faintly even in the bright sunlight, and the slender fiberglass hull of the boat rose free of the water and swung back in the direction of Westchester. As Phoenix concentrated, the hovering boat began to move forward, skimming along just above the surface of the river. It was fortunate that they weren't likely to run into any speed cops along the river; the powerboat was doing better than thirty knots, and still accelerating. As it brushed the waves, arcs of water jetted up from the stern; any on-shore observer would have been easily misled into believing that this was some sort of hydroplane.

"We should be there in half an hour," Phoenix called over the roar of the wind.

Cyclops nodded, but his face had already settled into the grim mask of duty. Playtime was over. Somewhere in the world, there was another job for the X-Men.

CHAPTER 4

The main conference room in the underground complex beneath the Xavier Institute for Higher Learning in Northern Westchester was fully occupied, though the total number of occupants was few, considering how many mutants called this mansion home. Only eight X-Men were present.

"Where *is* everybody?" Rogue asked, looking around in mild confusion.

"I've already sent them off," Charles Xavier said. "We have an enormous task ahead of us, my X-Men."

He was the most powerful telepath on Earth, one of the most formidable mutants. Professor Charles Xavier appeared to be a man of average build and middle years, confined to a wheelchair. In a room filled with extraordinary men and women, the only extraordinary things about Charles Xavier were his completely hairless skull—his hair, lost while still in his teens, had been blond—and his piercing blue eyes. Though an accident had confined him to a wheelchair—or, when away from public eyes, an alien-built hoverchair—Xavier was far from helpless, as his legion of enemies knew to their sorrow.

"Sent them off?" Rogue said, in response to Xavier's answer. "Sent them *where*?"

"Take it easy, Rogue. I'm sure Charles has a good reason—and is about to tell it to us," Psylocke said.

The tall dark-haired Asian woman with the striking red brand across her face was the sister of one superhero and the lover of another. As all of them, she wore her battle-dress: a dark blue combat suit—an evolution of ninja harness—cut out over the shoulders and high on the thighs to allow for maximum freedom of movement. Like Jean Grey, Betsy Braddock—Psylocke—was a telepath, but Betsy's psi-powers were focused into one formidable weapon: a psychic knife that she could use to immobilize a foe in seconds. Combined with her martial arts abilities, her psionic weapons made Psylocke a formidable enemy . . . but her checkered past made her a very troubled woman.

Xavier smiled faintly. "Yes, of course, Psylocke, and I'll come to that soon—but first, I want all of you to see what Rogue and Gambit saw a part of a little earlier today. Scott, if you'd get the lights?"

Scott Summers—Cyclops—reached to dim the lights, and in a moment all eight X-Men watched a replay of yesterday's proceedings of the International Conference on Genetic Research, held in Berne, Switzerland. They watched in silence as Dr. Arnold Bocklin presented his paper on "Selected Treatment Applications of Auto-Iatrogenic Somatic Morphology Reversal in Homo Sapiens."

The wind-riding mutant elemental Storm watched the image on the screen. Her arms were folded across her chest, bringing the long silver wings of her battle-dress around her and giving her the look of some exquisite, dangerous flower. Her eyes, narrowed now with the suspicion of danger, were startlingly blue against her dark skin, their slit pupils narrowed. As co-leader with Cyclops of the X-Men, she looked for danger everywhere, hoping to find it and avert it before she or any of her comrades must offer battle. Her long white hair cascaded forward, hiding her face from the other X-Men. Years of solitude—as an orphan on the streets of Cairo, stealing to survive; as a goddess, living among her mother's people on the Serengeti—had prepared her for the loneliness of command, but not for the fact that she must constantly risk the lives of those she had come to love.

Storm glanced across the room at Cyclops. The face and

eyes of the X-Men's other field leader were forever masked behind his gold-and-ruby battle visor, whose cybernetic controls allowed Scott Summers pinpoint control of his deadly optic blasts, but the woman who had once been only Ororo Munroe could sense a similar bleak mood in him. A new threat had surfaced out of the turbulent sea of life in which they all swam, and once more the X-Men must rise to fight it.

Wolverine studied Ororo without turning his head. His blue-and-yellow costume gave him the absurdly cheerful look of a harmless tropical fish, but it had been designed by his overseers to keep him visible under even the most inauspicious circumstances. The man who now answered to Wolverine more easily than to his own name—Logan—had been fashioned as a weapon, and any sane person liked to know where their weapons were at all times. He'd experimented with other rigs—he wasn't so fond of Canada's Project X that he exactly wanted a memento of his time with them—but he always returned in the end to the garish blue-and-yellow.

It was safer for the men and women he fought beside.

Wolverine didn't need to listen to Bocklin's presentation. He already knew the bad news—somebody else had discovered a cure for mutants. A weary anger gripped his bones like gravity. Fifty years—a war that had cost millions of innocent lives and scarred millions more irrevocably—and humanity had not learned to stop meddling with itself. Call it evolution, eugenics, selective breeding . . . someone was always coming up with a new reason to decide who should live and who should die. And who should be changed.

We shall not die; we shall all be changed. A line from a burial service spun through his mind—and hadn't the man called Wolverine buried enough friends and allies in his life? His mutant healing factor did nothing to mend those kinds of wounds. The deadly adamantium claws that he could extend from his knuckles could not cut away the grief. An animal's enhanced senses could not point out a path that led away from it.

Losses. They mounted up through the years, like nacre forming an ever larger pearl. Because someone always wanted to meddle with the way human race was—humans with humans, humans with mutants, mutants with humans.

Nobody's hands were clean.

And now here was Arnold Bocklin. Wolverine shook his head, impatient for the travelogue to be over so that Chuck would cut to the chase. The tension in the room was palpable—he could smell it.

Cyke was pretty calm—but he'd been through a lot in the years since Chuck'd recruited him, and he knew enough, even for a young punk, not to borrow trouble. Jeannie usually kept her feelings pretty much under wraps; no action there. 'Roro was angry, but government meddling put her on a short fuse, something nobody knew better than he did.

Betsy was the calmest of them—nothing like a little ninja mind-over-body-control to fool your enemies into not even thinking you were there. Whatever came down, 'Locke would rip its throat out. Said it discouraged recidivism.

Wolverine would put it more bluntly: dead men didn't shoot back. But he was an X-Man now, and he played by their rules when he could. The trouble was, everybody who said that violence never solved anything was wrong. Violence solved quite a lot—just ask the dodo, the passenger pigeon, any of a hundred species that human bloodlust had wiped from the planet. The trouble was, violence only made more problems.

After all, look at Rogue. It'd taken Chuck years of banging it into the steel magnolia's head that a fist in the face wasn't the best initial approach, and Rogue was apt to forget the lesson the moment she got excited. She looked like she wanted to punch something right now, and didn't look like she was going to be too fussy about what it was. The leather jacket with the X-team flashes that she wore over her green-and-gold battle-dress gave her a faint resemblance to a fighter pilot; young, cocky, and reckless.

That part was right. But Rogue didn't need a plane—or a bay full of bombs—to do as much damage as any F-18, Harrier, or Tomcat. She could fly, she could hit—while she'd still been running with Mystique she'd taken on Ms. Marvel and walked away the winner. And she had a pretty short fuse.

Her little Cajun buddy was just the opposite, at least on the surface. Gambit leaned against the wall just behind Rogue, making playing cards appear and disappear between his fingers in the way that an ordinary man might fidget with a pencil. The long leather trenchcoat he wore concealed his costume, making him look almost normal.

But then, Wolverine reflected, all the X-Men were passing for normal, and some of them were better at it than others. Remy LeBeau liked everyone to believe he bought in to the myth of the Big Easy: no problems New Orleans, where Gambit had first run up against Storm. But the easygoing façade was only that: a false front. Wolverine had seen Sabretooth make Gambit lose his cool completely. There was more to the Cajun than Gambit wanted anyone—even his teammates, especially Rogue—to see.

He supposed he could sympathize, Wolverine thought. God knew he had enough unshared secrets of his own to fill the books in Chuck Xavier's fancy library upstairs. But secrets always came back to haunt their keepers—and when the time came they exacted a blood-price.

He hoped Gambit's number was a long way from coming up, for all their sakes.

Gambit saw Wolverine watching him—on the tape, Bocklin was going on about more things than any man had a right to know about the human body, and Gambit let his mind wander just a bit—and knew that Wolverine watched him because the bloodthirsty little *Canadien* didn't trust him. But that was a fine joke, because sometimes Gambit didn't trust himself.

None of them really trusted each other. Oh, maybe Scott and *la belle Jeanne* and their friend *le Bête*—and Stormy had a good heart. But down deep inside Psylocke was hard— much too hard for a poor Cajun boy like Remy to feel really relaxed around—and it was difficult to forget how Wolverine had run with Sabretooth and the *vaurien* Maverick for years before the X-Men had taken him in.

Of course, there were things Gambit had done that he wasn't too proud of, and things he'd rather his new teammates didn't ask after any too hard. And there was trust and trust. He trusted the others to stand up with him in a fight—to help when things got down to the dirty end. If he needed a rescue—and even Gambit was willing to admit there were times you couldn't do it all yourself—he didn't doubt that any of them would put their lives on the line for the slimmest chance of saving his.

But trust, to Gambit, meant even more than that. Trust was about forgiveness. There were some things he wasn't sure he could forgive his teammates.

And there were some things he was certain they couldn't forgive him.

The tape rolled to a close and Cyclops moved to bring up the lights. The last image, that remained frozen on the screen, was a close-up of Bocklin's face.

There was something about Bocklin's face that made it the face of a dangerous man.

"Yesterday morning," Professor Xavier said, "Dr. Arnold Bocklin presented that paper to the World Council on Genetic Research, an international information-sharing organization currently holding its annual meeting in Berne,

Switzerland. Dr. Bocklin believes he's discovered what amounts to an on/off switch for human mutation, and current events lead me to believe that his discovery will have the direst consequences for mutantkind.''

An electric thrill of dismay coursed through his listeners at Xavier's words, and Gambit took a step closer to Rogue. For as long as any of them had known him, Professor Charles Xavier had been steadfast in his belief that human and mutant were one race who could live together in harmony. For him to draw a distinction between human and mutantkind—even in the most neutral terms—argued that the outlook for *homo sapiens superior* was grim indeed.

''Cut to the chase, Chuck,'' Wolverine growled.

''Please be patient, Wolverine. I've been watching matters coalesce for several months, and the situation is rather complex. Since Bocklin's name first surfaced in connection with HR-485, the Emergency Intervention Bill, I've done some investigating into his past. Arnold Bocklin seems to have appeared out of nowhere about twenty years ago and rose swiftly in international scientific circles. He has no past; no existence outside his work, which has been uniformly brilliant.''

''That's not completely unlikely, Professor,'' the Beast said after a moment. ''You know these Type-A Geniuses; all science, no philosophy.'' His words were light, but his broad furry face was drawn into an expression that resembled savage anger but was in reality deep concern.

''That is, of course, a possibility I'll bear in mind, Hank, and I hope that it's the case—but I suspect our Dr. Bocklin of being a cover identity,'' Xavier said.

In other words, Chuck, you've already made up your mind. So stop makin' us jump through hoops and lay it out, Wolverine thought irritably. He already had suspicions of his own about Bocklin, and they made him uneasy. But he wasn't ready to share them with the others. Not yet.

''But if the Bocklin identity is only a cover, who is it a

cover for?'' Phoenix asked, voicing the question many of the X-Men had. ''Who would go to all the trouble of masquerading as a famous scientist? What's the point, Professor?'' She glanced at her husband, as if he might be the one who had the answers.

''Not masquerading, Phoenix,'' Xavier corrected her gently. ''Whoever he is in reality, Bocklin is a fabulously gifted researcher. It may be that this identity conceals someone who has a tainted past. Or the truth could be something more sinister.''

''Or he could be jus' what he looks like—a workaholic science geek without a life,'' Rogue burst out impatiently. Her expression and her stance both indicated smoldering anger—and the bulldog stubbornness that made her such a dangerous foe. ''I'm sorry, Professor, but for the life of me I just can't see what all the fuss is about.''

Wolverine looked as if he were about to speak. Storm stared at him questioningly, but he shook his head, looking away.

Storm said, ''What it means, Rogue, is that Bocklin has given humanity the power to meddle in people's lives—indeed, in their very destinies. And it is a power I do not think that fragile humanity is ready to arrogate to itself.''

Rogue still looked puzzled—and truculent.

''Indeed, Ororo,'' said Xavier. ''Whether Bocklin is who he appears to be or not—and he's remarkably difficult to locate—his research has already borne more bitter fruit than any he mentioned in Berne. Not only has he isolated the x-factor in human DNA, my sources tell me that apparently Bocklin has already developed a form of experimental gene therapy to convert mutants into what the report I saw refers to as 'normal human beings'.''

''In other words, friends, Bocklin's treatment can convert any mutant into *homo sapiens*,'' the Beast said.

''Yeah?'' Gambit said, a little uneasily. ''The X-Men, we been in dat fix before. Can't no one reshuffle de hand we been dealt at birth, I t'ink me. Not for keeps.''

"That's the point," Hank said impatiently. "This time it *is* for keeps, my friends. Reconfiguration on a genetic level—which is what Arnie, in his quaint scientific fashion, means by iatrogenic somatic morphology. What Bocklin has discovered is a more insidious technique than simply suppressing or removing the mutant powers. He uses a retrovirus for delivery, and with this recombinant-DNA gene-therapy he's pioneered, the subject's neurochemistry itself is reconfigured. In other words, my kinetically-charged Cajun friend, not only your powers would be gone, but so would the part of your brain that told you how to use them. *Tabula rasa*—or, in the lingua franca of the people, back to square one.''

"That doesn't sound particularly friendly," Psylocke said in neutral tones. The British-born ninja looked and sounded calm, but, like so much about Psylocke, it was an act, a deception. To be a ninja was to embrace the art of deception. "But so far his research is only that, isn't it? Research?''

"No, it—'' Jean began, but Rogue interrupted her.

"So just tell me where the downside is in all this?'' Rogue demanded. "Why's everyone so hot and bothered about somethin' goin' on in *Switzerland*, f'heaven's sake? So this guy Bocklin's got a magic pill that will turn any of us human. What's so *wrong* with that? What's so wrong with bein' human? Haven't we all wanted to just be human at one time or another? Tell me that y'all haven't dreamed about it just once.''

No one answered her. There was too much truth in Rogue's words. Scott, Jean, Logan, Ororo, Betsy, Hank, Remy, and Rogue herself—each one of the X-Men had prayed at some time or another in their lives for the cursed blessing of his or her particular mutant power to be taken away. Cyclops's deadly optic blasts that he could not turn off, the Beast's grotesque furry form, Wolverine's half-bestial nature. And Rogue who, since she was a young girl in Mississippi, had not touched another human being bare skin to bare skin except as an act of war.

"That isn't the point, Rogue," Phoenix said soothingly. Though she had a temper as fiery as her red hair, Phoenix was often the peacemaker, making X-Men from a spectrum of different backgrounds—and, sometimes, universes— work together in harmony. She was Storm's dearest friend, and Logan still loved her. But despite her best efforts, she and Rogue had never quite managed to make a personal connection.

"The point," Professor Xavier explained, cutting across the others, "is that nobody is going to be given a voluntary choice about accepting Bocklin's 'therapy' and reverting to *homo sapiens*. Bocklin's research is backed by a private-sector group called the Center for Genetic Improvement, a Georgia-based multinational corporation that my sources tell me will be awarded one of the many government contracts that the passage of HR-485 will necessitate."

"But HR-485 is about emergency medical treatment," Phoenix said. "What does that have to do with mutants?"

"In relation to the bill itself, nothing," Cyclops said slowly. "The body of the bill is very specific about what it covers: genetic defects, catastrophic illness care, inherited conditions. They're very specific because the bill also provides for the refusal of treatment to be considered a federal felony. Treatment is *compulsory*—but there's nothing about mutants there. Only a rider to HR-485 was added late last year while the bill was coming up for its vote in the Senate. And it specifically classifies mutation as a genetic defect."

"Indeed, Cyclops," Professor Xavier said. "And once the bill and its rider classifying mutation as a genetic defect—a medical condition, in essence—have passed—"

"—every mutant who refuses to submit to Bocklin's process becomes an automatic criminal, and gets the gene therapy anyway," Scott Summers said grimly.

"Sounds more like shock therapy to me," Psylocke muttered.

"Yes, my X-Men," Xavier said. "It seems so innocuous: a simple bill—one of thousands placed before the government each year, its intent buried beneath pages of legal terminology. Without Bocklin's breakthrough, the bill is no threat—if there *is* no treatment, how can it be a crime to refuse it?

"But the bill is being rushed through the legislative process with frightening speed, backed by its sponsor, Senator Stewart Chisam. There's already an arrest list of known mutants who are to be taken into government custody and 'treated' as soon as the legislation rendering the action legal has been passed. I've sent the rest of the X-Men to get as many of them to safety as they can against the possibility of the bill's passage. It is up to us to stop its passage—or at the very least, to find and persuade Bocklin and CGI to withhold the gene therapy until the law can be overruled."

"Quit jerking around," Wolverine growled. "Why don't we just go down to CGI headquarters and rip the place apart—an' how do we know this stuff even works?"

Wolverine crouched where he stood, the formidable weight of muscle across his shoulders and arms making his body seem almost as distorted as the Beast's. His fists were clenched, the six deadly foot-long claws housed in his forearms seemingly on the verge of popping out. None of the X-Men were strangers to violence, but Wolverine carried an aura of violence always with him like a deadly cloak.

"We don't know, Logan. At this point, Bocklin's therapy has only been used on volunteers: criminals who have—technically at least—agreed to undergo the treatment. What happens to them afterward is something I haven't yet been able to find a satisfactory answer to."

None of the X-Men liked this answer. Wolverine growled, deep in his throat.

"As for launching a preemptive strike at the Center for

Genetic Improvement,'' Xavier continued, ''we have no right to take such extralegal actions, Logan. Consider the level of intolerance that allowed HR-485 to proceed as far as it has. Any overt assault by mutants at this time would influence public opinion to the point that it would very nearly *guarantee* the bill's passage.''

''Speaking of results, computer simulations I've run using Bocklin's data suggest that the reversion process is potentially lethal,'' the Beast said, struggling for a dry academic tone. Despite his efforts, the outrage still sounded in his voice as he added, ''Which means that Bocklin's gene therapy is about as safe as Russian roulette. As for how many people would die if it went into use nationwide—that I can't tell you. The computer model is only as exact as the published information, and the good doctor may be playing coy with us.''

''Garbage in, garbage out,'' Rogue grumbled sullenly.

''Even one death from Dr. Bocklin's gene-therapy is unacceptable,'' Cyclops said unyieldingly.

''Unfortunately, the bill's more radical advocates don't see things as clearly as that, Cyclops,'' Professor Xavier said. ''The question of the retrovirus's potential harm has already been raised more than once; Bocklin's advocates say that fatalities are irrelevant, since its victims are, in any event, not human beings. Even so, the potential fatality rate is one of the things that has kept the bill mired in committee, though it seems now that this last barrier will soon fall.''

''And then they start rounding people up,'' Psylocke said. ''Here. In America.'' The others could hear the bafflement in her voice—the legacy of the bone-deep English belief in fair play and right. Whatever strange paths Psylocke might have travelled to adulthood, as a child, Elisabeth Braddock had believed that God was an Englishman.

''Oh, they already have, darlin','' Wolverine said cynically. "*I* would, before I went this far public. It's basic strategy."

"And the more people they do it to, the fewer are left to complain," Phoenix said. "Professor, can't you stop it?" she said. There was a note of pleading in her voice.

"I'm trying, Jean. I'm flying to Washington tomorrow to see if I can get Senator Chisam to withdraw his support for the bill—and to see if there is any way to contact Dr. Bocklin through him, as my attempts to reach him through CGI have not been fruitful. You, Scott, Ororo, and Betsy will accompany me.

"Hank, you, Rogue, Logan, and Gambit must attempt to discover the location of Dr. Bocklin's research facility—is it in Atlanta, or located elsewhere? You may go to Atlanta if you must, but I must stress that extreme circumspection in your activities is vital at this time. If the X-Men should be seen to be acting in an extralegal fashion, attempting to block this bill outside of Constitutional means . . ."

"We do their work for them," the Beast said.

"So de X-Men, we fin' de *sce'le'rats* who ruin such a lovely day," Gambit said sarcastically. "An' den we ask dem ver' nice if dey stop bodderin' us, *hahn*?" He ran his hand over his unshaven chin and looked skeptical.

"And if they don't, well, I guess I'll just have to get a little personal," Rogue chimed in savagely, clenching her fists.

The Beast opened his mouth to argue with her—why wasn't Wolverine saying anything? He was the one who usually jumped down Rogue's throat when she went shooting her mouth off like that—and then closed it again. Let her blow off some steam; the immediacy of this new threat was a shock to all of them.

And when he glanced at Wolverine, Wolverine was looking away from Rogue, toward the image of Arnold Bocklin still captured on the screen.

Henry McCoy was not normally a fanciful man, but for

a moment he almost thought he'd mistaken the look on the feisty Canadian X-Man's face. But no. It was there, and Hank knew what it was.

It was fear.

CHAPTER 5

I t was evening at the Xavier Institute for Higher Learning, but the mansion hummed with activity, as Xavier prepared for his trip to Washington on the midnight flight, and the other X-Men—Psylocke, Storm, Rogue, Wolverine, Phoenix, Cyclops, Gambit, and the Beast—either helped Xavier with preparations for his trip or aided Hank McCoy in his attempts to pin down Bocklin and CGI.

The Atlanta location—CGI's world headquarters—apparently had a small laboratory complex attached to it, but nothing of the size that the Beast felt was capable of producing the work that Bocklin was claiming he'd done.

There had to be a second lab. Hank McCoy meant to find it. And then he meant to give Dr. Arnold Bocklin a severe talking-to about ethical research.

Bocklin must have known about the pending Emergency Intervention Bill—CGI was angling to be awarded one of its contracts. And genetic research was one thing—even the moral gray area of applied genetic research—but research tailored to genocidal ends was quite another.

Bocklin's research had no other purpose than to give humanity a sugarcoated chance to put an end to the *soi-disant* ''mutant menace'' forever.

So Hank was quite anxious to speak to Bocklin.

But, while CGI's corporate headquarters were in Atlanta, the location of the company's—and Bocklin's—research facilities was apparently a very closely guarded secret. For every dead end Hank ran down, another dozen leads appeared. And all of them had to be checked out, one by one. He'd given Rogue and Gambit a list of pharmaceutical supply houses to run down—Bocklin had to buy his supplies from somewhere—and the other X-Men were trying to trace CGI's presence through cyberspace.

All X-Men but one.

Standing on the terrace, looking out into the dusk, Wolverine lit another of his gnarled black cheroots and sucked the harsh smoke deep into his lungs. As the nicotine hit his bloodstream, it was blotted out almost immediately as his mutant healing factor flushed the toxins from his system. Sometimes the one thing that had kept him alive all these years had real drawbacks.

Wolverine was a loner, an outlaw, an outsider. In a world where his memories were an unreliable tissue, half lies and half amnesia, that much was truth he could hold fast to. He was who he was, and even after he'd given his whole loyalty to the X-Men, he kept much of his deepest self apart. He trusted most of them, loved some of them—but when you came right down to it, they couldn't understand him.

Take Scotty, for example—their stiff-necked, sanctimonious Mutant of the Month poster boy. Logan respected Cyclops—nobody knew better than Wolverine what it was like to live with destruction always at your fingertips—but that kind of inflexibility had its price. Someday Cyclops would meet something he couldn't defeat or even run from—and on that day he'd shatter into a thousand pieces.

But the thing that usually got Logan's goat—and had been at the root of most of his clashes with the senior-most X-Man through the years—was that, in the most profound sense of the word, Cyclops was naïve. He was forged in a more innocent time. Cyclops still played by the old rules. He would not kill.

And he couldn't—or didn't want to—understand a man who could.

Logan's hands had been far from clean when he'd come to the X-Men. For years he had been something less than either mutant or human—he'd been a weapon, a killing machine for Canada's Project X. Him and Sabretooth and Maverick, the closest of enemies.

If there'd been good times he no longer remembered them. He'd seen his comrades slide off the edge of the blade, one by one—Sabretooth into an uncontrollable murderous psychosis, Maverick into the queer failure of nerve that meant a field agent was finally broken. Wolverine was the only one who'd survived.

If, like the man says, you can call this survivin'.

When he'd joined the X-Men, he'd done his best to play by Cyke and the Professor's rules, only to find that it wasn't always possible. Maybe the flaw was in him. Maybe it was only that times had changed too much for the old rules to still apply.

If they ever did. Trouble is, Scotty, you think killin' is some big thing, and it ain't. What it is, is too flamin' easy.

And maybe Cyclops was right to shy away from even the thought of it the way he did. Maybe the only way to stake out a homestead on the moral high ground was to close your eyes to the existence of some kinds of darkness.

But Logan couldn't do that. His eyes had been pried opened too long ago. He took another drag on his cheroot, reducing most of its length to ash, and exhaled sharply, sending jets of thick white smoke into the twilight. For a moment, the scent of burning tobacco masked the myriad subtle smells his enhanced mutant senses brought him with every breath. A moment later, he crushed the glowing coal of the cheroot out between his fingers and snapped the butt over the terrace railing. He turned back toward the house.

He had to go and do some eye-opening of his own.

As Wolverine had expected, through common sense and the information passed to him by his enhanced senses, Xavier was in his study, with Cyclops. Just as well. Scott had to know sometime.

"You got a minute, Chuck?" Wolverine said, pushing open the door of the study.

Professor Xavier had been working at the VDT at his desk. Wolverine got a glimpse of columns of scrolled numbers as the founder of the X-Men turned in his hoverchair to face him. Cyclops was still wearing his blue-and-gold battle-suit; after all these years, it was more familiar to him than civilian clothes.

Wolverine turned up the collar of his buffalo-plaid jacket and regarded Xavier and Cyclops with unwavering blue eyes.

"If it is important, Logan, of course," Xavier said.

"That depends. You hot on running down this Bocklin or not?" Wolverine replied. He heard the anger in his own voice; pure nerves. He was edgy about opening up this antique can of worms, but it was something that had to be done.

"Do you know where he is?" Cyclops demanded, as if Wolverine kept biogeneticists stashed under his bunk by the case.

"No. But I maybe got me a line on someone who does," Wolverine said.

"Go on, Logan," Xavier said calmly. Though Xavier could easily have scanned the information from Logan's brain telepathically in seconds, the Canadian X-Man knew that Xavier's own sense of ethics kept him from doing so except in time of greatest need—and even then with great reluctance.

"Well," Logan began, almost hesitantly. "You remember how Alpha Flight used t'wander down here every once in a while to try and shanghai me back for the home team, right?"

"It isn't something we're likely to forget," Scott said impatiently. "Come on, Logan—we don't have time to waste."

"This *is* the point, Cyke. I ain't a man who likes bein'

blindsided like that. So I keep an ear to what's happening up in my old stompin' grounds. They ain't lost interest up there in rounding up paranormals for government use, even if it ain't worked out right for 'em yet.''

"Humanity has ever been as ready to exploit what it fears as to eradicate it," Charles Xavier said sadly. "There are times when I wonder which is worse—genocide or slavery?"

"That's like asking a man if he'd rather be shot or hanged," Cyclops said, making a rare grim joke.

"Anyway," Wolverine said, "there's some things I been hearin' lately—pretty vague, but I'm kinda thinkin' that if I trace things back through the Black Budget boys up there in Canadian Intelligence, could be I'm going to bump into Bocklin pretty quick."

"Are you sure, Wolverine?" Cyclops said reflexively.

Wolverine shot him a look of disgust and didn't answer. Cyclops knew as well as he did that nothing was for sure when you played catch with the smoke-and-mirrors types.

"How quickly do you think you can find this information, Logan?" Professor Xavier asked. "Assuming, of course, that there's anything to find."

"Well, I ain't going t'be subtle," Wolverine said, showing his teeth in a wolfish, predatory grin. "If there's somethin' t'find, I'll flush it out pretty quick."

"We need to know about Bocklin—be sure he's exactly who he appears to be," Scott said.

"Not that that's any great prize," Wolverine commented. "But the way I figure, if a guy's that ready to start rollin' dice with human lives, he has to've started somewhere."

"Very well," Xavier said. "Go to Canada and see what you can find out about Bocklin's involvement with the intelligence community there. But come back as soon as you can—our resources are stretched to the limit, and we will need every X-Man available to stand together when the time comes.''

"Aw, don't worry, Chuck. I'll be back before you've had time t'miss me. See ya around, Scotty.''

With an ironic salute, the feisty Canadian turned and walked from the room.

"He knows more than he's telling us, Professor,'' Cyclops said when the door had closed behind Wolverine.

"Granted, Scott. But our first priority must be doing all we can to derail the Emergency Intervention Bill before it becomes law—and the platform it will create, to which the antimutant faction in this country can rally. I trust Wolverine to do what he can to solve the mystery surrounding Dr. Arnold Bocklin, and return as soon as he can.''

"Of course, Professor,'' Scott said automatically. "So do I.''

But the words came with great reluctance.

Atlanta, crown jewel of the Peachtree State. Home of the 1996 Olympics, Scarlett O'Hara, and the Center for Disease Control.

And home of the Center for Genetic Improvement.

Coming here had been a bad idea.

But then, Crown Clarendon reflected sourly, practically everything in his life for about as far back as he could remember had been a bad idea. They taught you physics, biochemistry, and engineering in college—they didn't teach you life. He thought he could use a remedial course in that.

Crown Clarendon was twenty-three years old. He'd been working for CGI for five years now—the last three directly under Dr. Arnold Bocklin—ever since CGI had cruised and cherrypicked him out of Cal Tech's doctoral program. He'd been eighteen and just finishing up the accelerated track for a Ph.D. in biomechanics. His third Ph.D., as it happened. The others were in genetic research and chemistry. He used

to brag about going Dr. Frankenstein one better any day of
the week. The joke had long since ceased to be funny.

*I turned down S.H.I.E.L.D., Stark Enterprises, and SAFE
for this?*

Maybe it was just because it was Monday. Crown hated
Mondays, especially Mondays that started at five a.m.

He sighed, and shoved his long blond hair out of his
eyes. He knew he looked like a kid—a baby-faced techn-
ogeek who was tolerated for what he could do, and mis-
trusted for the same reason—but there was no dress code
in his department, and he didn't intend to give up blue jeans
and Megadeth T-shirts just to pretend to fit in. He had a
plain blue sweater in his locker to wear when the FDA
watchdog from rec.gov.smoke&mirrors got here in about
an hour for her all-expenses-paid guided tour of the Center
for Genetic Improvement.

Crown propped his chin on his hands and stared at nothing. He ought to get some sleep. He'd been here all night
just to make sure that the fussy, complex, and tempera-
mental delivery system would perform today. They had to
simplify it before it moved past the prototype—but without
the failsafes Crown suspected the mortality rate would sky-
rocket, something he didn't consider acceptable.

A half-empty cup of bad CGI coffee and a ravaged box
of donuts shared space on his console with a circuit tracer,
a hydrospanner, and a batch of printouts from the last no-
load test run. He hadn't found any problems with the monitor and containment equipment. He hoped there weren't
any to find, because as soon as the watchdog got here they
had another live package run on the menu.

Crown hated live runs.

He turned to the computer and pulled up the database.
When the package came in, the telemetry would match the
package specs against its files to determine treatment protocols. At least, that was the excuse Crown had been given

when he'd seen the database—and it was an excuse, he knew that much.

But the database also made a pretty awesome toy, so he wasn't complaining. He riffled through it on a random sort: hundreds of costumed adventurers—some he'd never even heard of—graded human, mutant, mutate, construct, cyborg, alien, alleged deity, and even unknown; rated lawful, evil, neutral, chaotic. A setup for playing the world's largest live-action role-playing game—and for every nut in a monkey suit that the government knew about, some number cruncher in the Bureau of the Census had projected somewhere between ten and a thousand mutants who either had really useless powers or just wanted to live quiet normal lives. Something like two percent of Earth's population were mutants—and how many people did that make in round numbers?

It didn't matter. Because soon they'd have their chance to be human, just like the other ninety-eight percent.

Nobody'd told Crown that in so many words, but they didn't need to. Most of the people working here thought he was just a bright mechanic. It had never occurred to them that when you were as smart as Crown it meant living surrounded by people with whom you could never have any sort of meaningful conversation.

Which in turn meant you had a lot of time to think.

When Crown had first been hired, Project Level Playing Field had been pure genetic research: cure diabetes, cancer, the Legacy Virus, even AIDS. He'd worked almost alone, following hints and directions mapped out for him by Dr. Bocklin, the man that Ronnie Ploog, their quondam supervisor, persisted in calling "our mysterious Dr. Bocklin."

All Crown knew was that the man was brilliant—when he'd begun working directly with Bocklin, for the first time in his life Crown had felt the way he guessed normal people felt around people like him: baffled, amazed, maybe even a little daunted. Bocklin was almost supernaturally gifted—

for him, research didn't mean wrong turns, dead ends, wasted experiments. It was almost as though he wasn't researching, but *retracing* previous work, and that with almost contemptuous ease. In fact, Bocklin was spooky as hell, but at first that hadn't mattered to Crown, and he guessed it still didn't matter to CGI.

And when Bocklin had found a single genome address for mutation, that was good too: it meant the therapy he had developed could neutralize really bad mutants so they could go into conventional therapy; let involuntary and unwilling mutates revert. Things had been really exciting then—Crown had worked almost as an extension of Bocklin's will, building the equipment, formulating the retro-mutagen to turn Bocklin's pure research into concrete fact—a perk of the engineering degree he'd picked up around the time when most kids were wondering what high school was going to be like.

Exciting times—but that had been before Crown had found out where all of Bocklin's work was going. Before he'd found out about live package runs. Before he'd *participated* in live package runs.

Crown didn't know what the packages had done before they got here, and he didn't want to know. He'd asked once, and Dr. Bocklin said it was none of his concern. Nobody argued with Dr. Bocklin. Crown had found that out early on.

Which didn't, of course, mean that Crown *agreed* with him.

Fortunately he'd only been present for two such runs so far, and that only because he'd had to learn the new delivery equipment. The Atlanta facility could only handle one package at a time, but Crown had now seen blueprints for a twenty-package installation, and he was going to have to be the one that made sure they worked when the time came to install them at facilities all across the country.

Which they wouldn't, unless he managed to stabilize the retro-virus or simplify the delivery system.

But the thought of what he'd seen here being repeated all across America—to watch grown men and women plead, and beg, and cry because of what was about to be done to them—to watch them . . . *dim.* . . .

Crown closed his eyes, shuddering at the thought. And today he got to watch it again.

Crown stared at the clipboard with the package transfer doccos in disgust. So much for the paperless office—CGI had a mainframe the size of a planet buried in the basement, and every corporate twitch was still accompanied by a pile of hand-annotated xerographed forms, just as if the same information hadn't been uploaded to the master database on paranormals. Paperless office. Yeah, right. And trees died for *this?*

The tag on this one read PSYCHOSTORM, who was going to rejoin the human race with an audience: one Roberta Everett of the Food and Drug Administration, whose mission in life was to give them final approval to use the retromutagen.

Crown gazed unseeing out through three layers of bulletproof, shatterproof, radiation-proof glass into a small, heavily armored room barely big enough to contain its vibranium-clad table. The room was at negative pressure, surrounded by a series of containment chambers and some of the most sophisticated antiparanormal devices going. If one of the packages got loose before it'd been treated with the retro-virus it wouldn't get far.

It. But they weren't "its." Each of the packages was a living, breathing, sentient being—each a mutant, but still, in the last analysis, human.

Just different. But could anyone who'd entered college at thirteen and graduate school at fifteen really say *he* was an average sort of guy?

You know the answer to that, boyo. But your DNA is

human, so that makes you all right. But down deep, where it counts, two-hundred-plus IQ and all—what makes you more normal than the average mutant on the street?

Nothing but public opinion, for all that was worth.

Did public opinion make what they were doing here right? He knew the packages were murderers many times over, but how many people did you have to kill before you forfeited your basic human rights and got turned over to a place like this as an experimental animal?

Crown knew the real answer—the right answer—and wished he didn't. The end never justified the means. And he suspected that the upgrade he'd seen meant that now the government was backing a plan to change over *all* mutants so that everyone could be equal.

Only all humans weren't equal either—Crown was a prime example of that. And once they'd remade *homo sapiens superior* in their own image, who would be next on the procrustean bed? Blond technogeeks with hypertrophied IQs?

And the worst thing was, it was all out in the open. There was some kind of bill in Washington right now that would make it perfectly legal. Majority rule. Democracy.

Might makes right? Crown asked himself with a grimace.

He knew the real answer to that, too.

He ought to leave, wash his hands of this place and let Bocklin get another butcher's boy. Unfortunately, the contract he signed when he came to work at CGI prohibited him from seeking related employment—and with Crown's job description, that meant nearly anything—for five years after termination. Which meant he'd spend five years twiddling his thumbs, while everyone else in his class—and in his *field*—raced past him, leaving him facing a lifetime of playing catch-up.

It wasn't worth it. Probably. If he didn't do this work, they'd get someone else.

Wouldn't they?

•   •   •

The room's walls, ceiling, and floor had the brushed-
aluminum finish of expensive cookware. At about one a.m.,
three-fifths of the Ohio Mutant Conspiracy had arrived at
what would be—if this was a book or a movie—a place
simply labeled *Unknown Destination.* The trio had gotten
glimpses of security lighting and a lot of barbed wire as
they were hustled inside by the men in the black armored
exoskeletons. They'd gone from the landing pad to an elevator, from the elevator to a corridor, from the corridor to
this room.

The room was about ten feet square and held four bunks,
a sink, and a toilet in a tiny cubicle. The three of them had
plenty of time to explore it completely in the last seven
hours. It was now eight o'clock in the morning.

"Do you think they're going to feed us?" Charade
asked.

Her face was puffy with crying—and from where one of
the men in black had hit her when she'd first regained consciousness and started trying to talk her way out of this.

"I've got a candy bar in my pocket," Lloyd offered, his
southern twang more pronounced than usual, his voice still
hoarse from the tear gas. His eyes and nose were red and
swollen from constant rubbing, and he looked as if he had
a bad cold. He kept his voice low—as Charade had—out
of unconscious expectation that someone would come in
and make them stop talking. Somewhere between Ohio and
here he'd lost his gimme cap, and his dishwater-blond hair
stuck up in random cowlicks.

"They didn't take any of our stuff," Slapshot said. He
still had his wallet and his house keys, everything he'd been
carrying. The men in black hadn't even searched them.

Lloyd began turning out his pockets on the bunk. Coins,
bus transfers, ticket stubs, keys, rubber bands, and a slightly
battered candy bar that he handed to Charade. She un-

wrapped it and bit into it with a doleful sniff, before passing the remainder back to Lloyd.

"But what did we do?" she said. "I mean, we were trespassing, but. . . ."

"But those guys weren't the local cops," Lloyd said. He took a bite out of the candy bar, and offered it to Slapshot. "Want a bite, Jase? It don't look like the lunch mobile is going to be along any time soon."

Slapshot shook his head. He was too wound up to think of eating. "They just came in, grabbed us, and brought us here. It was like they knew right where to go."

"But what do they *want*?" Charade wailed. "I was supposed to be home *three hours ago*. My dad is going to *kill* me!"

"Yeah," Lloyd said, sitting down beside her on the bunk again. "My folks aren't going to be any too pleased either. I told them I was going to the movies."

"Your folks let you go to the movies on a school night?" Charade said, momentarily diverted.

"Charade, that isn't the point here," Slapshot said gently. "Why did these guys pick us? Their uniforms said U.S. Marshals, but I don't think they're really feds. We're all mutants, but I don't think we're exactly powerful enough to qualify as hidden assets."

"At least the others got away," Lloyd said dolefully. He rubbed his nose again.

For a while. Slapshot didn't say it aloud. If the others hadn't thought of it, let them think that last night had been a one-shot deal. But personally he didn't think that guys with that much equipment—guns and explosives and helicopters and trucks—were going to have that much trouble rounding up two high school kids on the run in Cleveland, Ohio. Pipedream and Rewind didn't know the guys weren't real federal marshals, and neither would their parents.

We have to get out of here, Slapshot thought, *and tell somebody this is going on.*

Even as he formed the thought, a great weariness descended on his heart. *Tell someone. Sure.*

They were mutants. Who would care?

"Three more packages!" Crown tried to keep his voice down, but the cute brunette in the dress-for-success suit—Roberta "Call me 'Bobs'" Everett from the FDA—glanced toward him with interest. Mr. Ploog—her minder *du jour*—frowned.

"I don't make the rules," one of the other techies—a gangly, black-haired fellow named Infantino—told him, dropping the paperwork in front of him. "They just told me you should be ready to go again as soon as we get the first package out of there."

"I can't be ready for at least two hours," Crown said automatically, "unless you want to give me two more Crays and another sequencer. Remember, science isn't pretty." He glanced at the top form. Instead of a name, all it said was *Package 47*. Crown winced and dumped the clipboard into the nearest drawer. *Forty-six before this one?* "Is Dr. Bocklin back from Berne yet?"

"Tomorrow," Infantino said. "And don't bother trying to drag your feet on this one, Clarendon, because this is on Bocklin's orders—we're stepping up production early. Gonna really start to move!"

Wonderful.

"Everything all right over here?" Call me "Bobs" asked.

Standing next to the FDA official, Ploog shot Crown a murderous glance, daring him to say anything. Crown had seen Ronald Ploog once or twice at staff meetings—the usual sort of half-bright management type who wanted twice the results with half the budget. Right now, he wanted Call me "Bobs" to think everything was just fine here at Team CGI so she'd sign off on the process.

"They're just getting ready to bring the package in, sir," Infantino—ever the brownnoser—said.

Crown got up and stretched, trying to work out the kinks of a sleepless night. Six a.m. Another mutant, another chance to play God. He wished it didn't make him feel so guilty, because he couldn't see any way to get out of it. And he certainly couldn't see any way to stop it.

"Do you suppose you could tell me in your own words what you're doing here?" Call me "Bobs" asked, coming over toward Crown's chair.

She had a nice smile—Crown was willing to grant her that—and she didn't seem to be that much older than he was. And she must have at least a rudimentary science background, or else she wouldn't be able to see through a management snow job. Which was one of the reasons why she was here.

He glanced over at Ploog. The baby blue Land's End Drifter sweater that Crown's mother had given him for his birthday was not fooling Ploog into thinking that Crown was a safe team player, but he could hardly jump in and drag Call me "Bobs" away from Crown without committing the sort of social solecism that made government watchdogs highly suspicious.

"Well, Bobs," Crown said expansively, "as you know, the retro-mutagen, developed by our own Dr. Bocklin for Project Level Playing Field, is designed to allow mutants to revert to human, by removing the x-factor from the genome. Unlike other methods used in the past—such as Forge's neutralizer, which only served to suppress mutant powers—Dr. Bocklin's method completely rewrites the genetic code and the associated neurochemistry. After treatment, these people are no longer *homo superior* in any sense of the word." *And a lot of them aren't alive either, but what's one more dead genejoke, right? God. I wish I'd majored in origami. . . .*

"I heard you've been having trouble with the delivery system," Bobs said, leaning closer.

"Problems?" Crown was honestly surprised. "Not with delivery." Over her shoulder, Crown could see Ploog going nearly purple with the effort to control himself. "The treatment Dr. Bocklin's developed involves introduction of a collection of designer retro-viruses suspended in an artificial plasma medium. Once we hit a vein, reversion is almost instantaneous. It isn't a stable compound, however, and the proportions depend on the subject. It has to be mixed just before delivery—which is my job."

"Interesting. So you're implying you have problems with something other than delivery, Dr. Clarendon?" Bobs said. Crown opened his mouth to reply—let them fire him, if they didn't like the truth—but Ronnie beat him to it.

"Dr. Clarendon isn't really involved with the overall project," Ploog said quickly. "I'm sure that if you speak to Dr. Chaykin or to Dr. Bocklin himself, they'll be able to more than satisfy you as to the safety of CGI's anti-mutagen. Now if you'll just—"

A light on Crown's console flashed, and he forgot all about peaching on his employers. Inside the room visible through the triple glass, a massive set of interwoven blast shields began to iris open.

"Here we go," Crown said, interrupting Ploog. He reached for his mouse, and began clicking icons on the display screen. With his left hand, he groped for the holographic goggles, found them, and slipped them on. The familiar green standby grid appeared in his field of vision, spectrally superimposed on reality. His left hand hovered over the array of buttons that determined content and dosage to the limbic and arterial feeds. As soon as the package was in range, the grid would be replaced by feed from the telemetry on the package, and it would be his turn to do his part.

"This is what I came to see," Bobs said. There was an

eagerness in her voice that almost made Crown turn to look at her. He wondered if she'd ever met Psychostorm in the outside world—if she or someone she knew was one of his victims.

Not that you know whether he's got victims or not, boyo. But face it, people don't go around calling themselves "Psychostorm" if they're going to be Certified Public Accountants.

"The observation post—" Ploog began.

"Oh come now, Mr. Ploog, do you think I was born yesterday?" Bobs snapped. "I'm going to watch this from right here."

Crown heard Ploog take a step toward her.

"You, on the other hand, can go to the observation post," Crown snapped absently. He didn't want anyone in here at all during the live run, but even more than he wanted privacy, he wanted five minutes alone with the FDA observer.

Four white-suited CGI techs were wheeling a massive gurney into the chamber now. They wore gleaming psi-blocking helmets which—with the accompanying power packs around their waists—gave them something of the look of visiting space aliens. Two exoskeletoned security guards followed, and Dr. Chaykin brought up the rear.

Crown's eyes widened. Bobs Everett whistled low in surprise.

This package was huge—nearly seven feet tall, and muscled like the Steelers's entire offensive line. Psychostorm wore some kind of black and red costume, and his flowing hair was a weird silvery blue. A shimmering effect surrounded his body, a faint blue-green glow, but most of his face was covered by a heavy silver visor, with a cluster of small flashing LEDs at each temple. Crown recognized it as a neural disrupter, which—along with the psi-blockers everyone was wearing—placed Psychostorm in the psionic or parapsionic section, despite the fact that the guy looked as if he didn't need any mutant powers to tear Cadillacs in half.

"Whoever you are, you're going to spend the rest of your lives in hell!" Psychostorm yowled. The cords in his neck stood out as he strained against the metal bands that held him to the gurney, and the audio pickups in the chamber brought their creaking sound clearly to Crown's ears.

"Come on—move it, move it, move it." The tech's strained voice came clearly through the speaker into Crown's control room, and he moved the servomechs out of the way as the gurney was wheeled into position in the center of the room and locked down.

"Come on, come on, come on," Crown chanted under his breath in unconscious unison. His doubts about the rightness of the project had been temporarily swept away by the sheer fear that Psychostorm's presence evoked. He had the information he needed; all they had to do was sink the half-dozen feeds into the package and he could go to work. He focused for a moment on the holographic display of the package's vital signs. All were relatively low. Sedated and psi-scrambled, the package couldn't be much of a threat.

Could he?

Crown refocused, past the colored web of sensor readings, back to the chamber itself. The techs were having some trouble with the lockdown of the gurney into the floor clamps, which had to be done to trigger automatic release of the delivery system. *Come on, forget it, he isn't going to move much. Get that arterial tap in there so we can get going.*

There was a pinging sound, the kind that metal pushed to breaking strain makes just before it snaps. The displays hanging in front of Crown's eyes flickered.

"Guys, I'm getting a spike here," Crown said. *Ronnie is not going to be happy about this.* "Let's go to manual delivery, okay?"

He felt Roberta Everett lean forward, over his shoulder, though without her own set of goggles, she had no way of seeing what he saw.

Crown released the delivery system. Needle-tipped tubes began to descend over the gurney like the tentacles of a hovering octopus, but none of the technicians seemed to take any notice.

And a moment later, something happened that everyone could see whether they were wearing holo-goggles or not.

One of the wrist shackles confining Psychostorm to the table snapped open. The blue-green glow around the enormous mutant killer intensified. The readings on Crown's telemetry soared off the scale.

"We have Situation Yellow. Repeat: we have an emergency condition in Treatment Area One," Crown said into an intercom.

Psychostorm strained against his fetters. Crown could see the big man's face—what was visible below the psi-scrambler—turn almost purple with the effort he was making, and Crown could almost sympathize. The gurney tipped and fell.

Crown wrenched up his holo-goggles and hit the panic button. Inside the chamber, he could see Dr. Chaykin scrambling for the door, trying to get away. The two black-uniformed guards flanking it did not even turn their heads. Their guns were up, their attention was focused on Psychostorm, waiting for the money shot.

Dr. Chaykin hammered on the door. It didn't open, and Crown remembered with a pang of guilt that the moment he'd hit the panic button he'd sealed the chamber, trapping everyone there inside. In that moment it didn't matter to him that he'd done what he'd been trained to do, or that his action meant safety for the several hundred CGI employees outside the containment chamber. At that moment, Crown felt like a murderer. He fully expected that the next thing he would see would be Dr. Chaykin's blood.

He glanced up at the Washington observer. The sounds coming from the room were a mixture of shouted commands and the howling of the package as Psychostorm tried to tear himself loose from the gurney. Bobs was staring into the chamber intently, her face rapt and still. Crown pulled the holo-goggles back down over his face and slid the volume control on the audio pickup to minimum. The sounds from the chamber became faint and meaningless, like the crashing of waves on the shore.

There was no time to do this right. Fast and sloppy beat dead in his book. Crown shut out the faint bray of the alert klaxons and the flashing lights, concentrating wholly on the spectacle inside the chamber. He retracted all the feeds into the ceiling except for the largest arterial catheter. He purged the reservoirs of their previous loads and put everything behind this one—a Satan's cocktail of nanomachines, tailored retro-virii, artificial toxins, the lot—and lowered it again.

"Ah, Dr. Chaykin, I've, ah, simplified the delivery package." *Do it, guys,* Crown prayed inarticulately. *If you don't neutralize the package, you're toast. He doesn't look like a reasonable man, somehow.* "It's stable for the next ninety seconds. . . ."

One of the techs had moved in close and ripped the arm of Psychostorm's gaudy red-and-black suit loose. There was blood on Psychostorm's arm where the metal band of the chest restraint had cut into the muscle, and the veins were engorged, standing out blue and pumped against his skin. Crown quickly lowered the delivery system farther, to where the tech could reach it.

Seventy-five seconds. . . .

Psychostorm fought like a man possessed. Blood and foam flecked his cheeks as he whipped his head from side to side, and his free hand scrabbled at the neural disrupter that masked his face.

Sixty seconds. . . .

The technician held Psychostorm's arm down against his side. It took the strength of both hands to manage it, and even so it was a struggle. Dr. Chaykin—Crown hadn't seen him give up on the door, but he must have—grabbed the tube and pulled it the rest of the way down.

Forty-five seconds. . . .

As soon as Chaykin's hands touched it, Crown released the chemical cocktail into the system. The needle was already leaking as Chaykin slid it into the carotid artery on the side of Psychostorm's neck. The technician knelt on Psychostorm's free arm.

"Get the tap." The words came crisp over Psychostorm's howling and cursing, audible in the control room even at the reduced volume. "We may still be able to draw a good archive."

"Readings heading down," Crown said, feeling the tension in his chest ease. Crisis averted by Dr. Bocklin's magic bullet.

"What does he mean?" Bobs asked. "Tap? Archive?"

The sound of her voice startled Crown. He'd forgotten she was here. He took a deep breath, mentally pulling back from the scene. Things seemed under control, but Ploog was not going to be a happy corporate flack.

"The retro-mutagen compound is usually delivered to several sites at once in about a liter of artificial plasma suspension. We partially exsanguinate the package to improve delivery and speed up the effect. Of course, if the treatment were to go into general release, conversion speed wouldn't be so much of a factor. Dr. Bocklin is working on a broad-spectrum one-shot therapy that shows initial effects within one minute of delivery—" and Crown had just successfully field-tested it, thank you very much "—but at the moment we can only get that kind of speed with a direct aortal cannula."

What am I saying? If she listens to me, this'll be released to vaccinate schoolkids with inside of a month!

Inside the chamber, Dr. Chaykin had found the tap, and inserted it into Psychostorm's other arm. Dark red blood rushed through the tube and pulsed into the transparent receiver. The man was silent, his breathing slow, a result of the tranqs that Crown had slipped into the delivery. At the moment, he was still a mutant, but the glow about him was fainter now, almost an illusion, and as Crown watched, it flickered and died completely.

The four white-suited techs struggled with the gurney and its weighty burden, finally setting it upright.

"Readings just exceeding normal human range, and dropping."

Crown leaned back and sighed, realizing only now that he was drenched in sweat and shaking from adrenaline overload. He looked up at the digital clock over the door, and was surprised to discover how little time had passed. It had seemed like the longest five minutes of his life.

Crown hit the codes to cancel the alert, but he had to try twice before the computer would accept his verbal confirm; there was too much stress in his voice. Finally the screen flashed VOICEPRINT CONFIRMED.

Once it did, he saw the light go from red to green over the door inside the chamber. One of the black-suited guards saw it and gestured to the other. They both removed keys from their pockets—one a short gleaming metal cylinder, the other a magnetic passkey similar to the one Crown himself carried—and unlocked the door.

Crown watched with quiet respect. Whoever the chief of security was, he trusted his people to stay inside a potential killing jar even when they had the means to get out. Crown wasn't sure whether knowing this made him feel safer, or not.

"Well," Bobs said brightly, as Crown shut down the sensor interface and leaned back in his chair, "it looks like CGI's product delivers."

"Yeah." Crown gave Psychostorm's telemetry one last

look—he had just about rejoined the human race—and pulled off the goggles. Over the next several hours, Psychostorm's vital signs would continue to drop as his genetic code rewrote itself, until at last—at least, according to the documentation Crown had seen—they would stabilize in the normal human range.

Unfortunately, reports weren't all that Crown had seen since Project Level Playing Field began.

He glanced around the room. He and Everett were alone. Even if Ploog knew the complex was off lockdown now, it would take him a few minutes to get back here.

This is your only shot at getting the truth out, boyo. Don't blow it.

"Oh, sure. Worked fine—this time." Crown tried to sound casual, not like a turncoat employee with a grudge to hone. "But what about the rats? That's what you've got to consider when you're assessing the viability of the treatment in terms of wide-scale use."

"Rats?" Bobs said blankly. She'd been staring into the chamber, where Dr. Chaykin and the techs were clustered around a now-quiescent Psychostorm, but now she looked directly at Crown. There was a hard light in her brown eyes. "Vatranoff didn't say anything about rats."

Arthur Vatranoff was CGI's Chairman, and Crown doubted that he knew what a chromosome was, let alone anything about dominant and recessive allele pairs and the x-factor that governed human mutation.

"Project Level Playing Field is designed to turn mutants human, but like any similar project there has to be a way to test the methods of treatment before they're tested on humans."

"You mean 'tested on mutants,' don't you, Mr. Clarendon?" Bobs said. "Not on humans?"

Crown looked at her narrowly. Maybe he wasn't interested in dating her after all.

"On mutants, sure," he agreed, "which are a human

subspecies, *homo sapiens superior*. You know the old rule of thumb: if it can interbreed, it's the same species. But that's not important right now. The important thing is that we mutate rats as a control group to test the retrovirus. It's fairly easy, and safe as long as you remember to put them in adamantium cages afterward. And then we change them back—it's a cross-check for the computer simulation, so we can build a statistical effectiveness curve for the retro-mutagen."

"But I was told it was one hundred percent effective," Bobs said. "It sure worked on Big Boy in there. What went wrong here today, by the way?"

"I really couldn't say," Crown sidestepped. *The sedatives probably wore off—or else somebody told him what we were going to do to him.* "You'd have to talk to Mr. Ploog or Dr. Chaykin for that. But as for the retro-mutagen being effective, it all depends on how you define effective, really. The thing about the rats is, they mutate just fine— but when we change them back with the treatment, about half of them die."

And I've got three more packages coming through here in the next seventy-two hours. And each of them only has a fifty percent chance of making it through till Wednesday.

"Let me explain a few things about Project Level Playing Field that might have been left out of your information package," Crown said. Speaking quickly, he attempted to explain to Roberta Everett about the rats.

CHAPTER 6

R.CRUZ

The thing hardest for out of towners to grasp about Manhattan is how quickly it ends. Once you cross the river into any of the four outer boroughs, Fun City's particular magic is suddenly gone; wiped away. You could be in any major city from Chicago eastward—elevated trains, old buildings, bad neighborhoods.

Or sometimes not even all that bad, but when the workforce leaves at the end of the day—and all you're left with is a couple of acres of blacktopped parking lot and about a hundred thousand square feet of storage space beneath a sheet-iron roof—a warehouse that was only boring in daylight takes on a decidedly sinister aspect by night.

Case in point: Gotham Industrial Pharmaceuticals, somewhere in the borough of Queens, New York.

Here beneath the tracks of the El, surrounded by the crumbling façades of prewar row houses that have never known a yuppie renaissance, Manhattan seems a thousand miles away. This is Son of Sam territory: a place of ethnic neighborhoods and old blood feuds. In daylight, it's shabby-quaint; by night, the gloves are off. You lay your stakes on the table and you take what comes; it's a hard place, and what comes probably won't be very pretty.

In fact, make that a dead solid certainty.

"Shee-oot!" Rogue's sibilant exclamation cut through the night, making Remy LeBeau wince. He was sweet on Rogue—the Cajun would be the first to admit that, loudly, flamboyantly, and often—but his *p'tite chere amie* had all the subtlety of a truck, as Wolverine would say.

When you were hanging out in plain sight, ten feet off the ground and facing a glittering coil of razor wire, it was *not* the time to announce your presence to the world—at least in Gambit's opinion.

"*Ma chere,* if you do not lower your voice it will not only be your Remy who hears your words of love," Gambit said. The trick with barbed wire, so his teachers in the Thieves' Guild had always said, was not to be afraid of it. If you were too cautious, you got hurt. Gambit gritted his teeth and reached for the top of the fence. Boldly.

"Words'a love?" Rogue echoed in an outraged—and carrying—whisper. "Not hardly, chum. Why couldn't't'cha have scooted over this here fence all on y'lonesome, an' let me do the flyin'?"

Gambit inched his arm through the glittering coils of wire, reaching for a secure grip on the top of the fence beneath.

"Because, *chere, Charles* wish us to be inconspicuous, which mean dat if you fly in—or rip de fence from his foundation wit' dose pretty 'ands—we might attrac' more attention den I would be 'appy wid, me."

Carefully, keeping low, Gambit eased himself over the razor wire. The faint scraping sound of its glittering points passing across his leather coat and metal greaves was loud to his Thieves' Guild-trained ears, but in a moment he was over, hanging by his hands from the inside of the fence. He dropped to the ground, glad that the tricky part was past.

"They probably ain't even watchin'," Rogue grumbled from above him.

Gambit shook his head, smiling to himself at his lady fair's stubbornness. He glanced around. The warehouse was dark—at this time of night, once they'd gotten past the fence, they would only have to deal with one or two trifling locks and an easily evaded security guard.

But you didn't live as long as Gambit had by taking the opposition for granted.

"C'mon, *chere*," he called softly. "Come to Remy's arms."

There was a moment when Rogue stood crouched on top of the fence, the saffron blaze down the front of her battle-suit shining bright as a signal flare to Gambit's watchful eyes. Then she vaulted over the fence, not finessing the razor wire so much as blithely ignoring it. Instead of making the jump into Gambit's arms as he half-expected, she used her flying ability to float gently to the ground.

But still within reach.

"Ah, at las' we are alone toget'er, *ma p'tite*," Gambit said. He took the step forward that allowed him to put his arms around her. The thin fabric of her battle-suit was enough to insulate him from the deadly effect of Rogue's uncontrollable mutant power, but he could still feel the heat of her body, even through the palms of his fingerless gloves.

"Let *go!*" Rogue's voice was frightened, and she shoved Remy away with enough of her super strength to make him stagger back. "Do y'*wanna* die? Can't y'get it through y'thick Cajun head that nobody—"

"Hey, *chere*, I was only foolin'," Gambit said quickly. "You know your Remy wouldn't do anyt'ing to hurt you, Rogue."

"But I would," Rogue said bleakly. "I'd hurt you real bad, Remy. Now come on—use those magic fingers o'yours on a couple of locks so we can get inside. This place gives me the creeps."

A quarter of an hour later, Gambit decided that the place gave him the creeps too.

Getting in had been as easy as he'd thought, and now they stood inside Gotham Pharmaceuticals's enormous warehouse. The echoing open space was dimly lit—probably more because of state regulations than due to any idea of convenience for the night security staff. The vast storage area was broken up into aisles and cross-corridors—a baffling, mazelike complexity—by towering shelves stacked with boxed components, carboys filled with liquid, and drums full of strange powders. For Gambit, it was as if they wandered through the kitchen of some gigantic, cybernetic voudoun priestess who could bespell them at any moment of her choice.

This was the third warehouse they'd checked since Monday night for any connection to either CGI or Arnold Bocklin, and it was the last of the local ones. The Beast—who ought to know if anyone would—had explained to them that few suppliers handled the specialized materials needed by genetic researchers and fewer still sold to non-government-affiliated buyers. Which CGI, despite the fact that it seemed to be working hand in glove with Washington's political agenda, was. If CGI or Bocklin were buying from Gotham Industrial Pharmaceuticals, there'd at least be a shipping address to trace back.

Something here didn't make sense. Gambit shook his head, dismissing the thought. In his experience, trouble very rarely made any sense.

"Are we there yet?" Rogue whispered mockingly in his ear.

Gambit half-turned, bringing her into the corner of his vision. Most of his attention was still concentrated on the door at the far end of the warehouse which led to the warehouse office and the records they'd need to examine. Its trifling lock would be an insult to a thief's skills and panache, in Gambit's far from humble opinion.

"In a moment, *ma belle*. Firs' we wait for de watchman to go off on his roun'. Den we go quick like de bunny an' see what we fin' in de office. Pouf! We be in an' out before he see us, him."

"Ought to be right up your alley," Rogue grumbled,

"but I didn't join the X-Men t'become a glorified file clerk."

Gambit grinned at her, his white teeth flashing in the dim light. The scarlet glow in his eyes might have been mistaken for the light of love, but Rogue hardly noticed it anymore. She'd seen too much—things that made Gambit's glowing red eyes look positively normal. She'd been too many people.

None of the others could really understand what happened when she touched someone. It wasn't only that she stole their abilities and the memories that allowed her to make use of them. She stole *everything*—hopes, fears, dreams. When it happened, it washed over her like a tsunami, washing her own personality away.

Who *was* Rogue? The special hell of it was that even she wasn't sure anymore. Who had she been before her mutant power had given her the hellish gift to sample other people's lives? Did she like Patsy Cline, peanut butter and banana sandwiches, riding bareback in the rain? Or were those the plundered preferences of all the people she'd touched, with those things that made her uniquely herself gone forever? "*Where are the snows of yesteryear?*" Rogue quoted bleakly to herself, and then tried to remember if it was she or one of her victims who had read and loved Villon's poems.

Ahead of her, Gambit moved noiselessly forward, blending into the shadows as he slunk along the back wall of the warehouse. Rogue followed him as quietly as she could, though she strode more than slunk. Slinking just wasn't her style; never had been.

If anything I am is really me. If there's anything left. She put those thoughts out of her mind—they'd keep—and concentrated on the job.

Another night, another warehouse. They were running out of places to look, and they weren't any closer to finding the mysterious Arnold Bocklin than they'd been on Monday. And it seemed, from last report, that the others weren't doing any better in Washington. For a moment she wondered where Wolverine had gone—no one had said—and wished she'd gone with him. Wherever he was, there was likely to be a lot more action than Rogue was seeing at the moment.

"I'm bored," she muttered under her breath. But Gambit heard her.

"Bored, *ma p'tite?* You wound Remy to de heart, you," Gambit said with a smile.

Rogue felt a rush of—what?—at the sound of his voice. It was immediately suppressed by a dull resentful anger that made her stomach hurt. There were times that she couldn't stand these games of his. Remy knew what she was, but somehow that didn't make him respect the self-imposed No Man's Land that Rogue had been forced to erect about herself to survive. Her relationship with the mercurial Cajun was one long game of keep-away, and it hurt. At least he'd been married once—Rogue hadn't even had a proper kiss since her early teens.

Sometimes she wondered if Gambit would still be interested in her if she weren't so inaccessible.

"I just don't see what all the fuss is about," Rogue said plaintively. "Here we are tryin' t'stop this Bocklin fella. But it ain't exactly a no-win situation, y'know. What if we fail, Gambit? How bad could losin' our powers possibly be?" *At least then I could kiss you, Mr. LeBeau. And probably see you run like a rabbit in a New York minute.*

"But *M'sieur* Bocklin does not mean for us to choose. An' me, I am de one who chooses what I wan' to be. T'ink, *ma belle*—what de difference between a few scientists helpin' de governmen' to play God—an' a *galeux vaurien* like Sinister doin' de same t'ing?"

"Safety in numbers?" Rogue cracked, but her heart

wasn't in it. Hesitantly, she reached out and touched Gambit's sleeve.

"It ain't like I don't enjoy bein' able t'juggle pianos and fly and all—bein' superstrong an' invulnerable really does things for a gal's self-confidence—an' I purely do love the X-Men. It's just that sometimes . . ." Rogue stopped, not quite able to put her thoughts into words. *It's just that sometimes I'd give anything to be . . . human.*

Gambit took both her gloved hands in his, pulling her close. "Rogue, Remy swears to you dat—"

At that moment, all the lights in the warehouse went on. Both X-Men reacted without conscious thought. Gambit pushed Rogue away from him, into the cover of a stack of cartons, as he faded back into what shadows remained with a thief's ease. Already he fanned out his ever-present deck of playing cards in his right hand, glowing faintly as he charged them with his own biokinetic energy. Gambit's thieving abilities were the result of years of painstaking training, but the joker in his genetic deck had been handed to him at birth—the power to turn any ordinary object into an explosive weapon through the use of his mutant gift.

"Mr. LeBeau? Ms., er, Rogue? Could you come out, please? We know you're there. Nobody's going to hurt you," a bland corporate voice said anxiously.

That's the stupidest thing Remy hear in all his born life, Gambit thought. He risked a peek between the jars on the shelf. He could only see one man, but he knew there had to be more, tucked away somewhere out of sight.

The man was perfectly ordinary looking, wearing a dark business suit and dark glasses. His long brown hair was pulled back into a trendy ponytail, and an ornate silver dragon earring dangled from his left ear. Gambit could see the wire hanging from the earplug in his right ear and disappearing into an inside coat pocket, confirming Remy's guess that the crazy stranger wasn't alone. His kind were the sort of faceless professionals who populated the field arms of an uncounted number of alphabet organizations from S.H.I.E.L.D. to A.I.M. to Hydra, and they weren't in business for themselves. It didn't matter to them whether they were sent out to capture the X-Men or get a quart of milk from the corner deli; they did what they were tasked to, collected their security clearances, and, if they were lucky, their pensions.

Dangerous men. But Gambit, too, was a dangerous man.

"Folks? My name is Keithley, and I'm getting pretty tired of hanging out here by myself. All we want to do is talk. My employer has a proposition for you—it could save you a lot of time and trouble," he added coaxingly.

Keithley! Suddenly Gambit understood why this man seemed so oddly familiar, even though he'd never seen him before. Keithley was a member of an organization called Black Team 51. Some of the X-Men had encountered them a few months back in connection with an unfortunate mutant who'd called himself the Wheel of Fortune. Gambit had seen the name in the computer records of the incident.

"Well, I'm all in favor of that, sugar."

To Gambit's horror, Rogue stepped out of concealment and stood in the passageway, facing Keithley down.

Rogue's heart beat fast as she sized up the man Keithley. He dressed like a male model and talked like a lawyer, and Rogue didn't trust him an inch. But it was supremely unlikely that a high-powered shark like Keithley would be doing security for an ordinary medical supply house. Her instincts told her that this was the break they'd been looking for, and that they'd better grab it by the tail while it was in plain sight.

"I'm delighted to hear it, Ms., ah—"

"You can call me Rogue, sugar pie," Rogue cooed in her best honeyed magnolia accents. She knew it would make Remy smirk, but there were times when old-fashioned Southern charm was as effective against a threat as mutant powers.

"Very well, Rogue." If Keithley had been put off balance, he certainly didn't show it. "I'm pleased that at least one of you has decided to be reasonable. Any idea where your partner is?"

Rogue's smile hardened, but the coo in her voice remained as she said, "Oh, Gambit's around here somewhere, Mr. Keithley. I do declare, there's just no keepin' up with that boy sometimes."

"Why don't we just assume that he's within the sound of my voice, then?" Keithley's easy diplomacy didn't waver, making Rogue even more suspicious. What sort of backup did he have to make him this confident?

"Before I get started on my pitch, I'd just like to mention that our employer, CGI—a perfectly legitimate private research lab, may I remind you?—is aware of your interest, and finds it rather alarming in view of the fact that both you and Gambit are fugitives from the law, with several outstanding warrants against each of you. It really undermines the X-Men's credibility in the court of public opinion to find them constantly extending sanctuary to people with such questionable backgrounds. No offense meant, of course."

"Of course." Rogue's smile was gone now, and her eyes were narrowed. In the harsh light of the warehouse, she looked like exactly what she was—a very dangerous woman who was rapidly running out of patience. "So, Mr. Keithley. You know what we want, or you wouldn't be here. What do *you* want? And I'd better like y'answer, sugar pie, or little ol' Rogue just might mop up the warehouse with y'all."

Keithley's smile, if possible, grew broader.

"It would be a shame to resort to violence, Ms. Rogue. We're certainly not your enemies. Oh, the Team may have had a few differences of opinion with the X-Men in the past, but we're just the errand boys, remember? Even the United States government is handing off more and more of its functions to private-sector companies like CGI. Privatizing is good for everyone, really. Mr. LeBeau? Are you sure you wouldn't care to join us?''

"You was jus' followin' orders? Dat your excuse, *hahn*?" Gambit growled, stepping out from between two shelves almost at Keithley's elbow. In his right hand he held aces and queens, fanned out and glowing with a deadly energy.

"Isn't it yours, Mr. LeBeau?" Keithley said blandly. "And once again, consider me only the messenger. But there's someone here who'd really like to talk to you, if you don't mind."

Gambit snorted eloquently. Rogue folded her arms across her chest and glared at Keithley.

"All righty, then," Keithley said with mendacious cheer. "Let's begin by bringing on our mystery guest. Folks, I'd really appreciate it if everybody was calm here, because toys like this two-way hololink I'm about to bring out don't grow on trees, and I'd hate like hell to spend tomorrow explaining to my supervisor where I lost it."

Rogue and Gambit exchanged identical glances. Making Keithley's life easy was not exactly high on their list of priorities at the moment. But tracing the link between Gotham Industrial Pharmaceuticals and Arnold Bocklin was.

The two X-Men watched warily as two more members of Black Team 51 appeared at Keithley's radioed summons, wheeling a tall black object that looked like a space probe between them. They brought it to a halt and began unlimbering its long spidery arms and locking them into position.

Rogue's attention was split between the Teamsters and Remy. From the way he held the cards in his hand, the so-called hololink would be yesterday's breakfast the moment Gambit decided it was a threat.

"We're going to power it up now," Keithley said. "I'd just like to warn you—if either of you has decided to grow a brain—that the signal originates from the other end and can't be traced from here, so there's no point in either breaking or stealing the nice machine."

Rogue didn't know Keithley well enough to be sure it was apprehension she heard in his voice—but she suspected it was. So beneath that cool Armani exterior, the hired boy was rattled, was he? Rogue smiled widely at the thought.

"Get on wid it," Gambit growled.

"As the man says," Keithley said unctuously. He gestured theatrically.

One of the other nameless Teamsters threw a switch. Multicolored lights came on all over the body of the slender black device, and red lights on the points of four of the arms began to glow. In instants, optical lasers had woven a web of light between the four pickups; a shimmering white screen that faded into color . . . and a familiar face.

"Greetings, Rogue and Gambit. I am Dr. Arnold Bocklin, of the Center for Genetic Improvement."

Bocklin was a vigorous man, somewhere in his late forties or early fifties—it was impossible to really tell—with the pallid skin of someone who spends too much time indoors, and swept-back black hair. His dark eyes seemed to meet Rogue's with a surprising intimacy.

"Which is where?" Rogue shot back.

Bocklin smiled. "In Atlanta, of course. That's common knowledge."

"Y'know that ain't what I meant."

"Ah, yes, of course, you wish to know the location of our laboratory facilities—information that I would be a fool to provide in light of the fact that the X-Men seem once more to be fulfilling their terrorist mandate and resorting to brute force in defiance of the law. What crime is it that I am supposed to be guilty of, Rogue? So far as I know, neither I nor my organization have done anything illegal.''

''You're experimentin' on mutants, ain't ya?'' Rogue shot back, but suddenly she wasn't as sure of her ground.

''I'm engaged in testing a certain drug on mutants—with their consent—yes. And I arranged this meeting in order to invite both of you to join my program.''

''Join you—be your guinea pigs, y'mean!'' Rogue said.

''An' Gambit don' t'ink much of de company you keep,'' Gambit said.

''Let us not descend to mudslinging, Gambit—and I'd remind you, in particular, of the old proverb about glass houses. Your presence among them could only reinforce the perception of the X-Men as not-too-selective terrorists. But let us return to the subject at hand.''

Bocklin paused for a moment. The warehouse was silent except for the humming of the hololink. Neither of the X-Men spoke. Rogue could feel Gambit staring at her, not at Bocklin, but she refused to look away from the face of the man on the screen.

''Apparently you have realized the connection between my research and the government's Emergency Intervention Bill and made a typical knee-jerk response to perceived mutogenocide. But is there any reason—other than your own petty self-interests, that Earth should not enjoy genetic homogeneity?''

This time Rogue darted a glance toward Gambit. His face was set, a mask of bleak anger unlike the carefree face Remy LeBeau usually showed the world.

''Y'doin' a great job of explainin' y'self so far, sugar,'' Rogue drawled mockingly.

''Then let me put it this way, Rogue—who's being hurt by this? It isn't as if the government is endorsing racial, ethnic, or religious purity. I find such notions contemptible—it is as if the ants on an anthill were to choose some among their interchangeable number to be superior to all the rest.''

• • •

Gambit stood in the shadows, watching Bocklin as the man spun out his glib rationalizations. It seemed so sensible, so reasonable, the way Bocklin laid things out. But then, totalitarian regimes always did, at first.

And there was something about Bocklin, something that nagged at Gambit more with every moment he heard Bocklin speak. As if the Professor had been right, and Arnold Bocklin truly had no real existence. As if the man who called himself Bocklin was in reality someone Gambit knew . . . and loathed with every fibre of his being.

"But is it not equally disturbing to live in a universe populated by walking H-bombs and mentally unstable anarchists with unimaginable power?" Bocklin went on. "All the government is trying to provide is a level playing field—a world in which no one would have any unfair advantage. A world where one more roadblock in the way of international brotherhood would be eliminated—without violence. Is that not a noble aim?"

"You from de governmen' an' you here to help us, *hahn*?" Gambit sneered. "Now, why you t'ink I b'lieve somet'ing like that, *cher*?"

His unease grew by the moment, though the members of Black Team 51 did not seem to present any real threat— and if they tried, he and Rogue could certainly deal with them.

"I don't know," Rogue said slowly. "Dr. Bocklin, you make it sound so easy, but we've all been hearin'—"

"About the retrovirus's mortality rate upon conversion, I expect," Bocklin said confidently. "I won't deny that we've had heavy losses among our experimental animals while we were refining our technique. And certainly some of our subjects require extraordinary medical support while the conversion is taking place. But we're prepared to provide that. CGI doesn't want the kind of trouble that frightened, misinformed people could start. This is America, after all, and cooperation with the program is voluntary.''

"Until y'get that bill passed!" Rogue said, and Gambit relaxed. For a moment he'd been afraid that his headstrong Dixie darling was going to buy Bocklin's pitch—and if Gambit's suspicions were at all true, that kind of gullibility would be fatal.

"Surely you aren't in favor of coddling criminals, Rogue?" Bocklin said, and there was a dark humor in his voice that made Gambit shiver. "Those who step outside the law forfeit the protections of society. Removing their extraordinary power to do harm—safely, humanely—can only benefit them, and society at large as well.''

Gambit saw Rogue shake her head slowly, chewing at her lower lip as she frowned indecisively.

"But until the Emergency Intervention Bill is passed, all cooperation with Project Level Playing Field is completely voluntary. And because that's the case, Rogue, I'm in a position to make you an extraordinary offer. Come in from the cold, submit to treatment with my retro-mutagen, and you'll walk away human, and with a full pardon for all the criminal acts you've ever committed.''

Bocklin was speaking only to Rogue now, as if somehow he knew that Gambit was not going to buy what he was selling.

"Think of it, Rogue. I'm not asking you to betray your friends—just to dare to be human. To live a normal human life out in the daylight, free to enjoy the same human freedoms as anyone else.''

She wouldn't do it, Gambit thought confidently. There were too many holes in Bocklin's story; too much riding on the unsupported word of a man none of them knew. It didn't match what the Beast had told them about how this gengineered retrovirus worked—and when push came to shove, the volatile Cajun X-Man knew whose word on how things were he'd rather trust.

"A full pardon?" Rogue said doubtfully.

"That's right. Submit to the treatment voluntarily and you gain a full pardon—and a normal life. If you agree, Keithley's team will bring you back to the laboratory with them. It can be all over within twenty-four hours."

Gambit readied himself for action. When Rogue refused Bocklin's so-generous offer, Black Team would certainly try to change her mind by force, giving Rogue and Gambit the opening they needed to take Bocklin's hired muscle apart.

"All right," Rogue said, so softly that Gambit nearly didn't hear her. "I'll do it."

"You will?" Keithley sounded nonplussed, though he struggled to conceal it.

"Excellent." Bocklin smiled like an attacking shark. "Mr. Keithley will conduct you back to my laboratory."

The screen of the hololink went dark, and the two Teamsters standing next to it began to power it down in preparation for taking it away.

"*Jamais!* Rogue, *ma chere*, you can't mean dat!" Gambit cried.

In that moment of Bocklin's triumph Gambit's suspicions had crystallized. He knew who was really behind the cover identity of Arnold Bocklin—and he knew also that to give any hint of his suspicions would be to doom himself and Rogue, and possibly all the other X-Men as well, to irrevocable disaster.

"Don't try t'stop me, Remy," Rogue cautioned in a low voice. "I've made up my mind t'do this thing."

She took a step toward the three Teamsters, her expression solemn and determined.

"But dat is somet'ing Gambit cannot permit," Gambit said glibly. With a casual practiced gesture, he flicked one of his charged cards at the hololink, sending it flying over backward in a shower of sparks and fried circuits.

"I told you not to do that!" Keithley yelped in genuine

anguish. "Stop him—now," he ordered his teammates as he drew his gun.

"Back off an' nobody get hurt, *mes amis*," Gambit warned. He had the rest of the cards in his hand, fanned out like a cobra's hood.

"Don't hurt him," Rogue said swiftly. "That ain't part of our deal." She turned to Gambit, fixing him with a steady warning gaze. "I'm a big girl now, Mr. LeBeau, an' I can make my own choices. An' I'm choosin' this—so back off."

"*Jamais de la vie, ma belle*," Gambit said. *Never*. He flicked another of the cards toward Keithley's feet, forcing the man in the corporate Armani to jump back hastily, though Gambit had no intention of hitting him. "I cannot let you do dat, *chere*," Gambit said stubbornly.

"Didn't you hear the lady, Cajun? Back off," Keithley said. One of his accomplices was gone—for reinforcements, inevitably—and Keithley had unholstered a bizarre-looking hand weapon and had it trained steadily upon Gambit.

Rogue took another provocative step toward Keithley, but her eyes were on her partner. "I'm tellin' you one last time—" she said.

"But *ma p'tite*, when 'as Gambit ever listen to reason?" Gambit answered, smiling coldly.

And threw the rest of the cards into her face.

What had been a handful of ordinary playing cards exploded as they touched Rogue's upflung hand. The force of the explosion sent her flying, though it did nothing to harm her, as Gambit had known it would not. At her best, Rogue was as close to invulnerable as made no never mind.

And now she was angry as well.

"That *tears* it!" she shouted, struggling to her feet, her moonlight and magnolias accent growing thicker as she lost her temper. "Mr. Keithley, you jus' stay outta the way an' let little ol' Rogue settle this Cajun trash's business.''

She looked around for Gambit. He was nowhere in sight. Then, suddenly, an entire range of storage shelves began to glow with the eldritch orange light of Gambit's biokinetic power.

''Oh no y'don't,'' Rogue muttered, half to herself.

She started toward the glowing shelves, and hesitated. The moment she touched them, she'd release their explosive charge of biokinetic energy. It wouldn't be enough to harm her—Rogue knew that Gambit was not trying to do that—but it might force the Teamsters to retreat and leave her behind, which was what the Cajun X-Man wanted.

Don't you see, Remy? Rogue pleaded silently. *This is my only chance to help the X-Men.* But there was no Phoenix or Professor X here to carry Rogue's thoughts to Gambit, and so she searched for some way to defeat him without harming him.

Briefly she took to the air, flying down the corridor to where the burnt-out hololink rested, abandoned by the Black Team. Though it weighed more than a hundred pounds, Rogue lifted it easily in one hand.

''I told ya t'scat, Mr. Keithley—I'll be along just as soon as I've pounded some sense into that thick Cajun skull.''

''Oh, no, Rogue,'' Keithley said fervently. ''I've lost the camera—I'm not letting *you* out of my sight.''

''Suit y'self,'' Rogue said, shrugging. Someone like Keithley could certainly take care of himself—and if he couldn't, Rogue wouldn't waste any tears on him.

She turned back to the glowing rack of shelving, and hefted the camera in one hand as if her awkward burden was a javelin. Then she threw it with all her might. It hit the shelves and exploded.

The noise was tremendous, echoing through the vast cement and steel cavern like the sound of Judgment Day. The contents of the shelving—liquid, glass, and steel—sprayed backward and away from the explosion. If Gambit were in the path of any of it, he'd surely be unconscious now.

But Gambit had not been behind the shelving. Even before he came to Xavier's, Gambit had been a master of feint and misdirection, and frequent Danger Room sessions had put the final polish on perfection. He would not be caught out so easily.

"There!" Keithley said.

Out of the corner of her eye, Rogue saw Keithley raise his bulky, peculiar hand weapon to a firing position. Red lights flickered along the barrel, and she heard an almost imperceptible whine as it powered up. She had no idea what it did, but she knew she didn't want it to hit Gambit. Turning, she grabbed the first thing that came to hand—a large plastic jar filled with something that had a very long name—and flung it at Keithley with an unerring overhand pitch she'd learned not in the Danger Room, but on the softball field.

It struck his forearm, sending the gun flying. She heard Keithley stifle a curse as it clattered to the ground in a shower of sparks, all the diodes on the barrel going dark.

"Aw c'mon, Janey Reb, don't you know the war is over?" Keithley shouted.

"Maybe," Rogue admitted through gritted teeth, "but y'know what they say, sugar—the South will *rise* again!"

And then Gambit landed on her back.

The impact flung Rogue to the floor, and even if it did no real damage, it surprised her. For an instant she forgot that her opponent was Gambit—her teammate, her friend— and fought back with everything she had. Rising to her feet, she reached back, grabbed Gambit's leather duster, and flung him over her shoulder with every ounce of her strength.

Only then did she realize what she'd done. Gambit's thieving skills were only what any normal human could attain through diligent training, and his mutant ability to charge an object offered him no extraordinary protection from Rogue's strength.

He'd counted on her to remember that, and she'd betrayed him.

Gambit crashed into a wall of shelving with enough force to topple it. As it fell, it hit the one beyond it, a domino effect that would have been funny if it hadn't been Gambit who was the human missile that caused it.

"Can we go now?" Keithley said, before the clatter had completely stopped.

Clouds of powder rose from the scene of the destruction. There were faint pings and groanings of metal as the collapsing shelves settled into their new positions, and beneath those sounds Rogue could hear other dripping, plopping, clattering noises.

"I have to make sure he's all right," she said. *Please, Lord, let him be all right.* "Then we can go."

"Fine," Keithley said. He held a .45 automatic in his hand, now, and did not replace it in its holster.

Two more Teamsters had arrived. One of them was wearing a power pack harness over his suit, which looked odd enough to claim Rogue's attention for a moment. In his hand he carried a long complex-looking silver cylinder that bore a vague family resemblance to Keithley's gun.

"The Moebius Lance, sir," he said to Keithley.

"You brought *that?*" Keithley said.

Rogue stopped listening. She had to be sure Gambit was all right.

There was movement beneath the pile of debris.

Gambit rose to his feet. In one hand was a length of metal, obviously one of the stanchions torn from the industrial shelving. He was covered in the spilled powders and liquids stored on the shelving, and looked as if he'd arisen from his own grave. His eyes glowed with red fire.

He wasn't happy.

"All right, *chere.* If dat de way you want t'ings, den

Gambit happy to oblige. But you not goin' wid dese men, *p'tite*, an' I mean that, me.''

''Remy, I—'' Rogue held up her hand, her own anger gone. Wanting to reason with him. Still so confident of her own ability to hurt him . . .

. . . that it never occurred to her that the reverse was also true.

Gambit charged and threw his makeshift bo-stick in an instant. It sizzled through the air like a red-hot thunderbolt from heaven, catching Rogue squarely in the solar plexus.

It hit with the impact of a giant's war hammer, driving the breath from her lungs, sending her flying backward. She didn't just knock over two shelves as Gambit had done. She knocked them all over, coming to a stop in a tangle of twisted metal jammed into the warehouse wall. Rogue shook her head groggily, slowly pulling herself loose from the wreckage.

But Gambit didn't let up. With all the debris scattered around the warehouse, he had no shortage of missiles available to him, and he peppered Rogue with a constant barrage of them. The tiny explosions did no particular damage to her near-invulnerable hide, but they kept her off balance and made it impossible for her to either attack him or take to the air.

''Get out of here, you!'' Gambit shouted at the Black Team. He flicked a handful of ball bearings at them—a trick he'd picked up from an old friend, though Gambit's steel spheres were far more deadly than Roger's had ever been—bracketing the four men in a cascade of explosions like the Fourth of July come early.

He did not stop to see what effect they'd had; he could not afford to let up on Rogue for an instant, lest his southern-fried sweetheart mop up the floor with him.

Keithley smiled slightly in response to Gambit's words. His smile faded in the moment that his backup fired the contraption he'd called the Moebius Lance at Gambit.

Gambit felt the blast of invisible energy as a sickening chill across his skin, one that made all the small hairs on the back of his neck stand on end. It had missed him, whatever it was, but that didn't make Remy LeBeau a happy man.

And worse, the hesitation it had caused him had given Rogue time to recover.

"That *hurt*!" Rogue bellowed in outrage. There was the squeal of tortured metal, and then a hunk of wreckage went flying as she clawed her way free of the cocoon of twisted metal. In another moment, she was aloft.

"Put that away!" Keithley shouted, grabbing the barrel of the lance and jerking it down before his fellow Teamster could get off another shot. "You and Berkowitz go get the chopper warmed up; however this goes, we're outta here in ten. Gein, DeSalvo, stay hot."

Gambit stood his ground only long enough to make sure that Rogue saw him—then he ran. He didn't care what anyone thought of his courage; he'd proved it to his own satisfaction many times in the past—and in this game, winning was defined as anything that would keep Rogue from getting on that helicopter.

He could stop her with a single sentence. But it was a sentence that—if he uttered it aloud—could doom all of the X-Men and everything they were fighting for.

Gambit gritted his teeth and ran.

He dodged like a rabbit fleeing an attacking hawk, doubling back to confuse her. If she followed him far enough, he won by default. Rogue liked to finish her fights. He was pretty sure he had her safe.

The door to the outside he'd brought them through less than an hour before should still be open. He'd unlocked it, after all.

He slammed into it full-force, wrenching at the handle.

It was locked.

"Goin' somewhere, lover?" Rogue called mockingly from behind him.

Gambit turned, his back to the door. Those Black Team *sce'le'rats* must have locked them in—who could have suspected that slumming male models would be so clever?

"Not wit'out you, *ma p'tite amie*. Rogue, sweetheart—"

"*Don't you call me that!*" Rogue shouted.

She landed just out of his reach—a little tousled from Gambit's love taps, but still a glorious, powerful woman. She pushed the hair out of her eyes with one hand and glared at him with those Scarlett O'Hara-green eyes.

"I'm not y'sweetheart," she went on, more quietly. "How can I be? I can't even kiss you—an' you're a man who needs kissin', Remy LeBeau, an' often. I can't even hold your hand."

"Rogue," Gambit said in an urgent undertone, "dis is not de way." He glanced over her shoulder. Keithley and his two fellow goons were waiting impatiently.

Behind his back, concealed from Rogue's sight, Gambit's right fist began to glow. What he planned was risky—both to himself and to Rogue—but if it worked, it was worth it. Once they got home to the mansion, *le Bête* could contact Xavier in Washington, and let him know that the danger was more terrible than any of them had dreamed.

"It's m'only chance t'be human, Gambit—t'get outta this damned bell jar. Don't try t'stop me. Y'owe me that much."

"Ver' well, *ma p'tite*. Gambit will be de perfect *gentilhomme*." He summoned up his most charming smile and began to walk toward her, praying to all the gods who watched over wayward thieves and Cajun vagabonds that she'd let him get close enough.

"Gonna kiss me goodbye?" Rogue said sadly. She held out her hand.

Gambit swung at her with his glowing fist. Rogue was stronger than all but a few of Earth's paranormals, but Gambit was as fast as the best.

Though his power worked only against inanimate objects, Gambit was betting that the discharge would be enough to shock her unconscious. Then all he'd have to do was blow the door and leave.

But Rogue dodged aside as if she'd been expecting his trick, grabbing his fist and yanking it aside.

"You shouldn't'a done that, partner," Rogue said sadly. She cocked back her own fist, her other hand holding him prisoner.

And for Gambit all the lights went out.

"All right," Rogue said. Her soft Southern drawl was made harsh by anger and regret as she lowered Gambit's unconscious body to the floor of the warehouse. "He's out like a light."

"Two for the price of one," Keithley said.

Rogue pointed a minatory finger at the Black Team leader.

"Oh, no, Mr. Keithley. I'm doin' this for myself— Gambit ain't got no part of it. You leave him right there."

There was a long moment in which Rogue could see Keithley weighing the odds in favor of taking Gambit along anyway, and her blood ran cold with dread. She knew she wasn't the best tactician among the X-Men—she could fill the fingers of both hands with the names of people who had more field experience or leadership training than she did. She'd come up with the best idea she could on the spur of the moment, and she was seeing more holes in it by the instant—but it was the only idea she had, and she was committed to it now.

"Anything to please a lady," Keithley finally said.

Rogue smiled and walked toward him, brushing the dust of battle from her clothing as she did so. She walked out of the warehouse toward the waiting helicopter without a single backward glance.

CHAPTER 7

They took Rewind's car back to her house. Pipedream didn't want to face his family right now, and Rewind's dad was away on a business trip, so her house was empty. He'd figure out some way to get back to his own car later.

Rewind had a new Mustang, metalflake lacquer purple as a bruise. It looked fast even when it was standing still, and Rewind didn't let it do much of that. She zipped onto the first on-ramp she saw and treated the freeway like her own private LeMans. Soon they were away from the river, out of the downtown, and on their way to Forest Hills. Pipedream lived there—he supposed it only made sense for Rewind to live there, too. *Golden lads and girls all must, as chimney sweepers, come to dust.* A line from English Comp suddenly haunted him. He didn't know what it meant—he never had—and he didn't understand poetry anyway. But it seemed somehow meaningful and depressing.

"Hey, slow down, would you?" Pipedream protested, as Rewind whipped around a Honda and cut back over into the far left lane. What long-haul truckers called the hammer lane, as in "put the hammer down."

Well, someone had sure put the hammer down on them tonight, all right. So much for the Ohio Mutant Conspiracy. Pipedream thought of the wreckage of the factory, and shuddered.

The easiest thing would be to pretend nothing had happened, to slip back into their own lives for as long as they could. It was a seductive thought, even though Pipedream knew it was stupid. The marshals hadn't just come for the other three—they'd come for all of them. He and Rewind had gotten away, but it didn't mean they weren't still wanted.

"It doesn't make sense," he muttered.

"Why should it?" Rewind said, even though he hadn't been speaking to her. "Life sucks, then you totally die."

She spotted the off-ramp she wanted and slewed across four lanes to reach it. Pipedream heard the chorus of horns faintly in the distance, as the sounds and light of the freeway dwindled behind the purple Mustang.

Forest Hills was an upmarket suburban development of what realtors liked to call "better homes"—though Pipedream's mom, who was a realtor, had never been able to tell him what they were better than. Four and five bedrooms, two and three baths, two-car garage and landscaped lot . . . each one looked different, but they all had an eerie sameness beneath the surface, and sometimes Pipedream wondered if he was the only one who saw it. Was that what growing up meant—turning your back on anything that might possibly be different?

Rewind turned into her driveway with a last hair-raising flourish and braked to a stop inches from the closed garage door. She turned off the ignition and turned to look at him for the first time.

"We're here. Welcome to *chez* Conway."

"The lights are on," Pipedream said, and immediately cursed himself for saying something so completely stupid.

"Timer," Rewind said, getting out of the driver's seat and slamming the door with a noise that made Pipedream wince. "Dad's off someplace," she added with a dismissive shrug.

Pipedream got out of the car and followed her as she walked up the front steps. He tried not to keep looking around, tried to believe that men in black were not hiding in the ornamental shrubbery that landscaped the house.

At the front door, Rewind punched a code sequence into the touchpad beside the door and swiped a magnetic key to enter. Once she'd opened the door and they were both inside, she closed the door and entered another set of codes. When the light burned green again, she sighed deeply.

"I always think I'm going to forget one of the stupid numbers and then we'd have every cop in the county here in about five minutes," Rewind muttered.

Pipedream looked around, and found several additional things to worry about.

Adults always assumed that kids his age knew nothing about where money came from or what it did, but that was naïve. Pipedream knew perfectly well that the car, the house, the security system, and the living room furnishings he could see through the archway, all added up to plenty of money—more than his folks had. Big-time money. *Serious* money.

The kind of money that ought to mean that—even if you *were* a mutant—people would not come knocking on your door in the middle of the night with guns.

"There's food in the fridge if you want. Cook's gone home, though," Rewind said.

"That's it?" A desperate anger he hadn't known he was capable of welled up in Adam Kirby. "That's it, have a nosh, you'll drive me home? And what about Slapshot, Lloyd, and Charade? We just write them off, right?"

"What am I supposed to do?" Rewind cried, whirling to face him. "Do I turn back time—erase the last two hours? Those guys will still be out there, *Pipedream*—they'll still be after us! But I forgot! Real superheroes don't care about things like that! So why don't I try it anyway?"

She clenched her fists. Pipedream felt a faint uneasy ripple in the fabric of reality as Rewind pulled at it. Without thinking about what he was doing, he closed the distance between them and shook her—hard. She squeaked in surprise and fell against him, and he could feel the frantic hammering of her heart under the aborted strain. The feeling made him grow cold with fear. Rewind was headstrong, willful, and stubborn. And she could very easily be dead.

"Don't be stupid, Pey! Not even you can turn time that far back—so don't be an idiot." If she tried to rewind time by more than a few seconds, the strain would kill her. "Do you want to die?"

"Yes!" she screamed. "I want to die before they come and kill me!" She burst into tears—shocking and noisy and much unlike the cool collected ice princess Pipedream had come to know. He held her against his chest, and wished that boys were allowed to cry, too.

"Well, c'mon," Rewind said, pushing herself away a moment later. She sniffled, and dragged a Kleenex out of her jacket, scrubbing at her face. "If you tell anybody I did that I'll deny it, right?"

Without giving him a chance to answer, she turned and ran up the stairs. Pipedream followed more slowly. He didn't think he was going to understand women even if he lived to be eighteen.

Rewind's bedroom was as big as Pipedream had expected, but the resemblance to his suppositions stopped there. While one end of it was filled with a typical bed, dresser, and stuffed animals, the other end was something he wouldn't have expected.

Two computers, a short-wave radio, and a police-band scanner—all on and chattering, the computers both scrolling through online chat rooms—competed for space with other things that Pipedream could not identify offhand. There were a stack of programmers' manuals, a half-open roll of small tools, and CDs scattered everywhere.

"Neat, huh?" Rewind asked without interest. She tossed her jacket onto the bed without looking and sat down at the desk, pulling one of the keyboards over to her.

"Your dad buys you all this stuff, huh?" Pipedream said,

looking over her shoulder. She'd checked out of the chat
room and was hunting around in DOS for something.

"Overcompensation," Rewind said. "Mom bailed and
he's on the road most of the time so I get prototype soft-
ware in lieu of quality time. So long as I'm a good little
girl and don't rock the boat, I get whatever I want."

"Does he know . . . what you are?" Pipedream asked
awkwardly.

Rewind's shoulders hunched as though she'd received a
blow. There was a long pause. "Daddy's little girls don't
grow up to be mutants," Rewind said, and now there was
baffled helplessness in her voice. "I don't know how to tell
him. He'll just get mad."

Pipedream wanted to say something to comfort her, but
he couldn't think of anything, and the moment passed. Rewind turned back to her machinery.

"What are you doing?" Pipedream finally asked, over
the crackle and blatt of the police scanner.

"Finding out what happened down on River Street thirty
minutes ago," Rewind said grimly.

"You mean . . . with us?" Pipedream asked.

"Don't you want to know?" Rewind sneered, and Pipedream flushed.

"Yes," he said evenly. "I want to know what happened
to my friends."

Now it was Rewind who was silent, her fingers flying
over the keys. Pipedream tried to imagine what she was
thinking, how she felt, but he couldn't. He couldn't get
away from the idea that what happened tonight was all his
fault.

They hadn't done anything wrong—well, as long as you
didn't count a little trespassing. All they'd done was find
each other, and take the first steps toward discovering
who—and what—they were. That wasn't a crime, was it?
And they were a long way from being superheroes, even if
they did have super-villains after them.

Super-villains? Those were the U.S. Marshals. The good guys.

But they hadn't acted like the good guys. They hadn't shown a warrant, or yelled "halt" three times, or anything—they'd just waded in with tear glass and bludgeons to a room full of kids.

Something wasn't right here.

This was not the way the good guys played it.

"Got it," Rewind said, drawing Pipedream's attention back to the screen.

Several colorful screens unfolded and were banished before Pipedream could see what they said.

"What it is, is I have a voice-recognition program hooked up to the scanner for when I'm out. I used to just tape the stuff, but you can read faster than you can listen, y'know?" Rewind said.

"Police scanner?"

"Police, fire, FAA. Whatever's going on. An informed populace is the first defense of freedom, right?"

"Uh . . . right." All Pipedream was sure of was that he didn't understand Rewind at all. "You ever rewind your computer?" he asked at random.

"Nope. I don't know if I could make all of it rewind at the same speed . . . and I don't want to find out what happens if I don't."

A flourish of keystrokes sent the file to the printer. Pipedream picked up the first sheet as it fed out.

"Let me." Rewind plucked the page from his hand and scooped more from the printer's out bin. "I've got it set up to insert a line return for every pause, but it's still sort of scatty. I've got to fix up that program one of these days." She was talking almost to herself as she skimmed down the pages of dense type. "Nothing . . . nothing . . . nothing . . . police band, but that isn't what we want . . ."

Pipedream handed her a new stack from the printer. Rewind threw the ones she'd already scanned into the waste-bin impatiently.

"Okay . . . here we are. Look."

Pipedream looked at the page she held out, but it seemed to contain a lot of phrases like "Tango Foxtrot," "Freedom Bird," and "Back Door" and not much else.

"So, what are we looking at?" he said weakly. Rewind shot him a mocking glance, as if to say she knew very well he couldn't decipher the transcript.

"Well, they aren't police or local—look at the frequency they're using. And they aren't talking in clear . . . this stuff about picking up five packages at the Batcave is probably . . . yeah, here. They're reporting that they picked up three packages, but the other two were out of stock."

"Lloyd, Charade, and Slapshot," Pipedream said grimly.

"Yeah," Rewind said, but she wasn't listening. There were a couple of moments of silence, then she did speak to him. "Pipedream—look."

He glanced down at the page again, where her finger was.

"Go to 1440?" he asked.

"That's the frequency for the tower at Cleveland Airport. And look, here's where they identify themselves to the tower."

"But that says they're a commercial courier," Pipedream said in confusion. "Are you sure that's them?"

"Sure enough," Rewind said grimly. "And you know what that means?"

"They aren't Feds. Feds would have identified themselves."

"Yeah," Rewind said with a bitter laugh. "It isn't like they were exactly inconspicuous."

"What they were, was quick," Pipedream said, taking the pages away from her and looking over the time-signatures. "They were there and gone in less than ten minutes.'' In and out quick, like a last-minute shopper stopping at the 7-eleven for just one thing.

He'd been right. They hadn't been the good guys at all.

Rewind got to her feet and began to fiddle restlessly with the techno-toys on her desk. After a moment she turned to Pipedream.

"What do we do, Pipedream? Where do we start looking?"

Pipedream didn't want to answer her—didn't want to tell her that he didn't have the faintest idea where to start. And in his desperation not to say it, he found the key.

"You've got the tower's transmission, right? Well, they have to have filed a flight plan, whoever they are. So where did they go?"

Rewind tapped several keys in succession. After a moment—and after a great deal of text incomprehensible to Pipedream scrolled by—she said, "Atlanta."

Then she got up and left the room. Pipedream followed her—they wound up in what had to be Rewind's father's study.

Whatever he did for a living, he must do it very well. Large uncurtained windows on the back wall looked out over the landscaped backyard. The desk was one of those enormous Hollywood models with a black leather top and a VDT beneath an inset glass panel. The chair behind the desk looked like it belonged on the bridge of the *Enterprise,* and there was a similar, smaller one facing it across the uncluttered expanse of desk. There were bookshelves built into both the long walls of the room, and a leather couch and high-tech coffee table completed the room's furnishings.

"What are we doing in here?" Pipedream asked.

"Seeing what came in the mail, maybe—and buying two tickets to Atlanta." She sat down and began to spin through the extensive Rolodex on the desk. That and a rosewood tray containing a stack of unopened mail were the only

things on the leather and glass surface. It was big enough
to set up a train set on.

Atlanta was a big place. How would two high school
students be able to find three other high school students
there? They could be anywhere.

Pipedream glanced at his watch, stunned to discover that
it was just a little after ten o'clock. So early! There was
still time to go back to his life; phone his mom and have
Dad drive over and pick him up. Pretend nothing had happened—or tell them everything, let *them* handle it. But if
it was so crazy *he* didn't believe it, why should they?

Assuming, of course, they were still there at all. Assuming there wasn't a man in black holding them at gunpoint,
waiting for him to call in.

Pipedream shook his head. He wasn't going to panic—
not yet—but he knew he was close to it. Nothing in all his
entire life had prepared him to deal with something like
this. He'd never asked to live in *The Twilight Zone*.

Of course, he'd never asked to be born a mutant, either.
And the ability to send people off to their own private Idaho
didn't seem to be of any particular use at the moment.

Pipedream picked up the mail, just to have something to
do with his hands. One envelope stood out—thick, stiff,
and creamy, and about as expensive as this home office.
The foil-embossed return address had a postmodern logo
over the words Center For Genetic Improvement . . . in Atlanta.

"What's that?" Rewind asked.

"Letter to your dad." He handed it to her.

After everything else he'd seen tonight, watching her
carelessly rip the envelope open should not have the power
to horrify Pipedream, but it did.

"That's your dad's mail!" he said.

"So?" Rewind said. "It's probably some kind of fund-
raiser; he'd throw it out anyway." She pulled two sheets
of thick paper out of the envelope and began to read.

Pipedream had been watching her, so he saw the moment when she went completely still, like an animal caught in the headlights of an oncoming truck. The color drained from her face, and a tiny part of his mind noted with detached interest that he could see the makeup standing out against her skin quite clearly.

Without a word she handed him the letter, and then sat down in the large chair as though she couldn't stand up any longer.

Someone named Ronald Ploog, who was a project manager at the Center for Genetic Improvement, wanted to tell Richard Douglas Conway, Esq. all about the medical miracles gene therapy had made possible. It looked like a standard begging letter, but Pipedream kept reading. A request for charity wouldn't have gotten that kind of a reaction out of Rewind.

At the top of page two, Ronald Ploog said that Richard's daughter Peyton was a mutant.

"... standard genetic screening has identified your daughter as an x-factor carrier ... new medical advances make this an easily correctable condition ... we invite ... new legislation pending ... treat her as part of a pilot program before the widespread implementation of this treatment ... absolutely confidential. ..."

Down deep inside him, in a place he didn't go very much, Pipedream felt a growing sense of outrage. There wasn't anything wrong with Rewind!

"He's gonna do it," Rewind said. "It doesn't matter if I tear it up. There's probably a copy waiting for him at his office. He's going to ship me off to them the moment he gets that."

"He doesn't have to. The letter says he can call and have you picked up." The joke fell flat and neither of them laughed.

This is not right. Pipedream couldn't say where the conviction came from. It was almost as if a force greater than himself was speaking to him, but he knew it was true.

"He'll come back . . . he'll get this and he'll just hand me over to be a part of their lousy 'control group'! It doesn't matter what I want—I'm not *old* enough to have opinions; I'm just supposed to do what I'm told," Rewind said furiously.

Rewind was on her feet again, anger galvanizing her. Pipedream could almost see the energy vibrating through her entire body; she was beautiful the way a stalking lynx or a thunderstorm was beautiful. Better . . . faster . . . stronger—wasn't that the *real* reason *homo sapiens* resented mutants? Not the flashy sideshow superpowers that some of them had, but the fact that they were just . . . *better*.

No. Don't think like that. Equality doesn't mean that everybody's all the same. It means everybody is treated the same way by the law, even if they're rich, or famous . . . or a mutant. Not better. Different.

"How long has your dad been gone?" Pipedream asked. He heard his voice as if from a long distance, the outrage and the anger filling him so full they seemed to push the world away.

"Almost two weeks," Rewind said dully. A tear welled up in her eye and trickled slowly down her face, carrying small flecks of mascara with it. "He'll be back day after tomorrow. And then he'll call them. And they'll . . . Adam, what will they do to me? I was *born* this way—what part are they going to cut off to make me just like everybody else?"

Pipedream looked at the envelope the letter had come in. It was dated ten days ago.

"I wish tonight had never happened! I wish none of this had ever happened! I wish it was still yesterday!" Rewind wailed frantically.

"So do I, but like it or not, we're here, and the rest of the team's been kidnapped. We've got to do something."

Rewind snorted derisively through her tears. "Like

what? Do we phone up the Fantastic Four and ask them to investigate? Maybe ask the FBI if they'd like a new X-file? The transcript I captured isn't proof of *anything* except me breaking the law. Who's going to take *our* word for what happened? The police? And once we tell them we're all mutants? Get ready for your guest shot on *America's Most Wanted*, football star.''

''Well, it isn't like what we are is much of a secret anymore, I guess,'' Pipedream said defensively. He looked back down at the letter lying on the table. ''Pey, do you think Jase and 'Vette and Lloyd's families all got letters like this from CGI?''

Had his?

Rewind looked directly at him for the first time since she'd read the letter, life rekindling in her eyes.

''You think *they're* the guys that took the others? To 'treat' them? A bunch of biotech weenies?'' Rewind asked. There was an uneasy mixture of horror and belief in her voice.

The moment she'd said it, the idea made perfect sense— perfect horrible sense—to Pipedream. The fake marshals had filed a flight plan for Atlanta—CGI was in Atlanta. Who else would have any interest in five not-particularly-powerful mutants, only three of whom were old enough to drive? But CGI had a use for them, it said so right there in that letter. Grab them and use them as guinea pigs for its pilot program, just like they planned to use Rewind.

And if CGI had managed to track down Rewind, it had probably located not only all the rest of the Ohio Mutant Conspiracy, but dozens of other mutants all over the city and state—and nation—that Pipedream didn't know about.

How many mutants *were* there in America, anyway? Was CGI planning to ''cure'' all of them? Weren't some of the Avengers mutants? What about the X-Men—they were all mutants.

"They can't do this," Pipedream said slowly. *This is not right.*

"Oh yes they can!" Rewind said angrily. "They think they can do anything they want, because they're a great big fat multinational with a lobbyist in Washington and a record of big fat contributions to all kinds of political parties! But they're not going to do it to us. C'mon, Pipedream— we know where to go, now. We're going to Atlanta."

"Atlanta?" Pipedream almost yelped, startled out of his conspiracy theorizing. Atlanta had been the address on the letter. "But . . . we can't. How will we get there—and what if CGI *doesn't* have Lloyd and the others?"

"Look, my dad's a corporation lawyer. He hangs out with guys like these all the time, and I know all about them. If CGI *doesn't* have them, they know who does. And they're either going to tell us, or the whole world is going to see us asking where our friends are on a live CNN special."

"What if they, you know, do it to them before we can get there?" Pipedream asked weakly.

"They won't have," Rewind said, and in her voice Pipedream heard the iron determination of someone who would stop time in its tracks if she didn't like what she found in Atlanta.

"Besides—if we don't rescue our friends, who will?"

CHAPTER 8

Welcome to the Great White North. The last frontier, the last legendary land. Never mind that it's an up-to-date Commonwealth nation with a longer settled history (in parts) than its flashy southern neighbor; all most people think of when they envision Canada are Mounties and gold fields. Jack London, Robert Service, and other wordwrights now forgotten staked out claims to this literary motherlode, and it's their nineteenth-century version of the truth that starry-eyed southerners still take as gospel even in the final decade of the twentieth. Humans against nature, humans against humans . . . it doesn't matter if you believe in myth or truth; it's still all here, every kind of battle you could ever hope for.

And in some places, the myth seems more real than the truth.

Calgary looks like an American city, but not quite. Not really English either; it's that particular elusive cultural identity that's challenged preconceptions for centuries. Natives take it for granted, tourists learn to. But in one place that nagging cognitive dissonance fades. In the district that belongs to no city, and to every city.

Logan had hit the city twenty-four hours before, and since then he hadn't slept. Too many people to see. Too many words to drop in the right ears. Like a spider in the center of an enormous web pulling on the strands to bring in the prey.

It was a way of working alien to his essential nature—loner, tracker, hunter—but it was disturbing how easily it all came back to him. Walking out of the airport had been like walking into a theater filled with an invisible audience, all looking at him as he strutted his brief hour upon the stage. All ready to be manipulated.

Now he sat in the Silver Slipper Saloon nursing a beer and a smoke, thinking over what he'd learned and waiting to learn something more. In his Stetson, denim jacket, buffalo plaid shirt, and boots, Wolverine looked a little like a rodeo cowboy—maybe not a top-money rider with a big silver buckle, but at least like a circuit regular who wasn't afraid to take a fall. He wasn't out of place among the Silver Slipper's clientele, most of whom were dressed much as he was. Calgary, gateway to the mythic West, a land that no longer existed except in dreams.

And, sometimes, nightmares.

Many years before, his life had ended in a place much like this one—in a cheap saloon out under the Northern Lights, where men who had thought he could be useful to them had come and taken him against his will. Changed him, turned him into a weapon, making him more than human, and less.

But then, he'd never been quite human, had he? Mutant born, with a healing factor that stopped entropy and let him wander—an unaging ghost—through lives and decades. His mind choked with memories of all the lives he'd led.

Memories that had been ripped away in chunks, leaving him a bitterly defended sense of self, but not a lot of personal history. He remembered Project X very clearly, though—Project X, hell-bent on creating a bionic super weapon for domestic use.

He knew the way the people who ran projects like that thought. The paranormals who were fodder for their programs were not human to them, they were playing pieces. Playing pieces could be sold . . . traded . . . horded. And if the X-Men knew nothing else about Arnold Bocklin and the Center for Genetic Improvement, they knew that Bocklin and CGI were receiving a steady stream of mutant experimental animals who checked into the project, then disappeared.

Where?

That was one of the questions Wolverine had come north to answer. Where did the mutants come from, where did they go? Who rounded them up for Bocklin? Who did he owe favors to, and who was paying off favors to him? Where had he done his apprenticeship in the sordid trade of butcher of souls?

And strange as it might seem, Wolverine's contacts had all been expecting him. They were, if not anxious to talk, at least resigned to talking. As if it had only been a matter of time before Wolverine appeared and began asking questions.

He'd been too good an operative in his day to tip his hand by asking leading questions or showing the least surprise. His own questions could wait. He'd let them tell him what they thought he wanted to know, instead.

And what they thought he wanted to know about was something called Project Trapdoor. A big, scary, dangerous code name, for . . . what?

He had no idea.

But he didn't intend to remain in ignorance long.

"Sorry I'm late." The petite Chinese woman who slid into the seat opposite Logan had the practiced charm and dramatic grooming of a professional escort. Against the sordid glamorousness of the Silver Slipper, Connie Lau stood out in her blue satin dinner suit and elaborate makeup like a visitor from another planet.

Wolverine flagged down the waitress and ordered a drink for Connie and another for himself. He'd worked with Connie before, though he had no idea who she reported to. Connie was a problem solver. She never appeared until the situation had gone beyond serious and was heading for irretrievable.

He ground out the stub of one cigarillo in the tin ashtray and lit up another, striking the wooden kitchen match on the sole of his boot. He hoped she wasn't here to try to kill him. He would sincerely regret what had to happen after that, if it were true.

"Connie," he said, cautiously greeting her.

The waitress brought their drinks. Connie tasted hers and made a kitten face. She didn't look a day older than she had the first time he'd seen her, and that was . . . well, a long time ago, anyway. He wondered idly how old she was—and what she really looked like behind the exquisite mask of makeup. The kohl made her brown eyes startlingly light, like the eyes of a lynx, or a Kodiak who's just decided you're dinner.

"Logan. It's been a long time," she said, just as if they were the old friends—or business acquaintances—they seemed to be.

Yeah, Con, a long time. And I was expecting someone to meet me here tonight, but not you, babe.

"A long time," he said aloud.

"And I suppose you've come about the project. You always were soft, Logan—too many scruples—but I don't think there's anything you can do this time." She sipped her drink.

The description of him as "soft" charmed Logan momentarily, but then he considered the source. Connie Lau was a stone-cold killer, completely without a conscience. Her one concession to morality was to sell her services exclusively to the country of her birth, Canada.

"Is that what you've come to tell me, Connie? To go home?" Wolverine said. He flexed his fists, feeling the points of his claws move just below the skin, wondering if she was holding something on him beneath the table. Wondering which of the escape routes he'd take if this turned dirty. Wondering about her backup. Wondering.

Connie's eyes flickered for a moment in recognition of

her danger. But Wolverine didn't smell fear on her. He
never had. Only the scent of her makeup, and a faint flow-
ery perfume. Jasmine and cordite. It had been a joke between them—the sort of true, unfunny joke that
professionals shared about things neither of them could
change.

"No, Logan. I haven't come to tell you anything. I've
come to give you Project Trapdoor."

Instantly all Wolverine's senses strained to greater alertness. He'd expected information, but Connie was saying
she'd give him everything—location, approaches, names.

"Why?"

"Those were my orders." Connie sighed, and for a moment her shoulders slumped, as if she were tired. "Come
on, Logan, you know me. That's what I do. I follow orders.
I was given the information to pass to you—do you think
I spend my spare time riffling my control's files?"

No. As long as they worked her and paid her and kept
her out of the official eye, Connie did what she was told
without question. Another difference between the two of
them.

"You worked for the government, last I heard," Logan
said, taking a pull on his drink. "Project Trapdoor's a government project. Why rat them out?" His eyes flicked left,
right, trying to decide where her backup was. He couldn't
see anyone, and in a dive like the Silver Slipper he sure
couldn't smell them. If Connie had a backup, he or she was
either good . . . or far away.

"Don't you ever watch *The X-Files* where you are, Logan?" Connie said impatiently. "It doesn't matter if we all
work for the same side on paper. Whatever Trapdoor is,
someone doesn't mind if you quash it. So here I am."

It was reasonable enough—interdepartmental feuding
wasn't always a bloodless affair conducted behind closed
doors in high offices. Involving him might even be a cover
for somebody else's own strike against it. And whatever

happened to Project Trapdoor, it would be Wolverine, the rogue operative, that the blame fell on.

Of course, a lot of people would be happy to just settle for retiring Wolverine—permanently.

"One last time, Connie, and make it convincing—why you?" Logan growled. Connie Lau wasn't a messenger. She was a cleaner. That meant no bodies, no traces, no comeback, when Connie Lau worked.

The petite woman opposite him drained her drink, then regarded him steadily, a weary light in her cold brown eyes. A look that suggested that, for Connie Lau, there was no way in from the cold.

"My jacket says we've worked together. I could ID you and not be sandbagged by your polished charm, lover. That's all they told me. I don't even know anything about Trapdoor, okay? I brought you a briefing package; it's in my evening bag. Logan, lighten up, can't you? We were *partners*."

Logan smiled, knowing what everyone around them ought to see. The cowboy and the hired girl, and a little discussion that was—probably, inevitably—about money.

"Connie, you'd try to kill me without batting an eyelash, if they ordered you to."

She smiled. It lit up her face, making her glow. Masking the stone killer for a brief moment.

"Sure," Connie Lau said readily. "But I'd miss you, Logan. I really would."

As if she'd be the one who survived.

She smiled again; a meaningless gesture that did not reach her eyes. "Take it or leave it, lover, this is what I've got for you. I'm only the messenger."

Wolverine glanced toward her evening bag. It was a little envelope clutch in silver lamé. On the table in plain sight.

"It was good to see you again, Connie." Maybe she was telling the truth. "Get out of the life. It's going to kill you one of these days." It killed them all. Everyone Logan loved who had walked in the shadows had been eaten by them in the end.

"You should give up smoking, Logan. It'll kill you first." Casually she propped both elbows on the table and leaned forward. The bag was swept back, off the edge of the table and onto the seat of the booth. "Got to go powder my nose, lover man. Back in a few."

She got to her feet and walked toward the back of the room, her sky-high heels going *tik-tik-tik* on the Silver Slipper's worn linoleum, looking like an elegant locust. Wolverine reached under the table and snagged the evening bag. Under the cover of the table, he pulled the bag to him and opened it, assessing the contents by touch.

A miniature cassette recorder, the kind that held about thirty minutes of notes. A five-by-seven envelope that felt like it held a few pictures. The bag held nothing else. Wolverine transferred the contents to his jacket pockets and tossed the bag back onto Connie's seat.

No one had seen.

He nursed his drink and lit up another cheroot, and waited for Connie to return so they could play out the end of the act.

A few hours later in a rented room in a transient hotel, Wolverine got the chance to look at the photographs and listen to the tape. The photographs began to fade the moment they were exposed to the light—in half an hour the image would be gone. When the tape had played to the end and self-destructed, Wolverine began to laugh.

It was a harsh sound, and there was no humor in it.

"Look. There's no point in sitting around here waiting. We've got to get out of here," Slapshot said.

He said it because neither of the others would say it, and because it had to be said. More than that, he had to act on his words.

"How?" Lloyd asked bluntly. It was nine o'clock in the morning. He was wedged into a corner of one of the bunks, holding Charade in his arms. Slapshot couldn't tell whether she was asleep or not. "There's nobody around for 'Vette to convince, and the superpowers of a dog aren't worth . . . well, a heck of a lot." His voice was bleak.

"Don't give up yet, Cosmic Canine." Slapshot made his voice sound more cheerful than he felt. "There's still Slapshot, the Kinetic Avenger."

"You?" Lloyd Englehart tried not to sound doubtful and failed.

"Yeah. Me. I think, if we can punch a hole through that lock assembly, the door might open automatically."

"We'll still be in here," Charade said, sitting up and wrapping her arms around herself. "I mean, out-there-in-here, you know, Jase—I mean Slapshot."

Is this what all leaders feel like? Slapshot thought. *Panicking inside, and still trying to seem confident to the people they lead? If only it didn't seem so much like lying. . . .* "That's where you come in, Charade. You tell the first person we meet that they've decided to let us go. He'll believe you."

"Until he runs into somebody else," the petite black teenager said. She gazed up at Slapshot with worried hazel eyes. "You know they don't believe me once they think about it." She ran a hand over her hair, pushing the beaded braids back from her face.

"Well, Lloyd can make sure we don't run into anybody that contradicts you," Slapshot said soothingly, remembering that Charade was only fourteen, still a kid.

"And you're gonna get the door open," Lloyd said. Disbelief was patent in his voice, and Slapshot kept himself from snapping back at him with an effort. *Why can't you at least pretend to believe me, Dogbreath?* But he didn't say the words aloud. "Turn out your pockets, Lloyd. I'm going to need your spare change."

With all three of them contributing, they had almost two dollars in pennies, nickles, dimes, and quarters. Charade and Lloyd were looking at Slapshot as if he were their last hope.

Which might have been the truth. Because if the three of them didn't get out of here, Slapshot suspected that what was going to happen next was not going to be very nice at all.

He glanced back at the door. The lock mechanism was halfway down the left side of the door. If he could break that, the door *had* to open. He picked up a quarter.

"Jase." Lloyd was pointing. Slapshot's gaze followed his finger.

At the opposite end of the room from the door, up near the ceiling, was a small black lens, set almost flush with the wall. Preoccupied with their own fears, none of them had seen it before.

"Some kind of camera?" Slapshot wondered aloud. He tossed the coin in his hand up into the air and then caught it.

Then he threw it. It had nearly reached the camera eye when Slapshot stopped it and sent it flying toward the door. Back and forth, until its trajectory was a silvery blur and it took all of Slapshot's concentration to keep track of it.

Then at last he let it go.

The small silvery disk—legal tender for all debts, public and private—slammed into the lens of the camera with all the force of a speeding bullet. There was a popping explosion that made all three of them jump, and when the smoke had cleared, all that was left of the spy camera was a square hole in the wall.

"Now let's get to work, okay, guys?" Slapshot said.

They'd caught a late-night flight out of Cleveland, arriving at Atlanta International Airport in the early hours of the morning. The rental car Rewind had reserved on her father's card was waiting for them, but once the clerk had gotten a look at both of them, they wouldn't have gotten it but for Pipedream hitting her with his powers. While the rental clerk stood, silently lost in her reverie, Rewind had gone behind the counter in the kiosk and spent a brisk few minutes on the keyboard, getting their paperwork and the keys. They were gone before the woman woke up. With luck, she wouldn't even remember seeing them.

They were tired, and neither of them was familiar with the city. Rewind drove while Pipedream tried to decipher the street maps. CGI was outside the city limits, on the opposite side of the city from the airport. They took the wrong turnoff almost immediately.

"I think we—" Pipedream began.

Rewind jerked the wheel hard, pulling the car off to the side of the road. As Pipedream stared, she pounded on the steering wheel, weeping with fury.

"Stupid—stupid—stupid—" she raged.

Awkwardly, Pipedream tried to comfort her. But when he put his arm around her he only succeeded in drawing her fury to him instead.

"Leave me alone!" Rewind shrilled. "This isn't going to work! They're already dead!"

"No they're not!" Pipedream shouted, equally fiercely. He refused to believe in any other possibility. "They were alive a few hours ago. You saw that letter—they just want to change them." His voice sounded hollow in his ears.

"Maybe they already have." Rewind sat hunched over the wheel, her head down. Her voice was exhausted, defeated.

"No." A crazy intuition possessed Pipedream—but crazy or not, this was what Rewind needed to hear. "Look at your watch. It's four o'clock in the morning. Those fake marshals may work around the clock, but they're not the ones who're going to do it, are they? It won't be until after nine o'clock in the morning, after whoever does it gets to work." He cast around for something else to distract her before she thought to question him further. "Look. There's a McDonald's down there.'' Pipedream pointed toward the middle distance, where the red and gold sign could be seen floating in the darkness, a lure to weary and hungry travelers. ''We could both use something to eat. Why don't you take the next exit, we'll get some food and go over the map together?''

For a long moment he thought she was going to refuse—and if she did, Pipedream wasn't sure what he'd do. They'd called themselves a superteam in fun, and he'd been the de facto leader, but it wasn't really true. If any of them refused to follow his suggestions, there was nothing he could do to compel them. He was no leader.

And they weren't superheroes. They were high school students who happened to be mutants, targeted by their heritage for adult insanity just because of what they were.

It wasn't fair.

''Okay,'' Rewind said finally. Her voice was hoarse, as though she were holding back tears. ''You're the boss, Pipedream.''

After that, things went more smoothly. They retraced their path, found where they'd gone wrong, and reached CGI a little after six o'clock.

They were on a secondary road, approaching a turnoff. There was a big sign at the edge of the road that said CENTER FOR GENETIC IMPROVEMENT on it. A sign on the opposite side of the turnoff identified it as a private road. In the distance Pipedream and Rewind could see a complex of low white modern buildings—none over six stories—that obviously belonged to CGI.

''It looks too normal to be true,'' Rewind said, looking at CGI's Atlanta corporate offices.

''I know,'' Pipedream said. They reached the turnoff. ''Keep going.'' Rewind stared at him for a moment in amazement, but obeyed.

When they pulled off a mile or two later, Pipedream said, ''It's like this—I think maybe I can bluff our way in there, with your help, but if we do that, what about the car? If they do anything to it, there goes our only chance of getting away—and if they connect it with us, and trace it, it's on your dad's credit card, isn't it?''

"So," Rewind said, drawing the word out as she thought, "we need to find some place really close to hide the car where we can get it again, and then we go in and get them out, right?''

"And then we go in and get them out," Pipedream agreed. But in his heart he felt it so much more likely that they would simply all die together.

"I'm bringing Peyton Conway here to drop her off, like it says in the letter." Pipedream spoke slowly and soothingly, wishing desperately that Charade were here. She could convince anyone of anything—all he could do was make them dream.

The main entrance to CGI looked more like the entrance to a military base than that of a corporate office park. There was a high fence with warning signs on it telling passers-by that the fence was electrified, and a checkpoint that every vehicle that entered the complex had to pass through.

And so did Pipedream and Rewind.

"Everybody already knows about this. You just have to let us go on in," he said soothingly.

Pipedream was using the smallest portion of his pipe-dream power he could manage. They didn't want the man oblivious—they needed him awake and willing to operate the motorized gate.

And he had to do it soon. It was after eight A.M. They were running out of time.

"Let us in," Rewind urged, adding her wholly human persuasion to Pipedream's.

And finally the gatekeeper, his eyes turned inward on visions of his own, turned back to the gatehouse and

pressed the button that sent the mechanical gate sliding
backward on its track.

"Come on," Pipedream said to Rewind, taking her hand.
"We have to get inside before he wakes up."

And before Rewind thought to ask him how they were
going to get out again.

Slapshot had never been so tired in his entire life. It was a
weariness that seemed to come from a deeper source than
physical exertion, almost as if he were expending some
unrenewable part of himself. His muscles ached, but he
forced himself to toss another coin into the air, to play it
as it flitted back and forth like a demented dragonfly, and
at last to aim it at the lock on the door.

But at the last moment his concentration failed him; the
coin hit at an angle, several inches off target, and bounced
off the wall to hit the floor.

Slapshot clenched his fists and barely kept from swear-
ing.

"Hey, uh, Jase—maybe you ought to take a break?"
Lloyd suggested quietly.

The well-meant suggestion only irritated Slapshot. At the
opposite end of the room, the lock assembly looked like
the surface of the moon—pitted with craters the size of
nickels, dimes, and pennies, but still intact. He'd been
working at it for the hardest fifteen minutes of his life, and
he hadn't been able to punch through it.

"I could see if I could maybe get it open now that you've
softened it up," Lloyd went on.

"Save your strength, Dog Star," Slapshot said. *Who the
heck's writing my dialogue?* "You ain't seen nothing yet,
as the actress said to the bishop."

*There you go again, your mouth writing checks your
body can't cash.* But this was one promise Slapshot *had* to
make good on, for all their sakes.

He inspected the small store of change still spread out

on the bunk. If something was going fast enough, it didn't matter how much it weighed, but at the moment Slapshot was feeling insecure enough to hedge his bets.

"Lloyd, you still got your lucky piece?" he asked.

"Sure do." Lloyd sounded puzzled. He fished it out of his pocket—a brightly-polished golden disk about the size of an old-time silver dollar, with the word STRIKER embossed several times around the rim of the reverse. The obverse side had an enamelled atomic energy symbol stamped into the surface. It looked lethal.

Slapshot took it and hefted it in his hand. It weighed about an ounce, and was probably the densest item any of the three of them could come up with.

"What're you going to do with that, Slapshot?" Charade asked.

She'd been very quiet this last hour—too quiet, in the opinions of anyone who knew Charade at all well. Slapshot worried, with a clinical detachment he hadn't known he possessed until now, that she'd fold up if the pressure kept on, becoming a liability to the team.

The team. Hah. We're not any kind of team—we're just . . .

Victims? Mutants? Slapshot wasn't too pleased with either answer. Refusing to think any longer, he tossed the striker up into the air.

"I'm going to get us out of here, Charade." *This time for sure.*

The golden disk sailed up and then began to fall naturally. Slapshot knew the limit of his power—he couldn't add momentum to an object; he could only change the direction it was going. It wasn't even really telekinesis as he understood it. But it was going to have to be enough.

Up—down—up—the disk began to blur. Terminal velocity was his outside limit—the speed an object would reach falling through infinity.

Up—down—up—the air was humming now with the

passage of the disk speeding through it. The coin itself was a flickering golden flash in the blurred pillar of its movement, speeding too fast for anyone but Slapshot to see it. *Maybe I can push it just a little faster . . .*

He'd never tried that before—but he'd never been this desperate before. Reaching deep into himself—into the place where the x-factor twisted him irrevocably away from the baseline of humanity—Slapshot reached for *more*.

The humming sound the disk made became higher, louder. Lloyd and Charade flinched away from it almost unconsciously. Slapshot could feel his heart race with the effort he was making, could see the blackness infiltrating his field of vision, but he wouldn't let up.

Faster—faster—*faster*. . . . He was going to lose it any minute now, but he could feel that Lloyd's striker was still accelerating. He had to judge his moment carefully. This was all he had to give—if he failed here, there would be nothing left.

The piercing whine that the hurtling coin emitted seemed to hit right behind his eyes, darkening his vision until sound and color merged into a red fog. He closed his eyes, willing himself to stay conscious as he held on until the last possible minute.

And then let go.

There was a sound like a gunshot, louder than any of the previous impacts had been. Slapshot jerked back from the edge of unconsciousness and stared at the door.

It was opening. And as it rolled back, he could see a neat round hole just the size of Lloyd's striker, punched dead-center through the locking mechanism.

For a moment his blood ran chill, one terrifying thought uppermost in his mind: if he could do that to a door, he could do it to a person . . .

Please, Lord, don't ever let anything like that happen, Slapshot prayed wildly. "Okay, guys, c'mon, let's go," he said aloud, pushing himself to his feet. "Lloyd, show us the way out of here."

"Where are we going?" Rewind whispered.

I wish I knew, Pipedream thought.

It had been fairly easy to get inside the building—it had a keycard lock, but it had been simple enough to lurk until someone else opened it, and then have Rewind go back far enough so that they could go through, too. The guards who had just—so they thought—seen the two of them use a keycard to enter didn't bother Pipedream and Rewind as they passed through the reception area, and, following in the wake of CGI's early arrivers, they made their way deeper into the building, navigating by means of the cryptic signs posted where corridors crossed one another.

Which way should they go? Where were the others? If they could find the person in charge of the project, maybe they could run another bluff—and maybe not.

Chutzpah could carry you exactly so far. Now they needed a miracle.

"Come on," Rewind said, dragging him into an office with a half-open door.

"What are you *doing*?" Pipedream demanded in a whisper.

The office was empty, fortunately. It was one step up from a *Dilbert* cubicle: a window, a potted plant, a bookshelf, and a desk with a computer, all in various shades of white. Rewind slid into the seat behind the computer and began riffling the drawers.

"Lock the door, Pipedream," she said abstractedly.

"What are you doing?" he repeated, even as he moved to comply. There was a button in the middle of the brushed aluminum knob; he pushed it in, locking the door. It would protect them—at least until somebody on the other side came up with a key. He looked at his watch. Almost nine o'clock. Whoever's office this was, they'd be showing up to claim it soon.

"Got it!" Rewind crowed. "Morons always leave their password written down somewhere—security? We don't need no steenkin' security." She dropped both hands to the keyboard and began to type in a rattle of keys. "We're in," she said a moment later. "Ooh, this loser's got supervisory access to the system."

Pipedream moved around to the other side of the desk, where he could watch the screen. The CGI logo dissolved into menu after menu as Rewind clicked on each button just as if she knew what she were doing.

"Rewind," Pipedream said, in a tone that demanded, *Tell me what you're doing—and right now.*

"I'm looking for me," she answered. "Because they sent my dad a letter, so I've got to be in here somewhere. And wherever I'm filed, the other guys should be, too."

And then we can go there. Pipedream felt a sudden surge of gratitude that Rewind had figured out what to do next. Maybe that was what being a team was about, each of them filling in what the others lacked.

"They're here," Rewind said in a choked voice.

Pipedream looked down at the screen. There was a long list of names he didn't recognize—real names and code names both—and down at the bottom, three he did: Davetta Mantlo, Lloyd Englehart, and Jason Gerber.

Theirs were the only names on the list colored red.

"Scheduled for conversion?" he said, his voice harsh and strained.

"But not converted yet," Rewind answered, her voice equally harsh. "And this thing's got a modem."

Pipedream figured out what she meant a few moments later, as Rewind dialled her own computer back in Cleveland and began to download a file.

"It's a real nasty virus," she said happily. "Usually it'd just get eaten by the security measures on the system, but not if a supervisor downloads it himself. I can disperse it as random-generated e-mail, and once it's activated, it'll eat the hard disk and then go looking for other hard disks—and mainframes—to eat. CGI has a LAN, which means the virus should be able to take down most of the in-house system before anyone catches it.''

"Won't they be able to trace it back to you?'' Pipedream asked.

Rewind looked at him as if he were out of his mind. "Sure; just as soon as they scope their phone bill, sometime next month. But I don't actually think that's our major problem right now, do you, boss?''

"I suppose not,'' Pipedream said doubtfully. He supposed he ought to get used to thinking of this as the end of his life, but he still kept hoping that this whole nightmare was something that they could all walk away from and go back to life the way it had been before.

He'd be happy to give up a not-particularly-useful mutant power if that was the price he had to pay. He just couldn't convince himself that whoever had planned their kidnapping was going to stop with the five of them. And it might start with mutants, but where was it going to end?

"They're in the other building—there's a lab, see? There's tunnels connecting all three of the buildings.'' On the screen now was a multicolored schematic of the CGI complex. The mouse arrow flashed with white light, heartbeat-swift, in the bottom corner. "C'mon.''

Rewind half-rose from her chair, then dropped back down into it again. Quickly she typed a string of letters and numbers and hit RETURN.

"Bye-bye, CGI,'' Rewind said. "Don't mess with the best.''

Pipedream grabbed her and dragged her out of the chair. Behind them the VDT flashed like a malevolent idol's eye.

They got to the door. Pipedream closed his hand over the knob.

As if on cue, every alarm in the building went off at once.

"Quit stalling, Clarendon."

Ploog's voice was harsh and unexpected; Crown jumped, banging his head on the top of the access panel. He glanced surreptitiously at his watch. Almost nine o'clock. Maybe he could plead the fact that he'd been here more than eighteen hours and go home.

But they'd just find somebody else to run the equipment—and not as well.

"Stalling?" Crown echoed. "You wound me, Ronnie. Why would I stall?"

Ploog didn't have an answer to that; he changed tactics. "The check-through only takes ninety minutes to run. It's been three hours. What's the holdup?"

The fact that I don't want to kill a fourteen-year-old girl. "Well, in the first place, there's the fact that the last package really tuned up the equipment," Crown improvised. "And with a federal observer on site, do you really want to chance one of the packages going *splat* right before her eyes?"

"She's at breakfast with the Chairman," Ploog said, as if that made a difference. "And Dr. Bocklin called from Berne—we have to run these packages pronto to make room for a new shipment."

Terrific. "We'll run them as soon as I've checked out the delivery system completely," Crown repeated stubbornly.

Ploog smiled then—not a pleasant sight. Too late Crown realized that he should have trashed the system while he'd had the chance.

"I think we can save you the trouble, Clarendon. After all, we're testing the equipment for reliability in field conditions. Why don't we just run the first package as is?"

"Why don't you get off my back, Ronnie?" Crown snarled, knowing even as he did so that the sound was one of helpless defiance.

Ploog knew it, too.

"Why don't I just call down and have them prep the first package?" *And keep an eye on you and the equipment at the same time,* his expression plainly said.

"Oh sure," Crown snarled bitterly, "and while you're at it, you can think up a really good explanation for Dr. Bocklin about why all four packages we ran today died."

It was a shot fired at random, but Crown saw from the flicker in Ploog's eyes that he'd been right—Psychostorm was dead.

And he'd helped kill him.

Though Crown hadn't expected it to help, oddly enough, the invocation of Bocklin's name actually slowed Ploog down. The corporate hatchetman hesitated, searching for a properly annihilating response.

And at that moment, every alarm in the building went off.

The sound—a clashing cacophony of a dozen different alarms—was the loudest thing Slapshot had ever heard, and he could see that Lloyd was in agony. The canid mutant reeled down the hall as if he'd been blinded, hands jammed over his ears.

That couldn't be helping much. The sound seemed to beat in upon them through the skin itself. Distantly, Slapshot could feel Charade clinging to his arm. Now that they were free, they must not lose each other.

And every minute counted.

"Which way?" Slapshot shouted over the din. "Lloyd!"

Slowly Lloyd Englehart turned back toward him. The lanky Georgia-born mutant's eyes were narrowed to slits, and his nose was still red from the tear gas he'd inhaled hours before. For the first time, it occurred to Slapshot to wonder if Lloyd's scent-tracking abilities were even functioning after the hit they'd taken last night

"Can you lead us out of here?" Slapshot demanded. *And*

fast. Before they come to investigate. Lie if you have to, Dogbreath.

Slowly Lloyd nodded. He turned and took off at an unsteady trot. Slapshot followed, pulling Charade on after him.

Rewind didn't even let the noise slow her down. She pushed past Pipedream and yanked the door open, then headed off down the corridor at a brisk trot. Toward the tunnel, and the lab beyond. Toward the others.

Crown didn't know why the alarm had gone off and, deep down, he didn't really care. As Ploog still stood frozen, Crown jumped to his feet and bolted for the door. Fortunately it wasn't the containment chamber alarm—that meant the control room wasn't automatically locked. And as long as Crown could stay missing, he could buy a little more time.

But in his heart, he knew he meant to do more than that. As terrified as he'd been by Psychostorm's narrow escape, the man's retro-mutation and death had somehow been the final unforgivable straw. He'd told Roberta the truth about the hidden costs of Project Level Playing Field—that up to fifty percent of the treatment's subjects would die—but he wasn't sure that would have any effect on government support of CGI's work.

Even if, as far as Crown knew, mutants could still vote.

If he didn't want this place on his conscience for the rest of his life—and at twenty-three, he expected that he had a lot of it left—he knew he had to do something to stop Bocklin. Now.

Before Ronnie could barrel out of the control room after him, Crown had turned down the nearest cross-corridor at a dead run. Heading for the place the packages were kept.

•   •   •

The lesson to extract from all this, Pipedream thought to himself, was that while Rewind was plenty decisive, her choices might not always be the smartest ones.

Take this tunnel business, for example. While it was true that this was the shortest way to get to the place where the others were being held, there was also the minor problem of them being able to check in . . . but not check out.

The tunnel ran maybe a quarter of a mile, and was almost as wide as a one-lane road. Fluorescent lights along the sides of the ceiling gave adequate—if greenish—illumination, and there'd even been a go-cart waiting inside the door for them to steal.

That was the good part of Rewind's plan.

The bad part was that the doors at the opposite end of the tunnel were sealed, and the keycard Rewind had lifted from the burgled desk was having no success at opening them.

At least down here the two of them were away from most of the klaxons, although Pipedream could still hear them faintly through the doors at either end. Pipedream leaned back against the side of the go-cart and stared at the sealed doors. It had seemed like such a lucky find at the time— but now it only appeared to have helped them reach the site of their ultimate failure that much faster.

"No!" Rewind slammed her fist into the door, unwilling to accept defeat now, when they were so close.

"Chill out," Pipedream said urgently. "This won't help."

"*Well, what will?*" Rewind snarled, rounding on him.

As she turned, she caught sight of the go-cart. Her eyes kindled, and Pipedream had a sudden horrible suspicion he knew what she was thinking.

Only the oath all five of them had sworn to never use their powers against each other stopped him from wrapping Rewind in a pipedream right now. Before he could make up his mind as to whether it might be a good idea to bend that promise just this once, Rewind had scrambled into the driver's seat. Pipedream jumped away from the hood and found himself staring after her as she backed the cart up down the corridor at its top speed.

"Hey! Pey—*Rewind!*" Pipedream shouted. His voice echoed off the walls.

The cart drifted to a halt, still sliding gently backward.

"Get out of the way!" Rewind yelled, her voice almost buried beneath the faint howls of the sirens.

Pipedream shook his head, waving her to a stop. "Don't do this!" he shouted back.

Rewind shifted the cart into forward and jammed the accelerator all the way down.

When the balloon went up, Chessman jerked like a galvanized frog and dumped an entire sixteen ounce carton of hot coffee (light, two sugars) all over the legs of a very nice silk-mohair three-piece Dior on its very first outing. He didn't even stop to register the disaster, grabbing his big-game handcannon out of the desk drawer and bolting for the door of his office.

The only reason for that many alarms to go off at once was because something with an x-factor in its chromosome map had gotten loose.

And somehow, Chessman didn't think it was Clarendon's rats.

They were toast.

Slapshot was too rushed with his attempt to escape to have the opportunity to really *appreciate* their failure, but he recognized it. Lloyd was stretched to the max just trying to keep them out of the way of the people looking for them—and Slapshot himself was completely exhausted.

If they could just hole up for five minutes and *think*— but down here there weren't that many places for them to duck into and hide. Just more cells like the one they'd busted out of, a lot of blank walls that looked like the corridors on the *Enterprise*, and some double-doors leading into laboratories that didn't look like places the Conspiracy ought to be bottled up in.

At least somebody'd turned off the sirens. That was something to be grateful for.

"Lloyd!" Slapshot hissed, in a tone that was half command, half prayer. *"Get us out of here, homeboy, or we're going to become Graydon Creed's Official Poster Victims."*

"I'm trying," Lloyd protested. "Maybe—no, wait. Someone's coming."

Turning about, he began to lead them back the way they'd come. But Slapshot knew their luck couldn't last.

And it didn't.

The first place Crown stopped was the security hotlocker. It was password-and-key secured, but Crown had broken the sequence a couple of weeks ago when he'd gotten bored and been looking for random challenges. One swipe of his keycard and he was in.

Technogeeks with 200 IQ's and too much free time got to know a lot of strange things; Crown didn't even blink at the sight of advanced weaponry that would be the envy of any police or national guard unit in the country. He had about fifteen seconds to grab what he needed and vanish before the security unit that used this armory showed up.

He grabbed a crash helmet with sensors, one of the rifles, and a spare battery pack for it. As he did, the lights flickered once, and the LEDs on the hotlocker faded out and then came back displaying a string of nines.

All the sirens stopped.

System crash? If it was, it'd picked a dandy time for it. And it had to be one primo hack—the security programs living in the CGI mainframe were extreme.

No time for that.

He slung the rifle over one shoulder and took off in the

direction of the package check, praying that was where the alarms had been triggered.

The cart slammed into the doors at the end of the corridor at its top speed. Pipedream gritted his teeth in unconscious sympathy as it bounced back, leaving the doors unmarked.

Then it seemed to flicker, and suddenly the cart was hitting the doors again.

And again.

This time there was a dent, and Pipedream realized what she was doing. She was rewinding time around the cart, but not the doors. Each time the cart hit the door, it was the first time—but for the doors, it was as if they were being hammered repeatedly by an enormous ram.

And slowly they began to buckle.

Pipedream watched helplessly, unwilling to do anything to distract her in the middle of such a delicate manipulation, trying not to think of what he knew too well—that Rewind's use of her mutant power put an enormous strain on her heart . . . and even the strongest heart could break.

But now there was daylight showing at the place where the doors joined.

Chessman was actually enjoying himself, but then, Chessman liked to kill things. And he thought he had a pretty fair justification for scragging any targets he happened to see; loose mutants running wild were not something the boss—the real boss, not those figureheads in the corner office—would approve of, now, was it?

He was sure it wasn't. Especially since this batch were corn-fed civilians, young and sassy and still believers in Truth, Justice, and the American Way. They'd been on the watch list for about the last six months, and now the word had come down to reel them in and trust everything to be covered up with legality later. In another two months it'd probably be legal to shoot genejokes on the steps of the

Capitol Building, but little details like that weren't Chessman's problem.

He got to shoot them *now*.

Chessman's official designation was Off-Site Security; the movements of his in-house colleagues was not something he was being paid to scrutinize. He ignored the armed and armored troops heading to secure all the exit points from the floor and worked his way inward, to the detention area.

Just as he'd expected, the kids had gotten out. Chessman looked at the half-retracted door and slid it out along its tracks again. There was a two-inch diameter hole punched through the several layers of steel and ceramic armor that protected the electronic lock assembly.

It was never a good idea, in Chessman's opinion, to place too much faith in the power of electronic devices. On the other hand, he would have been willing to bet that none of those three kids had smuggled a carbon laser in there, and of the three of them, only Jason Gerber had any potential to do something like this—and he didn't have anything like this kind of power.

A little snooping around, and Chessman found out what had made the hole in the door. There was a brass disk—melted and warped, but still recognizable as a foreign object—embedded in the wall in a direct line from the door.

Well, I take it back. I guess that dink kid has what it takes. He didn't even want to think of how fast that chunk of metal had been travelling when it hit the wall—and that was after going through the door. Chessman revised his opinion of the kids from Ohio upward several notches. If Gerber had done this to an armored door he could do it to a human body just as easily.

Not if I see you first, kiddo.

Chessman went hunting.

•   •   •   •

His ID badge—whatever Management thought of him in
its more unguarded moments, he had clearances out the yin-
yang—got Crown past two patrols that didn't even blink at
the amount of armament he was carrying. He glanced at
his watch, and was surprised to see it was only five minutes
since the alarm had been raised. He didn't think the packages could stay out of Security's way much longer.

He reached the holding cell and saw the hole in the door.
Had a fourteen-year-old girl done that?

And where was she now?

The corridor lights had been flickering for the past several
minutes, as Lloyd led them around in circles. Slapshot realized that the plan he'd had possessed several flaws. Sure,
the Human Pup could find them a safe way out if there was
one—but what if there wasn't one?

"Hey, Power Pooch, what's up?" Charade asked, sounding a bit more like her old self. "We've already seen this
hallway—twice, I think."

"Three times," Lloyd corrected. "But it's the only place
they aren't looking for us right now."

"Guess again, Canine Commando," Chessman said,
stepping out of a doorway.

The three teenagers stared at him in horror. Chessman
was holding a silvery pistol shape that looked more like a
flare gun than a firearm, but whatever it looked like, it was
pointed right at them.

Charade drew breath to speak, and in that instant, Slapshot realized in horror that whatever she was about to say
wouldn't do any good. The man in black had already made
up his mind to shoot, made it up beyond Charade's power
to affect it.

"Say goodnight, kids," Chessman said, and fired.

Slapshot was already wavering on his feet with exhaustion, but imminent death was a great motivator. With the
last of his strength he deflected the bullet—only barely,

since there wasn't much there for his power to grab hold of—so that it went just above their heads. He felt the last of his strength flow out of him with the effort, and slid to his knees, barely conscious.

Chessman looked up and past them. "Clarendon, get out of my fire line. I could have hi—"

His words were cut off by a flash of green light that went right through the space that Slapshot had been occupying, and the man in black flew twenty feet backwards down the corridor to fall in a twitching heap, and then lie motionless.

"I hope that was the stun setting," said a mild voice from behind Slapshot, "but frankly, I've never liked that guy. Are you—"

"We're nothing to do with you," Charade said quickly. "You aren't interested in us at all—in fact, you're just going to walk away and pretend you haven't seen us, right?"

Slapshot saw this Clarendon person shake his head as if he'd just been struck, and move to sling the strange rifle back over his shoulder.

"No, wait, Vette. I think he wants to help." He tried to get to his feet and failed.

Clarendon had actually turned and taken several steps away from them before he stopped and turned back. Either Charade was slipping, or Clarendon was one of the small percentage of people naturally immune to her powers.

"Don't . . . do that," Clarendon said. He regarded them with less friendliness than he'd shown a moment before.

"She won't," Slapshot said quickly, and Charade shot him a murderous look. Lloyd held out his hand and she went to him, taking an ostentatious detour around Clarendon.

"Mister, I can rip your throat out right here if you give us any grief," Lloyd said.

"Look, we don't have time for this," Clarendon said.

"Do you want to live, or do the three of you want to be guinea pigs on toast points?"

"What do you care?" Charade snapped shrilly.

"Because if you stay here, I'm the guy who has to kill you," Crown said.

Slapshot made another attempt to get to his feet.

"Hey, kid, are you all right?" Clarendon said.

Slapshot glared up at him. "I am *not* a kid," he said brusquely. Charade moved to help him, and on the next try he made it to his feet.

He almost wished he hadn't. Lights flashed behind his eyes, and his head pounded. He leaned heavily on Charade.

"And because I'm stupid," Clarendon said, continuing. "And because I'm not a mutant, but I know what it's like to be a freak. And because I don't really like killing people. So come on."

He turned around and walked away. Lloyd and Charade looked at Slapshot.

Why me? he wondered, although he knew the answer. Do any job twice and it's yours. He'd given the orders, he'd gotten them out of the cell. Now he had to decide whether to trust a stranger in a place where all the strangers were enemies.

"Let's do it," he said. Still leaning on Charade, he followed in the direction Crown had gone.

By the time that Rewind had exhausted herself and lay back against the seat of the cart, sweat-drenched and panting, there was a gap almost large enough to pass through in the sliding doors. The power had flickered on and off several times while she was banging away, and Pipedream guessed that Rewind's computer virus was starting to work. He ran over to Rewind's side. She seemed barely conscious.

He shook her, not knowing what else to do. He could see her eyes darting back and forth beneath the closed lids, as if she were dreaming, and she grumbled unintelligibly but did not rouse.

Stupid . . . stupid . . . this is all so stupid . . . he told himself. But he didn't know what else they could have done, any step of the way. They had to rescue their friends.

It was just that Pipedream thought it might be a good idea to throw in a rescue for themselves while they were at it.

He went over to the doors and put his hands on either side of the gap. Being a football hero had to count for something, and it did—he was able to push the doors open enough to wedge his body in between them and, with that additional leverage, he pushed them open almost far enough for the motorized cart to pass through the gap.

And certainly far enough for him and Rewind.

When he extricated himself and turned back to the cart, Rewind was conscious again and on her feet, though still holding onto the cart for support.

"Come on," Pipedream said, taking her hand. "We're almost there." *Yeah, just like Butch and Sundance. It's not Bolivia, but I bet it's going to be a major ambush.*

With Rewind following, Pipedream walked forward into the laboratory wing of the Center for Genetic Improvement.

Slapshot heard gunfire in the distance—which was a little crazy, he thought, because, if the guys with the guns weren't shooting at *them*, who *were* they shooting at?

Lloyd was right behind Clarendon, scoping out his every move. The four of them were headed into territory they hadn't covered before, but at least it was away from security. Clarendon's keycard got them into an enormous lab that was chilly and smelled of ionized oxygen and mice.

"Now we wait a couple of minutes to make them think you've gotten past them," Clarendon said, "and then we try to sneak you out into the parking lot. I've got a car—I can drive you back to the airport and then it's up to you.

Do your parents know you're mutants, at least?''

They shook their heads. Slapshot was pretty sure his parents wouldn't *mind* . . . but he just hadn't gotten around to mentioning it somehow. Lloyd and Charade had their own reasons for keeping silent, and he didn't think that Rewind and Pipedream had told, either.

''Tell them,'' Clarendon said grimly. ''And then tell them to get you out of the country to any place where the Emergency Intervention Bill won't become law in about fourteen days.''

''Why?'' Slapshot said. He knew this guy was older than he was—college student, maybe—but he wasn't *enormously* old. Maybe he'd be willing to tell them what was going on.

Clarendon ran a hand through his hair. He looked tired.

''Okay, let me make this as simple as possible.'' He glanced at his watch. ''I don't know how much of this you'll be able to understand—''

''Why?'' Charade demanded. ''Because we're mutants?''

''No,'' Clarendon said. ''Because from my point of view, you're normal, and I don't have that many conversations with normals that go beyond 'and a large fries with that, please.' ''

Lloyd snorted, and even Slapshot had to smile. He kind of liked this guy, even if he was weird. Maybe it was because he seemed to understand what being different without your own consent was like.

''Yeah? So?'' Charade was not soothed.

''Okay. CGI specializes in gene-tech, DNA therapy, all that sort of moral-gray-area stuff. With the work they've been doing, pretty soon we're going to be able to cure all sorts of inherited defects—hemophilia, diabetes, Alzheimer's—with just one injection of the right stuff, because what it will do is rewrite the part of the genetic blueprint it's targeted for in its own image. Now, a couple of years ago my boss, Dr. Bocklin, discovered a single genome-address for the x-factor—''

At that point, Slapshot was pretty sure he stopped following the conversation—except for the fact that this was CGI's Atlanta facility, in Atlanta, Georgia—though Charade stayed with it, asking questions that Clarendon seemed to think were sensible.

"But it doesn't work very well, does it?" Charade said.

Clarendon smiled crookedly. "A fifty-percent gross mortality rate doesn't do it for me, kiddo. I guess it depends on whether you think the only good mutant is a dead mutant.''

"Do *you*?" Lloyd asked boldly.

Crown shrugged. "I don't know. There's a difference between being *lusus naturae* and having the power to side-step the rules—play with someone's head, for example, just because you can.''

Charade hung her head, flushing, and tried to look as if she didn't think he was talking about her.

"But you saved us," Slapshot pointed out.

"I hate people who falsify test results to get their own way," Clarendon said inadequately. "C'mon. I think the sweep's moved on. It's time to go.''

At the first branch in the corridor, Rewind and Pipedream came face to face with six guys in black coveralls who looked awfully familiar. If they'd needed any more proof that something hadn't been right about the abduction of the others, they had it now. CGI had made the snatch start to finish, not the U.S. government.

The man in the lead stared at Pipedream and Rewind for a moment too long, uncertain if these two kids were the enemy. By the time he'd recovered enough to bring his weapon to bear, Pipedream had had time to overcome his shock as well. He hit the lead goon so hard with a dream that the man lost his balance and fell backward into his comrades.

Pipedream and Rewind ran the other way as fast as they could. As they did, the lights in the corridor flickered and died.

Everything was darkness.

"What was that?" Charade said nervously.

As Clarendon had opened the doors of the lab again, all of them could hear the weird sound of energy weapons being fired in the distance.

Suddenly all the lights in the corridor flickered and died.

"Great," Crown muttered. There was a sound of groping in the dark, and Slapshot felt Lloyd move past him unerringly.

"Here," Lloyd's voice came out of the darkness.

"Thanks." Clarendon switched on the flashlight, and suddenly a bright beam of light illuminated the room. "How did you know what I was looking for?"

"Well, with the lights out, it only stood to reason you'd be wanting a flashlight. And I could smell the batteries."

Slapshot could see Clarendon trying not to respond to that, and wished he'd give up trying to be so cool about everything. They already knew that they were the weird kids on the block.

"Right," Clarendon said. "Come on then, and don't dawdle."

The only good thing about the total blackout, Pipedream thought, was that even if they couldn't see anything, neither could anyone else.

"So how did your dataworm turn off the lights?" he asked Rewind quietly.

"I don't know." She sounded more upset than she would have wanted him to know. "It should just be taking down every computer it can find—but who runs the lights through the computer?''

CGI does, Pipedream thought, but he didn't say it aloud. How much time did they have before another death squad found them?

"Come on," Rewind said. "The map back in that office said that the guys were being held down this way." She took his hand and led him forward through the dark.

"We've already been here," Charade said dangerously.

"Probably," Clarendon snapped, "but you're going to be here one more time, because it's on the way to the tunnels."

"People," Lloyd announced. "Up ahead. Hey, guys! It's—"

But Clarendon had already pushed past him, flashlight in his left hand and rifle in his right.

Rewind squealed in shock as the beam of light hit her full in the face, dazzling her. Pipedream yanked her back, but the damage had been done; they'd seen her. And no amount of pipedreams would do any good against a blast-rifle.

"Come out with your hands up," a strange voice snarled.

Then a familiar one said: "No—wait. It's Adam and Pey—they're friends." The voice belonged to Lloyd.

Slapshot hadn't thought he'd ever see the day—Rewind fell on each of them in turn and hugged them as if she'd sincerely missed them. When it was his turn, Slapshot smelled *Muget des Bois* and a faint after-scent of McDonald's french fries that made his stomach rumble with hopes of breakfast during what ought to have been the peak experience of his life.

But he had truly never been so glad to see anyone as he was Pipedream. Pipedream was the Ohio Mutant Conspiracy's leader—they'd all voted on it. Let *him* worry about everything for a while.

"You know these guys?" Clarendon said.

"They're the ones *your* guys missed picking up last night," Lloyd said drily.

"He *works* for these creepo-maniacs?" Rewind said in revulsion.

"Not anymore," Crown said. "I just quit."

After that it was almost easy. There was only one brief clash between them and a security team, of which they were warned long in advance by the other side's flashlights. Rewind and Pipedream hit them with everything they had, and even Slapshot had recovered enough by then to make a couple of plasma blasts go wildly off target.

And having Clarendon on their side—with a big gun and no fear of using it—counted for a lot.

They got to the entrance of the tunnel that connected this one with the administration building. Its interior was lit by battery-powered lights, so a dim glow was visible through the twisted doors.

"Guys, what did you *do*?" Charade squeaked. "This is so cool!"

"I guess I got a little carried away," Rewind said, but the lightness of her words was contradicted by her harsh, edgy tone.

"Can we get out through here?" Slapshot asked.

"I think so," Pipedream said. "Pey and I have a car stashed—"

"Then this is where we kiss and part," Clarendon said. He handed the rifle to Pipedream. "Ever fired a gun before? It's set on 'Leave No Evidence,' so don't aim it at anything you want to keep." He handed the flashlight to Charade. "You might need that—and it makes a good blackjack if you don't need to see where you're going."

"Where're you gonna be?" Lloyd demanded. "I thought you was going to drive us to the airport." His Cracker drawl started to show through more than usual, so he was obviously tired. But they were all tired right now, Slapshot thought. He was almost ready to let them shoot him so he could just get some sleep.

"Pretending I never saw you. I hate to do it, but if I ditch you now I might get away with it. This thing is bigger and nastier than I thought; I've got places to go and guts to spill, and I can't do either one from jail—or with a bullet through my head. What CGI's gotten mixed up in is wrong, and I don't think anybody cares about stopping it but me. I'll probably blow my pension plan all to hell, but I can live with that more than you guys could live with what they're doing."

"Right," Slapshot said, before Pipedream could speak. "Good luck, then—and thanks. And could you tell our folks we're okay?"

"I'll tell them you were here," Crown said. Charade darted forward and gave him an embarrassed hug. He smiled, and turned away without saying anything.

"C'mon, guys," Lloyd said from the entry to the tunnel. "It's clear, I think."

Pipedream was the first to follow. He was the one with the gun, after all.

Lloyd led, on foot, two or three car lengths ahead of the others. The go-cart didn't work too well anymore, and they wanted to move silently and unnoticeably anyway. Charade had turned off the flashlight—here in the tunnel the faint emergency light from the slowly draining battery packs that powered the fluorescents on the ceiling were sufficient to navigate by.

He was very conscious that the others were all depending on him, and he'd never been more worried in his life. They were depending on him—a guy with the mutant superpowers of a dog.

Stronger. Faster. Able to hear bats and dog whistles and

supersonic alarms, as well as whispers a block away. Able to smell what was happening and what had happened—to follow a scent for miles just like his grandpa's favorite coon hound.

It didn't seem all that useful, somehow. And things the others could just ignore knocked him flat. Terrific.

He concentrated on what those useless senses could tell him. Scent of metal, fluorescent lamps, tired recirculated air, burned rubber and grease, metal, fried insulation, Adam and Peyton passing this way about fifteen minutes before. No one else. No threat.

And when they got out of here, where did they go? They were in. . . .

Atlanta. Lloyd thought back to what Crown had told them while he'd been hiding them in the lab. They were in Atlanta. That meant there *was* somewhere for them to go if they could just get out of here.

In his heart, Lloyd wanted to run back to the others, to hide in the middle of his self-chosen pack and let someone else choose what they should do. His mutation might have caused him to drift the farthest from human of any of them, but that didn't make him an alpha anything. It just made him think that most human ideas were stupid.

The thought scared him. If he didn't fit in with humans anymore—and he already knew he didn't fit in with animals—just where *did* he belong?

Don't try to think deep thoughts just now, Lloyd counselled himself sternly. *Just think about how good it's going to feel to be out of here, safe and free.*

The lights had dimmed all the way to darkness without his noticing. Lloyd bumped into something solid, and froze—had he wandered off-course and into a wall?—before he realized what it was. Carefully, his fingers traced the seam where the doors met.

"Folks? We're here. And we're alone."

●   ●   ●

Charade flicked on the flashlight and shone it on the doors. Their silvery surface was bland and unrevealing.

"Should we have brought the cart?" Rewind wondered.

"You *broke* the cart," Pipedream reminded her.

"Could we just, like, *go*? And maybe get breakfast?" Charade said, fear underneath her words.

"Let's get this door open first," Pipedream said. He swung the rifle awkwardly down over his shoulder. The other four scrambled to get out of his way.

"Hold it right there!" a voice barked behind them.

Pipedream fired.

The gout of pale blue-green fire washed over the doors like a thrown bucket of water, and as it began to fade, the others could see that it had washed the door away too. Pipedream fired again, then again, not waiting to see the effect of the shots.

"Down!" he said, whipping the gun around in the other direction and pulling the trigger. Memory of what Crown had told him about the setting on the rifle made him fire high, over the heads of whoever followed, but the thought that he could easily kill them with only the slightest mis-calculation made him feel ill. The shots caromed off the ceiling and walls, dissipating with each successive ricochet, until at last the thing only clicked when he pulled the trigger.

Rewind was dragging at his arm. "Come on, come *on!* Pipedream! Adam!"

He realized he'd just been standing there, staring at the destruction he'd caused as if it were something worth looking at. He flung the useless rifle as far from him as he could and followed the others through the slagged doors.

CHAPTER 9

ime to come out and play, Arnie, Wolverine said silently.

The area had been known as the Northwest Territories once, and before that—around the time everything west of Chicago belonged to Spain—it had been part of a land grant to the Hudson Bay Company, merchants and gentlemen all. Now it was just a godforsaken stretch of chilly wilderness somewhere between Yellowknife and the Bay.

Winter came early here.

There might be a few more weeks of autumn scheduled for south of the fiftieth parallel, but up here, King Cold had already been settled in for a couple of months, and nobody would be shoving him out of the driver's seat much before next April.

The weather didn't bother Wolverine at all. His namesake—as well as being one of the most ruthless predators of a harsh land—had an almost supernatural resistance to cold. The Native tribes here still lined their clothes with wolverine pelts because the fur would not freeze, no matter the temperature. Wolverine snuggled down in the powdery snow on the lee side of the rise overlooking Trapdoor Base and raised his field glasses to his eyes once more.

Project Trapdoor looked like any other military base stuck out in the middle of nowhere—a conglomeration of shacks and Quonset huts set up in a pattern that hadn't changed much from the days when Imperial Rome had made its camp at Rimini.

But the sno-cats under the tarp at the motor pool were top-drawer rides, and the forest of antennae sprouting from the roofs of the shacks sure weren't scooping broadcast power for anything as small as a toaster oven. Wolverine was willing to bet that ninety percent of Project Trapdoor was hidden underground, in puzzle-palaces and mazes and one first-class biolab.

He thought about the contents of the packet Connie Lau had passed him, and as he did he felt a cold fury leech like acid into his blood. It was tempting to think of going down there and slaughtering them all—biotechs, trainers, brass. It was as much as they deserved, opening this particular Pandora's Box again.

Once upon a time, a very long time ago, there'd been something called the Weapon X Division. It found—or made—weapons out of human beings. Elite weapons. Unthinking tools in the right hands. But even unthinking tools can break. Wolverine had survived the longest, but if Xavier hadn't recruited him, who knew what he would have become by now?

But Xavier had made the offer, and Wolverine left without a single backward glance.

Which left his former employers, what with one thing and another, fresh out of cat's-paws. The team known as Alpha Flight (which Wolverine was being groomed to lead when he resigned) had been the next attempt to start a government-sponsored paranormals program, and in the end, that team had fragmented as well, its disparate members going off in a dozen different directions.

But Canadian Intelligence's interest in having superheroes of its very own had been as lively as ever.

The report Connie passed him said that some group here in the Great White North had taken an interest in rolling their own—using mutates, not mutants. And they'd had more than enough DNA lying around to work with. Project Trapdoor had been up and running for about thirty-six months, and was just getting set to expand. The current

super-soldier prototype was female, but other than that,
Wolverine didn't know anything about her.

*A girl. So she'd be more tractable, I guess. Sheesh, didn't
any of these guys rent* Species *down at the video store?*

He stowed the glasses away—nothing to see, anyway,
and the wind was blowing toward him, bringing him a
scent-picture nearly as detailed as a photograph.

He had no fear of discovery, even if the base were to
have mounted a proper perimeter guard and not just trusted
to the harshness of the wilderness to protect them. He was
dressed for infiltration. His gloves, parka, and the rest of
his outer garments were a dusty grayish blue, perfect for
blending into the snowfields. At the moment his body temperature was low enough to make most thermosensors think
twice about registering him as a human intruder.

Which, of course, he wasn't.

He glanced at the sun: three o'clock. It'd be getting dark
soon. Another hour and he'd make his move.

The sun had vanished behind the peaks of the mountains
to the north when Wolverine began to move. The wind was
rising, and he could smell a storm on the air. It would be
here in an hour or two, providing perfect cover for his escape. He should have discovered everything that he—and
Xavier—needed to know by then.

Illegal research on human beings was the only way to
come up with conclusions like Bocklin's, and it was real
unlikely that a big fish like Bocklin wouldn't have his fingers in a whole lot of pies that CGI didn't know about.
Which meant that Wolverine was willing to bet that some
of that research had been done here—at Project Trapdoor.

He passed the outer sensor pickets without raising a
blip—probably they were set to go off at the proximity of
motorized transport, and not just for moving heat-shapes
that might be bear or moose.

Or Wolverine.

The fence gave him even less trouble—in this weather,

the sentries had their own little bungalow near the gate, and were sensibly staying inside it—and one slice of his claws opened up the fence. Only the tripwire at the top was electrified—in this kind of country, you didn't want to risk shorting out your fence every time a half-ton of herbivore decided it might be good to scratch an itch on. Wolverine slid through the gap he'd created—taking time to press the edges of the chain-link fence back together—and started looking for a way into the underground complex.

The big Quonset hut was the mess building—his nose told him that much—and at this hour most of the base's complement was there. That left Wolverine an open field for his search.

Where would it be? There had to be at least two entrances, but he only had to find one. Not in the commander's office—there'd be people going in and out all the time. Not in the barracks—same reason. Mess tent, hospital—ditto.

Now, what was here that wasn't any of those things?

He sighted a promising building and began to trot toward it, silent as a ghost in the gathering dusk.

The underground complex was nearly deserted—he'd found it on the second try—its lights set low for night. The place brought back too many bad memories, even though he'd never been here before. But he'd been in a place like this one—the place where Project X had warped his body and mind almost past saving . . . and possibly past redemption. There wasn't much in his long life that Wolverine was willing to say was truly evil, but that place—and all the places like it—qualified. In spades.

The air smelled of disinfectant and chemicals, with a faint undertone of ionized oxygen. There were people somewhere off in the distance, smoking and eating and drinking strictly forbidden beers. Most of the time this place was probably pretty boring. Wolverine smiled ferally to himself. Maybe he could change that.

Where was their guinea pig being kept? That was where he needed to start. She might be able to supply everything he needed—or be able to tell him that this was a dead end. But it was the only lead he had—if Bocklin wasn't here, then his whole trip North had been pointless.

But he didn't think it had been, somehow.

Wolverine faded into the background as two men walked by, talking loudly. These were the beer drinkers; he could smell it on them.

"—prize package all bedded down for the night," one said.

"Good. She gives me the creeps."

They were both dressed in fatigues, wearing flashes with a colorful elaborate symbol that looked to Wolverine as if it were meant to represent a DNA helix crossed by a sabre. Cute.

"Come on, Paulie, what can she do? Brass has so many safeguards in place she can't turn around without permission. You know they aren't ever going to run her flat out."

Their voices became fainter as they passed Logan's hiding place and continued toward their destination.

"Yeah, maybe," the one called Paulie said. "But I seen the way she looks at me—and safeguards can fail."

His companion shot back some easy refutation, but Logan didn't pay any attention. He didn't care where they were going.

But he was very interested in where they'd just been.

Their scent trail led back to an elevator. Wolverine didn't care much for the idea of being boxed into something that could become a killing box with the flick of a switch. Luckily, he found a ladder that led in the same direction. He stopped on each of three levels, casting about for fresh scent trace of Paulie and his companion.

He found it on the bottom level, four levels below the surface. That argued a pretty extensive complex, but Wolverine knew from bitter experience what such complexes were like: research labs, training areas, medical facilities extensive enough to put the ruined hero back together after yet another head-on collision with destiny. That the complex had a certain family resemblance to the labyrinth beneath Charles Xavier's Westchester mansion disturbed him a bit, as though there could be some continuity of method between Xavier's pursuit of his dream and the methods of these faceless people.

Wolverine rejected the very idea sharply. Chuck was an all-right guy who was much too soft-hearted for his own good. There was simply no comparison possible.

Was there?

He shook himself. There was no reason to let this place give him the creeps, just because it reminded him of Old Home Week at Hell House.

Just because some part of him didn't want to find what he was looking for.

However, this was definitely it.

The trail he was following passed through a portal that had a hatch like a submarine pressure door. It was spiked with a bar to keep the wheel from turning, but once he removed it, Wolverine had no trouble opening the door. He hadn't yet tripped an alarm. He knew he would sooner or later, and for a moment he pitied the guys that would show up. Just now he was spoiling for a good nasty fight, and he didn't think his temper was going to improve any time soon.

The door was harder to shift than he expected, and when he finally broke the seal, he realized why: air whistled through the gap and into the chamber, filling the vacuum. Negative pressure, just the way biohazard labs were kept.

Why?

As soon as the air pressure equalized Wolverine shoved the door the rest of the way open without any difficulty. When he had, he was looking at a round chamber about sixty feet across. The scent trails of the two men crisscrossed the floor, as distinctive as if they were limned in fluorescent paint.

Another compartment sat in the center of the chamber, as squat and armored as a hyperbaric oxygen chamber. There was another armored door set into its side, but opening this one wasn't a simple matter of brute force. A computer keyboard jutted out of the wall beside it, and Wolverine suspected breaking its codes would take several hours and probably trigger every alarm in the place.

Fortunately, he didn't have to.

He tapped the ''activate'' code that Connie had given him into the keyboard. Immediately a number of lights came on—including lights inside the room itself. He looked through the window. The interior was as stripped-down as a kennel, with only a single bed for furniture. On it lay a young woman, restrained by straps that would certainly have confined Frankenstein's monster—or at least Hank McCoy. She stared at him, the expression in her black eyes unreadable.

Her long black hair lay spilled across the pillow; her features had the faintly asiatic cast of one of Canada's native population, the Inuit, probably full-blood.

She also didn't have any obvious mutation. Wolverine wondered if she knew what had been done to her—and why.

And what *had* been done to her?

That's the sixty-four thousand dollar question, ain't it? Wolverine thought, and punched in the string of codes that would unlock the door.

The air inside was far warmer. He shrugged off his unzipped parka, snow boots, and cargo pants, and tossed them into the corner. In the heat of the confined space he could scent her clearly. Drugs. And beneath that a bitter musky smell that raised the hackles on his neck and started a rumble deep in his throat. She didn't smell human.

''You can talk?'' he growled.

There was a pause, as if she had to translate his words into some unknown language. "Yes," she finally replied.

"You gonna give me any grief if I let you outta those straps?"

Another pause. "Let me out?" she asked.

The scent of the chemical cocktail coming off her skin was chokingly strong, and he could see an IV drip snaking out of the headboard of the cot into a clear plastic shunt in her arm. Why sedate someone who was strapped down and sealed into an armored room besides?

"No . . . trouble," she said when he didn't respond, and Wolverine moved to unbuckle the restraints.

When she sat up, he saw that she wore a dull-colored jumpsuit with the same project flashes on the left shoulder and right breast as Paulie and his companion had been wearing.

"You aren't with the project," she said, pushing her hair out of her face and regarding him with the dull incuriosity of the drugged. She was inches shorter than he, a real pocket Venus, but with the heavy, solid musculature of a weight lifter.

"No. I came for information about the project. What's your name?"

"Mantrap," the woman responded promptly, as though it were an answer she knew well.

More testosterone-loaded BS from the House of Ideas, Wolverine sneered to himself.

"Wait . . . no. My real name—" she stopped, staring at him as if she were afraid he was going to hit her.

We don't have time for this. "Tell me your real name," Wolverine said gently.

"Roane. It was . . . they used to call me that. A long time ago."

"Tell me about the project, Roane," Wolverine said.

He had to push her to keep talking, badger her with questions to keep her on the right track, but a nastily coherent story began to emerge.

What was Trapdoor's mandate?

Trapdoor was a plan to take ordinary people with minor mutations—such as Roane had been—and convert them to supercharged playing pieces that the government could use in the international "favors for favors" game.

How many subjects were there?

She knew there had been others involved with Trapdoor. One of them, code named Psychostorm, had escaped early on. She knew she was the only one who had survived. There had been fifteen of them three years ago.

Where did the mutants come from?

A private-sector multinational called Black Team 51 was the organization doing Trapdoor's shopping for them. Black Team 51 was an international broker in mutants. Some came to them freely, some they kidnapped. All were traded, sold, and leased as if they were property.

"And so nobody's . . . responsible, are they?" Roane shook her head, trying to make it all make sense to herself. "Because they just buy us, and don't care it isn't . . . legal. What they do. Nobody . . . knows."

They'd know if they had a lick of sense, Wolverine thought sourly. But that wasn't quite true. The government and the project didn't know what Black Team 51 was up to because it didn't want to know. It was so much more convenient that way.

But Wolverine had heard of Black Team 51. Scott, Jeannie, Warren, Bobby, and Hank had run into them a few months back. With what Roane had told him, that whole adventure made a lot more sense. Black Team 51 had been trying to add the Wheel of Fortune to their sale catalogue, a buying spree the X-Men had foiled.

"Okay, Roane. Tell me about this man." He pulled a picture of Arnold Bocklin, captured from the Berne broadcast, out of the pocket of his baggy white cargo pants and showed it to her.

"I hate him." The words were flat, but an ugly sort of life had kindled in her eyes. "He's been here. He's the one. He tells them how to change me. I was—"

She stopped, lost in her own private dreamworld. Impatient with her vagueness, Wolverine reached out and pulled the IV tube out of the wall and tossed the leaking end into her lap.

"Wake up, darlin'. We've got a few things to do, here."

She stared at the end of the tube with dreamy curiosity. A sharp chemical scent came from the leaking end, and thin trails of blood began to leak into the fluid from the place where the shunt entered her arm.

"You're not supposed to do that," she said, puzzled, absently pulling the shunt out of her arm. It came easily, drawing a long arterial catheter with it, still dripping colorless fluid, but a moment later the angry red wound on the inside of her elbow was gone without a trace.

That was one thing they'd done for her. Mutant healing factor, just like his.

"Big deal. In case you hadn't noticed, I'm not exactly with the program here," Wolverine said. "Now, tell me about this guy."

She rubbed her temples, as if she were trying to summon memory, but when she answered, it was not directly.

"I could always find my way home, you know? Tell how the weather was going to be? Grandfather said that made me . . . special. I was going to join the Tribal Police, do some good for the Nahane. But some men came with a car, said that my country needed me. This was my country before it was theirs—why should I help them? But I came here. They shot my dogs."

She fell silent again, staring off into space.

"And then?" Wolverine barked. His escape plans were more complicated, now that there were two people to move, and he had no idea how well Mantrap would hold up out-side of glasshouse conditions.

"Then I met him—the man in your picture. I never knew what his name was. Some kind of visiting consultant from America, but from his voice he used to be English, a long time ago. His scent—" She stopped, shaking her head as though she were trying to banish the thought. "He was the one who got the stuff they were giving me and the others to work. Him."

"And then?" Wolverine asked, when she stopped.

"He said I was a mutant, that he'd turn me human, and then it would work. But they didn't like the results." She closed her eyes and shuddered, and Wolverine wondered exactly what the results of the first trial run had been.

"So they turned me back—made me human—and tried again." She stopped, looking out the window into the larger room. In the increased illumination, Wolverine could see that her pupils were widely dilated, the dark brown iris only a thin ring around the edges.

There was something in what she'd told him that sounded disastrously familiar.

"Wait a minute. They been turning you human—then back into a mutant? That's just the same thing as mutatin' regular humans. . . ."

"You're from outside." There was more awareness in her voice now, as her body purged the drug. She looked down at her hands and flexed them.

"Right. An' that's where you're going," Wolverine said.

"No. I can't." She got to her feet. "I was never rated field operational. That's what they said. Just a playing piece. Never for use. Go on. Find the man in the picture. Kill him for me. Cut him up."

Pocket Venus, he'd thought, but maybe pocket Morrigan would be more to the point. Morrigan, Celtic goddess of slaughter.

"You're comin' with me. There's folks what can help

you. Maybe even make you human again, if that's what you want," Wolverine said. If Chuck would open the Xavier Institute to someone like Wolverine himself, he'd surely accept . . . a playing piece.

"I was never human," Roane said. She looked at him sullenly, but with increasing alertness. "They wanted another Weapon X, but they missed. They couldn't afford to do skeletal bonding, so my bones break."

Wolverine stared at this woman who was, in fact, his mirror image. He knew what she was now, and where Bocklin had gotten his raw material for this experiment. Closer than a sister, a daughter—how much difference would a genescan show between them, now that Bocklin and the project had enhanced her DNA with his?

They had no right.

"But they heal, too," she finished, and charged.

Her heart rate doubled, and doubled again until her heartbeat was over two hundred. Respiration increased with it, her lungs working like bellows as they dragged oxygen out of the air in a hopeless race to supply the new demands of the body. Adrenal glands began dumping adrenaline into her racing bloodstream, increasing strength, sharpening reflexes; neurochemical balance shifted in the brain, shutting out pain messages, constricting blood vessels to minimize damage. Blood sugar rose, glycogen reserves were mobilized, providing energy that oxygen could not. Body temperature rose, wasting heat as fast as it could from the biological inferno Mantrap's body had become.

The perfect predator.

Mantrap was as fast as Wolverine, and overlaid with the chemical cocktail as it still was, her scent had given him no warning of her intentions.

She hit him high in the chest, going for his throat and a quick disable, but she'd underestimated his agility. Wolverine simply rode the force of the blow, rolling backwards, bringing his feet up to plant them in her stomach and fling her out the door.

Fighting room.

She rebounded off the wall and was on her feet in the same motion. The wiser move would have been to go for the door—Wolverine was sure she could find an alarm to trigger before he could stop her, but she simply charged again.

He tried to grapple with her—to hold her still so he could talk sense to her or at least knock her out—but Mantrap lifted him as though he weighed nothing and swung him like a Louisville Slugger at the side of the containment chamber, smashing the computer and slamming him into the sharp edges and protrusions of the open steel hatch.

Unlike Mantrap, he had gone through the skeletel bonding procedure that laced his bones with adamantium, the same substance that his claws were made of, so this treatment didn't hurt as much as it might have. But it did hurt enough to destroy any temporary impulse of mercy. Blood ran into Wolverine's eyes from a myriad of cuts that healed almost as soon as they'd opened, but he was blinded momentarily and Mantrap pressed her advantage, landing on him with both feet as he lay half-conscious on the floor and then doing her best to twist his head off.

He flung her off again, knowing this little tussle blew all chance of his getting any more information from the project or getting out of here on schedule. And even of taking Mantrap with him, unless he could manage somehow to knock her unconscious.

He popped his claws, hoping he didn't know how this was going to end. "Roane, don't make me hurt you. You're good, girl, but I been doin' this since before you were born."

"I'm Mantrap. And you talk too much."

She came in again, right over his claws. He spread his hands at the last minute so they skated along her ribs instead of skewering her, but he still felt adamantium grate against bone and smelled the blood.

But she'd picked up a shard of glass from the shattered window, a big blunt spike that cut her hand even while she tried to hack him open with it. Her lips were drawn back from her teeth, the *rictus sardonicus* a parody of a smile that would have frightened anyone else.

It was an expression Wolverine could see in the mirror any day of the week.

Well, he'd tried the easy way. It would have to be the hard way.

The shard she was using slid between two ribs and jammed. Wolverine retracted his claws and backhanded her with his full strength, the sheathed claws adding even more force and weight to the blow. Her head snapped sideways with a crunching sound; the impact of the blow itself was the sound of wood against wood. She fell, the force of the impact making her slide along the floor.

Wolverine was pretty sure he'd broken her jaw—the question was, how long would it stay broken? He pulled the glass shard free from his chest and flung it away. The bleeding had already stopped, and any fragments left in the wound would be forced to the surface by the process.

He didn't wait to see the effect of his first blow, but she was already trying to get up when he landed on her again.

It took several minutes to put her down all the way, but Mantrap never tried to break off the unequal combat. Disengagement must be the one thing they'd never taught her—though they'd taught her every way to fight dirty that there was. She was good.

Wolverine was the best.

Finally he slung Mantrap's inert body over his shoulder. He'd gotten a comparatively easy win through superior size and strength. If her project had had the guts to armor her up the way his had him, it would have been a longer fight.

With Mantrap on his back he couldn't use the crawlspaces to get back to the surface. He had to risk the elevator.

That was where they caught him.

The doors opened on the top floor, revealing a semicircle of scared men with rifles. Wolverine didn't hesitate. He bent forward and flung the unconscious woman lying across his shoulders at the soldiers directly in front of him. The dead weight knocked three of them sprawling, and opened up a space for Wolverine to work in.

The fight with Mantrap had taken the edge off his anger at the very existence of this place. He didn't want to kill any of these guys, but he didn't mind hurting them a little and scaring them a lot. With a blood-chilling yell he flung himself into their ranks.

His fists and feet connected solidly with bodies; he was deliberately keeping so close to them that none of them could use a rifle for fear of hitting his own side. Wolverine wanted them hurt, panicked, unconscious.

They knew who he was, just as Mantrap had. The knowledge worked in his favor—in their minds they were already defeated and waiting for death. He slammed head against head with brutal force, used slack bodies as battering rams to clear his way. He no longer worried about attracting attention—speed was the only thing that would gain him and Mantrap freedom from Trapdoor.

In only a few minutes, half of the soldiers were unconscious and the rest were down, offering no more resistance. Just as he'd expected, the alarm had been raised and "silent" alarms were beginning to shrill, their ultrasonic clamor making Wolverine's hackles rise.

The way was clear. He turned back, looking for Mantrap.

She was on her feet, though not quite conscious. In her hand was a bayonet removed from one of the rifles and she was looking around for a target.

Wolverine slapped the bayonet out of her hand with enough force to send it spinning harmlessly down the corridor. Then he grabbed her by the wrist and took off at speed, hoping she wouldn't fight.

She didn't. And once they'd gotten topside she was distracted by fresh targets; any place fooling around with paranormals would have to keep something around that could deal with them, and Trapdoor was no exception.

Full night had descended while Wolverine had been underground, and the freshening wind blew a thin hail at the ready room's insulated windows. Two armored figures waited for them.

Their dully shining cybernetic casings were eerily reminiscent of the armor of those mutant-killing peacekeepers, the Sentinels, the normal human shape of the people inside blurred and distorted by the sheer amount of telemetry, sensors, and weapons packed inside their armored shells with them. Stronger, faster, nearly invulnerable.

But not as smart as a cornered animal.

And not nearly as savage.

Wolverine moved sideways, clearing space for Mantrap to operate. Two goons. The suckers didn't have a chance. And while Wolverine knew he'd been on a lot of people in Canadian Intelligence's "better dead" lists for years, he was betting that the megabucks they had invested in their little playing piece would be enough to keep them from just hosing both of them down.

It was.

The ready room had no other purpose than to function as a gateway to the underground complex. Both long walls were lined with hooks where outdoor cold-weather equipment could be hung and benches on which personnel could sit to remove heavy snow boots. The corners of the room were cluttered with the kind of equipment that collects in a place that everyone uses and nobody stays in—coils of line, a fire extinguisher, rock salt, a can of paint.

And an axe.

Mantrap went for it as if it were the only thing in the

room. Maybe for her it was. As soon as he saw she was fully committed to the armored figure nearest to her, Wolverine focused his attention on the person in front of him.

"Why don't you just surrender peacefully?" the man inside the monkey suit sneered. "You're playing way out of your league here, Weapon X."

"Ain't you heard? The name's Wolverine, bub. An' I don't do *anythin'* peacefully."

Claws fully extended, Wolverine leapt to the attack.

He ducked beneath the weighted steel fist that skimmed the air past him with the deadly force of a trip-hammer, only to rebound off an electrified force field surrounding the armor itself. He'd half-expected it, but contact with it *hurt*; it slowed him enough that the follow-through blow nearly connected as he lay crumpled against the wall.

Years of special training and his own accelerated healing factor enabled Wolverine to twist away at the last moment, but the force of the blow was such that the fist that dealt it was buried up to the wrist in a section of wall that now more closely resembled a bomb site.

Given his unbreakable bones and his healing factor, all the blow really served to do was make him mad.

Few opponents ever realized how strong Wolverine really was, because by preference he chose either a slashing attack with his claws or a direct confrontation with his fists. But he was perfectly able to tackle the seven-foot, five-hundred-pound bulk and lift it from its feet—then fling it through the wall. The force field burned against his skin, but this time Wolverine was prepared for it—and he wasn't trying to punch through the armor's protective shield.

Wind-whipped sleet and frigid arctic air poured in through the hole in the outside wall. Wolverine saw that the armored faceplate of his supine target had frosted over, and the tingle on his skin told him that the man had switched to radar imaging to see in the dark.

Wolverine heard a howl from behind him where Mantrap

was engaged, but there was no time to stop and see what it was. He threw himself through the gap in the wall in the direction of his prey just as a hatch in the man's chest armor opened, revealing a rack of launchers pointed directly at Wolverine.

Training and instinct combined in one lightning decision: he charged. The extended claws of his right hand sheared through the top of the open carapace, shredding delicate wires and circuitry and causing the faint powerful hum of the miniature missile launchers to suddenly stop. But Wolverine wasn't through. He pulled back with all his strength, and there was a tortured squeal of sundering metal as the ventral weapons pod tore loose from the rest of the armor. There was a brilliant display of multicolored sparks, and the faint glow from the force field went out.

Unfortunately, that left most of the armor's passive systems intact. Wolverine dodged backward across the icy ground as the man in powered armor came for him with swinging fists, waiting for the instant to make his move.

At the wall of the bunker he turned and dodged. Obediently the other man followed—until that moment when Wolverine turned and all but leapt into his arms. The suits were fast, but they weren't agile, and that gave Wolverine the edge against something that was now no more dangerous to him than an armed man in an armored car.

Which meant—to Wolverine—that his opponent wasn't dangerous at all.

As the armored man thrashed and tried to grab him, Wolverine clambered over him until he was seated on the behemoth's shoulders, ankles locked beneath what would have been its chin.

Then he set himself to smashing open the Plexiglas faceplate.

Between the night and the storm it was cold out here. He'd left his winter gear in the underground chamber. All he wore now was his blue-and-yellow battle-suit, which was insulated, but left his mouth, chin, and arms bare. Only Wolverine's extraordinary stamina kept him moving under these conditions, and his opponent didn't have that. When Wolverine finally tore open the faceplate, his opponent floundered, freezing, disoriented, and blinded. Heat fountained out through the opening as the suit's environmental systems worked to compensate, but it was a hopeless attempt.

"Open up and say 'ah,' bub," Wolverine snarled, the points of his claws less than an inch from the technician's unprotected eyes.

The man froze.

"Now. Shut down the suit. Or get ready for a real extensive lobotomy," Wolverine snarled.

The man simply stared up at him with the helpless fascination of a chicken watching a cobra.

"Do it!" Wolverine roared. He lowered his claws until the points rested just below his opponent's eyes, just barely breaking the skin. The technician quivered and moved to obey, and within seconds the armor was an inert unpowered hulk.

Without its internal gyroscopes to compensate, it fell helplessly forward, unbalanced by the weight of the man riding on its shoulders. Wolverine rode it down, and at the last moment added to its impact with an impact of his own—a double-handed blow to the back of the helmet that left a perceptible dent in the metal. Even if the technician were able to power the armor up again, he'd hesitate long enough for Wolverine and Mantrap to get clear of the base. Next stop, the motor pool.

Assuming, of course, that Mantrap was still alive.

Disabling his prey had taken less than five minutes start to finish. Wolverine raced back into the building to see how his doppelgänger was doing against the armored machine.

As it happened, the machine hadn't had a chance.

At some point Project Trapdoor must have taught Mantrap something about these attack suits, secure in the knowledge that if they ever had to use them against her, the odds would be two to one. But when that day came, those weren't the odds they got. There'd been only one of them, and she had a weapon.

The heat-diffusion vents were between the shoulders at the back of the suit, a grate that looked like an old-fashioned ice tray, and kept the hyperinsulated soldier from frying in his own juices.

Burn marks and craters along the wall told of how he'd tried to stop her, but she'd been mercilessly patient. Once she disabled the grille using the axe, she only had to wait a minute or two for him to go down, as the heat his own body radiated was turned against him, raising the interior temperature of the suit well over two hundred degrees in only ninety seconds. All she needed to do was stay out of his way until he went down.

But she hadn't done that.

The heat vents were also the weakest part of the armor; she kept on at the damaged section until she'd cut through the armor. He must have been down by then—judging from the angle of the cuts—but she hadn't stopped. Chopping and tearing, Mantrap had gotten through all the layers of the armor to exposed flesh.

She hadn't stopped then, either. The white walls of the ready room were spattered with blood in high feathery arcs, as if they were the work of some abstract painter on a butcher's holiday. The tattered remains of the gray jumpsuit Mantrap wore was soaked to the elbows. So was the front.

There was blood on her chin.

She looked up when he entered, and for a moment he saw fear and despair in her eyes—until it was replaced by the cold bloodlust that was all the project designers had left her with their meddling. She reached slowly behind herself, feeling for the axe handle but unwilling to take her eyes off the new enemy.

Wolverine knew the reason for the drug delivery system now. Something had gone wrong with this incarnation of Project Trapdoor, too—and the planners hadn't had the brains, the guts, or, maybe, the resources, to pull the plug. They'd kept Roane alive—as something with all the cunning of a human—and no more rationality or self-restraint than a rabid wolf.

"Kill them all," she said, as if it were an explanation—or an apology.

If he could get her back to Xavier, there might be hope.

"You gotta start with me, darlin'. We've got unfinished business, remember?" Wolverine said.

She did. He'd counted on that. It would get her to follow him. He turned and ran.

She followed.

The motor pool was guarded, but even with the base on full alert, deep in their own territory, at night, in winter, the project and its security weren't quite expecting someone to materialize out of the shadows and bash them over the head. To the three guards, Wolverine seemed to appear out of nowhere. He hit them at a dead run, knocking them flat and incapacitating them in moments.

Fast as he was, he nearly wasn't fast enough.

He heard the crunch of her bare feet on the frozen sleet as she leapt. He grabbed the rifle from one of the unconscious men, turning and whirling it by the barrel to catch her in the midsection as though she were a curve ball and he were Joe DiMaggio. Her momentum was reversed in midair; she flew backward in a short curve and fell to the ground hard, fighting for breath. Wolverine dragged her back under the cover of the motor pool tarpaulin and finished her with a swift blow to the head from his rifle.

He would never have hit a normal human being the way he'd just hit Mantrap unless he meant to kill them. Shattered ribs and concussion would mean a lingering but inevitable death. But he knew that such injuries wouldn't kill

Mantrap—he'd already seen her accelerated healing factor at work.

It should just slow her down for a while.

There were a couple of trucks and a van in the motor pool along with the sno-cats, but neither truck nor van would be much good offroad. Wolverine checked the sno-cat nearest the back, then loaded Mantrap on board and headed for the fence. He'd have liked to disable the other sno-cats, but there was no time. He'd first breached Trapdoor's perimeter about forty minutes ago, and they'd known he was here—and been hunting him—for the last fifteen.

Time to go. Wolverine had what he'd come for—the information that Bocklin's hands weren't clean at all . . . and that Bocklin almost certainly wasn't who he said he was, but someone else. A master of manipulation: of people, of DNA. . . .

Someone he knew?

Wolverine stopped at the fence long enough to rip an opening big enough for the sno-cat to pass through. He was running without lights, but the pause was long enough for the snipers posted on the compound's roofs to find him and open up.

They were a good distance away, probably using night scopes; he heard the impact of the bullets around him before he heard the sound of the shots. A moment later one of the bullets hit him, but it was a fully-jacketed military round and didn't do much damage. The hole in his shoulder had started to close by the time the expended bullet hit the snow. Wolverine's only worry was that something might puncture the sno-cat's gas tank.

Then a few minutes later the sno-cat was running flat out and without lights across the open snow, heading due south, and he figured he'd left Trapdoor behind.

Wrong.

He'd been careless, they'd got lucky. They'd been so

clueless up till now that he hadn't thought that Trapdoor could field a serious threat. But either they'd just been a little slow on the uptake, or they'd been angling to get Wolverine out here where there was elbow room all along. Either way, three sno-cats surged out of concealment on the trail ahead and faintly, over the sound of their engines, Wolverine could hear more closing up behind. A neat little pincer movement that ought, by rights, to trap him between them.

But the best hunters are those who can become the most elusive prey. Wolverine turned off the trail, heading east. Into the storm.

He still had the rifle. He aimed the sno-cat at a relatively clear stretch and set it running flat out, then turned around, half-standing in the seat. Mantrap was slung across the back half of the seat, and he took a moment to pull her closer to him before lifting the rifle to his shoulder.

His pursuers had grouped together to follow him—he could see their lights—two men to a vehicle on the lead three sno-cats, and the driver able to concentrate on pursuit while his companion took aim and fired. Bullets whistled past his head, and Wolverine returned fire, but being jounced along as he was, he wasn't any better a shot than they were, and none of the rounds connected.

The other three machines, with only one man aboard each, started to pull ahead of the shooters. He would have tried for one of them, but the sno-cat hit a concealed rock and nearly went over. Wolverine grabbed the steering yoke before the machine capsized, and steered it to safety before making a sharp left into a copse of trees.

If he'd been running this ambush, there would be another part to it, and since there was only one quick and easy way in and out of inaccessible wilderness like this, he wondered where their helicopter was. It might be a half-mile overhead, pinpointing him by radar, or it might be hovering down at treetop level waiting to take him apart with a brace of Stoners. The fun was in figuring out which it was before it was too late. But there was one way of defeating the usefulness of the helicopter completely—wherever it was.

Wolverine turned east again, into the direction of the oncoming storm. A real back-country blizzard, his senses told him, probably the first of the season and likely to drop three feet of snow by morning.

In other words, tactically perfect. Choppers couldn't fly through that, radar imaging was confused, and snowmobiles would bog down in that much loose-packed snow. But Wolverine could move through it with comparative ease, cover thirty miles in a night, and be on his way back to civilization before they'd figured out where he'd gone.

When he cleared the thicket the renewed wind was like an arctic hammer, cold enough to make his eyes tear and then freeze the moisture to his lashes. The searchlights of the pursuit picked him up almost at once, and the shooting began again, but Wolverine didn't hesitate. He shoved the throttle forward, made sure of his cargo's presence, and crouched down as far behind the minimal windscreen as he could.

Unfortunately he was carrying double, which meant that he was evenly matched with half his pursuit, and out-matched by the other half. On a straightaway they would inevitably be faster.

So the way to win was obviously not to take the straight and narrow path. He wrenched the wheel in a circle and headed the 'cat straight for the nearest pursuit.

The driver wasn't expecting that. Through the glare of the headlights Wolverine could see that he had a rifle slung over his shoulder—impossible to grab—but what he pulled from beneath the cowling and aimed was a bulky, light-weight pistol that looked as if it ought to fire Ping-Pong balls.

Flare gun. And even the most rapid-healing flesh would be in a world of hurt with a chunk of burning phosphorus embedded in it. Wolverine waited until he saw the man's finger pressing on the trigger, then jerked the wheel sharply to the right.

The burning flare passed neatly over his left shoulder and arced off into the storm, burning with a pinkish radiance. Wolverine hauled the steering yolk back, veering leftward again. The nose of his 'cat kissed the back end of the other vehicle, making it flip and roll down the slope in the direction of another stand of trees. Thick—sturdy—tall—the trees might make a good place to den up and pick them off one at a time before heading into the blizzard.

The lead sno-cat was stopping to see what was wrong with his companion. Wolverine turned in his seat to make sure Mantrap was still out; stupid kid would probably insist on going back and duking it out with one of the sno-cats.

She wasn't there. And, looking behind him, Wolverine couldn't see her anywhere.

She was still in pain, but the snow was cold and welcome on her skin and the last of the injuries were fading even as she moved slowly toward the concealment that would guard her from another attack. The unintelligible buzzing in her ears became the sound of a pack of snowmobiles, chasing each other through the dark.

She took a deep breath, forcing the still-plastic ribs out to their proper shape. Stupid, to think that she could take Wolverine without her equipment. He was the bad example her trainers had always held up to her; the success story she had been created to beat. And she *could* have beaten him, Mantrap insisted to herself, if she'd only had her weapons. Or if the shard of glass she'd grabbed back at the base had only been thinner, she could have shoved it between his ribs and left it in his heart. Let him deal with *that* while she was ripping off his head. Decapitation was the only sure way to kill their kind.

But Wolverine was running away, and as long as he was

far away, he wasn't her problem. There were plenty of other targets within range.

Live targets.

Because anything living was her target.

Mantrap was field-operational at last.

And on the hunt.

Trapdoor was nearly deserted, with every available person out chasing Wolverine. The cargo copter was gone, and the motor pool was empty as well. Mantrap slunk back into the ready room that led to the underground lab complex without being seen.

The men in the suits were both gone, which she thought was a pity. She'd taken down her man, but she hadn't had time to make sure that the other one was dead.

She wanted to shut down Project Trapdoor once and for all, and with a little luck, she'd get her chance. She might not be able to take Wolverine out, but she was confident of her ability to kill any normal human with her bare hands. No one would be able to keep her from her goal.

Wolverine had taught her that her tormentor had a name, but he hadn't told her where Bocklin was. She intended to find that out.

And then Trapdoor would become . . . history.

Down below all the lights were up as if it were daytime, but Mantrap ignored that, heading for the armory where her kit was kept. As she did, she inhaled deeply, searching for human smells, and found none close by. The interruption of the drugs seemed to have enhanced all her senses—she could not recall a time before this that she'd been off them. Even when she trained, they only stepped down the dose to where she could operate, and one punch of a button on the control-box held by her handlers would deliver a paralyzing dose of tranquillizer through the permanently-implanted shunt on her arm.

But the shunt was gone, and so were her handlers.

Permanently.

Her equipment was waiting here for her just as she expected it to be. She pulled off the ragged remains of her blood-encrusted jumpsuit and took down the black skinsuit from its frame. She shook it out like a set of long underwear and stepped into it, smoothing it upward over her hips. When she was dressed, Mantrap was covered from her throat to her toes in a substance halfway between rubber and leather. A back cut-out exposed her shoulders and left her arms bare for freedom of movement. She flexed her hands, then pulled on long black gloves that fit like a second—tougher—skin, and regarded the blunt fingertips with regret. They'd given her all the rest, but they hadn't been able to give her claws.

At least they'd made other arrangements. She slid her feet into her boots and reached for the rest of her equipment.

Knife-sheaths that buckled around the outsides of both thighs. A hip belt that held a number of things from line to grenades, but also held two sets of brass knuckles with razor-edged knuckle guards. And the cream of her collection. Her long knives.

Two rings twelve inches apart, the smaller of the two bisected by a crossbar. Connecting them was a steel shank, and welded to that shank was a long, tapering, half-moon of a blade. Once she slid them over her gloves, the outside of each forearm became a cutting edge from fingertip to elbow. She tried an experimental swing.

"Hold it right there!" a voice shouted from behind her.

She turned, baring her teeth in a feral grimace. The man had his service automatic drawn and aimed, and the moment he saw her face he fired.

The first round went high, but the next two connected, one shattering her collarbone where the left shoulder joint connected to it and the other taking her just below the heart. She howled with the pain—shock, cold *weakness*—but by then it was too late.

She'd reached him.

She drove her right knife up through the underside of his jaw, and saw the blood blossom behind his eyes. He might not have been dead then, but he dropped the .45. It fired one last time, uselessly, as it struck the floor, but by then she'd pulled the knife free and used it to open him from groin to sternum.

When his buddy showed up two minutes later, her shoulder was well on its way to knitting back together. She made quicker work of him than of the other one, and this time she didn't get shot. When she was done, she dragged both bodies inside the armory, closed the door, and turned out the lights.

A warm glow of purpose suffused her. Her primary mission was clear: kill them all, destroy the base, find Bocklin, kill Bocklin and everyone with him.

And then . . . ?

There were a lot of live targets in the world.

Enough for a lifetime.

The sound of the explosion made Wolverine whip the sno-cat in a small arc so he could see in its direction. His pursuers had managed to cut him off from the forest; he hadn't been able to shake them, and his transportation wasn't exactly inconspicuous. He was on the run . . . but eastward, steadily leading his pursuers into the heart of the storm. The sleet had thickened and mixed with heavy wet snow, and visibility was almost nil. Fairly soon the air intakes on the sno-cats would clog and freeze, and then they'd all be walking.

But even with the blizzard, the fireball that blossomed where Trapdoor had once been was easy to see—a baleful golden apple that turned snow to steam and earth to glass.

Looks like somebody triggered the self-destruct mechanism that all these kinds of places have. Was it you, kid? Helluva exit, I'll give you that.

And now his hunters were cut off from their home base. Wolverine wondered if they had the sense to realize it. The remnant of the envelope of superheated air that had been pushed outward by the blast reached him, a hot wind at his back that melted the sleet and made the snow spatter against his face as drops of rain.

Time to leave this party. Setting the sno-cat to full throttle, Wolverine flung himself off and away from it. The sno-cat's engine wailed as his weight was lifted from it, and the little vehicle skimmed over the surface of the snow on the course he'd set for it. Wolverine scrambled into the cover of some scrub trees and lay very still.

But his pursuers weren't pursuing.

After a moment he backtrailed himself and found them. When they'd seen the blast, they'd pulled their sleds in together and were arguing, pointing back in the direction of the base. All there was in that direction was a blackened ring of destruction dotted by a few smoldering fires—and without it, these men were marooned in some of the most inhospitable terrain on earth with little more than the inadequate clothes on their backs. No food, no medicine, no communications equipment, and no way out.

In fact, without the fancy broadcast equipment transmitting back at base, they probably didn't even know where they were right now—and with the weather closing down like this, the helicopter wasn't going to be any use. And Trapdoor was gone for sure, along with everything living that had been in range of the blast.

There was no reason for the hunters not to join them. Wolverine slipped away from his pursuit and headed south, leaving the men to argue in the storm.

CHAPTER 10

R. CRUZ

Crown Clarendon was a very lucky man, but at the moment he didn't like himself very much. He wondered if the kids had gotten out all right. Had it really been necessary to abandon them that way? Dr. Bocklin was back in the country now, but he was in New York and wouldn't return to Atlanta until tomorrow at least.

Crown had managed to get up to the cafeteria in Building One without being noticed, which was where he found out that the local area network was down due to some kind of malfunction. The news gave him a little more hope that he'd get away with this; if the system was corrupt, so were all the files from the surveillance cameras and keycard checkpoints. He got himself a cup of coffee and a plate of fries—and signed a makeshift list that the cashier was using because the reader wouldn't accept anybody's ID card.

I have to get out of here, Crown thought as he carried his snack over to an empty table. He didn't think he was home free—not by a long shot. Chessman had gotten a good look at him, and might remember it when he woke up.

And Crown had seen the packages—the *kids*—that Bocklin was proposing to work on. To kill, perhaps—but at the very least, to rip away their essential *difference* and turn them into cookie-cutter normals. He'd been kidding himself all along, pretending it was okay to do it as long as it was just to scum like Psychostorm, but even at the time he knew it was a lie. Bocklin's retro-mutagen process wasn't okay to do to *anyone*.

But the most important thing right now was that Crown

had to look as if he weren't running away. Then he could vanish, and decide who to give his information to.

Now there was a question.

X-Factor was a government agency—they might be backing Project Level Playing Field for all Crown knew. Not them.

The Avengers were out of the country (he'd seen that on the Hero Watch Page on the Internet, a site he hit frequently) and the Fantastic Four were on some mission in outer space, no one knew where exactly (ditto).

Spider-Man? What could a lone web-slinger do about a major multinational corporation that was acting more-or-less legally—and had billions of dollars and lawyers to prove it? Plus, there was the problem of getting in touch with him—the Avengers and FF at least had toll-free numbers he could call.

It had to be the X-Men. He'd known that all along, but he'd been looking for a way out. Crown didn't want to meet the X-Men.

Like anyone in applied genetics, mutant rights, and a number of allied fields—as well as New Yorkers who read the papers—Crown had been familiar with the X-Men for years. Mutant outlaws for justice, who often fought to save the world from their own kind—most recently when Magneto reprogrammed a bunch of Sentinels and used them to take over Manhattan. Mysterious and shadowy—no one was quite sure where they were based or who their membership was, though Crown had heard there was a spinoff team operating now in Europe. And one of them, the Beast, had been an Avenger once. The X-Men would care about what CGI was doing here, and maybe they could even figure out how to stop it.

All he had to do was find them and get them to listen. Unfortunately, like Spider-Man, they weren't listed.

Crown bit into a french fry morosely. He was still brooding over that minor insurmountable obstacle when Ploog found him.

"Hi, Ploogie, how's tricks?" Crown favored the management flunky with his sunniest smile.

Ploog sat down at the table, scowling. Crown prudently removed his coffee from Ploog's vicinity and ate another french fry.

"Where the hell did you run off to?" Ploog finally said.

"Here," Crown answered easily. "I didn't want to be trapped underground just because some security program ran amuck."

"You were supposed to be at your station," Ploog said. Crown supposed he was trying for a magisterial aura of dignity, but he sounded more like a sulky debutante.

"I was. I checked out the lab to make sure none of the rats had gotten out. The ones with the wings are pretty harmless, but there was one rat two batches ago that kept exploding, and I was worried that we'd gotten something like that in the latest run. Sometimes the mutations don't show up first thing."

"I don't like your attitude," Ploog said, having run out of other accusations.

"Well, I don't like yours either," Crown admitted generously. "But I don't work for you, Ronster. And since the Core Memory has gone down, there's nothing for me to do here. I've been in this place since three o'clock yesterday afternoon, so what I'm going to do with my afternoon is leave."

I might be carrying the brat-brain act too far, Crown thought, but it was hard to tell with people like Ronald Ploog. Ploog thought *incomprehensible* meant *stupid*, and that wasn't such a good mistake to make.

"You can't do that," Ploog sputtered weakly.

"Watch me," Crown said airily. In fact, he wondered if all this might not just be a learning experience for their Mr. Ploog.

Eventually.

Crown was out on the highway and tooling down the road in his antique E-Type before he really relaxed, however. He might not be James Bond, but he was a regular viewer of *The X-Files*, and he certainly knew better than to go home when a sinister multinational with a conspiracy was after him.

The Jag was distinctive. It would have to go.

Crown drove to the center of Atlanta and pulled into the first parking garage he found. Since when they found that, they'd know he'd been here, he stopped at the ATM two blocks away and pulled as much cash as he could. In scruffy jeans and a heavy-metal T-shirt, his laptop slung over his shoulder (it had been in the trunk) he looked like any other college student on the planet.

He flagged a taxi next. It took him to the Peachtree Mall, where he checked in at a cybercafé, ordered a latte with raspberry, and used their internet account and his Visa to order first-class air tickets to Chicago, Dallas, Los Angeles, and Tokyo. He also checked the departure times of all the Greyhound buses to Washington, and the online news service to see if there was any report of the kids, but there wasn't. He'd pretend that was good news; at the moment, there was nothing more he could do for them.

If anyone was chasing him—if Chessman had woken up and fingered him—they'd be able to catch the Visa use, and maybe even a record of the place he'd used it from if they could find a good enough tame hacker—but it would take them a while.

Next he wandered through the mall, buying a backpack, underwear, a toothbrush, a really ugly jacket, a complete outfit at *The Gap* that made him look like a Young Republican, and a two-pound bag of M&Ms. Then he took a series of buses around the city, stopped at a barber shop, got a haircut, got back on the bus, and wound up at the bus station around three o'clock. He went into the men's room and changed into cuffed tobacco-brown, wide-wale corduroy pants and a heather-purple, waffle-weave Henley with leather elbow patches. His own clothes went into the backpack, on top of the M&Ms.

If you were trying to vanish, taking a mode of transportation that required you to show up an hour early and provide photo ID was not the way to go, so scratch air travel. But a bus was almost as anonymous as a car, and you didn't have to buy it to use it.

Crown Clarendon, boy genius, boarded the Greyhound bus to Washington, D.C. at 3:47 p.m. Atlanta time, and was asleep long before they reached the state line.

By morning, he'd be in the nation's capital.

Somebody in Washington must know how to find the X-Men.

Connoisseur of the bizarre Charles Fort always said that one could measure a circle beginning anywhere, and for the last two and a half days, that was what Xavier and his team had been doing in the nation's capital.

Psylocke, Storm, Phoenix, and Cyclops had accompanied Xavier to Washington, D.C. escorting him to the numerous meetings he had planned with Washington luminaries and researching background information on HR-485 and its backers for him on their own. Soon they had uncovered the history of The Emergency Intervention Bill, soon to become Public Law 105–485.

The Emergency Intervention Bill had been sponsored by Senator Stewart Chisam upon its introduction into the House two years before, and in its original form had borne little resemblance to the version that had been in and out of committee and was now on the verge of becoming law. That older version of the bill had been an attempt to allow the government to directly cover the cost of medical treatment for victims of catastrophic medical emergency—cancer, AIDS, leukemia, the Legacy Virus. No one thought it would pass the Senate, but everyone wanted to be seen to be in favor of it, so fourteen months ago HR-485 passed the House with a respectable margin on its way to the Senate.

It was in the Senate that HR-485 began to . . . change. A rider defining mutation as a medical condition was added without difficulty, and then the real horse-trading began. To have teeth, its supporters argued, HR-485 must make medical treatment *compulsory*.

With the final changes in Senate subcommittee added on to it, HR-485 returned to the House to have its final form voted upon—and once again it had passed. Now it was back at the Senate awaiting final approval. Its next stop would be the Oval Office.

And nobody's noticed that "compulsory" anything is next door to a police state, Jean Grey mused.

It was a neat bit of smoke and mirrors, she decided, hefting a copy of HR-485. The bill's sponsors had played on people's fears—fear of plague, fear of bankruptcy, fear of greedy insurance companies—to make them see this political time bomb as their savior. But it wasn't.

She dropped the inch-thick pile of paper in the blue paper cover on the corner table in the hotel suite. Their rooms were in the Watergate Hotel—now there was a little political irony, considering they were here to save democracy, not to blast it—and the others were all out at the moment.

Scott and Betsy were accompanying Professor Xavier on his visit to Senator Chisam. Jean knew that Xavier had put off this difficult interview as long as he could, hoping that the other things he'd discovered would make it needless.

But what he'd discovered instead was that a lot of people owed the powerful and influential Senator Stewart Chisam favors, and none of them saw any reason that blacks, gays, and women shouldn't get what was coming to them. Free medical care—nobody could really object to that, right?

The poisoned fist in the sugared glove, Jean thought, glancing back at the bill. Professor Xavier had gotten a copy from his representative. Not an official copy—that would only come from the Government Printing Office once the bill was passed by the Senate and on its way to the Speaker of the House—but a reading copy, as it was any American's right to request a copy of any pending piece of legislation.

It was just too bad that more of them hadn't asked to see a copy of HR-485, Jean thought, although she had to admit herself that without a careful explanation of the pertinent clauses she probably wouldn't herself have been able to separate the meat of the bill from the clouds of Washington lawyerese.

And if *she* couldn't—with time, motivation, and an excellent education—why should she expect anyone else to be able to?

Maybe Chisam doesn't know what his bouncing baby bill's turned into. It was a forlorn hope, and Jean didn't place much reliance on it. From all she'd seen and heard in the last few days, Stewart Chisam was a canny political animal who never put a foot wrong, and certainly didn't lend his support to legislative time bombs. So he must benefit—but how?

Maybe that's what Charles will find out today.

Restless, Jean paced the expensive suite—filled with flowers and fruit baskets from Xavier's friends and from favor seekers—wishing she were anywhere else, and not faced with a problem her mutant powers and finely honed battle skills didn't seem to have a hope of solving.

She wanted to go jogging, or shopping, something to work off her restless energy, but Ororo—not one to spend time indoors if there was any other option—was out sampling the pleasures of the Mall, and they'd agreed that someone needed to cover the room all the time. The tenuous psychic link she maintained to all the other X-Men while on missions told her that Ororo was well and happy, revelling in the crisp fall day, and certainly not in need of rescue.

So here she was—stuck. With a sigh, Jean flopped down in a chair, turned the television to CNN, and picked up HR-485. Maybe a second reading would let her find some loophole in it somewhere, some reason why its passage would not be the disaster Charles Xavier feared.

Maybe—though she doubted it.

She wondered how the other three were doing.

Scott and Betsy stood behind Professor Charles Xavier, who, as an internationally known authority on mutation, could ask for—and receive—an appointment with an important man like Senator Stewart Chisam in a matter of hours. Both X-Men could have passed for aides or staff in any office on the hill, dressed as they were.

In their early days together, as Xavier's first X-Men, Warren Worthington III—known then merely as the Angel—had often gibed at Scott's "Young Republican" clothes sense, assuring him that he'd never get any girls if he continued to dress like a neonatonic Jimmy Stewart. But Scott had never wanted "girls." He'd wanted Jean Grey.

And Jean had wanted him. She hadn't cared how he dressed. And as a matter of fact, today a dark blue wool three-piece suit and a maroon rep tie were the perfect thing to wear; suitable camouflage for this urban jungle.

He glanced sideways at Betsy, who was standing behind the Professor's chair with a bland expression of meaningless approval on her face. Her long dark hair was pulled back in a severe chignon at the base of her neck, the ninja marks on her face concealed by expert makeup, and her own dark suit and high-necked pink blouse a symphony in *haute* Brooks Brothers couture.

The office itself—one of hundreds in the Senate Office Building on Capitol Hill—had the hushed respectfulness of a high-class undertaker's parlor. The receptionist's desk was a colonial reproduction in cherry, the walls were coffered maple, honey dark with age. Two leather couches that would not have been out of place in an exclusive men's club from the turn of the century faced each other atop a fine reproduction Oriental carpet, and the green-shaded lamps in the corners completed the illusion of a Victorian parlor washed up on the beach of time.

An aide came out through one of the three discreet private doors and smiled warmly, with a sort of all-encompassing impersonal friendliness.

"Senator Chisam will see you now."

Betsy pushed Professor Xavier's chair forward. Scott followed meekly.

"Charles! How are you? It's good to see you."

Senator Stewart Chisam—the man who would be President, insider sources claimed—came up from his chair and around his desk as if he were surging to meet his opponent in a boxing ring. He shook Xavier's hand enthusiastically.

Stewart Chisam was a vigorous man in his early sixties, the product of a well-bred Georgia family. Scott knew from his voting record in the Senate that Chisam liked to be characterized as a conservative with heart. He kept himself carefully far from extreme positions—unlike some others, such as Graydon Creed and his Humanity First party—and until now, had stayed out of all the political brawls about mutants' rights to exist.

"It's good of you to see me on such short notice, Senator," Xavier answered. "These are Scott Summers and Betsy Braddock, my assistants."

"Mr. Summers, Ms. Braddock," Senator Chisam said courteously. "Please sit down; make yourselves comfortable."

Chisam, suiting his own actions to his offer, sat down in one of the comfortable chairs ranged in front of his desk, putting himself courteously into Xavier's eyeline.

Scott, taking his cue from Xavier, removed himself to a couch at the far end of the room. From there he had a breathtaking view down the length of the Mall, with the

Washington Monument framed in the middle distance, a flashing ivory spire of purity in the clear autumn air. Anyone sitting opposite Senator Chisam at his desk would see it.

Somehow that image crystallized Scott's nebulous dislike of the senator. Chisam *manipulated* people with a sort of psychic bullying that Scott, no pacifist himself, found disturbing and offensive on an unconscious level.

His attention was drawn back to the real world when Chisam spoke again.

"But tell me, Charles, what can I do for you today? I'd hoped to be able to at least offer you lunch at my club, but I'm afraid I'll be lunching today in committee."

"Then I'll do my best to be brief, Senator. I came about a bill you're sponsoring: HR-485, the Emergency Intervention Bill?"

Senator Chisam looked wary, as any politician might.

"I suppose I should have expected this sort of thing from someone in your profession, Charles," Chisam said, still imperturbably urbane. "Very well, let's discuss HR-485."

"To begin with, I'm rather concerned that the bill defines human mutation as a life-threatening medical condition, subject to compulsory treatment."

"Well, that's direct enough! So let me ask you a question, Charles. What is your objection to actual equality for all Americans, regardless of the circumstances of their birth?"

"Equality by any means? I have quite a few, Senator, and I'm forced to wonder what the phrase *actual equality*, as you use it, means—especially when you use it to justify the suppression of the civil rights of millions, mutants included."

"That's hardly fair, Professor. This bill offers free medical care to those who would otherwise go without—and offers mutants a chance to be cured of painful and potentially embarrassing differences that can lead to sometimes fatal persecution. If we don't give HR-485 a few teeth, it'll be nibbled to death by the states, and then thousands—the poor, the elderly, the disenfranchised—will go without the basic medical care that's surely every American's right?'' Chisam smiled.

"It's every American's right not to be executed by his own government in the name of political expediency," Xavier said evenly. "Yet HR-485 is a loaded gun leveled at the head of every mutant in America, as you are well aware. Is that the sort of actual equality you mean to provide?"

Scott stiffened at the sudden upswing of tension in the room, though neither man had moved.

"I'm afraid I don't take your meaning, Professor. HR-485 is a bill I was proud to sponsor, because it paves the way for *real* equality at last. What good are the laws that the Framers of the Constitution left us if mutants break them at whim through their more-than-human abilities? Our entire system of laws and justice is based upon the principle that no *one* individual should be able to take that life or death power into his own hands—yet mutants and other paranormals do that very thing every day: a band of vigilantes and masked anarchists running roughshod over the fabric of daily life, without the least consideration for the innocent bystanders who are inconvenienced and even killed by their theatrical grandstanding."

"These so-called vigilantes and anarchists have saved this world from destruction a thousand times over," Betsy Braddock burst out, unable to keep silent. "Where does *that* fit into your equations, Senator?"

Professor Xavier held up a minatory hand, and Betsy subsided, still angered.

"Perhaps the young lady has something of a point," Senator Chisam said graciously, "and certainly some so-called super groups have shown the inclination to function successfully under a governmental aegis. But the point is, Ms. Braddock, that your 'costumed avengers' tend to create the very threat they then boast of having saved us from. Where's a super-villain without a superhero to fight? Half of those costumed hooligans will vanish the moment their partners in crime do, and for the rest, we now have task-forces equipped to deal with them on the federal, state, and local levels. Exhibitionists in pajamas simply aren't needed anymore.''

Scott saw Betsy clench her jaw muscles, holding her tongue with an effort.

''And this . . . theoretical benefit justifies genocide in your mind, Senator?'' Xavier asked quietly.

''Genocide!'' Chisam got to his feet, good humor vanished, all the stern lawmaker now. ''I would appreciate your showing me exactly where HR-485 advocates killing anyone—if you would be so kind, Professor Xavier,'' he finished with steel courtesy.

''Forgive me if I am laboring under some misapprehension, Senator Chisam, but I've made some inquiries, and I was under the impression that the research team headed by Dr. Arnold Bocklin at the Center for Genetic Improvement, a company based in your home state of Georgia, had developed the 'treatment' protocols that would be used on the American mutant population when HR-485 becomes law.''

''Yes, of course.'' The tension had faded; Senator Chisam gave Charles Xavier the benign smile reserved for fools and idiots. ''I'd forgotten you'd have your inside sources. I'm very proud of the work CGI's been doing in my home state with Dr. Bocklin's help. I'd never have introduced such a rider to this bill in Congress if I hadn't known that a safe, effective, and humane solution to the mutant problem hadn't been available.''

''Do you call fifty percent mortality a humane solution, Senator Chisam? And what of—''

''In *rats*, Professor Xavier,'' Chisam all but snapped. ''In the early stages of the research. I'm afraid you'll have to do a bit more digging before mounting your scare campaign to kill this bill. You don't have all the facts.''

''I have enough facts to know that this bill must not pass. I was hoping I could call upon you as an ally,'' Professor Xavier said quietly. ''Are you so determined to have peace that you must purchase it at the expense of human lives?''

Chisam was now angry enough to show it. Scott got to his feet as Chisam strode past him, to open the door to the outer office in a conspicuous hint that the interview was over.

''And where does it say in the Constitution that a mutant who constantly flouts its laws is allowed to claim protection under them?'' Senator Chisam said. ''I'm sorry, Professor, but I'm really very busy, and I don't have time to listen to ill-informed fear-mongering. If you don't like HR-485, I suggest you exercise every citizen's right—and write a letter to your Congressman.''

As soon as they were out of the building, Betsy burst out, ''What an unpleasant man!'' The characteristic British understatement in her voice was at odds with her exotic—and dangerous—appearance.

''It isn't hard to guess where Chisam stands on the issue,'' Scott said.

''I only wonder,'' Xavier said, ''If Senator Chisam has all the facts. He seemed surprised when I mentioned Hank's findings about the mortality rate of the treatment. As if he had been told otherwise.''

''Could CGI be lying to him about the results?'' Scott asked. Both he and Betsy were well aware that their mentor held the inviolability of the human mind sacred; though Charles Xavier, the most powerful telepath on the planet, could easily broach any person's psychic defenses and read his most personal thoughts, it was the one thing Xavier would never permit himself to do—for in doing it, he would cross that invisible line that separated his dream from Magneto's. Xavier believed that the good end did not justify evil means . . . and Eric Magnus Lehnsherr believed that any means, no matter how vile, could be turned to serve a good end. Those ideals had been sorely tested when Magneto took over Manhattan a few months previous.

"He probably knows every sordid detail," Psylocke said crossly. "Masked hooligans . . . exhibitionists in pajamas . . . costumed vigilantes—that man makes me ashamed of every time I, or Brian, or any of the X-Men, have put our lives on the line for him and people like him."

Brian Braddock was Betsy's older brother, who, as Captain Britain, was a member of Excalibur, the European superteam.

"Inflammatory rhetoric, deployed as bait," Professor Xavier answered with a chiding tone in his voice. "But I see the limousine up ahead; we might as well save the rest of this conversation for the hotel, so that Jean and Ororo can be informed."

"That stinks," was Jean Grey's succinct response as, half an hour later, the four X-Men and their mentor gathered together in their suite at the Watergate Hotel to review events. Ororo had returned from her walk, looking windblown and cheerful, but the coleader's air of calm serenity had faded under Xavier's impassive recounting of the interview with Stewart Chisam.

"And that," Betsy said, "seems to be our good senator's final offer. Whether he actually believes that CGI's retromutagen has no side effects, or whether he secretly thinks its okay if thousands of mutants die 'for the good of the people,' he isn't withdrawing his support from the Emergency Intervention Bill."

"And he is its sponsor," Ororo said. "If he will not yield, what chance is there that others will?"

"And from all we've heard here in the past few days, the Senate vote isn't even going to be close." Scott Summers added gloomily.

"Why should it be?" Jean Grey asked in frustration.

"It's already passed House and Senate once; as soon as it comes out of conference committee it goes back to both houses for final approval—which it's likely to get very quickly, considering that everybody wants to go home for Christmas."

"There's always the possibility that the bill will die on the President's desk," Scott offered. "If Congress adjourns while HR-485 sits on the President's desk—and the President doesn't sign it during those ten days—the bill's dead."

"Darling, that just isn't going to happen," Jean said. After Magneto's takeover of Manhattan, this President was hardly likely to back down on any issue involving mutants.

Scott smiled slightly. "I know. I was hoping to cheer you up."

For a moment the frustration in the room lightened, the spirits of the others borne up by the sight of Scott and Jean's love for each other. As two of the original X-Men, the pair had been hunted outlaws since their teen years—the passage of HR-485 would be business as usual for both of them.

But for thousands of others—the rest of the two percent of America's two hundred eighty million who had been born mutants—the passage of HR-485 would spell destruction, mayhem, and death.

"In any case, it is far too early to despair," Xavier said. "Anything might happen, from the bill failing to pass in either house, to the President vetoing the bill during the two-week period he has to consider it. I believe that enough public outcry could influence the President against HR-485, and unless the bill reaches his desk by next Friday, it faces an automatic pocket veto. There is still time to—"

At that moment the room phone rang. Jean moved automatically to answer it.

"Yes?" She listened for a moment, then lowered the phone, cupping her hand over the mouthpiece. "Professor, it's a woman named Laura Severn. She wants to come up. She says you know her."

A rare smile of hope lightened Professor Xavier's grim expression. "Yes, Jean. Laura's an old friend of mine. Tell her to come up."

As Jean Grey relayed the information into the phone, the Professor turned back to the other three X-Men.

"I think this is the light at the end of the tunnel that we were hoping for, my X-Men."

Laura Severn might have been a longtime friend of Charles Xavier's, but Laura herself seemed only to be in her middle thirties; not an "old" friend at all. She was brisk, blonde, and friendly, wearing the Washington uniform of blue suit and white shirt. She carried a heavy shoulder-strap briefcase.

"Charles! It's so good to see you again," Laura said, stooping to embrace the man in the wheelchair. "You should have told me you were coming; I only heard yesterday and it's taken me forever to track you down."

"As a matter of fact, I was planning to give you a call in just a few minutes, Laura," Xavier said. "I've just returned from a rather disappointing meeting with Senator Chisam. But before we deal with that, allow me to introduce my associates."

Introductions were quickly made, and then Xavier summarized the morning spent with Senator Chisam.

"That . . . man," Laura said inadequately. "Even leaving the mutant issue aside—though I know that's your central concern, Charles—HR-485 is just one more erosion of civil rights in this country. Its wording takes the right to determine appropriate medical treatment out of the consumers' hands—and just what form is this 'emergency intervention' supposed to take? Euthanasia? The bill is remarkably vague, and going on the basis of what's going to happen to mutants—internment, forced relocation—it isn't a very pretty picture."

"I know," Xavier said quietly. "But we mustn't give up hope. What is Amnesty International's official position on the bill?"

"Oh, we oppose it on civil rights grounds of course, but we're just trying to whip up opposition to it before the final vote. The ACLU has already got the mechanism in place for the court challenge once the bill—as we expect—passes, and we'll be coplaintiffs when that happens. So will WorldWatch and M.O.N.S.T.E.R." WorldWatch was a California-based group that, like Amnesty, worked for human rights; their chief spokesperson was the superhero War Machine. The latter organization's acronym stood for Mutants Only Need Support, Tenderness, and Equal Rights. It grew out of a visit by the Beast and Iceman to a college campus, and had developed into a small but potent nation-wide mutant rights group. "But until they can get an injunction," Laura continued, "the bill is law—and I'm afraid that isn't good news for your people."

Scott traded a surprised glance with Ororo. Did this woman know Xavier's most closely guarded secret: that Charles Xavier was the secret leader of the outlaw X-Men? But Xavier's next words dispelled that fear.

"Don't paint me as having more influence among mutants than I do, Laura. I've always believed that human and mutant can live together in peace—but there are many who disagree."

Laura Severn smiled tiredly. "I know, Charles—and frankly, I wish there *was* one spokesperson for all mutants, worldwide. I tell you, I'd be willing to do a deal with Magneto himself just to get this bill killed. The rest of the world—Genosha, particularly—is just waiting to see which way the U.S. is going to jump on this one. And of course, Bocklin would pick *now* to make that presentation in Geneva. Even if the bill fails here, there will be others worldwide who want what he's got—and CGI has no reason not to sell it to them if there's no government contract in the offing.''

"We must hope for the best—and work with what tools we have to hand," Xavier said comfortingly. "Meanwhile, I find myself rather interested in Dr. Bocklin and his motives. It is he, in a sense, who has made all of this possible.''

"And don't I know it! We've tried to appeal to him, but we haven't even been able to *find* him. Bocklin's the original Teflon boy," Laura said tartly. "He just popped up out of nowhere about twenty years ago, but there isn't a hint of coverup in his background. Once CGI got him on board, their focus changed. They went private, bought back all their stock—and terminated several lucrative government research contracts. All their financing comes from 'private investors' now, although they're working hand-in-glove with a couple of very scary government agencies. And if HR-485 goes into effect, they'll definitely be awarded the contract to 'cure' the mutants, thanks to Bocklin's research.''

"Through a process that will leave half of them dead," Xavier said.

It was a shocking statement, but none of the X-Men was really prepared for Laura's reaction. Her face went white, and she clutched at the arms of the chair as if she expected to fall off.

"So it's true, then," she said in a whisper. "I didn't believe it . . .''

"What do you mean?" Jean Grey asked. She glanced at the others, all of whom looked equally watchful.

"I'd heard . . . a rumor . . . that CGI was massaging the confidential reports to the Hill and the FDA." She was leaning forward in her chair, her entire body vibrating with tension. "And now you say it's true.''

"All I can say, Laura, is that all the independent testing of Dr. Bocklin's theory that certain associates of mine can manage tends to indicate that the mortality rate for such a treatment would be high. We know so little about how mutation works, and simply annulling it with a wave of a biochemical hand is bound to have unimaginable consequences. Even if I did not disapprove of such a line of research on purely moral grounds, I would wish to see it undergo years, not months, of trials before being offered to the public . . . and even then I would utilize it with extreme caution.''

''And the FDA's going to approve it,'' Laura said bitterly. ''I know that the FDA was planning to send down Bobs Everett to check out the operation on-site in Atlanta, but she was supposed to be back on Tuesday— Wednesday at the latest—and there hasn't been a whisper of what her findings were.'' The activist seemed to hesitate for a moment, then come to a decision. ''Charles, could you come to a sort of, well, a council of war, tonight? I'd intended to ask you anyway, and now it's vital. I have some friends who'd like to meet you, very quietly, and I'd also like you to be my guest for dinner.''

The four X-Men exchanged glances. Laura Severn's reaction was certainly enough indication that the truth about the retro-mutagen was not common knowledge. If they could *prove* its deadliness, might that not be just the information Professor Xavier needed to tip public opinion against the Emergency Intervention Bill before it became law?

''It would be my pleasure, Laura,'' Charles Xavier said. ''And if I may bring two of my young associates? Scott? Ororo? I think it's important for you to be there as well.''

Scott nodded, gravely. Ororo merely smiled wistfully, as though she were remembering truths she'd rather forget.

Laura looked at the four X-Men with a cold considering eye.

''I'll assume they're as discreet as you are, then. Because I tell you, Charles: tonight you're going to have a table at

Ground Zero of the most explosive American issue since the Civil War.'' She stood to go, and smiled, a reflexive meaningless flicker. ''So shall I come by to pick you up around six?''

''I am *not* just going to sit here while Scott, Ororo, and the Professor eat rubber chicken with a Political Action Committee,'' Jean Grey announced a few minutes after the other three had left with Laura Severn that evening.

''And you're suggesting?'' Betsy Braddock said. Psylocke—like Jean Grey herself, was a telepath, though one whose mutant gift had taken a very different turn—slouched in a chair pulled up in front of the television, looking for all the world like a sulky adolescent.

''What I'm suggesting is a little fishing expedition to find out just how much Senator Chisam really knows about CGI's retro-mutagen and its effects. If we can find proof that he and CGI both know about the so-called 'unfortunate side effects' of the treatment . . .''

''They'll be fair knackered, and so will their bill,'' Betsy said excitedly.

With the benefit of long experience, Jean was able to translate *fair knackered* as *in a world of hurt*, as another of her teammates might have expressed it.

''That's the idea,'' Jean said.

For a fleeting moment she wondered where Wolverine was and what he was doing. He'd left for Calgary Monday night, but no one had heard from him since then. And in this case, no news was bad news.

On the other hand, the news from Hank, who was masterminding the search for Bocklin from the X-Men's Westchester HQ, was frequent . . . and all bad. If Rogue and Gambit didn't hit paydirt tonight, they'd have to widen the scope of the search.

With a ripple of thought, Jean Grey transformed the

clothing she wore to the blue-and-yellow battle-suit of Phoenix.

"I thought I'd start with the good Senator's office—his real office, not that showpiece you were in today."

"I'm in," Betsy said quickly, going to the specially hidden compartment in her suitcase to begin her own transformation into Psylocke. "But I've got to ask: are you sure you haven't quite lost your mind?"

"Oh come now," Jean said, her light tone belying her sober expression. "It's just a little self-interested snooping. It isn't as though Chisam were running for President or anything."

The Senator's other offices—something that most of official Washington had—were located inside the Beltway but far from the pristine splendor of Capitol Hill. Here in this shabby downmarket office building was where the real work got done—there were desks for aides and secretaries, and whole walls filled with file cabinets containing most of the voluminous correspondence a senator received during a working year. In addition to this office and the showplace Betsy had visited, Senator Chisam would have a third office, back in his home state, where still more work was done.

Cloaked in darkness, their passage eased by their mutant psionic gifts, Psylocke and Phoenix walked down the darkened hallway heading for the private office within Senator Chisam's administrative suite. The outer door, with its complex and efficient array of locks, had already yielded to a little telekinetic persuasion.

"Supposing we do find something—what's the Professor going to say about this?" Psylocke asked.

"I contacted him on his way to the meeting with Laura Severn, while you were getting dressed. He didn't like it, but he agreed, providing we stick to our mandate."

"No nicking naughty pictures of our Stewart in compromising positions with a Capitol page, then?'' Psylocke said in hopeful tones.

"Not one,'' Phoenix answered, smiling faintly. "Just his relations to CGI.'' The inner lock yielded just as its counterpart had, and the two X-Men stepped into the inner office.

"Ah, you Americans. 'What did he know and when did he know it.' Well,'' Psylocke said. "This shouldn't take long.'' She gazed in faint trepidation around an office filled with paper.

The luxurious appointments of the office the mutant ninja had been in earlier in the day were almost completely absent here. Dark green curtains were drawn shut over white venetian blinds. Bookshelves and a utilitarian credenza filled most of the room, leaving scant space for the magisterial mahogany desk and its leather chair, and the carpet underfoot was worn.

"Cheer up—if there's anything to find, it won't be out in the open,'' Phoenix said.

"So all we have to find is whatever Chisam doesn't want us to find,'' Psylocke said. "Sounds perfect.''

But forty minutes later, it was Psylocke who was still cheerful, and Phoenix who was losing hope. She'd begun to feel that even if they found what they were looking for, they might not recognize it. And they hadn't even found any compromising photos.

"Here's something,'' Psylocke offered, brandishing a sheet of paper with CGI's corporate logo embossed upon it in gold.

"What does it say?''

"It's from Bocklin to Chisam, thanking him for his support, yadda, yadda. Here's the letter it's in reply to; looks like our Stewart took a trip down to CGI last year, and CGI in return made a healthy donation to the senator's favorite charity.''

"Great. That'll be a lead story on CNN,'' Jean grumbled.

"And it doesn't prove that Chisam knew any more than they wanted him to." She sat down on the edge of the desk, brandishing a file folder in frustration.

"C'mon, Betsy. We'd better start putting all this stuff back where we found it. I don't think the Senator *has* any dark secrets. Finding anything out in this town is like arm wrestling an amoeba, and even if we *do* find something, who are we supposed to punch out: the Clerk of the House? Even if we can find out who the enemy is, we can't fight him directly. It's like battling an octopus."

"Perhaps," Psylocke replied absently, leafing through the folder of correspondence. "But cut off the tentacles, and the head usually starves to death, wouldn't you say?"

"What *I'd* say is 'halt three times, ladies; you're under arrest'."

Both woman whirled and stared in stunned surprise at the intruder.

I thought you were supposed to be bloody psi-scanning! Phoenix had no trouble in hearing Psylocke's topmost thought.

And what about you, *Betsy Braddock?* But there was no point in slinging recriminations now. She stared at the man who had entered, for one of the few times in her career not quite certain what to do. And she could not hear his thoughts at all.

The man in the dark business suit was wearing a mesh cap on his head; as she watched, he removed it, and suddenly Phoenix could clearly perceive the background noise of his thoughts. She skimmed their surface. His name was Chessman, and he worked for Black Team 51.

Phoenix recoiled mentally, keeping herself from lashing out at him with an effort. She—and the rest of the original team—had encountered Black Team 51 for the first time last August, when they'd hounded to death an innocent man—David Ferris—whose only crime had been to be born with a mutant ability that allowed him to shuffle through alternate realities the way Gambit might shuffle a deck of cards. Since then, the X-Men had heard nothing more of the organization . . . but here it was now.

"Clever little device, isn't it?" Chessman said, brandishing the cap. "Suppresses transmitted brain waves, allowing someone like me to sneak up on a couple of someones like you, ladies." He tucked the cap into his coat pocket. "The only trouble is, it gives you a helluva headache."

Psylocke opened her hands and let the file she was glancing through drop to the floor. Papers spilled everywhere in a wordless but eloquent commentary. Bottled up in this office, the man in the doorway neatly blocked their only escape route.

"Cut to the chase, Chessman. I know your organization, and I know what it stands for. And you know I can turn you into a grease spot in five seconds or less," said Phoenix. Like her husband and teammate, Phoenix had been trained to fight by the old rules; as much as she loathed him, until Chessman attacked, she wouldn't either.

"Temper, temper, carrot-top. Politics, someone once said, is the leveraged application of superior force, and at the moment I'm holding all the aces. Well, one ace, anyway, and I think she's kind of cute."

He reached into the pocket of his black cashmere polo coat and withdrew something, tossing it at Phoenix's feet.

"We picked up that—and all that goes with it—earlier tonight," Chessman said.

With a simple mental command, Phoenix levitated the glove into her hand. It was yellow, of a leatherlike synthetic, and short; cuffed at the wrist.

It was Rogue's.

"Harm one hair on her head, Chessman—" Phoenix began dangerously.

"*When* are you people going to move into the twentieth century? Aren't you supposed to be two of the X-Men,

humanity's self-proclaimed saviors from the evil mutants?
Rogue qualified for the evil mutant list last I heard—there
are warrants out on her from agencies ranging from Interpol
to the Boy Scouts.''

"Nevertheless," Psylocke said coolly, "we would not
like to see her harmed."

"That's just the attitude I've been talking about, here,"
Chessman said. "All of this kill—hurt—harm—would it
surprise you to hear that we had a reasoned conversation
with Rogue earlier this evening and she came with us voluntarily?''

As a matter of fact, Chessman . . . yes.

Phoenix wanted to reach out mentally to Rogue, find out
where she was and if she was safe, but she dared not risk
such a major distraction with Chessman present.

"Rather," Psylocke said drily, answering for them both.

"I'm hurt, ladies," Chessman said. "But let me proceed
in good faith and make you the same offer my colleagues
made Rogue earlier this evening—and which she accepted."

"And that is?" Phoenix asked. While Psylocke had held
Chessman's attention, she'd risked taking a moment to brief
Scott on the trouble she and Psylocke were in and where
they were. He and Storm were on their way.

"To turn yourselves in and submit to Dr. Bocklin's treatment voluntarily. You will absolutely not be harmed, and
in exchange, you'll receive a full pardon for any acts committed while you were mutants. Think about it. You can
start a new life. Amnesty for an injection—it's a great
deal."

Phoenix smiled coldly. "The trouble is, Mr. Chessman,
I've heard something like your offer before—at a little
place called Dachau. In other words, no deal."

"Then I'm afraid you leave me no choice," Chessman
said, shaking his head in mock sadness. "It's certainly going to look bad for your side tomorrow morning when the

world wakes up and finds out that the X-Men have been burglarizing a U.S. senator's office in order to keep a vital piece of legislation from being passed,'' Chessman said.

''But you're not going to tell them, are you, Chessman?'' Phoenix said. ''You're going to go to sleep, and when you wake up, you'll be back in your own bed with no notion of how you've spent the evening.'' She took a step toward him.

''Back off!'' Chessman cried.

There was an odd-looking gun in Chessman's hand; before Phoenix could snatch it from him he'd pulled the trigger.

A weird blue-green fireball launched itself from the muzzle, expanding as it went. Phoenix sprang back, away from Chessman. It missed both Psylocke and Phoenix but burned through the curtains and the blinds, melted the window, and soared off into the Washington night.

''That's torn it!'' Psylocke said, grabbing for her sword.

But Chessman had taken advantage of the moment to replace his psi-blocker, and his gun never wavered.

''That's you folks all over. The moment the going gets rough, you genejokes start cheating. Is it any wonder that normal people can't stand you? You're like the schoolyard bully,'' Chessman's voice was angry.

For one absurd moment, Phoenix almost wanted to apologize for being what she was. Was this truly the way that humans felt about mutants—jealous and resentful to the point of psychosis?

''Chill out, Chessman. I may not be able to get to your mind now, but I can get to your body just fine,'' Phoenix said.

''Trouble,'' Psylocke said, glancing out the window. Jean plucked the image from her mind: two black unmarked cars and a black van, pulling up to the curb in the street below.

''Expecting friends, Chessman?'' Phoenix asked.

"Don't bother to surrender, mutie," Chessman snarled. "We'll be taking you out of here in boxes."

It had been a mistake to frighten him, Phoenix realized ruefully. Even if she didn't want trouble, Chessman was going to see to it that she got it, now.

"Psylocke—want to take the air?" she said.

"Gladly," Psylocke answered. "It's getting a bit close in here." With one heave, she wrenched the melted casement window open. Chill night air spilled into the room.

"Come on," Phoenix said. As soon as Psylocke had vaulted through, Phoenix followed, levitating herself gracefully into the air. She looked around.

Psylocke seemed to have vanished into the shadows, setting up the next assault.

Disengage, Phoenix sent to her teammate. *We have to lose them and get back to the hotel.* Tonight's adventure would be a black mark against the X-Men, but at least they hadn't left any proof of their visit behind. People would have to take the Black Team's word for it that the X-Men had been here. Some would, some wouldn't.

But Chessman does have proof: Rogue's glove. He can drop it there and say she was the one who wrecked the office. Could Black Team 51 really have her? Rogue isn't an easy target.

Behind her, Chessman fired, leaning out the window. The bolts from his weapon lit up the night like flares, and in their harsh illumination Phoenix saw the men on the ground scatter. All of them were wearing psi-blocking headgear.

Well, there goes one strategy, Phoenix thought unhappily. A wide-focus psi-bolt could have dropped all of her targets instantly, and let Phoenix and Psylocke disappear in peace.

We'll just have to outrun them, then, she decided. A blazing and very public battle between two X-Men and the Black Team was the last thing they needed on the eve of an important mutant rights vote.

Although such a battle might be exactly what Black Team 51 was angling for.

And we walked right into it. But how did they know where we were? Phoenix wondered. *How could they know?*

Then she heard a mental summons from Psylocke and changed course.

Psylocke had a problem, or, more precisely, three of them. The telepathic ninja had climbed the four stories to the roof of Senator Chisam's offices and had crossed to the roof of the neighboring building. Phoenix had said they were getting out of here, and Psylocke was willing, if not eager, to obey.

But just as she'd chosen her next destination, she'd been confronted by three more members of Black Team 51, looking oddly out of place in their fashionable business suits and dark coats—sort of like the GQ version of the CIA. The armament they carried, however, did not look out of place at all—gleaming energy rifles that looked as if they carried a nasty kick.

"Good evening, gentlemen. Lost?" Psylocke asked coolly.

"Not precisely," one of the men said. "I don't suppose you'd be willing to reconsider Mr. Chessman's offer?" he added hopefully.

Psylocke smiled and shook her head distantly. A few early snowflakes scudded along the chill wind as Psylocke backed toward the edge of the building. She knew that Phoenix didn't want to fight, but disengaging didn't seem to be much of an option at the moment.

"I don't believe so," Psylocke said briefly.

Almost as she spoke, Psylocke was bracketed in a crossfire—both of conventional slug-throwers and high-tech energy weapons. Aside from her ninja training and mutant psi-powers, Psylocke was as vulnerable and mortal as any human being; either weapon could hurt her badly.

But only if they hit her. She flung herself backward off of the building's roof just as the gunfire reached the place where she'd been, trusting to her teammate's timing to save her life.

She fell twenty feet before Phoenix caught her.

"Left it a bit till the last minute, eh?" Psylocke said with relief.

"I was busy," Phoenix said, automatically dodging a renewed burst of gunfire on the rooftop.

Looking down, Psylocke could see that Chessman had reached the street—and she could see more than that.

"Phoenix—look!" She pointed.

From the van below, the Black Team was removing small, one-person flying platforms. Several of them were already airborne.

At that moment, a roof-mounted spotlight on the van flared to dazzling life and locked onto Phoenix. She took automatic evasive action, but the actinic glare of the flood-light's beam followed her unerringly.

"Whoever they are, they've bought the best," Psylocke said.

"So they're rich murderers," Phoenix answered. "But a well-stocked toy box doesn't worry me as much as the mind behind it."

Still carrying Psylocke, Phoenix headed southwest, back toward Capitol Hill and the open green spaces of the Mall. It was only little after eight o'clock at night, but at this time of year the Mall should be fairly empty. If the X-Men were going to have to give these guys a fight, at least they'd have some elbow room.

"We'd better split up," Psylocke said, but Jean was already landing on a roof, now that she'd shaken the spotlight.

"I don't want to do that," Jean said reluctantly. "While they're wearing those psi-blockers, I haven't got a clue about their intentions or their location—and if they actually managed to capture Rogue, I don't want to make the mistake of underestimating them."

"But at least the evening hasn't been wasted. We do know that if Black Team 51 is mixed up with Chisam, his hands are far from clean," Psylocke added.

"There they are!" The voice came from above both women, accompanied by the weird rushing sound of a stealth-configured helicopter. Reacting without thought, Psylocke and Phoenix dove in opposite directions.

As soon as she had some altitude, Phoenix glanced around, but the helicopter was already rising into the sky. The air around her was far from empty, though—two flying platforms were closing on her, and on the ground below, others were taking to the air. The moment she saw them, Phoenix realized she'd made a tactical error in coming out of the cover afforded by the rooftop.

There was the sharp crack of a conventional pistol, the reports sounding flat and phony here in the open air. Quickly Phoenix threw up a telekinetic shield, using her mutant power to stop the bullets and make them fall harmlessly to the street below. It was just as well that she'd taken this elementary precaution, because the Black Team's van had finally reached her new position. The arc light and the plasma beam struck her at the same moment.

The impact of the bolt was referred by the psi-shield over her entire body, but the effect was still the same as if Phoenix had been hit by a fire hose turned on full blast. Unable to maintain the mental concentration necessary to keep herself aloft, she was flung away by the impact, falling helplessly.

"Attention, X-Men! You are under arrest! Please halt your resistance immediately and surrender to the U.S. Marshals! You will not be harmed!"

The blaring bullhorn voice made Psylocke cling harder to the shadows on her rooftop. From her vantage point she

could see three men on flying platforms, flitting like silver
dragonflies through the wintery air. There were more on
the ground, she knew, and the blast from the energy
weapon behind her had severed her telepathic link with
Phoenix.

Though Psylocke—as her name implied—was a psi herself, her particular abilities were aligned more in the direction of attack, especially the formidable psychic knife that
allowed her to strike down her enemies with a single blow.
A psi-screen wouldn't stop the psychic knife, but even so
perfect a weapon was of no use if it could not reach its
intended target.

And she was pretty sure that Phoenix's hopes of a swift
and silent undetected retreat were history.

"Attention, X-Men!" the amplified voice returned,
mindlessly repeating its message.

There was a bump behind her on the roof as one of the
platforms landed. Psylocke's right hand began to glow with
baleful scarlet light as she readied her psychic knife, and
the red mark across her face seemed to brighten in sympathy. She darted a quick glance around her, and saw that
to move out of shadows would bring her directly into the
restlessly questing searchlights.

There was the crunch of a footstep behind her.

It began to snow harder.

Storm had arrived.

Thank you, windrider, Psylocke thought in Storm's direction; Storm briefly acknowledged the telepathic gratitude. Trusting to the snow to conceal her, Psylocke stepped
out of cover and turned to face her stalker.

Storm and Cyclops had received Phoenix's mental summons only minutes before, but Laura Severn's dinner party
was fortunately located only a few blocks from Senator
Chisam's secondary offices. It had been the work of only
a few moments to transform themselves from Xavier's self-
effacing aides to members of the outlaw X-Men, and in

seconds Storm had been borne aloft to reach the place from which Phoenix's summons had come.

High in the air, Storm could look down and see silvery flying platforms crisscrossing below her. Some were mounted with spotlights, and other searchlights reached up from the ground below, giving the zone some of the false theatricality of a movie set. She could also see the bright crossing fire of tracer rounds and the beams of discharging energy weapons, but she could not see either Phoenix or Psylocke.

Time enough to locate them later. The first order of business was to neutralize the enemy. Though Storm had never faced Black Team 51 herself, she was vividly aware of their potential threat through Jean's description of the other X-Men's encounter—an engagement that had resulted in a needless, senseless murder.

At her mental command, the scattered cloud cover over the Capitol began to thicken. Sparse flakes of snow became plentiful and fat, and in less than a minute dense white curtains of snow were falling in a six-block area centered on Storm herself.

Jean! Storm called through the psychic bond that linked them. *Where are you, my friend?*

There was no answer.

Landing hurt.

Holding herself aloft with her telekinesis required concentration and effort; but building a simple shield was one of the earliest defenses that Phoenix—known as Marvel Girl in those days—had learned. With her last ribbons of consciousness, she pulled her telekinetic shield around her now, and turned a potentially fatal landing into merely a rough one.

I suppose this is where Sly Stallone would say something like "Now it's personal"—but frankly, it was already personal, Phoenix thought.

On the other hand, I'd say the ante has just been upped.

At that moment the blustery autumn night turned frigid, a rolling front of icy air—like the opening of some celestial refrigerator—bringing cascades of thick snow in its wake.

Storm? Phoenix queried mentally, and was rewarded with a burst of relief as soon as the psi-link was re-established. Wincing slightly, the red-headed telepath got to her feet and shook out her hair, reflexively brushing herself off. Then, summoning her concentration, Phoenix rose into the air as gracefully as her namesake, returning to the fight.

We're blown. We're definitely blown, Psylocke thought.

Above her, the loudspeaker message—now muffled and distorted by the snow—continued its mindless hectoring, while here below, Psylocke faced her opponent.

It would have been child's play for her to simply slip away through the veils of shifting snow and disappear, but in her heart, Psylocke wanted the physical confrontation. She'd been on edge ever since the Professor had informed the X-Men of this new infringement on their right simply to exist, and now—as Wolverine might put it—Psylocke was spoiling for a fight.

The man facing her was wearing the psi-blocking net on his head, and carried one of the bulky, silvery handguns she'd seen earlier in his left hand. His right fist was clenched as well, as if it held something, and his eyes were covered by dark glasses. Psylocke assumed they were simply a screen for a holographic display or even a set of "smart" night-eyes—at any rate, he seemed to have no trouble locating her as soon as she stepped out of cover and began moving toward him.

He didn't do her the insult of assuming she was anything less than lethal; the moment he saw Psylocke he began firing. Having seen the effect of Chessman's weapon back in Senator Chisam's office, Psylocke exerted every effort to stay out of the way, and was confirmed in her assessment: brick was vaporized, metal slagged, and tar paper turned to bubbling cinders wherever the bolts hit.

But every evasion brought her closer.

When she was less than ten feet away, Psylocke threw herself into a forward roll, a maneuver that took her onto her back in a perfect position to plant both feet in her opponent's stomach in a debilitating mule kick. He went flying, losing his grip on both his pistol and on whatever he'd held in his left hand. Psylocke had a peripheral glimpse of a small black object going flying.

But her opponent was no amateur. With professional grace, he collected himself and drew a knife, advancing on her in a knife fighter's crouch.

"Mine's bigger," Psylocke told him mockingly, unsheathing her katana. The samurai sword's smoky silk finish shimmered in the snow light as she flashed the blade at him, and—as she'd known it would—its lethal sharpness drew his attention for the vital moment she needed to attack with the sheath.

And in that moment, the flying platform exploded.

Dead man's switch, was all Psylocke had time to think as she was flung backward, toward the edge of the rooftop.

If you don't like my driving, get off the sidewalk, Cyclops thought with uncharacteristic dark humor as he pushed the rental car to its limits. But in truth there were no pedestrians and few vehicles to impede him as he raced to the site of the battle.

It wasn't hard to find. The crossing searchlights and the occasional flares of energy weapons gave him little doubt of where the action was. No, where was not the problem.

What he was wondering was why.

Why was Black Team 51 providing security for Senator Chisam—and if they weren't, how and why had they picked Jean and Betsy up at Chisam's office? In the several months since the David Ferris incident, there hadn't been a peep out of Black Team 51—certainly no indication they were spoiling for a return match—and even an intensive search of the open files of various law-enforcement agencies had failed to turn up any trace of their existence.

Still, here they were now. And Cyclops guessed that was why they were going to have to wait for the postmortem.

At that moment, the car around him vanished.

One moment Cyclops was driving as fast as he could toward the lights and the gunfire. In the next moment he was flying backward, surrounded by the burning magnetized fragments of his borrowed car.

In a practiced combat maneuver, Cyclops tucked his body in tightly, converting his momentum into a backward roll that ended with the X-Men's co-leader on his feet and ready for action. He looked up the street, searching for whatever had hit his car.

And found it.

Jean? Cyclops queried. *Phoenix?* There was no answer.

His enemy was a black stretch limousine with tinted windows and a large plasma cannon jutting up out of its sunroof. It had fired the shot that had pulverized his car and, as Cyclops watched, the cycling LEDs along its barrel all stabilized, burning green-for-go, and it swiveled on its mounts to bring Cyclops in range.

But Cyclops fired first.

His cybernetic battle-visor required no manual operation, only his wish that it should open and unleash the deadly optic blasts that the first X-Man had lived with almost every day of his life. Fuelled primarily by the cosmic furnace of the sun, his power might be slightly weaker at night, but it was still more than enough to stop this crew.

His first blast sheared the plasma cannon free of its roof mount. His second stripped the undercarriage away from the limousine, leaving it resting on its frame in a pool of brake fluid while four tires bounced off down the street in the direction of the main battle.

Cyclops didn't hesitate, running past the marooned limo toward the sound of the megaphone and the veils of thickly drifting snow.

Now that Phoenix was back in the fight, Storm was able to pinpoint Psylocke's location—though not that of the members of the Black Team. She could have easily blown all of the Teamsters who were on the hover-platforms out of the sky, but to do so might have killed them, and that she would not do under any circumstances. Storm valued the sanctity of life and, though her ethics had often been strained to the utmost during her years with the X-Men, that was a line she promised herself never to cross.

As it was, the X-Men would surely be blamed for the destruction here, even that which they had not committed. The megaphone continued to blare its false message of amnesty, a deception staged for the sake of any innocent citizenry who might be listening, to give them the illusion that the X-Men were fighting against legitimate government forces.

Hearing that, Storm's serene features grew hard. It was true that she refused to resort to deadly force, but her years with the X-Men had taught her to be as hard and implacable as nature herself when there was need. With a wave of her hands, Storm dismissed the snow and summoned the rains. Just as she did, a spotlight fixed on her, illuminating her silver costume with a bright flash like lightning.

The rainstorm hit Psylocke like a thrown bucketful of water as she lay, groggy and disoriented, on the edge of the roof. Her ears were still ringing from the proximity of the flying platform's explosion as she dragged herself upright, looking around for her adversary.

He lay facedown on the wet gravel roof. Blood pooled

on his clothes, but the rain had washed most of it away and he was not bleeding now.

He was dead.

Psylocke withdrew her fingers from his neck with a faint feeling of mingled disquiet and triumph. She would not have hesitated to kill him in the heat of battle—in her own way, Psylocke could be as ruthless as Wolverine—and she did not exactly grieve for him now, but the very randomness of his death left Psylocke with a sense of unfinished business.

"There she is! Smoke her!"

Psylocke heard their voices faintly through the pouring rain, and dodged instinctively. The rooftop where she'd stood was pelted with a barrage of energy-weapon fire. Psylocke ran.

Phoenix soared through the night like a glowing comet, her psi-shield ionized by the air molecules that struck it until it shed a pearly golden light.

She was worried.

All possibility of concealing the X-Men's presence in Washington seemed to be over. She saw from Psylocke's mind that there had already been one death; all she, Cyclops, and the others could do now was make the best of a bad bargain and get away before anyone else got hurt.

The trouble was, it didn't look as if the four of them could do that either. Cyclops and Psylocke simply couldn't move as fast as she and Storm could. The alternative was for her and Storm to carry the other two, which would slow them down and make all four of the X-Men easier targets.

Oh, well. Who said this job was easy?

Phoenix reached the edge of the rainstorm and flew into it. The driving rain hissed as it hit her psi-shield and bounced off in a million shattered drops. Phoenix reached out with her mind, scanning.

She'd already located Storm and Psylocke, and took a

moment to reassure Cyclops that all of them were safe.

But I can't tell you where the bad guys are, lover, or even how many. I think they're all wearing psi-shields.

Sounds like they cared enough to send the very best, came Cyclops's dry response. *I'm not sure I'm dressed for such a fancy affair.* Then his mental tone turned brisk: *Tell Psylocke and Storm to pull back. Disengage if they can, but if they can't, lead the Black Team west. If they overfly the White House's airspace, they'll have more than a few X-Men to worry about. I'll see what I can do to encourage their disinterest.*

Be careful, darling, Phoenix sent, and was rewarded by the psychic equivalent of a snort of amusement before the X-Men's first leader turned his attention to other matters.

She saw Storm ahead of her, hovering in the eye of the storm she had called. The Black Team had lights trained on her, and the mutant elemental flashed like a moth dazzled by a candle flame. As Phoenix watched in horror, the limousine on the ground below launched surface-to-air missiles targeted on Storm. Storm destroyed them easily, with the lightning that Phoenix could feel crackling through the very air, but they'd only been a distraction. The plasma cannon mounted on the roof of the van swung on a broad arc, its beam shearing through the buildings it struck as if they were warm butter, until it reached Storm.

There was an explosion, a blinding flash, and Storm's psi-signature vanished from Phoenix's mind.

Okay, kids—the gloves are off!

Hovering where she was, still blinded by the flash, Phoenix reached down and seized the van, dragging it up into the sky.

If I'm going to be the last X-Man as well as the first, I'm going to see the team out with a bang, Cyclops vowed. He hadn't let Jean know how worried he was by what he'd learned at the dinner tonight. There'd be time enough for that later.

But as he raced toward the fight, he couldn't stop thinking about it.

A Deep Throat inside CGI's Project Level Playing Field had confirmed that the kill ratio from the retro-mutagen was nearly fifty percent, just as Hank had speculated. And at the same time, the Washington insiders the Professor had met at the dinner tonight believed that the architects of HR-485 were willing to see all the bill's provisos struck out except the one dealing with the compulsory transformation of mutants into normal human beings. Despite the treatment's mortality rate, that one element would become law, bringing the entire formidable weight of the U.S. government into place behind the lawful suppression of mutant-kind.

Cyclops had been raised as the heir to Xavier's dream: more than perhaps any other X-Man, he believed in its potential to become reality. But—perhaps because he'd entered the fight in his late teens, perhaps because he simply possessed less natural optimism than his mentor—more and more often lately, Cyclops felt that Xavier's dream was doomed to fail.

If they'd only wait until the treatment was safer—or just make it voluntary . . . he found himself thinking—and knew that when such compromises were made, Xavier's dream was dead. Mutants such as Magneto would not accept even the most benign genocide for their fellows—whom they considered a separate superior race. And what of Genosha? Would news of this treatment bring peace at last to that troubled country—or plunge it deeper into murderous civil war?

Time to daydream later, Cyclops told himself brutally. Right now, his mission was to open up some space between the X-Men and Black Team 51.

He'd reached the street where the fight was. In the background he could hear the wail of emergency sirens, responding at last to the reports of the battle. Well armed as the Black Team was, the X-Men were a match for them—but the four of them weren't a match for the combined might of all of the District's security forces. The nation's capitol was one of the prime targets for terrorists from every nation on Earth, and it was guarded accordingly—if the X-Men didn't get out of here within the next ten minutes, they'd be giftwrapped and on their way to either the Vault or Dr. Bocklin before Charles even knew they were gone.

Suddenly Cyclops heard the whine of a discharging cannon, and all the world went white.

Psylocke had reached the ground safely, no thanks to the spotlights that kept returning to her despite all her stealth. She began to wonder if Black Team 51 had a telepath somewhere in its bag of tricks; she knew Chessman hadn't had the time to plant a tracking device on either her or Phoenix, and she could think of no other way for them to continue relocating her with such unnerving regularity.

The driving rain had slackened slightly, and, from her vantage point in the doorway, Psylocke could see that the Team was keeping Storm too busy to shape the tempest, and, like any unnatural weather pattern, it was dissipating once the windrider's attention was no longer directed to it.

Let's see if I can buy Storm some elbow room, Psylocke thought. She ventured out into the street, sliding up on her goal as stealthily as any shadow.

Her psychic knife found its target; the Teamster slumped to the ground unconscious. Psylocke had grabbed his rifle—one of the energy rifles—and was just checking its charge when she heard footsteps running toward her.

The wall above her head exploded with a rain of bullets. Psylocke swung the barrel of the rifle up, firing back almost at random. *They're tracking us—and I think I know how!*

And the world exploded in a blaze of white light.

Storm had robed herself in a protective cocoon of lightning, and the web of electromagnetic potential—millions of volts—was enough to deflect both bullets and the beams of the rifles. As she dodged and dived, riding the winds to escape from their sight, she felt her grasp on the tempest dissolve as the unseasonable monsoon began to unravel.

Let it. It had served its purpose. All that remained was for them to withdraw, as Cyclops had ordered.

Then the beam of the plasma cannon brushed her.

At that moment, the entire corona of potential energy she had gathered around her rushed to ground itself down the cannon's energy beam. Its dissipation caused a massive feedback explosion, flinging Storm from the sky as if she'd been slapped from the air by a giant hand.

Phoenix wrenched the van into the sky, spinning it and shaking it as a child might shake a box to dislodge the last cookie. But Phoenix was no child, and furthermore, she was angry.

With a reflex hammered home by years of training, she kept the van near the ground as she shook it. There might be injuries, but no deaths from what she'd done here tonight. When she'd joined the team, X-Men didn't kill. Ever.

But she'd changed, in the years since—all of them had. Her friends and comrades of today included those whom her younger self would have hunted down without a second thought.

We were so innocent then.

But though Phoenix had lost that innocence long since, old reflexes still held.

She could easily have flung the van into the Potomac, but with the psi-nets, she had no way of knowing if it still had passengers aboard. She settled for flinging it into the

Reflecting Pool in front of the Lincoln Memorial. The dazzle was fading from her vision now, and she could see—well enough to make sure the van hit its target, at least.

She looked around. From her current height, Phoenix could see that the streets for blocks around were choked with the flashing lights of emergency vehicles. Police were already setting up barricades, cordoning off the area. She plucked an idea from her husband's thoughts and added her concurrence: if they didn't get out of here within the next few minutes they were toast.

Storm?

No answer. She wasn't sure if that was bad news, or if the Team had just deployed some kind of broad-based psi-dampers. Phoenix swooped down to treetop level, trying to find Storm visually, and suddenly the street below was washed in crimson light.

Cyclops.

Cyclops had lost patience several missiles ago. He blanketed the street with a wide-angle low-intensity optic blast that knocked the standing Black Team 51 members off their feet like so many ninepins and rocked the remaining ground vehicle—the stretch limo with the missile launchers—backward as sharply as if it had hit a brick wall at speed.

He felt a ripple of telekinetic force as Phoenix cleaned up after him, deftly plucking hand weapons and any loose equipment up from the street and sending it to join the black van in the Reflecting Pool on the Mall.

Cyclops calculated the best route to his destination and began warily to move through the street. The few members of Black Team who were still on their feet—or had regained them—backed out of his way, unwilling to draw his fire.

Suddenly a pillar of lightning rose in the west like an early dawn. The raw cascade of EMP energy fried every piece of equipment using a radio or satellite link within a half-mile radius, and several nearby streetlights went out.

Your misfortune, friends, Cyclops thought to himself. *You've made Storm mad.* But his next thought was to Phoenix: *Jean, tell Storm to back it down—we're trying to sneak out of here, not call in a preemptive strike!*

Gotcha, husband-mine. Psylocke?

On my way, Jean. I think they're using some kind of Cerebro-like device to track us. Psylocke sent.

Not anymore they're not, Phoenix answered, and then there was an indefinable sense of *absence* as Phoenix concentrated her attention elsewhere.

Cyclops was clear of the Black Team members, who were regrouping around their only remaining transport. Cyclops began to run, reviewing his mental map of the Downtown area as he did. They had to get out of here and back to the hotel—and, if possible, stay away from the White House. The place must be lit up like a Christmas tree right about now.

They'd been suckered very neatly; Black Team 51 wanted a front-page incident that Senator Chisam could use to whip up even more support for a bill that was on the verge of passing—maybe even enough support to guarantee the Presidential signature. And the X-Men had almost given it to them.

But not quite. And if Cyclops had his way, not ever.

All they had to do was disappear.

But disappearing didn't seem to be very easy this evening. The four of them regrouped a few blocks north of the Black Team's position, while Cyclops reviewed their options.

"We're a couple of miles from the hotel, we may already be inside a security cordon made up of most of Washington's defense muscle, and whoever the folks are in those choppers up there, I don't think we want to tangle with them."

"For all we know, it's CNN on the trail of an exclusive interview," Phoenix said sourly.

"Which we *don't* want to give," Psylocke added.

"It looks like we walk, folks. Storm, can you lay down some weather cover?" Cyclops said.

"Easily, Scott," Storm responded. She raised her hands, as if reaching for the clouds themselves, and immediately the air began to grow misty.

"A good old-fashioned pea-souper," Psylocke said. "It makes me quite homesick, really."

"Let's go, folks," Cyclops said.

Then the spotlight hit them.

"Halt, X-Men—you are under arrest!" a familiar amplified voice shouted.

The X-Men ran.

For the next half-hour, that was how it went: no matter what they did to evade them, the four X-Men were always only seconds away from rediscovery by Black Team 51. It was as much as they could do to stay away from the rapidly thickening cordon wall, but each one of them knew that as soon as the cordon was complete, it would begin to close.

"How are they *doing* that?" Phoenix fumed at one of their stops.

"I'd thought for a while that it was some sort of mutant detection device like Cerebro, but I'm not sure anymore," Psylocke said. "They'd have attacked us by now if that was what it was—as it is, it seems they're somehow half a jump behind—but the margin seems to be closing."

"Whatever it is, we need to neutralize it before we try passing that cordon," Cyclops said grimly. "Ideas, people?"

"If I attempted to cause another electromagnetic pulse. . . ." Storm said slowly.

"Too risky," Cyclops answered instantly. "It's too late to be inconspicuous, but we risk too many lives if we cause a power failure in a major population center like this one."

"True, Cyclops," Storm agreed sadly. "I had hoped—"

"They're late," Phoenix said suddenly. The other three X-Men looked at her.

"They're late," she repeated. "The last few times we stopped they were on us almost immediately. Why not this time? What's different?"

"You know," Psylocke said, "I bet I can produce them in less than a minute." She looked at Cyclops for permission.

"Do it," the X-Men's field leader said. "And then you can explain how it works."

Psylocke clenched her right fist, concentrating. Her brows drew together as the fist began to glow, the brilliant ionized aura indicating the presence of the ninja X-Man's formidable psychic knife.

The distant drone of the helicopter suddenly became louder, closer. A white light shone down from the sky to the street below.

But the X-Men were already gone, gathered in a narrow alleyway just north of Franklin Square. They were only a few blocks north of the White House, and the cordon was thickest here. The small open space—Washington was a city of parks, even more than New York City—was choked with heavy security vehicles from several different overlapping jurisdictions.

"So they aren't tracking us—they're tracking the use of our powers?" Phoenix asked.

"That's what it looks like," Psylocke admitted.

"It's a hypothesis worth testing," Cyclops decided. "Without our cheering section, we at least have a hope of getting through the defense cordon and going to ground."

Whatever happened, they dared not risk leading their pursuers back to Professor Xavier and imperilling his secret.

"But . . . how?" Storm asked.

"It's simple, people—we walk," Cyclops said.

• • •

Sometimes it's nice to prove you're not just a set of mutant powers in a fancy suit, Jean reflected. They'd made it this far without using their powers once; the moment any of them slipped would be the moment the massacre began.

It hadn't been in the direction of their goal, but it was a course that none of the hunters had been expecting them to take: Cyclops had led them north and east again, back to the center of the evacuated area. His plan had been for them to slip through the cordon somewhere to the north, then work their way west (giving the White House a wide berth), toward the Watergate. At the moment, they were within yards of their goal.

Phoenix and Storm should be able to pass through easily—both of them could use their powers to transform the unstable molecules of their battle-suits to a semblance of civilian clothes. But Psylocke and Cyclops, in their distinctive costumes, would have a harder time.

"Easier for me," Psylocke said, and Jean smiled faintly. Psylocke's ninja abilities were not the product of any mutant heritage, but of training the human body to its limits. Unless she used her psionic powers, her ninja abilities would draw no attention.

"I'll manage," Cyclops assured them both.

It was after ten o'clock. The cordon had begun closing almost an hour ago, with Washington's mixed security forces moving through the area in several waves. The four mutants had avoided them by taking to the rooftops. That route protected them from the traffic in the street, but extra care was needed to keep them hidden from the eyes in the helicopters overhead. And it was only a matter of time until the buildings—as well as the streets—were searched.

At least the news media wasn't involved. The X-Men could see the brightly colored helicopters hovering in the distance, but the black "alphabet agency" machines flying directly overhead kept the newsmen at bay.

And either Black Team 51's bogus ID as Department of Justice personnel was holding up, or they had some ace in the hole or other, because both Phoenix and Psylocke had seen familiar Black Team faces among the patrols they'd evaded.

"Okay, Psylocke—you first," Cyclops said.

The other X-Men all had enough field experience to know what Cyclops was thinking: if Psylocke were detected crossing over, the others could use the diversion she made to cover their own passages through the cordon.

The loneliness of command isn't about physical isolation, Phoenix thought, looking at her husband. *It's about making choices no one should have to.* She dared not send him any message of comfort, however, lest even that small use of her mutant powers should lead to their rediscovery by Black Team 51. She glanced back toward Psylocke.

Psylocke wasn't there.

Psylocke moved from darkness to darkness, drawing on all her ninja training and combat experience. She did not think about those left behind. She did not think of the consequences if she should fail. She did not *think*. She became the wind.

The cordon was thinner in this direction, so far from all of the targets that would tempt a terrorist. The heavy guns were all to the south and west: here, all the X-Men had to contend with was a roadblock, two police cars, and what looked like a squad of National Guardsmen.

She risked a sprint across the open space of the deserted street. Downtown Washington was like Wall Street: when the sun went down, the streets—at least in some neighborhoods—resembled the streets of a ghost town. Good and bad: fewer eyes to spot her, but when she moved, she was the only moving thing—any eyes looking would be drawn to her.

Psylocke reached concealment on the north side of the street.

No one saw.

Now, all she had to do was pass the checkpoint itself. Psylocke faded back into the shadows, seeking the wind's way.

"Okay," Cyclops said, once Psylocke had vanished from sight. "Jean, you go next—then Ororo."

"And what about you?" Phoenix asked suspiciously.

"I'll improvise," Cyclops said with a faint smile.

Phoenix took a deep breath, squared her shoulders, and walked out into the street, directly toward the roadblock.

She'd morphed her battle-suit into a coat and slacks, and her red hair was pulled back under a scarf. She looked as much like an inconspicuous civilian as she could manage. Now it all came down to the bluff.

"Good evening, officer—what's all the excitement?" Phoenix asked. She'd stopped—just as any lost and bewildered civilian might—in front of the blue sawhorse stencilled POLICE with the marked car parked behind it.

"Just a drill, Miss," the uniformed officer answered unconvincingly. "We'd appreciate it if you'd clear the area."

"Sure," Phoenix said easily. He came around the front of his vehicle and pulled the sawhorse aside for her, and Phoenix smiled dazzlingly at him and walked past the squad of National Guardsmen. Behind her, the officer was on his walkie-talkie, explaining to some unknown superior that one more civilian had been evacuated from the area.

Some drill, Phoenix thought.

"Remind me not to play poker with the lady anymore," Cyclops said admiringly from his concealed vantage point. "Your turn, Ororo."

"Confrontation isn't quite my style," Storm said, smiling, "as our young colleague Jubilee might say."

"Meaning?" Cyclops prompted.

"I'll take a leaf from my early training," the windrider said.

As a child thief in Cairo? Scott wondered. But Storm had already turned away, moving deeper into the alley.

Cyclops's night vision was the worst of any of the X-Men's—day or night, he saw the world through the scarlet haze of his deadly optic blasts, and he disliked night fighting almost as much as Storm hated enclosed spaces. Almost instantly, the six-foot-tall goddess with the silver hair and costume had vanished from his sight, but by the faint whispery sounds that came to his ears, he could tell that Storm was climbing up the side of the building without using her powers: moving like a spider, using every available handhold.

Nothing left to do but wait.

Psylocke waited at the agreed-on rendezvous spot, hoping the others would join her soon. She was outside the cordon—she could see its lights several blocks south of her—and the street she was on had only the usual amount of late-evening pedestrian traffic.

That had both advantages and drawbacks. The presence of so many other people would confuse any tracking sensors the hunters might use, and in any large crowd of people there were almost bound to be one or two other mutants, which would confuse the X-Men's stalkers further.

Psylocke turned, looking behind her, as finely honed instinct warned her of someone's approach.

"Howdy, sailor—fleet in?" Phoenix said.

An hour later the four X-Men had regrouped and returned to the Watergate Hotel.

Too bone-tired to even fetch out her keycard, Phoenix telekinetically manipulated the electronic lock to let the quartet in. Barely a minute after they entered and collapsed on the various beds, sofas, and chairs provided by the hotel, the sound of a keycard in the outside door could be heard.

"Professor!" Jean Grey exclaimed on a note of edgy relief. He wasn't alone; Laura Severn was with him, as well as a lanky blond youth who looked as if he were barely old enough to be in college.

"Is everything all right?" Xavier asked—publicly, for the ears of his companions—while Jean filled him in telepathically on the evening's activities.

I'm sorry, Professor, she thought, while keeping her face serene. *I tried to help, but I seem to have just made things worse.*

It was a noble attempt, Xavier's mind-voice said reassuringly, *and a legitimate risk. Even failures can be instructive—I discovered tonight that Black Team 51 is providing security for the Center for Genetic Improvement. It is . . . interesting to discover they have an interest in Senator Chisam as well.*

By now the other three X-Men had rejoined Xavier and his guests, having changed to civilian clothes while Jean covered for them. Scott wasn't wearing what he had been at the dinner—those clothes had been destroyed with the car—but he hoped that neither Laura nor Crown would notice.

Crown Clarendon works for CGI? Jean asked, picking the information up from the surface of Scott's thoughts.

Until two days ago, Scott responded. *It's a long story.*

"I appreciate your seeing me home, Laura," Xavier said. "I find my plans have changed unexpectedly, and I must return to New York at once."

"But you'll get word to the X-Men?" Crown said anxiously. "They have to know."

He *was* as young as he looked, Jean realized when she heard him speak. He was wearing an obviously borrowed tuxedo, and had his hands jammed deep into the jacket pockets, as if this were the only way he could keep from fidgeting nervously. She touched the surface of his thoughts lightly, receiving an impression of distress so strong that it blotted out any other thoughts.

"It's a good thing you were surfing the Internet looking for them," Laura said to Crown, "or I'd never have found you. Now, if you're sure you're willing to testify before the subcommittee on Monday morning . . ."

"Sure," Crown said quickly. "Violate confidentiality agreements, disseminate proprietary technological information, whatever you want. But you've got to pull the plug somehow before CGI kills anyone else. I got the kids out, but they'll be only the first."

Psylocke and Jean stared at each other. So this was the reason for the anguish they both had felt.

"Charles will do what he can," Laura Severn said. "And I'm sure he'll do his best to get a message to the X-Men."

"He has to," Crown said bleakly. "Because wherever they are, they're just about the only hope mutants have left."

Westchester Airport wasn't exactly bustling at one o'clock in the morning, when Scott, Jean, Betsy, Ororo, and Professor Xavier arrived on the shuttle from Washington, but there was still a reception committee . . . of sorts.

"Logan!" Jean exclaimed, spotting him across the terminal as they emerged past the security checkpoint.

Wolverine wore a buffalo plaid jacket and his trademark Stetson. "We got trouble, Chuck," were the first words he spoke once he had crossed to the others.

"Indeed we do, Logan," Professor Xavier said. "I take it you have made some discovery on your own journey?"

"Somethin' like that," the Canadian X-Man agreed dourly. "An' not anything you'll like, either."

CHAPTER 11

ambit was pulled back to aching consciousness by the nagging thought that something was dangerously wrong. He opened his eyes slowly. He was staring up at an unfamiliar ceiling and lying on a cold hard floor.

Rogue!

The sudden memory galvanized him; Gambit leapt to his feet—every muscle ached—and stared around himself wildly.

The warehouse was empty. No one was here. The ruin he and Rogue had made of the place with their battle remained, but his thief's instincts told him the others had gone.

And Rogue had gone with them. Straight into the hands of the so-called Dr. Arnold Bocklin. Who was not Bocklin at all, but someone far more subtle and dangerous—and he had Rogue.

"No . . ." Gambit moaned. Not Rogue. She would never survive.

"No-o-o-o-o-o-!" he cried aloud, sinking to his knees under the weight of his pain and howling his despair to the emptiness. Rogue was stolen away—and all the X-Men were betrayed by his failure to save her.

His cry faded, but not into silence—and as the wailing sound swelled anew, Gambit recognized it for what it was: police sirens.

Coming for him.

Even in the depths of his anguish, the thief's instinct of self-preservation remained. The door to the building was still locked, as it had been when Rogue trapped him there, but it yielded to a few moments of manipulation. Gambit was out, free in the night air.

The sirens were louder now, the police cars only minutes away. Gambit sprinted for the fence.

He was halfway over it when the searchlight hit him. Gambit swore feelingly and redoubled his efforts. He did not fear the razor wire at the top of the fence this time; he didn't even notice it. His feet hit the ground on the other side of the fence just as the police unit screeched to a stop.

"Police! Halt!" a voice shouted behind him.

Gambit ran.

He heard the car start up again in pursuit and dodged down the nearest alley. He had one advantage, even if this wasn't the Big Easy, his home turf: these officers wouldn't randomly open fire.

He hoped.

Rats and cats scattered out of his path; Gambit slipped and nearly fell on some strewn garbage as he ran through the alleyway. He emerged on the street at the far end, and was just about to congratulate himself on his narrow escape—

—when another police unit, lights flashing but without siren, turned the corner.

Gambit didn't even pause. He turned on his heel and fled back up the alleyway. He climbed to the top of a dumpster and leaped, his fingers grazing the bottom rung of a fire escape ladder. He tightened his grip and pulled himself aloft, cursing the noise he made climbing the rusty structure.

But when the car reached the alleyway and shone its searchlight down it, there was no one there.

He'd lost his pursuit for only a few minutes, but Gambit's wild flight across the rooftops did buy him enough time to reach the place where he and Rogue had stashed his bike. Once astride it, zipping away from his pursuers,

Remy LeBeau would become *M'sieur* Ordinary Citizen, and evade the police presence with ease.

But his motorcycle wasn't there.

Gambit stared around wildly, unable to believe what he saw. But this was the street corner, and there was the vacant gas station he'd taken for a landmark.

But the Harley wasn't there. And he could see the police lights flashing off the buildings on the cross street. They were still looking for him.

Gambit turned and ran again.

Where could he go? Steal a car, perhaps, but that took time the so-zealous *policiers* would not give him. He thought, indignantly, that the police were taking far too much interest in a simple break-in, but then Gambit realized that they must have gone inside and seen the ruin he and Rogue had made of the warehouse. *That* would keep the *bonrien* interested.

Thinking of Rogue made the anger and pain in Gambit's soul waken anew. For a moment he felt like abandoning the X-Men, vanishing into the night and seeking vengeance on his own for what "*Docteur* Bocklin" would do to Rogue. He did not believe that he could save her—or that the X-Men could, either. Black Team 51 had too much of a head start.

The police car turned the corner, moving at a slow crawl up the block. Its light shone on the row of parked cars, on boarded-up houses, on anonymous businesses with their steel shutters lowered and locked for the night. Gambit slunk back into the shadows, concealing himself behind the abandoned gas station. It would be child's play to force a door, get inside. Maybe he'd get lucky and there'd be a pay phone inside the station that still worked, and he could call for backup—if he decided to.

But Gambit stayed where he was, not moving. The shock of the discovery he had made in the warehouse was like a mortal blow, paralyzing him. He could not purge his mind of Rogue's terror. Of her death.

And he'd done nothing to stop her from going to her doom. He should have voiced his suspicions despite the cost—but he'd been a loner too long. A lifetime's habit of caution and fabrication had doomed Rogue.

As he lingered there, he heard another vehicle turn onto the road, moving as slowly as the first. But this one had neither lights nor siren—Gambit looked out, seeing a long black limousine, its tinted windows preventing any sight of the occupants. It was as out of place here on these mean streets as Gambit himself. He retreated farther from sight.

The limousine came to a halt.

"My dear colleague, I would strongly suggest that you eschew any lingering farewells to the fine borough of Queens and make haste with all due celerity," Hank McCoy said.

The passenger door of the limo was open. Gambit sprinted for its haven and tumbled inside. The car began moving immediately.

McCoy was driving, a chauffeur's cap balanced ludicrously atop his blue-furred skull. "Where's Rogue?" he asked—though Gambit noted that McCoy had not waited for her. As if he knew she would not be coming.

"She gone," Gambit said bleakly. "Mam'selle Rogue will no' be joinin' us—maybe ever again."

"You brought us here, Captain Canine—what now?" Rewind's voice was edgy and hostile.

The five of them—Rewind, Pipedream, Charade, Slapshot, and . . . Captain Canine—had escaped CGI yesterday in Rewind's rental car. Lloyd had brought them here: his aunt's house in nearby Augusta.

But Aunt Shirleen wasn't here—and she hadn't come home yet.

Yesterday they'd all been too tired to care. But tomorrow

was another day, so the saying went, and tomorrow was here.

The five of them were gathered together in Shirleen Morrow's kitchen. Rewind had wrinkled her nose at the way it was decorated—a rooster-shaped clock, and matching canisters, salt and pepper shakers, refrigerator magnets, and spoon-rest (with coordinating gingham curtains)—but she hadn't said anything aloud.

Fortunately Lloyd and Slapshot both knew how to cook, or the five of them would have starved this morning; they'd finished all the cookies, crackers, cold cereal, and lunch meat that they'd found the night before, and all that was left was bacon, eggs, and frozen TV dinners. Now they were all gathered in the kitchen's tiny breakfast nook together, finishing their meal and looking for answers.

"What day is it?" Charade asked, as if it mattered.

"Wednesday, I think," Lloyd said slowly.

"Just since the day before yesterday?" Charade demanded indignantly, and Lloyd nodded.

"We can't go home," Slapshot said firmly, cutting through the other conversations. He'd had a lot of time to think this over—since Monday, in fact—and by now he had a few ideas. "Think about it, guys. The Center for Genetic Improvement is a major multinational corporation—but they kidnapped us, some of their people impersonated U.S. Marshals, and they shot at us when we tried to escape."

"With real bullets," Charade said sulkily.

"Obviously operating within the confines of the law is not, like, a major issue for them," Rewind said.

"So we shouldn't act as if it is," Slapshot continued stubbornly. "If we go back to Cleveland, we have to assume they're waiting for us. If we phone home—"

"The phones are bugged," Pipedream said reluctantly. "But why us, Jase? We haven't done anything to anybody."

"We were organizing," Rewind said slowly. "Remember? I was going to start that mutant BBS just like *NextNet* over in New York?"

"They're going to kill us for running a *bulletin board*?" Charade squeaked indignantly. "But I've got to call my folks—they're probably going to ground me until I'm *thirty* for this."

"You could send them e-mail. I could use this foreign remailer I know," Rewind said slowly. "But Lloyd's aunt doesn't have a computer and a modem."

"Pipedream?" Slapshot said. "You're the leader. Tell us what to do next."

"I don't *want* to be the leader!" Pipedream shouted, surprising all of them.

He'd been standing, leaning against the doorway eating poached eggs and toast. Now Adam Kirby flung the empty plate aside and stepped back.

"Hey!" Lloyd said. "You can't go breakin' Aunt Shirleen's dishes like that—"

"I resign," Pipedream said, ignoring Lloyd. "I never asked to be leader; I never wanted the job. The Ohio Mutant Conspiracy was just a *joke*, remember? It wasn't ever supposed to get real. Just what are five high school kids supposed to do about a crazed multinational corporation with real live bullets. Huh?"

"Pipedream," Slapshot said desperately. They couldn't afford to fall apart now.

"Fine," Pipedream snapped. "You want the job—you got it, Jase—oh, excuse me, that should be Slapshot, shouldn't it? Well have fun, Fearless Leader—I don't think you're going to have a long run."

Pipedream turned and walked out of the room.

"Pipedream!" This time it was Rewind who called his name. She struggled out of the back of the U-shaped breakfast nook—climbing over Charade—and ran after him, crying.

The other two looked at Slapshot.

Just as if they think I'm a real leader, and we really are a superteam. But we're not. It's like Pipedream said: we're high school kids.

"Lloyd?" he said hopefully. "You're the oldest."

"You know I can't do anything like that, Slapshot," Lloyd said reproachfully, his Georgia drawl thickening under stress. He turned away and began picking up the pieces of shattered china. "M'aunt's gonna kill me when she gets home an' finds this mess."

Slapshot looked at Charade—nobody's choice for leader, no matter how desperate they were. If none of the other three wanted the job, it was up to him.

Only a leader has to have followers, doesn't he? And none of the others'll do a blessed thing I say. Lloyd and Charade had followed his lead when they'd broken out of CGI only because the three of them had been running in the same direction.

"Y'know, Slapshot," Charade said seriously, "I've been thinking. Lloyd really needs to work on his code name. I mean, he's never really chosen one, and it kind of looks ridiculous for all the rest of us to have them and not him."

Slapshot stared at her, trying not to show his dismay. They were being chased by an army of gun-toting maniacs from hell and she was worrying about what kind of a *nom de guerre* Lloyd should have?

But Charade was the youngest of them—only a kid, really—and if anybody deserved an escape from reality, she did.

"Okay, how about Top Dog?" Slapshot asked.

Lloyd made a rude—relieved—noise as he dropped the shards of the broken plate into the trash.

And besides, Slapshot couldn't think of anything else to do right now.

They'd come up with—and rejected—Super Saluki, Power Pooch, and the Sub Woofer as possible new names for Lloyd by the time Rewind came back. Lloyd had cleared the table and left the dishes to soak, and they were sitting around the table—Lloyd with coffee, Slapshot with tea, and Charade with a Coke—when Rewind came in and plopped herself down next to Slapshot.

"Coffee?" Rewind said hopefully, and Lloyd got up to get some for her.

Slapshot looked at her, not daring to ask.

"Pipedream . . . Adam just wants to be alone for a while, okay?" Rewind said.

"Yeah. Sure," Slapshot said. He was just glad that the golden boy hadn't done something completely stupid, like leaving the house or using the phone. They didn't know what lay in wait for them out there—while they'd watched the news last night and today, there'd been nothing on about any trouble out at CGI.

And that was suspicious, wasn't it?

Lloyd set the cup down in front of Rewind—black, the way she liked it—and another can of soda down beside Charade's glass. She rewarded him with a sunny smile, but the other three could see the dark shadows under her eyes, giving her an uncharacteristically haggard look that was a reminder to all of them of the danger they were all in.

"So," Rewind said. "What do we do?"

For a moment Slapshot felt a flare of anger—why were they all so ready to turn to him? He was no better leader than Pipedream could be. But he pushed the feeling away. They were in too much danger. They couldn't afford any more fights or panics. All of them had to work together, or they'd all probably die.

"We have to figure out what will let us get away from CGI," Slapshot said slowly, feeling his way. "We know that what they're doing isn't legal. If we can make it public, they should have to stop."

Shouldn't they?

"But who's going to believe us?" Rewind said, her tone

just as tentative. "I mean: five kids—mutants—"

"This isn't about us, Pey—it's about CGI. It doesn't matter who they're picking on, if they're impersonating federal marshals to do it." Slapshot was sure of that much.

"Bad mistake," Lloyd agreed.

"So who do we call—the X-Men?" Charade said.

Rewind shuddered. "Don't they kill people? I heard they were all escaped criminals."

"Well, *we're* escaped criminals right now, so that doesn't mean much," Slapshot said. "But the point is, we've got to find someone we can *find*, for one thing—and who will listen to five high school kids."

"*Rolling Stone!*" Charade said. "I read it in this Stephen King book once, where there was this girl who had this mutant power and the government was chasing her, so she went to *Rolling Stone.*"

It sounds almost ridiculous enough to work, Slapshot thought. Turning to a rock magazine for help.

"CNN and Turner News both have bases here in my hometown," Lloyd said. "Why don't we just call them up an' give an exclusive interview?"

"Guys!" Pipedream yelled, bursting into the kitchen. "Come quick!" He led them upstairs to the second-floor front bedroom. "You can see it from up here."

From the window, they could see a line of ominous black Stealth-configured ground transports moving down the quiet residential street. It was eleven thirty on Wednesday morning, but there were people standing on their porches all along the street to look.

"They're coming for us," Pipedream said flatly.

Stand or run? Slapshot thought wildly. He knew the Ohio Mutant Conspiracy couldn't beat CGI Security if it came to a fight—and if those tanks belonged to anyone else, the odds got even worse.

The house had a storm cellar—Slapshot had seen it last night—but they couldn't lock the bad guys out of it for long if they were really trying to get in and he didn't think they could hide there in the first place.

Think!

"Get to the car," Slapshot said aloud. His voice sounded as if it belonged to someone else.

Fortunately Rewind had her purse—and the car keys—within reach. Slapshot chivvied the others along ahead of him mercilessly, with the result that they were backing out of the driveway in the rental car while the lead transport was still half a block away.

"Where should I go?" Rewind asked nervously.

"Go! Just go—*go!*" Slapshot shouted at her. Rewind yanked on the shift and floored the gas pedal.

There was a moment of skidding and squealing as the car hesitated before zipping backward out of the driveway. Pipedream, Charade, and Lloyd, who were jammed together in the back, complained loudly.

"Watch your elbow, Dogbreath!"

"Get back over on your own side of the car!"

"My jacket!"

A moment later they were barrelling down the street, leaving the transports behind.

For a moment.

"They're speeding up," Pipedream said, craning around to look out the rear window.

"Oh, yeah?" Rewind muttered. "Watch this."

She yanked the wheel to the left.

There was a bump as the front wheels of the car hit the sidewalk and bounced up over the curb. It skidded across the corner of somebody's lawn. Another bump for the back wheels. Two bumps as the car slid off the sidewalk again into the street beyond. Rewind clawed the wheel to the left, barely missing a parked car. The engine howled as she picked up speed again, racing for the end of the cross-street.

"This is a dead end!" Slapshot shouted over the engine noise.

"I know!" Rewind shouted back. "This is a car!"
What?
At the end of the cul-de-sac there was a curb, a sidewalk, and a wide grassy verge. Beyond that was the chain-link fence that bordered a school playground. Between the grass and the fence was a wide, beaten-down trough of red earth—a jogging path.

Rewind hit the grass at an angle and began driving along the jogging path not much more slowly than she had on the paved road.

"Rewind—" Slapshot couldn't think of what to say.

"They're here," Lloyd said.

Slapshot glanced back. The lead transport was turning the corner in pursuit of them.

Rewind jerked the wheel left again, jamming on the brakes.

They'd gone about a block, and there was an opening in the fence leading into the school playground. Rewind turned the wheel sharply, but the fence post still scraped off the right-side mirror and most of the paint on the door as the car passed through it.

"Hey!" Pipedream said. "Where'd you learn to drive?"

"The Han Solo School of Driver's Ed," Rewind snapped. "Do you want to go back and argue with them? I don't."

It wasn't time for the Winter Break, so school was still in session. Fortunately it wasn't time for recess either, and the playground was deserted. Their getaway car zoomed across it like the proverbial bat, heading straight for the other entrance. A short trip over the school's front lawn, a sharp right turn back onto the street, and they were rolling through the suburban streets once more.

There was no sign of their pursuers.

"We did it!" Charade crowed.

Too early to brag, Vette, Slapshot fretted silently.

"So what do we do now?" Lloyd asked.

"We've got to—" Slapshot and Pipedream said at the same time.

Slapshot felt a surge of relief. Maybe Pipedream was going to take over again as their leader. He was better at it than Slapshot was.

"Pipedream?" Rewind said.

"I think we've got to put as much distance between us and them as we can," Pipedream said. "If we can get home and tell what we know—"

"My dad's going to hand me right back over to them," Rewind said flatly.

"But my mom won't," Pipedream said. "My mom'll yell to everybody she knows. You can stay with us."

We can't go back, Slapshot thought to himself. *We haven't got a hope of getting back to Ohio in the first place, and we need help now, not in two or three days.*

But as he thought of saying something, Slapshot hesitated. They all wanted to go home. And why should they listen to him? Nobody was chasing them right now—and the Ohio Mutant Conspiracy only listened to him when they were actually under attack.

So he said nothing, hoping he could talk them around later, when they all felt safer.

But that time wasn't going to come.

Rewind got out onto a main street—two lanes each way, the sidewalks lined with shops—and was heading back toward the Interstate to pick up 495 East.

"Slow down, Pey, we don't want to get a ticket," Pipedream said.

Slapshot hunched his shoulders beneath his jacket, hoping nobody saw and said anything. He sat in the front passenger seat, hating himself for saying nothing about their plan but unsure of what else to do. He thought that what they ought to do was head for the downtown area, find CNN, and tell the world about this while they could. He just didn't think the others would go along with it—especially with Pipedream offering them such an attractive alternative.

Yeah. Run.

Why had Pipedream had to say anything, anyway? If the football hero hadn't spoken up, the others would have listened to him. Slapshot was sure of it.

Almost.

He stared morosely out the window, watching the image of their battered car pace them in the plate-glass windows of the shops. But there was something odd about the reflection. . . .

"Jase!" Rewind squealed.

He whipped around in his seat. One of the stealth transports was behind them, one car back. As he watched, the car between them pulled over to the curb.

"Floor it!" Pipedream shouted.

"I can't—there's too much traffic!" Rewind yelled.

"Pull over!" Slapshot bellowed over both of them. "We've got to run for it—make them scatter!"

The transport fired.

Lloyd yelped, and Charade squealed in reaction. But as far as Slapshot could see, there'd just been that weird moment—a weak glow as pale as a candle flame in the sun—

The car died.

Rewind frantically turned the ignition key, but nothing happened. The car coasted silently onward, out of control now that the engine had died and the power steering had locked.

The intersection ahead had a red light in this direction. They were moving—slower now, but forward still—directly into the cross-traffic.

"Get out of the car," Slapshot said.

He reached across Rewind and unhooked her seatbelt. His was already undone. They had to move—this was a two-door compact, and the three in the backseat couldn't get out until they did.

"Rewind, *move*."

Finally she did, moving as slowly as though she were under water. Slapshot waited a split second to see that she was clear, then bailed out the passenger side, trying not to look at the asphalt sliding by beneath the car. He hit hard, yanking his legs free of the door just in time, and watched the car roll on.

All around him cars were honking and swerving. The tank pursuing them rolled onward.

It was in motion.

And Slapshot's mutant gift was to change the direction of an object's motion.

He didn't know if it would work—he'd never tried to affect something this big before in his entire life—but he had to try.

Jason Gerber reached deep into himself and drew upon whatever it was inside him that made him Slapshot—and flung it at the transport.

There was a squawk. The transport rocked backward as if it had been hit. From the direction of the intersection came the sound of first one collision, then more. All around him, traffic began to snarl. He looked around the intersection, but couldn't see any of the others.

He'd done what he could. Nearly exhausted from his effort, Slapshot ran, dodging traffic.

She didn't want to play this game anymore. Rewind ran until her breath came short and her legs ached, even with all the hours of practice she'd put in on the Kirtland Cavaliers Cheerleading Squad. She slowed and looked around.

There was nobody in sight. None of the others, and none of those weird troop carriers. She slowed and stopped, the fear so much a part of her now that she could almost ignore it.

Across the street at the next corner there was a little grocery with a pay phone beside it. Rewind headed toward it, fumbling in her purse for her credit card. It wasn't hers, really, but it had her name on it—her father had given it to her so that she could learn to handle money.

Yeah, right.

She walked over to the phone and dialed 0.

"Operator? I'd like to make a credit-card call to Cleveland, Ohio. Yes, I have the number here—"

Lloyd had stayed with Charade. Neither of them were sure where to go, and they didn't have more than a few dollars between them.

"What are we going to do?" Charade whimpered. Lloyd put an arm around her, pulling her close.

"Don't you worry. Everything's gonna work out just fine."

She glared up at him, her tear-filled eyes indignant. "How?" she demanded.

"Well, I don't know. Jase'll think of something," Lloyd said desperately. "C'mon, we better keep moving."

Their headlong flight had taken them off the business streets, back into the residential area. Pedestrians weren't as common here, especially pedestrians who ought to be in school. Lloyd forced himself not to think about it.

Pipedream leaped out of the car and tried to roll, feeling as if he'd just been clotheslined by an opposing tackle. He heard the sounds of cars crashing and horns blowing, and, in the distance, the wails of sirens. He wanted to follow Rewind but didn't see her, so he picked a direction at random and ran.

He didn't want to get too far from the main street, either. His intention—such as it was—was to get under cover (hitting somebody with a pipedream, if necessary) and stay hidden for as long as possible. And then. . . .

He'd think about that later.

•　•　•

"Daddy, I don't *care* what the letter says! They kidnapped my friends and they were going to *kill* us!"

Rewind kicked the wall in fury, her long blonde hair bouncing with the movement. Why had she ever thought her father would listen?

"I'm a mutant, Daddy!" she shouted over the sound of his voice. "And you know what? It's heredi—"

A hand reached over her shoulder and took the phone from her hand. Rewind gasped in shock, turning toward them. The man with the phone in his hand looked almost normal—even if he was wearing black winter-weight Giorgio Armani in Atlanta and had a big dangly gryphon earring in one ear—but the four men standing behind him were dressed like the fake marshals who had kidnapped her friends two days ago.

She pushed at them with her Rewind power, but all they did was flicker. They'd been here for more than a minute, then, and thirty seconds was her top limit for reversing the time flow.

"Don't do that," the Man in Black said, giving her ponytail a yank.

Rewind hit him.

She'd been a cheerleader for years, she'd been "victim-proofed" in a nationally-franchised self-defense program and she had a brown belt in judo.

And she really, really wanted to hit somebody.

The man in the suit stumbled backward. Rewind bolted to the side. One of the faceless goons in armor raced after her, and she dropped him with a wheel-kick to the chest. She steadied herself, ready to run again.

A bullet flew past her ear. Rewind froze.

"Very good," said the Man in Black. He was still on the ground, but he was pointing a .44 AutoMag pistol right at her. "But I'm very good, too. And if you take one more step I'm going to blow your leg off."

Rewind stood there, frozen by the sight of the gun. She

hardly noticed when two of the faceless men came up to her and shackled her hands behind her, pulling her toward the transport.

The Man in Black got up from the ground and reached for the dangling receiver.

"I apologize for the interruption, Mr. Conway," the man said smoothly into the phone. "Peyton has to go now, but I'm sure she'll be able to talk to you again soon." He held the receiver away from his ear, wincing slightly, and then quietly hung up the phone.

Slapshot walked down the street, trying to look like somebody with someplace to be. He wondered how much the bus fare was in Atlanta—eventually every bus had to end up downtown, didn't it?

He was cold—he hadn't been wearing his jacket when they'd all fled Mrs. Morrow's house, and without it, he wasn't dressed for the weather. He was cold and he didn't know what to do and he had the feeling that he'd *failed* the others somehow.

And all around him life went on, as though nobody but the five of them even saw the ominous black vehicles.

Maybe no one else did. Maybe they weren't there at all.

Get a grip, Jase, he told himself.

There was the sound of a familiar engine behind him. Slapshot looked around wildly. He'd cut back over to the main street, several blocks away from the accident, and now he ducked down an alley, stopping halfway along its length. He didn't know if he could get through at the other end, and he didn't want to leave the relative safety of crowds and bustle.

And maybe they hadn't seen him at all.

He crouched down behind a pile of boxes filled with spoiled produce, and tried not to breathe—for any number of reasons.

The transport pulled up against the curb in front of the alleyway and stopped.

The side door opened. A man in a black suit whom Slapshot had never seen before stepped out. He was wearing dark glasses, his long hair was pulled back in a ponytail, and he wore a long silver earring dangling from one ear.

"Mr. Gerber? Jason? Or should I call you Slapshot? Are you within the sound of my voice? My name is Keithley; I'm fairly sure you know who I work for."

The feeling of rage that swelled inside him took Slapshot by surprise. He dug his hand into the pocket of his jeans and wrapped his fist around a handful of change. He could kill Keithley with any of the coins. One would do.

No! The revulsion he felt was as sudden as the anger had been, and the combination made him miss whatever Keithley had been saying.

". . . so we'll try a little persuasion," Keithley said.

Keithley gestured, and the back hatch of the transport raised. A man in the soft Kevlar armor and black helmet that Slapshot recognized from Cleveland climbed out, and then reached back inside for something else.

Rewind.

Her hair was a mess, and her leather jacket—she'd worn it at breakfast, otherwise she wouldn't have it now—was pulled half off her shoulders. She was struggling so hard that the goon who was holding onto her practically had to carry her.

Why didn't anybody see? Why didn't anybody stop them? Couldn't everyone see that what they were doing was illegal?

"This is Ms. Conway," Keithley said. "And this is my gun." He held the long-barreled silvery thing with the rifled top low, in front of himself, both to make it visible to Slapshot and to conceal it from the passersby. "I'm going to put a bullet through her knee if you don't come out on the count of five. It doesn't matter what kind of tricks she tries; I've got plenty of bullets. One—''

''Wait!'' Slapshot scrambled to his feet, raising his hands over his head. Only once he'd done it did it occur to him that he might have bluffed. Let Keithley fire, slapshot the bullet right back at its owner.

But what if he missed?

It didn't matter. He was already standing in plain sight, and Keithley had put away the gun.

''Thank you,'' Keithley said. ''Now if you'll come this way?''

After half an hour's walk, Pipedream had found a branch library. It was as good a place to hide as any. He took a magazine off the rack and pretended to read.

He felt sick.

He'd run out on the others. It was *his* fault they'd hadn't managed to escape, that they were all on the run again—if the others hadn't been recaptured already. He wasn't any kind of a leader—but if he didn't want the job then why had he started arguing with Jase, trying to upstage him?

Maybe because of Rewind? He knew she liked Slapshot—she'd only come running after him this morning because Jase had told her to, probably. It'd even been Slapshot who told them all to run when the other guys had stopped the car—and right now Pipedream wished Slapshot was here, because Pipedream didn't have the faintest idea in the whole wide world of where to run *to*.

The two of them were made for each other; Rewind was beautiful and brainy, with all that computer stuff—and Slapshot was on the Honors List. And Pipedream? He was nothing but a big dumb jock with about as much in the brain line as your average golden retriever. After all, they'd all ended up here on his advice, hadn't they?

Someone sat down beside him at the table.

''Mr. Kirby? It's time to go now.''

• • •

They'd gotten away, but all the away they'd gotten had been into a larger box. Both Lloyd and Charade had wanted to phone their parents, but neither had quite dared. Suppose Slapshot was right? Suppose the phones *were* tapped?

Suppose somebody had gone around Cleveland after they'd left and arrested their folks?

He hadn't said that aloud, not wanting Charade to get that idea if she hadn't already, but after they'd been wandering around for about an hour Lloyd realized that he had to know. So he hunted until he found a phone, and made his call.

"Hello?"

"Aunt Shirleen!" Lloyd's knees nearly buckled with relief. "You're home!"

"Well, where else would I be?" his aunt asked. "Lloyd, are you calling from Atlanta? I got home from going to see Carolee MacGregor to find everything turned inside out and all of my groceries gone. Have you been in this house, nephew?"

"Yes, Aunt Shirleen." And he couldn't even think of a way to begin explaining what he and his friends had been doing there.

"Well, you just get right back here, Lloyd Englehart— you hear me? You get back here right now."

"Yes ma'am. Right away." Lloyd hung up the phone with relief. They'd go back to his aunt's house, and they could get everything sorted out from there. "C'mon, Vette. We're going back to my aunt's."

They'd managed to wander fairly far from it, and the walk back gave Lloyd plenty of time to become suspicious. Was it really likely that the guys with the transports would have just driven off after them and not done anything about the house?

But they must have—otherwise, Aunt Shirleen would

certainly have mentioned it over the phone. Everything had to be fine.

But when they turned the corner and were on the street that led back to the house, he still hadn't managed to convince himself. Lloyd looked down at the ground, staring at the tire tracks that Rewind had left across old Mr. Ditko's lawn.

"C'mon, Wonder Dog!" Charade said excitedly. "Hurry up—maybe the others are back here, too."

That was what bothered him, Lloyd realized—that there was no one on the street at all at this time of day. Reflexively Lloyd took a deep breath, sifting the air for familiar scents.

And he found some.

"No! Wait, Vette—it's a trap!"

The moment Lloyd cried out, men in black leapt from hiding and began to race toward them, out of the concealment of cars and bushes.

Charade ran back the way they had come. Lloyd grabbed for her and missed, and then was grabbed himself. He heard Charade cry out as she was seized, and he growled, deep in his throat.

"Down, boy." A man in a fancy suit was standing in front of him. Lloyd wasn't sure who he was, but he knew this man was the enemy. He lunged for him and was yanked back.

"Hit him up with a trank, would you? He makes me nervous," the man said.

Aunt Shirleen came out on the porch. Her eyes were red with crying.

"Did I do all right?" she asked the suited man.

"Perfectly, Mrs. Morrow. And the FBI very much appreciates your cooperation."

"It's a *lie!*" Lloyd shouted. "They aren't the FBI! They're—"

There was a sharp stinging in his leg, and a tingling

coldness spread through his body. Suddenly his head felt heavy, and his neck muscles ached from supporting its weight.

"We'll be going now," the man in the suit said. "You'll receive an official letter of commendation in a few weeks."

Lloyd no longer had the strength to struggle. But as they led him toward the transport, he could turn his head to look back one last time at his aunt. Shirleen Morrow's hands were knotted in her apron, and she raised it to wipe her eyes.

They lied to her. And so she turned the two of them in.

It wasn't fair. Not to anyone.

And as they marched him away, Lloyd could hear his aunt's voice behind him. "Lloyd? What have you done? Lloyd?"

The killing had been good, but it was never enough, Mantrap thought sadly. Nothing was enough to satisfy the beast who lived inside her skin with her, and which thought about slaughter even when she was alone. Only a few hours behind Wolverine, Mantrap crossed the Canadian frontier— the world's longest undefended border—into Michigan's Upper Peninsula. A few hours after that she picked up a car with U.S. tags. Its former owner hadn't minded once she was through with him.

Other drivers on the road made her edgy. *Too close!* her instincts screamed, and every one of them a potential target. But she had to concentrate, focus. Bocklin was hundreds of miles from here. She couldn't afford any incidents that would let him get away.

She drove steadily west. According to the maps she'd gotten with the car, there was a small airfield a few miles from here. She needed a plane. Speed was vital.

Because she'd never been meant to be mission operational.

Never.

The gas tank's warning light began to flicker a few miles later, then to glow steadily, and at last the car coasted to a stop. Mantrap pulled it off to the side.

Out of gas, and too many cars on the road to make it easy for her to make use of a passing Good Samaritan. What else? She scanned her surroundings. Verge, ditch, rise, fence . . . and on the other side of the fence, a housing development.

Her arm blades were wrapped in the car donor's coat. She'd have to get camouflage for herself, too: the battle-suit was too conspicuous.

She slid out of the car on the passenger's side and went down into the ditch. She watched for a break in the traffic, and when she found it, went up the other side.

The high wooden fence had been designed for decoration, not to keep someone out. She slid through a gap and dragged her arm knives in after her. She wasn't sure she was as fond of them as the designers were. It was true they were showy, and effective in melee situations. But they were also awkward to carry, and useless in covert ops.

She'd have to think about it carefully.

Beyond the fence was more grass, followed by a series of backyards—some fenced, some not. She chose one at random—it had sliding glass doors letting out onto the yard, easy to get in through—and entered the yard.

The doors opened, a sliding sound that drew all of Mantrap's attention.

A woman stood in the doorway. She was youngish, with short blonde hair. She was wearing blue jeans and a sweat-shirt with a picture of a cat and the caption I AM SMILING. She held something down at her side—a weapon, Mantrap was sure, though she kept her eyes on the woman's face.

"You. Who are you? What do you think you're doing? Get out of my yard," the woman said. She sounded angry, and fear rose from her skin like an acrid perfume.

Target. A Target. Prey. . . . The woman took a step forward, holding the weapon down at her side.

"Back away," Mantrap said. She dropped the bundle holding her long blades to the ground. It clanked faintly. "Just leave." Her voice was ragged with the effort of control.

But the woman took another step forward, frightened to the point of attack by what she saw. "Get out of here," she said, bringing up the shotgun. "Or I swear I'll call the po—"

Mantrap sprang, drawing one of her thigh knives as she did. She knocked the shotgun away before it fired, and buried her blade to its guard in the woman's chest. The woman went down, twitching and clawing weakly at the wound for perhaps five seconds.

There was no blood.

Had anyone seen? Mantrap looked around quickly, but she seemed to be out of the direct sightline of the other houses in the tract. Better to risk it, then, but she couldn't stay long.

She grabbed the shotgun and the woman's body and dragged them both inside. She made a second trip for her bundle before closing the sliding doors carefully behind her and pulling the curtains. No one must see her—or survive to say they had.

Those were the rules.

What now?

Mantrap stood in the middle of the kitchen, staring down at the woman's body pensively. If she took her knife back, the body would bleed, but on the other hand, Mantrap wanted her knife back.

Better find a bathtub, then. She'd need to clean the blade before she put it away. She picked up the body again.

As she walked through the house, her enhanced senses brought her information about its inhabitants. *Dog—no, two; man (not here), woman (the target). . . .*

A dog rounded the corner, barking furiously at the smell of blood and predator musk. One of the small toy breeds; not a threat, but eventually someone would hear it barking.

Mantrap dropped the body on the hall carpet and turned. The dog backed away, still yapping.

The second dog had been in the basement, and it had been bigger. Mantrap stood at the kitchen sink, cleaning her knives and looking out over the backyard. The day was grey and overcast, but bright. She'd rather move at dusk, but time was running out, and she could count on only an hour here at best.

Now, what could she find here that she could use? Money, clothes, transport, ID. . . .

CHAPTER 12

t was three o'clock in the morning when Charles Xavier and the seven X-Men gathered in the briefing room.

No one asked where Rogue was.

"I think we can safely say that the situation has exceeded critical mass some time ago," the Beast said. Despite his teddy-bear demeanor, the blue-furred mutant looked exceedingly formidable at the moment. "Apparently its backers are determined to see the Emergency Intervention Bill passed at any cost, whereon it becomes the teeth of the amazingly forthrightly named Project Level Playing Field, intended to wipe out mutants in America . . . tidily."

"Never min' dat now," Gambit said. "Rogue has gone away wid dese men, but she does no' know who she goes to."

Remy LeBeau looked as if he had been physically beaten. His face was haggard, its lines drawn into a harsh mask of pain. He huddled inside his leather duster as if he was cold, an untouched cup of coffee on the table before him. A cigarette burned between his fingers, its blue smoke rising to join the smoke of many others that puddled against the ceiling in a misty cloud.

"We'll all need to pool our information, Gambit—" Cyclops began.

"You don' un'erstan', you." Gambit's Cajun accent grew thicker with his distress. "I know de *homme maudit* who 'as her." He drew a deep breath, as if steeling himself to say the words.

"It is Sinister, *mes amis*. Sinister is Arnol' Bocklin, an' he has Rogue."

There was a moment's electrified silence. They all had begun to suspect that Dr. Arnold Bocklin of CGI Atlanta was only a mask for some darker truth, but . . . Sinister?

Sinister had been born Nathaniel Essex, a mortal man in Victorian England. A scientist, ahead of his age, determined to unravel the mystical process of evolution, natural selection, and mutation. His humanity destroyed by the death of his wife and child, Sinister had given himself up to the machinations of the malevolent Apocalypse, a creature of fantastic age and evil, who had awakened in Sinister's time to once more pursue his agenda of world domination. But Sinister was an unwilling and rebellious servant, who fought against Apocalypse's control over him and, in fact, had been instrumental in foiling Apocalypse's attempt to take control of Earth there and then.

The X-Men knew this because two of them had been there, swept back through time by the power of Askani sorcery in a doomed attempt to end Sinister's evil before it had begun. Cyclops and Phoenix had failed in their attempt to change the past, and Sinister had proceeded along his foreordained course to become a foe the X-Men could fight but never defeat . . . because, as the decades had passed, the drive and ruthless brilliance of Essex's mind had been refined, distilling into a perverse cruelty that acknowledged no master but its own limitless desire to *know*. People— living or dead, mutant or mortal—meant nothing to the man who now gloried in the name Sinister; he used them or destroyed them almost without thought. All Sinister cared about was his research, the solving of that fateful riddle which had started him down this twisted and hideous path over a century before.

The riddle of human evolution.

Of mutation.

''Yeah,'' Wolverine said slowly. ''That sounds about right. I ran into one o' Bocklin's little extracurricular activities up North. A little black-budget op, t'give somebody a

mutant strikeforce of their very own—the same super-
soldier crap they been futzin' around with for the last fifty
years. The op I busted up was called Trapdoor—cute, ain't
it? Only now they've got a new spin on it, and it stinks.
They start by kidnappin' mutants—it don't matter what
they used to be good for, 'cause the first thing Trapdoor
does is hit them up with this voodoo cocktail of Bocklin's,
turnin' 'em human, an' then into whatever kind a' mutate
they think they'd like this week. It wasn't workin' out too
well, last I saw, but I got a positive ID on Bocklin from
their guinea pig, an' he's in it up to his navel. An' who
else do we know that specializes in turnin' humans into
mutates, an mutants into. . . ." Wolverine shrugged. "From
the MO, I'd hafta say it's our boy Sinister, like the Cajun
says."

"An' I 'ave seen 'im," Gambit said. "When he spoke
to us at de warehouse, preten'ing to be Bocklin, it was him.
I swear it."

All of the X-Men knew that Gambit had faced Sinister
several times, with and without the other X-Men. If Gambit
said Bocklin was Sinister, the X-Men could not afford to
disbelieve him.

"Gambit, how did they capture Rogue?" Phoenix said
gently. It had been a long and tiring day—and a strenuous
battle with Black Team 51 on top of it—but it didn't look
as if the X-Men were going to get a break any time soon.
Not if Sinister had Rogue—and was planning to use the
retro-mutagen on her.

"Dey did not capture her, *chere*." Gambit paused to
light another cigarette and suck half of it to ash on the first
draw. "De Team *Noire* set up dis holocam, dem, an' den
it was Bocklin who convince her to come to him. To let
him make her human, in exchange for a free pardon. An'
I cannot tell you wedder she meant to let dem change her,
or if she jus' want to fin' out where de *salaud's* lair is, so

we can follow her. An' I do not t'ink Rogue knows dat trut' any more den I do.''

Gambit was more rattled than any of them had seen him since he joined the team. But whether Rogue's peril or Sinister's involvement concerned Gambit more, no one could say.

''That's the same deal Chessman offered us in Washington,'' Psylocke said. ''Which would throw some doubt on CGI's claims to be operating independently from the federal government.''

''And it hardly matters, does it?'' the Beast said. ''It's a brilliant plan; get mutation classified as a medical condition, and the U.S. government will hand Sinister all the experimental subjects for his twisted eugenic theories that he could possibly want.''

''Hardly the point at the moment,'' Jean said. ''The question is, *why* did Rogue go—and why did you let her, Gambit?'' Phoenix's voice turned hard; fond as she was of Wolverine, it had been clear from the moment Gambit joined the team that one scoundrel was more than enough for her. Deep in her heart, she did not trust Gambit to put the X-Men's interests before his own.

The question seemed to take the thief by surprise. He pushed himself away from the table, and in that same moment, a playing card was in his hand.

He stared down at it as if he could not imagine how it had gotten there. ''Let her?'' he finally said, his voice rough. ''I try—I *tried*—to stop her.''

''But she went willingly?'' Cyclops asked. Gambit nodded. ''But that makes no sense,'' Cyclops continued, thinking aloud. ''Rogue can't possibly believe she can defeat Sinister one-on-one.''

''I did not tell her it was him.'' Gambit's voice was so low the other X-Men could barely hear him. ''I did not tell her it was Sinister.''

Silence in the briefing room.

"I did not dare!" Gambit protested, although none of the others had argued with him. "If the ot'ers heard—if *he* knew I knew . . ." Gambit's voice trailed off. "I tried to stop her, *mes amis*."

"Yeah, Cajun. I bet you—" Wolverine began.

"We can discuss Gambit's choices later," Cyclops said decisively, cutting off whatever Wolverine had been about to say. "We need to get Rogue out. If we are up against Sinister, we'll have to move fast, but carefully. The first thing to do is to find where Rogue is. Hank?"

"Earlier this evening—excuse me, last night," the Beast said, smothering a yawn, "When Gambit told me what had happened, I set Cerebro to scan the area around Atlanta, Georgia, where we already know CGI is located."

"And?" Psylocke demanded impatiently.

The Beast shrugged. "Nothing there—no energy signature that Cerebro is programmed to recognize, at least. Only the usual statistically average concentration of mutants in Atlanta Metro. Rogue might be there, and behind shielding that Cerebro's sensors can't reach through, but on the off chance she went somewhere else, I've set Cerebro for a whole-world scan. An alarm will sound when it finds Rogue . . . but that's going to take hours."

"Hours Rogue does not have," Storm said. "We must find her immediately." None of them was yet willing to consider the alternative explanation of Cerebro's failure . . . that Rogue was already changed beyond Cerebro's capacity to find her.

Changed . . . or dead.

"We also need to know what we're going up against," Cyclops said. "Gambit, you said that there was a Black Team waiting for you at the warehouse?"

Gambit brooded. "Dey mus' have been, *hahn*? Because we did not see de *sce'le'rats* going in, an' dey showed up mighty quick. Dis Keit'ley, he *knew* we would be dere."

"And Chessman knew exactly who was going to be at

the senator's offices in Washington—and when,'' Phoenix added. "He came prepared for me and for Psylocke, no one else.''

"They wasn't expectin' me up North,'' Wolverine said with grim satisfaction, "but then, I didn't see nothin' that looked like Black Team, neither. An' Bocklin—or Sinister, or whoever the hell he really is—was a consultant on Trapdoor. He ain't runnin' it.''

"But wherever the Black Team is involved, they're always a step ahead of the X-Men,'' Storm said.

"How?'' Phoenix demanded in frustration. "How do they know what we're going to do—before we do it? It's as if they're predicting it, or eavesdropping, or—''

Suddenly Hank McCoy bounded onto the table's surface. The blue-furred biochemist's gleaming fangs showed as he grinned with excitement at his sudden breakthrough.

"No,'' he said. "Not the X-Men, but an incredible simulation! Don't you see? Somehow the Black Team has access to equipment that allows them to use computer modeling against us—they've got their own private oracle.''

"And are using it just as the Defense Department uses computers to model nuclear war scenarios,'' Charles Xavier said. "Program in everything you know about your enemy, and the computer tells you what he will do next. It's something of a leap of logic, Henry, but I believe you to be correct. It is the only thing that makes sense.''

"So all we have to do to outguess Black Team 51,'' Cyclops said, "is think of everything we might possibly do—and then do something else.''

"That won't work, Scott,'' Ororo said quietly. "Because wherever and whoever they are, the Black Team will be expecting us to come to Rogue's rescue, and we cannot fail her.''

"They're the trap—an' she's the bait. Well, the X-

Men've got a habit a' bein' real hard on traps," Wolverine said.

"We've got to find her before we can rescue her," Psylocke pointed out. "And it doesn't look as if we can manage that any time soon."

Suddenly, the Beast looked like the proverbial lightbulb went off over his head. "Yes, we can!"

"What is it, Hank?" Cyclops asked.

"I've been a complete idiot. Back in the mists of prehistory when I was an Avenger and Rogue was with the Brotherhood of Evil Mutants, I was able to track Rogue down with a special scanner that could read her hybrid human/Kree genes."

Gambit frowned. "*Hahn*? Rogue is human, *mon ami*."

"Yes, but she permanently absorbed the powers and memories of Ms. Marvel, who *does* have that distinctive genetic signature, which Rogue got as part of the bargain." He turned to Xavier. "It shouldn't take an hour for me to set up a scanner. I'll keep the Cerebro scan going as well."

Xavier nodded. As the Beast bounded off toward the lab, Cyclops called out, "Good work, Hank."

Much earlier the previous day, Rogue was thinking that this wasn't one of her brighter ideas, and it seemed to be getting worse all the time.

It was cool inside the helicopter's cargo bay, and Rogue was glad she wore a jacket. No one spoke, to her or to each other. There was nothing to distract her from worry about what she'd done tonight, and what was still to come.

She was sitting between two members of Black Team 51, in the back of the jet helicopter that had been parked outside of Gotham Pharmaceuticals. It was formidably well-equipped, a masterpiece of modern aerial armor.

She could probably do a good job of ripping it apart with her bare hands. She could escape easily—they wouldn't dare shoot at her; they'd know that bullets and blasters wouldn't hurt her, and in fact would do most of the work of smashing the helicopter for her.

But if the helicopter were destroyed, the eight men inside would fall to their deaths. There was no way Rogue could catch them all, and none of them was wearing a parachute. They'd all die, and Rogue didn't want that on her conscience. Her fate had been sealed the moment the copter had taken to the air. In effect, she was powerless to act until the copter landed—the members of the Black Team were hostages for her good behavior, although she doubted the notion would ever occur to them. She was going to stay right here in this seat and behave—at least if she wanted to remain on the side of the angels.

And she did. Rogue had done many things in her life that she was ashamed of—the X-Men didn't know all the details of her past, not by a *long* country mile—but since she had left Mystique and the Brotherhood of Evil Mutants behind and gone to Xavier in a desperate gamble to help Rogue take control of the mutant power that had shattered her life, she'd at least *tried* to be good.

Only she never seemed to quite live up to her own expectations. She wished Gambit were here with her—even if he'd probably never speak to her again after the way she'd turned on him back at the warehouse. But nothing fazed the Cajun X-Man, and if he were by her side she'd feel better about this whole shebang.

She wished she'd been able to confide in Remy beforehand, instead of just springing this on him. She hoped he'd gotten away all right—she'd tried not to hit him very hard, but Remy LeBeau could get under her skin like nobody's business. And he'd made her mad, taking on at her that way. She'd gone along with the offer Bocklin had made in order to be brought to his secret base for treatment. Keithley's presence at the warehouse had clinched her impression of Bocklin's character: whether Bocklin really was Bocklin, or whether Bocklin was a cover identity—if he was hiring muscle like Black Team 51, he almost definitely was *not* an innocent scientist.

So Rogue told herself now. But at the time there'd been at least a part of her that hadn't been playacting at all. A part of her that honestly had meant to accept Bocklin's offer.

To be human. To *touch*. . . .

But it had been only a passing dream. She couldn't let Bocklin use his retro-mutagen on her. She didn't trust him.

But if she could. . . .

When the copter landed its side door opened automatically, and chill thin air swept in. Rogue zipped her jacket shut. They were in the mountains, then. But which ones?

Rogue looked around. It was night; she couldn't see much of her surroundings—just a lot of poured concrete with floodlights. The helicopter landing pad was marked out in bright red, yellow, and black paint on an otherwise featureless expanse of gray concrete the size of a football field.

A *large* football field, surrounded by a high fence topped with razor wire.

At the far end of the open area was a bunker, its façade as harsh and featureless as if it were a structure created by soulless alien machines. There were floodlights mounted on it and around the fence, all trained on the landing pad. Their pitiless illumination bleached everything to the stark uncompromising monochrome of the surface of the moon.

The contrast between this place and The Xavier Institute could not have been greater. *I feel like I'm in the place in those books Scotty tried to get me to read—Mordor, that was it*, Rogue thought.

"In the land of Mordor where the shadows lie. . . ."

Coming here had been a mistake.

"This way, Rogue." Keithley gestured toward the door.

She could fly. She could run. Find a nearby landmark— find a *phone*. . . .

"Gen'lemen, I hate t'disappoint you, but . . ."

She took a step away from Keithley, backing toward the fence. No one tried to stop her.

"This is a bad idea, Rogue," Keithley said. "You trying to break your promise to us this way, I mean."

There was a pulse; the sound of an energy weapon firing. Something hit her from behind and Rogue went down.

Blackness. For a long time.

Then voices.

"—Moebius Lance's good for something."

"Starkweather, you have the brains of a newt," Keithley said. "You should have used a stasis grenade. One, the Moebius Lance was designed only to work on parapsionics—we don't even know if Rogue *is* a parapsi. Two, the damned thing doesn't work right, and never has. And three, she's heavy."

Rogue opened her eyes. Her head hurt, and the ceiling was moving by at a good clip.

She was being carried by four of the Black Team down a corridor on a stretcher, and wherever they were going was no place she wanted to go.

"Heavy?" she said, sitting up and swinging off the stretcher. "Well-l-l, I'll just relieve y'all of the burden, then."

Rogue bounded to her feet, shoved the nearest man away from her, and ran. Behind her, Keithley pulled out a cellular phone and spoke into it quickly; suddenly there were red-flashing warning lights overhead and a faint rhythmic honking in the distance. Alarms. Rogue could feel a low vibration through her boot soles. Somewhere, heavy machinery was moving—probably the outside doors sealing.

She launched herself into the air, but a wave of vertigo overtook her and she crashed into a wall, then fell to the floor, unable to stay aloft or on course. Hastily she scrambled to her feet and ran on—it must be the effects of that

Moebius thing they'd been talking about; the one that had KO'd her earlier.

She'd have to get out of here on foot, then.

One of the stretcher bearers had almost reached her; sensing his presence, Rogue backhanded him. The blow connected satisfactorily and she heard him fall; only her flying ability was affected, then. She could use a good tussle to settle her nerves, but even more than that she wanted to get *out* of here—and once the security doors had closed, that was going to be a lot harder.

No one fired at her. Odd, but not odd enough to brood about. The hallway came to an end and Rogue glanced both ways quickly. A huge metal door started to slide into place on her left, sealing the corridor off. Rogue ran for it flat out. If they were sealing off this corridor, it probably led someplace she wanted to go.

Gripping the edge of the sliding door in her hands, she dragged at the massive piece of metal, trying to force it backward in its tracks. Her boots skidded along the floor as the door dragged her with it—she could be as strong as she wanted, but without traction she couldn't get the leverage to stop the door.

The door dragged her inexorably toward the wall. Closer . . . closer. . . . Until, raising her left foot, Rogue could brace the sole of her boot against the wall.

Now she had leverage. Her muscles swelled as she strained, all of her effort concentrated on saying no when all the mass of metal was saying yes.

The door stopped moving forward. There was a grinding sound as the machinery forced it one way and Rogue forced it the other. Slowly the gap between wall and door began to widen again, until it was almost large enough for her to slip through. Rogue glanced back the way she had come. Over the groaning and complaints of tortured metal, she could hear the sound of running footsteps. She wormed her body through the gap. Almost there. She slapped the door shut behind her. It was broken; she had to drag it, but it moved easily under the impetus of Rogue's strength.

Safe.

But safe *where*? Rogue looked around.

She was in a corridor just like the last one. Concrete walls, concrete floors, recessed metal doors—the place was done in Early Modern Bunker, and there were no more clues to which way the exit lay than there had been before. She couldn't hear the klaxon any longer—when had it stopped?

A faint banging sounded from the other side of the door. The boys were probably just now finding out that their overrides weren't going to work. Too bad.

Rogue smiled, but the smile vanished almost as soon as it had appeared. Going this way had seemed like a good idea because the door had been closing, indicating that there was probably something on this side the Black Team didn't want her to reach, but as Rogue walked slowly down the corridor, she began to realize that this direction was a dead end.

Literally.

Rogue rested her forehead against the concrete wall. Well, she'd just have to go back the other way. She looked back at the door. Only one way to do that.

Rogue turned, and leapt into the air. Flying full-speed, she charged the blast door, fists outstretched, and hit it head-on.

And bounced.

Must not be as up to snuff as I thought, she decided. Rogue got to her feet for another attempt.

"Please cease your futile posturing, child. It is both unappealing and useless," Arnold Bocklin said.

His voice came from behind her. Rogue whirled, pressing herself back against the blast door. One of the hallway doors was open, and Bocklin stood in the doorway.

No, not Bocklin.

The man in the doorway bore a strong resemblance to the man she'd seen on television four days ago and on the hololink this evening . . . but the resemblance ended abruptly.

This man's skin was dead white, the diamond-shaped scarlet mark in the center of his forehead echoing the crimson fire in his eyes. His short black hair dipped to a profound widow's peak that nearly touched the diamond, and more closely resembled a cap of burnished ebony metal than human hair. His head was framed against the high scarlet collar of a cape that arched high over his back to swirl around him in a multitude of pointed black ribbons that echoed the trailing tentacles of a poisonous sea creature. The cape's style also repeated the design of the plates of blue armor that covered his body, their darkness unrelieved save for the repeating red diamonds down his torso that seemed to mock the patterning upon some venomous predator of the natural world.

As it was meant to—for Sinister understood the process of evolution and the natural world as few scientists ever had.

"Sinister!" Rogue exclaimed.

He smiled. "Indeed, Rogue. Welcome to the place that the X-Men have been so desperately trying to locate—Dr. Arnold Bocklin's research laboratory. But, as you may by now actually have guessed, there *is* no Bocklin, and never was. It was merely a . . . pose of mine."

"But you—CGI—the legislation—" Rogue sputtered.

She knew she was babbling, one tiny despairing part of her mind still frantic to gather any intelligence about the foe that she could in order to benefit the rest of the team. And as long as she could keep Sinister talking, she gained time to think of a way out of this trap.

"I, CGI, the Emergency Intervention Bill," Sinister agreed with diabolic geniality. "It is a matter I have been considering for some years—how to deal with this burgeoning population of freakish upstart paranormals that has been interfering so constantly with my work. But come this way, Rogue. Resistance is futile, and there's nowhere for you to run.''

Rogue looked around, but the corridor was still a dead end. A killing box. She dared not turn her back on Sinister for as long as it would take to get past the door.

Rogue took a reluctant step toward him.

''It was primarily a problem of the proper application of force,'' Sinister explained as he led her into a new room.

Rogue had hoped there'd at least be something to smash, but the room was white and featureless. It contained nothing save Sinister himself, though the walls were engraved with deep cuts that suggested hidden doors.

''I wanted these random mutations and crusading paranormals brought under control, but I did not wish to take the time to arrange it myself, nor did I wish several important long-running experiments disturbed in the process. Your eradication must be measured, orderly, restrained. So several years ago I activated the Bocklin persona as the first step of a plan to turn over the tiniest fraction of my research to the government of the United States, so that it could handle the administrative details of what would prove to be a large, if not terribly complex, problem. Once the Emergency Intervention Bill becomes law, the U.S. government will sweep first America, then the world, clear of these evolutionary false starts, and, when the time comes, I shall supplant my unwitting human servants with their successors—the true superman. Culled from those specimens I save from the obliteration of their fellows, carefully bred to embody the true successor race.''

He's nuts. Rogue could not remember the last time she'd been so terrified. There was a kind of elemental inhumanity that radiated from Sinister like a profane charisma, filling her mind with images of darkness, failure, and despair.

Any sensible person—Rogue thought—would be screaming and running for the door about now, but when had Rogue ever been sensible? She'd joined the X-Men, hadn't she?

"The X-Men've heard that one before, Sinister. And we're still here," Rogue shot back bravely.

"Ah, but the rest of your annoying companions are not here now, infant, so you may cease threatening me with them. Are you prepared to fulfil the promise you made to me earlier this evening?"

For a moment of pure shock Rogue could not imagine what he was referring to. Then she remembered.

Amnesty . . . a full pardon . . . accept the treatment.

"You must be outta y'cotton-pickin' mind!" Rogue yelped.

Collecting herself, the Southern X-Man threw herself at Sinister, intending to do as much damage as she could—

—and fell through him, colliding bruisingly with the unyielding white floor.

He was a hologram.

She scrambled to her feet. Sinister was still there, several feet away from where he'd been when she rushed him. Rogue shook her head, trying to focus. She still felt the effects of the Moebius Lance that the Black Team had used to take her down before, but that didn't mean she didn't have more than enough on the ball to turn Sinister into road pizza.

Providing he didn't cheat.

"Oh, come now, Rogue. No one's ever admired you for your intellect. Why should I expose myself to a dull contest of brute force when I can assign that task—like so many others—to one of my subordinates?"

Rogue stared at him mutinously.

"While I'm entirely aware that you'll have little interest in my research, it might interest you to know that in addition to the retro-mutagen I've achieved remarkable success in short-term, auto-reversed mutation," Sinister continued smoothly. "My test subjects have been delighted to give their all, you might say, to provide the raw material for this process, and a simple transfusion of augmented blood to any properly prepared recipient does the rest."

A door began to open in the far wall, revealing a figure standing behind it. Rogue focused her attention upon this person, while simultaneously trying to watch the entire room for an additional threat.

"This donor's code name was Psychostorm," Sinister— or his hologram—said. "He can't be here with you tonight, but his genetic inheritance lives on—in the person of Mr. Lieber. You should find the acquaintance . . . interesting." Sinister smiled, a chilling expanse of shark-white teeth. "In fact, I venture to say you'll be mad for him."

Rogue took a step backward, but there was nowhere to retreat to, and no backup to help her.

Well, fine, she thought. *Just me on my own again. Done it before, and I'll probably do it again.* Rogue bared her teeth in a defiant grin. She was going to do what she'd been trained to do, by Mystique and by Xavier—kick some serious butt.

Lieber stepped through the door. This, at least was no hologrammatic ghost; she'd heard the sound his boots made as they struck the floor. He wore an orange coverall and boots. Lieber glanced toward Sinister as if seeking information or assurance of some kind, and then turned toward Rogue.

She sprang at him.

And the world exploded.

The mutant who had called himself Psychostorm had risen to his position on the FBI's Ten Most Wanted List through the exercise of a mutant gift that was essentially a variation of telepathy, still one of the most common mutations. Psychostorm's variation, however, was a force of a different color.

Psychostorm could interrupt, intensify, or simply change
the electrical field in his victim's brain, pulling up buried
memories, evoking long-past sensations, or simply creating
the intense if unpleasant sensation that one's brain was lying in a hot skillet beside two strips of bacon with orange
juice and toast on the side.

Rogue didn't stand a chance.

She tried. If she could have hit Lieber, she might have
hurt him, but she couldn't see him. Using his stolen mutant
powers, Lieber simply pushed the neural conductivity of
her synapses to maximum and left Rogue to drown in her
own mind. It was over in less than a minute.

When Rogue lay still at last, Sinister—the real one, this
time—bent over her prone body and lifted one arm.

"Thank you, Mr. Lieber, that was most refreshing."

Sinister carefully worked the short yellow glove free and
handed it to his lackey.

"See that Mr. Chessman receives this, if you would.
Rogue won't be needing it anymore."

CHAPTER 13

They'd cuffed Slapshot's hands behind his back once they'd gotten him into the transport next to Rewind, and one of the guys in the goon suits had held a gun to his head while another one jammed a needle into his arm. He'd expected whatever they'd used to knock him out, but it hadn't. It had just made him drowsy and distant—if he concentrated hard enough, he could keep his eyes open and see what was going on, but he couldn't seem to *care*. That was worse, somehow—like having a nightmare you couldn't wake up from.

He opened his eyes, realizing he'd nodded off. What had wakened him? Oh, yes. They'd stopped.

Slapshot leaned forward, but his muscles were sloppy and loose. He might have fallen to the floor, except for the fact that his cuffs were shackled to a ring in the wall. Everything was organized. Just as if they did this all the time.

What if they did?

He looked over at Rewind. She wasn't wearing her biker jacket anymore, only the candy-pink sweater and matching skirt, black fishnet stockings, and silver Doc Martens that she'd worn to their meeting Monday night in Cleveland.

How long ago? Slapshot wasn't sure anymore. He just knew that he wanted to go home, to be home again; he'd pay any price to make all of this never have happened, he'd even give up having known Adam and Lloyd and Peyton and Vette. Just make it all go away. . . .

But the drug took control of his thoughts, bending time until he forgot what he'd been thinking.

Later—how much later?—the back hatch of the transport opened again, jerking Slapshot back to consciousness. The man in the suit, dark glasses, and earring—Keithley—appeared, herding Pipedream ahead of him.

Pipedream looked toward Slapshot beseechingly, a mixture of apology and appeal in his eyes. Slapshot didn't understand. What could *he* do now? What could any of them do?

Someone shoved him back in his seat, pinching his wrists against the cuffs. The pain spun out of his grasp as soon as he noted it, wrapped in the terrifyingly plastic nature of time.

No . . . Rewind was time. He was Slapshot . . . he was motion. And Pipedream was thought, and Charade was impulse, and Lloyd. . . .

Charade had been right. They had to get Lloyd a real code name.

Slapshot drifted away again.

He roused again, and this time found himself someplace he recognized. Another boring trip in another boring helicopter—at least, Slapshot would have preferred being bored to being terrified, but actually he didn't have a lot of chance to be either one. The drugs coursed through his system; he looked around, mildly pleased to be able to see all his friends. He counted them several times to make sure, before realizing that he shouldn't be pleased, because that meant that they'd all been captured.

His mind slowly began to clear, leaving him with the weird false clarity he recognized from those times his mind had woken up before his body. He couldn't move, and his emotions were curiously flat and unimportant, but he could think.

The five of them had made a mistake last night. They'd run for cover, as if the people who'd captured them in the first place wouldn't chase them. If they'd gone directly to CNN they might have had a chance.

*You've learned. You're still alive. Just don't make the
same mistake twice.*

It was as if something outside himself were speaking to
him, something older and more experienced. But there was
nobody there but him. *Okay,* Slapshot thought, oddly com-
forted by the hallucination, *no mistakes twice.*

What now? They weren't going back to CGI in Atlanta,
because they wouldn't be on a plane if they were. They
were being taken somewhere else then.

Home? For a moment the fantasy flooded through him.
It was all a mistake. They weren't the kids CGI wanted at
all; they were taking them home to apologize.

But Slapshot couldn't make himself believe it. If that was
what they'd meant to do, they wouldn't have done it with
guns and drugs. Not home, then.

Somewhere. Where?

Why?

The X-Men's specially-modified SR-71 *Blackbird* hurtled
west at 30,000 feet carrying seven X-Men into battle, following the direction indicated by the Beast's genetic scanner. Even Storm at her fastest was not as fast as the
Blackbird at top speed, and so she sat with the others inside
the *Blackbird*'s cabin.

The atmosphere was tense. All of them had faced Sinister
before; all of them knew that Sinister was perhaps the most
dangerous foe the X-Men had faced in the entire existence
of the team. And Rogue was in his power.

Every few minutes Phoenix reached out, trying to contact
Rogue, but wherever she was, Rogue was still out of her
telepathic range.

Phoenix prayed that that was the reason she could not
find her. That Rogue was out of range—not that she was
dead. Besides, if she was dead, she probably wouldn't still
be registering on Hank's scanner.

Phoenix glanced over to where Gambit was sitting, staring morosely out the window, an unlit cigarette in his hands. He looked miserable, but Phoenix couldn't find it within herself to be pleased that the scape grace Cajun was learning a sense of responsibility for his actions. None of this was his fault. There was no way he could have stopped Rogue from going with the Black Team, except by telling her his suspicions.

But if he'd really believed Bocklin was Sinister, why hadn't he done that?

Never mind. He was suffering now.

Phoenix unbuckled her seat belt and stood. Crouching beside Gambit, she put a comforting hand on his shoulder.

"It wasn't your fault, Remy. You did the best you could."

"But not good enough, eh, *ma belle Jeanne?* Rogue is in dat Sinister's clutches, an' Gambit mus' live wid dat, *hahn?*"

"We'll get her back," Phoenix vowed. But the words sounded hollow, even to her. Who—*what*—would they get back? Rogue? Or Rogue after she'd been subjected to Sinister's vile "treatment"?

She wanted to offer Gambit words of comfort, to make sure he could go into battle with his mind clear and his spirit at rest, but Phoenix realized Gambit would not accept them from her. Why should he? She had always judged Gambit—not unfairly, but mercilessly. And now, when Gambit judged himself, how could she tell him to stop?

Phoenix shook her head sadly, rising to her feet and returning to her seat.

She did not sleep.

As the hours wore on, Mantrap began to miss the drugs. The twilight imprecision of mind that they'd brought— the slowing of a metabolism that was a raging biological furnace.

Time had passed. She was airborne again, this time in a corporate jet.

From Chicago she'd picked up transport at a small private airfield. There hadn't been a lot of people there, so she hadn't had to kill many: the imperatives bred in the matrix that had remade her in its own image were unyielding. Everything that moved was prey.

And prey was for killing.

It had been a short hop from Chicago to Atlanta. She'd made a sloppy landing on the grounds of CGI itself and spent about two hours there. When she left, she knew more about Bocklin, including where he was now.

Wearing a disguise, armed with stolen identification, Mantrap had driven to the private airfield where CGI's jets were parked. Sealed inside one of the planes, her environment self-contained and self-referential, her body aching pleasantly from recent exercise, she'd been able to hold back the imperatives long enough to take off. Voices on the radio were different. Voices weren't targets, weren't prey. She'd answered back as though she were one of them. She'd been able to leave everyone at Butler Airfield alive.

Someone would be after her now. She'd been in too much of a hurry at CGI Atlanta to leave a clean back trail. She'd left too many people alive and too many scattered corpses—no one who knew what she was looking for, it was true, but the hunters who followed her would piece the picture together quickly enough. Then the governmental spider whose tangled web led ultimately to Trapdoor and her creation would know his playing piece had not died when the base's self-destruct mechanism had been activated.

They'd be after her.

But not yet. Even if they already knew, they were hours behind her. And she had miles to go before she slept.

• • •

Lloyd decided he liked being unconscious better as the plane landed. The guys in black had given him a heavier dose of drugs than they had the others, and even given him a booster shot a few hours later. But Lloyd Englehart's metabolism wasn't very close to human anymore—not that he was planning to announce that, or anything—and he felt completely lucid as the plane rolled to a stop.

Where had they been taken? Two or three hours west of Atlanta at least, Lloyd was sure of that much, somewhere in the Rockies. When the hatch opened, letting in sunlight and air from outside, he was sure of it: he could smell pines, and snow, and a multitude of things he had no human words for, though they made a detailed map in his head. It was late afternoon, and the fresh air had a wintery chill.

His hands, like those of the others, were cuffed behind his back, though of the five of them, Lloyd was the only one whose mutation had resulted in a physical transformation. If they hadn't been drugged, the other four could have fought back even all tied up.

But they were groggy, disoriented. Pipedream was blindfolded—as if that really mattered—and Charade was gagged. Their captors got them to their feet and moved them carefully toward the hatchway and down the stairs.

When it was Lloyd's turn, he tried to act as if he were still drugged, too. He didn't know how well he was doing with his act; he was too scared. Maybe if he'd worked harder, applied himself to this superdude stuff—gotten himself a fancy name the way the others had. Something to hide behind when he got scared, to pretend it wasn't him, wasn't Lloyd Englehart—a shy Southern boy whom genetic roulette had turned into a mutant dog—out there in a fracas with people yelling and getting hurt, but some gung-ho mutant in a fancy suit.

Something like Red Rover, his mind offered, desperate to think of anything but this. Red for his Cracker heritage,

Rover for his powers. *Red Rover, Red Rover, let Lloyd cross over....*

Fine. He'd be Red Rover. And Red Rover wasn't afraid of a bunch of guys with guns. Red Rover was the power-house of the Ohio Mutant Conspiracy, and the Conspiracy had weathered a dozen—no, a hundred—hair-raising adventures together, which they always won. Because that was what the good guys did. Win.

But to win you had to escape. Shake the bad guys up, make them wonder.

That was what Red Rover had to do now. He looked out the hatch and down the steps. The private jet had landed on a large open slab of concrete, several acres square. The open space was surrounded by a fence—impossible to tell its height this far away—and there was a big concrete bunker at the far end of the slab. If the five of them ended up in there, somehow he had a feeling they weren't going to come out.

Red Rover tripped on the last step of the rolling stairs, half by accident, half by design. He stumbled forward, opening up a space between himself and his minder. Then he yanked his wrists apart.

The shackles were police-style cuffs; good quality. The chain between the cuffs were soldered and the cuffs themselves were ratcheted and locked. Red Rover winced as the sharp metal cut into his wrists, breaking the skin.

But the chain broke.

His sense of balance returned as his hands came free. There was no time to wait and see if any of the others were able to back his play. He had to run. Now.

Red Rover ducked under the belly of the plane before all their minders really knew something had gone wrong. The fence was about six hundred yards away, and Red Rover was sure he could get over it, no matter how high it was. He didn't bother to wonder if he *could* get away. There was no time for second thoughts, only to *do*.

A greyhound can outrace a cheetah in the short run. A mastiff can stop a charging bull. Red Rover ran, pushing himself onward with his mind while his heart screamed that he was deserting his friends, his pack. . . .

He hit the fence and dug in with hands and feet. It towered above him—fifteen, twenty feet, and once he was on it he'd be an easy target for the men with guns. Red Rover didn't hesitate. It was the only way out. He climbed as fast as he could.

A hand grabbed his ankle.

The grip was crushingly strong; frightening in its very intent to damage. Red Rover glanced down—and recoiled.

The man holding his ankle was burly, massive—and farther from human than Red Rover could ever hope to be. His skin was a dead chalk white, as if it had been painted with white lead, and his eyes were a bloody glowing red. A cape made of ribbons licked around his armored body like black flames. A scent rose from his body that burned into Red Rover's brain like an alien thing—composed of pain and fear turned inside out, of inhumanity and a limitless capacity for harm.

"Come down, child," the man said. His voice was a match for his scent. "Resistance is futile, and it will be over soon."

Before Red Rover could make up his mind what to do, the hand on his ankle tightened. He felt something give way, some small bone buckling under the strain, and then he was airborne, his mind scrabbling for equilibrium seconds behind the facts.

He struck the side of the plane and fell. There was a moment's bright agony as he landed on his crushed ankle, and then there was nothing at all.

CHAPTER 14

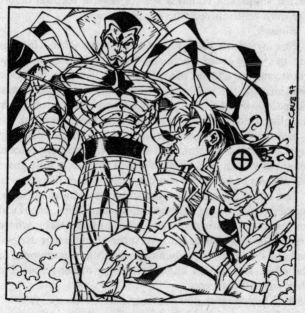

Rogue was a professional. She fought her way back to consciousness against her better judgment, her body testing the limits of the trap even before her eyes were open.

Things were bad. She struggled against the steel mesh of the straps that confined her for several seconds before she even remembered who the enemy was.

Sinister.

She lay on her back, lashed to a narrow table. This was not the white room where she'd fought Sinister and Psychostorm, but another place. It looked like the office of a mad dentist: the ceiling was inset with bright lights that glared down at her, and there was some sort of robot arm dangling from it almost in her face, purpose unknown.

But there were a handful of large bright needles dangling from the end of the arm, each attached to a brightly-colored length of tubing. And Rogue's gloves and jacket were gone, the sleeves of her battle-suit cut away to bare her arms.

She could not move. All her struggles did was cause the metal straps crossing her body at chest and hips, knees and ankles to creak slightly. There was no one nearby whose power she could steal, her own super-strength was useless, and she could not even fly away while she was strapped to the table. The X-Men might be coming to her rescue, but they weren't here now.

And Sinister was going to strip her powers away.

A fine dew of moisture appeared on Rogue's forehead. She did not fear the one-in-two chance of death. Rogue had made her peace with death a long time ago; it did not frighten her. What she feared was the loss of love. What place would there be for her in the X-Men if she were merely human? Would Remy love her—or would he move on to someone else—a fresh challenge for his vaunted Cajun charm?

Who would she be, if she was no longer Rogue?

She repressed a yelp of dismay as the mechanical arm began to move, rotating through two dimensions to hover just above her left arm.

There was someone else in the room. The atmosphere changed, as suddenly as if a stormfront approached.

"Good evening, Rogue. I trust you're fully recovered?"

Sinister walked into her angle of view, as calmly as if he were still being Arnold Bocklin in Berne. He took the cluster of dangling tubes into his hand and pulled gently, as though they were the strings of a bouquet of balloons. Working with the careful precision of a master scientist, he began carefully sliding the long hollow needles into the veins of her arms and neck. Rogue set her teeth. She would not give him the satisfaction of her reaction. Her skin crawled away from the burning intrusions, from needles expressly designed to penetrate her near-invulnerable skin.

She would *not* cry. And there was no use in begging an inhuman monster like Sinister for anything. He wasn't even doing this out of a spirit of vengeance. Only efficacy and science motivated the once-human creature.

As he worked, incredibly, Sinister began to speak.

"Permit me to expound upon a pet theory of mine in what may be your last moments of life, if you will," Sinister said. "Have you never wondered about the peculiar nature of the human mutations which surround us? The lack of pattern, of order, that it represents? Is this, we must ask ourselves, a commonality with the patterns of nature? In the animal realm when a mutation appears, it spreads throughout the population through genetic transmission if it is favorable, or at worst irrelevant to the animal's survival. The mutant dies if the mutation is lethal or self-destructive. And so the species evolves toward one perfectly adapted to its environment, able to change, if slowly, to meet the demands of a changing world.''

Rogue had not realized it was possible to feel more helpless, more frightened, but it was. *He's crazy. He's about to kill me—if I'm lucky—and here he is, lecturing little ol' Rogue like he's some kind of TV science teacher!*

''Compared to the bewildering variety of human mutations,'' Sinister continued, ''animal mutation is a simple, even elegant, process; conservative and ruthless, as nature always is. It offends all sense of order, of balance, that one species out of all the daily-fewer that populate this teeming cesspit we call home should respond differently to the touch of nature's merciless hand.''

''Do tell,'' Rogue managed to choke out. She could barely force herself to pay attention to his words, but the one thing she remembered about Sinister from the X-Men's clashes with him was his twisted but scrupulous sense of fairness. Maybe there was something in this demented lecture that could show her some way out.

Sinister smiled—encouragingly?—which was somehow more frightening than anything that had happened yet.

''And so, naturally, I sought for some commonality in all the vast spectrum of human mutation, some linkage to explain this seemingly senseless diversity. And I discovered it. There is only *one* constantly-recurring human mutation, my dear Rogue, and only one: self-actualizing homomorphism. To simplify it to even the level of your childish understanding, you have chosen—as each mutant on this Earth has—to be exactly what you are. Somewhere between conception and maturity, each of you makes this choice, impelled by what forces that drive the magnificent engine of human evolution I cannot say. Each mutant blossoms forth according to his or her nature, in a variation of the human template visible or invisible, explicit or hidden, to take his place as an architect of blind nature's steady groping toward the next step in evolution—the true *homo superior*: the superman.''

Rogue continued to strain against her bonds as Sinister spoke. She could feel the needles moving in her veins as if the metal were made of fire. As her muscles flexed, tiny drops of blood began to well up at the entry points.

Sinister continued to speak.

''And now the key is in my hands. To unlock the riddle—to direct the evolution of the race, to guide nature's hand, to erase the misfits and false starts that her method produces and replace her stumbles with the sure direction of a master intellect. I alone will guide the development of the race to come—and erase nature's freak show from the pages of history. I shall destroy mutantkind as humanity has come to know it—and then, when the time is right, I shall destroy humanity as well.''

Rogue wanted to say something, to hold his attention a few precious moments longer, but she could think of nothing after what Sinister had said. *She* controlled the form of her own mutation? *She* had chosen to be as she was—a lethal, destructive, untouchable, pariah?

How could anyone believe that?

What purpose could it serve?

Rogue! Hold on!

A voice. Phoenix's telepathic voice. The X-Men were here! Rogue allowed herself a small glimmer of hope.

Then she felt a faint vibration through the surface to which she was bound, as though an explosion or impact had occurred somewhere far away.

Sinister looked up as if someone had called him.

''And here, appropriately enough, are your hopeful rescuers. Unfortunately, the X-Men's arrival forces me to deny myself the pleasure of observing your miraculous transformation, but the procedure is thoroughly automated . . . and I will have other opportunities.''

He paused, looking down at her with a proprietary fondness that made Rogue's skin crawl.

"And now, I suppose I should greet my new guests. Who knows what marvel of transformation awaits them?"

"Heads up, people," Cyclops said as the *Blackbird* settled to rest. "We don't know what we're facing, but it's likely to be rough."

He popped open the hatch. "Phoenix, Gambit, Wolverine—get to Rogue. Beast, Psylocke, stay with me. We cover the others as long as we can, but we don't know what we're up against. Storm, keep the action local—I don't want to see any reinforcements or escapes if you can help it."

"Understood, Cyclops," the regal windrider said. There was a ragged chorus of assents from the other five X-Men.

"Okay, team, let's move," Cyclops said.

Pipedream stared numbly down out of the cage he crouched in. It was shaped like a giant birdcage, but the thin metal bars would not bend or break. The cage was not large enough to stand upright or lie at full length in; you had a choice of sitting cross-legged on the solid disk of the cage's floor, or crouching or kneeling. He'd found that rotating through all the possible positions was best. He'd had several hours to consider it, once the drugs wore off.

He'd never really been unconscious. He thought Lloyd had made a break for it, but the next time Pipedream had seen Lloyd, the Woofster had been wearing a bright red union suit . . . just like the rest of them, though they each got a different color. They'd been brought inside the cement bunker and separated, turned over to a bunch of guys in surgical scrubs. Everything they owned had been taken away, and they'd been re-dressed in these leotards that made them look like a *corps* of crazed ballet dancers.

Pipedream looked down at himself. He wished he'd at least been allowed to choose the color. Powder blue. It

made him look like a . . . he didn't know what. Slapshot
was in navy blue, Rewind was in bright yellow, Charade
in purple. And Lloyd was in red, which reminded Pipedream irresistibly of long underwear.

It was funny, the things your mind fixed on when you
knew you were going to die.

"Hey, Lloyd, you awake?" Pipedream whispered. Lloyd
was the one hanging nearest to him.

Lloyd raised his head and looked at Adam. His eyes were
sunken in their sockets, and there were dark bruises beneath
them. He looked five years older than he had Monday night.

"Tol' you not to call me that, Pipedream. M'name's Red
Rover now."

"Okay, Rove." If Lloyd wanted to be called Red Rover,
Pipedream wasn't going to argue. Besides Lloyd—Red
Rover—was in the worst shape of any of them. His ankle
had been broken, and even sheathed in skintight insulated
spandex, it looked swollen and painful. It also meant that
the only position that Red Rover could really assume in his
cage was to lie curled up on his side.

"We've got to get out of here, right?" Pipedream said.
He wasn't sure he really believed in the possibility of escape, but lying here silently waiting for their captors to
return was more than he could stand.

"Talk to Slapshot. *He's* the leader," Red Rover said
sullenly. He put his head back down on his pillowed arms
and closed his eyes.

Pipedream groaned to himself in a combination of exasperation and pity. He couldn't even do anything for Red
Rover—he'd tried giving him a pipedream a few hours before to make things easier for him, but his initial attempt
resulted in shooting pains all through his head. There was
something about these cages that made using their mutant
powers extremely painful.

He looked around the room, searching for answers once
more.

The five cages were suspended at various heights, but none less than thirty feet off the floor. The room was enormous—the ceiling had to be sixty feet high, and the room itself was immense—and equipped like a mad scientist's lab from the 23rd century, with filters and centrifuges and electron microscopes and something that Pipedream was pretty sure looked like the DNA sequencer he'd seen in his textbook in school. The lights were dim, and the addition of people in hanging cages gave the whole place a weird gothic chamber-of-horrors overtone, like the Island of Dr. Moreau.

Pipedream wondered who'd built this place, and for what purpose, and then decided he'd just as soon never know.

Red Rover and Pipedream were suspended on one side of the room, Slapshot and Rewind directly across on the opposite wall, and Charade at right angles to the rest of them. If he wanted to get Slapshot's attention, Pipedream would have to shout. He wasn't quite sure he was ready to risk it.

As Pipedream looked off into the distance, a red light flared where there had been no light before. It was a string of numbers—and as Pipedream stared at it, it resolved itself into one of those digital clocks, the kind that showed hours, minutes, and seconds.

01:00:00

For a moment he thought it was showing the time—it might be that late, or that early—but of the five of them, only Red Rover had a really acute time-sense, and he'd stopped answering that particular question a while ago.

The numbers shimmered and resolved again.

00:44:45

The seconds flicked methodically past.

00:43:59

It wasn't a clock.

00:43:15

It was a countdown.

"Jase?" The word emerged from Pipedream's throat in a strangled whisper, as though the silence of this place had substance and weight. "Slapshot?"

"Shhh-h!" Slapshot hissed. "Don't you hear it?"

Pipedream strained against the silence, but he didn't hear anything, not even the clicking of the digital clock as it ate the seconds and minutes. Was this place driving all of them mad?

"Slapshot?" he called again.

"Hit it, Rewind!" Slapshot said, over Pipedream's words.

Pipedream saw Rewind get to her knees, her face furrowed in concentration. She reached out her hands to the bars, not quite touching them. A faint silvery corona began to grow from her hands, and soon the bars were glowing. Rewind's face was contorted in pain—she obviously felt the same shooting pains Pipedream felt when he tried to use his powers, but she managed to work through it.

But Rewind makes time run backwards. How's that going to help? Pipedream wondered.

The cage began to rock, forty feet above the cement floor.

And now Pipedream heard the sound—no, more of a vibration that seemed to come through the cable that suspended the cage itself, as if somewhere else in this building explosions of tremendous force were being detonated.

Both Rewind and Slapshot's cages were glowing, now, as their occupants yanked them back and forth through space and time.

And far below, a stoppered beaker of green liquid was teetering on the edge of its table. In another moment it would fall.

They'd found a door leading in to the bunker, and the X-Men's field leader didn't seem to be in any mood to mess around. Motioning the others to step back, Cyclops opened

his visor and turned the irresistible power of his optic blasts
loose at maximum strength on the thin fissure where the
halves of the door met.

Nothing happened.

Where the ruby shaft met the door there was a radiance,
almost as though the light were splashing back, but nothing
else.

Then, slowly, the surface of the door began to change.

First the metal started to pale in a ring around the site
of impact. Cyclops didn't let up. The air around him began
to heat until the other six X-Men felt as if they were standing in the doorway of a blast furnace.

The surface of the door now resembled cottage cheese.
Heat radiated from it in waves: its surface was white-hot,
the friction-heated metal having passed all the way through
the spectrum into pure colorless incandescence.

And slowly, impelled by irresistible force, the door began to soften and bend inward.

An excellent party trick, comrade mine, but Mrs. Mc-
Coy's favorite child fears that once the recalcitrant portal
has made its final bows, the after-theater special is going
to be Roast X-Man Au Jus. The Beast stood behind Cyclops, trusting to strength and luck to save him from any
flying shrapnel. The heat was killing, and his furred hands
and feet were slick with sweat. He wondered how Scott
could stand it.

Overhead there was a sudden wild banshee howling, and
the top of the bunker was haloed in light.

"Cyclops!" Storm cried.

A giant helicopter rose slowly like some monstrous sen-
tinel above the roofline of the bunker. The X-Men could
not see inside, but the four who had fought Black Team 51
in Washington recognized a plasma cannon mounted on the
stealth copter's undercarriage among the racks of missiles.
They could see the lights begin to race along its barrel as
the cannon powered up for its first shot.

Storm raised her arms to the heavens. The weather elemental was at her most formidable as she summoned her birthright; her hands were gloved in lightning, and the X-Men nearest to her stood away as she flung a wind freighted with bone-numbing arctic chill at the molten door.

Cyclops swung his head back and up. The brilliant crimson of his optic beam sheared through the darkness, clipping the barrel of the plasma cannon off as if it were made from spun sugar. The impact flung the helicopter backward in the sky, and the X-Men could hear the sound of its engines howling out of synch.

At the same instant, Storm's arctic blast hit the white-hot metal of the door, and it shattered like glass as its temperature plummeted a thousand degrees in seconds. Storm rose into the sky to finish off the helicopter, as Phoenix's telekinesis made short work of the shattered wreckage of the door.

"Let's *go*!" Cyclops shouted.

Wolverine was the first one through the opening, running down the exposed corridor as if he had a destination in mind. Phoenix flew above him, the low ceiling keeping her only inches above Wolverine's head. Gambit pounded after them, intent on Rogue's rescue.

Cyclops waited a dozen heartbeats and plunged after the first three, Psylocke and the Beast at his back.

She was alone with her worst nightmare. A mortuary chill seemed to spread outward from the drug that was slinking through her veins, leeching away her *self*.

Rogue did not want to die, nor to be changed. She strained against her bonds, but was it already too late for escape to save her? Was she already weaker?

What had Sinister said? She knew he'd spoken nothing but the truth when he described the treatment's effects. Think!

"*There is only one constantly-recurring human muta-*

tion . . . you have chosen—as each mutant on this Earth has—to be exactly what you are. . . .''

Was that the key? Did he mean that somehow Rogue had chosen her own hellish isolation, doomed herself to be an outcast?

Did he mean she could choose it again—now, when it might mean the difference between freedom and slavery for all the X-Men?

Something wasn't right here, Phoenix thought. Other than the chopper outside, there'd been no opposition to their penetration of Sinister's sanctuary.

''Heads up!'' Wolverine shouted, putting on a burst of speed.

Blast doors were sliding out of the walls, sealing the X-Men in. She'd spoken too soon.

Phoenix heard the buzzsaw sound of Cyclops's energy beams clearing the way behind them. With her telekinetic power, Phoenix reached through the wall to the mechanism moving the doors, and fused the machinery. The doors directly ahead of her stopped moving, but there seemed to be more closing the corridor ahead, and no way of being certain which door Rogue lay behind.

The almost-imperceptible drone of the ventilating system ceased, and a heartbeat later a malignant hissing replaced it, as heavy yellow vapor began jetting from the thin strip of grille near the ceiling.

''*Jamais de la vie!*'' Gambit flung a handful of ball bearings first left, then right. They struck the gas jets with a sound like machine-gun fire, and the yellow vapor stopped—even from the jets Gambit had not touched.

But so has the ventilation, Phoenix thought. *We could suffocate in here. Time enough to worry about that later— when Rogue is free.*

There was a sound up ahead like someone dismantling a Buick with a crowbar dipped in nitroglycerine. Wolverine had reached the next set of doors and was clawing his way through them.

Suddenly the lights in the corridor went out.

"We got company!" Wolverine shouted.

It was like some live-action version of Dungeons and Dragons, Cyclops thought as he swept the corridor behind him with his optic blasts. Their ruby glare illuminated a bizarre vista—faceless men in black with silvery high-tech weapons. Phoenix and Psylocke both glowed, but their bodies and his force beams were the only source of illumination in the corridor, and likely to continue to be so.

"Sinister!" Cyclops cried. He wasn't interested in spear carriers. He wanted the main event—the man himself. All the Black Team did was slow them down, keeping them from reaching Rogue.

"Beast! Hold them off back here!" Cyclops shouted over the noise of battle. "I'm going to clear the way up front!" He heard the Beast shout something in assent, and the hiss of Psylocke's psychic knife and a cry when it found its target. He turned and ran toward Phoenix and the others.

He located Gambit by the handful of glowing cards the Cajun mutant held. "We got a problem, us, Cyke!" Gambit shouted, and then flung his cards forward.

But instead of the explosion Cyclops expected, the kinetically-charged cards fizzled and died as they reached their target. Cyclops heard Wolverine swear in disgust, his voice thick with effort.

"Phoenix! We could use some more light on the subject!"

In answer to Cyclops's call, the corridor brightened. Phoenix was on the ground, her body a pillar of light. The three X-Men stood facing something that looked like nothing so much as a wall of black Ping-Pong balls, filling the corridor from floor to ceiling.

It absorbs everything we throw at it—worse than the

doors—it just moves out of the way of Wolverine's claws— we can't get past it! Phoenix's voice said in his mind.

Let's turn up the heat, then, Cyclops sent back. *Phoenix, on my signal—hit it with everything you have . . . now!*

At that moment, Phoenix and Cyclops both attacked the wall. Seeing what they were doing, Gambit moved up and placed his hand against the yielding surface, forcing his mutant power to kinetically charge the floating spheres.

The wall held for ten seconds . . . twenty . . .

Then, suddenly, it reached its limit. Now-inert spheres flew in every direction as the wall simply disintegrated.

Behind it, a machine gun opened fire.

Phoenix flung up a telekinetic shield as the slugs sprayed off it, flattening against the walls and ceiling into silver-dollar-sized disks of lead. The machine gun was emplaced behind a shield-wall at the juncture of two corridors, its fusillade—fearsome though it was—serving only as a covering fire until the energy weapon beside it had powered up.

"I'm not asking you to surrender this time—" Keithley's amplified voice came from behind the blast shield, loud enough to be heard even over the din of battle "—but I'd just like to take this opportunity to point out that you X-Men are trespassing illegally, vandalizing government property and endangering government personnel. Your activities are being recorded, and—"

"Go!" Cyclops shouted at the other three. "Find Rogue!"

He turned his optic blasts against the hail of bullets.

It was easy to call in the snow, here among the mountains, harder to keep it away. But Storm knew—if the Goddess were with them—that they would need to leave more swiftly than they had arrived, and the *Blackbird* could not lift off if it were covered in ice.

Warily the windrider wove the strands of the weather,

calling forth from the potentialities at her command a cold clear night, in which the setting moon flamed golden and the stars sparkled like gems on black velvet. As good for their enemies as for them, but in a twenty-mile sweep of the area, Storm had seen nothing of Black Team 51 or any other hostile forces. In fact, the only signs of human life she'd seen at all was a small town, barely a dozen buildings, with the burnt-out wreck of a commercial jet lying just outside it.

Its passengers—if any—were obviously long beyond help, but Storm landed anyway, just to check.

The logo—still visible on the tail—was that of CGI— Sinister's minions. Storm approached the fuselage carefully, unwilling to believe this was a coincidence. Sinister's allies might be waiting here in ambush.

But there was nothing. The interior of the plane was gutted with the swift flashfire of its kind, but no one had been inside when it burned. Storm turned away, wrinkling her nose at the smell of charred synthetics. The fire was hours old—nothing to do with their attack upon Sinister's stronghold, for all that it had come from his allies.

There was someone lying in the street.

She could not see the entire body—only the outflung arm, its white skin ghostly pale in the moonlight—but she could smell the blood, even in the chill of the night. Cautiously, Storm stepped toward it—why did she already think of this as a corpse?

When she reached it, she realized that instinct had not lied. The body was nearly decapitated, but the cut had not bled. The blood—and the death—had come when the body cavity had been ripped open. The internal organs, like strange and dusty fruits, had been scattered in the street along the arc of attack.

Wolverine could have done this, Storm thought unwillingly. But that was not quite true. Her comrade was as deadly and savage a predator as any found in nature, but he was no wanton murderer, killing for the sheer joy of it.

And such thoughts are useless. He was not here to have done it, in any event.

But there were others whose attack pattern mimicked Wolverine's, and many of them might be in Sinister's employ—sent to his aid, as the wrecked airplane indicated. Indeed, one such person, Sabretooth, used to be one of Sinister's Marauders.

She needed to search for survivors before she rejoined the others.

Rogue strained against the invisible enemy with all her heart. She had to accept what she was—wish for it.

Strong, powerful, free. . . .

The chill spread through her body.

Isolated from every human touch.

But not from love! Rogue cried in her heart. *Not from friendship, redemption, change. . . .*

As long as I live, I can hope.

The door blew inward as though it were made of wet paper. Gambit, Wolverine, and Phoenix stood framed in the wreckage.

"No," Phoenix whispered. "Oh, no."

Gambit's face bore the look of a man who was seeing hell. "Rogue . . ."

But Rogue did not hear them. The cold had filled her flesh, her heart, her spirit. It was ending, the ultimate annihilation, despair. Darkness.

But she could still choose. Choose to be what she had been, embrace what she had hated and feared the most.

And she could hope.

Like the kindling of creation, like the spark in the heart of a newborn star, the embers in the center of Rogue's soul blazed up anew, fuelled by her unyielding will. Light—warmth—power rushed through her body with the pulse of her blood.

She opened her eyes, straining against her bonds. The unbreakable alloy cut into her skin, but she barely felt it. The strap across her chest came loose from the table with a sound like tearing silk.

Rogue sat up, ripping the needles from her arm and then the tubing loose from the mechanical arm above. She favored her rescuers with a sunny smile, bending forward to tear loose the rest of her bonds.

"I don't get it," Phoenix said. "Weren't you . . ."

"Y'know what they say, sugar—the South will rise again!" Rogue vaulted off the table, grinning from ear to ear. There'd be time enough for detailed explanations later.

Gambit started toward her, but Rogue waved him off. Without the protective layers of her costume, she dared not touch him. She blew Gambit a kiss instead and grinned.

"C'mon, fellas, let's *dust* these suckers! An' I got me an extra-special date with Mr. Keithley!"

The beaker fell.

Pipedream watched it fall, knowing that even if the object *was* in motion, the cage kept Slapshot powerless to affect the direction of its fall.

But that was no longer the case.

Rewind lay back against the bars of her cage, gray-faced and panting. But the combination of the tidal stresses of her power and Slapshot's had short-circuited both their cages' power.

The beaker fell *up*.

"Careful . . . careful . . ." Pipedream heard Slapshot mutter to himself. Pipedream didn't know what was in the beaker and neither did Slapshot, but he was willing to bet that it wasn't something anybody wanted to pour on themselves.

The beaker swung off at a wild angle.

"Pipedream!" Slapshot called. "You want to be Play-Mutant of the Month?"

Pipedream stood up as well as he could in the cramped confines of the cage. "Sure!" he shouted back, though he had no idea what Slapshot had planned.

"Here's the deal." The explanation came in disjointed phrases, as Slapshot focused on keeping the beaker in the air.

As Pipedream had thought, without knowing what it contained, he dared not use it to attempt to smash the mechanism that held each cage suspended in the air; once it was broken, the beaker's contents would rain down on the cage's occupant.

But Slapshot could use it to set in motion an object that he *could* use.

The beaker hit the worktable like a returning space shuttle, spraying glass and liquid everywhere. An overturned Bunsen burner crashed to the floor, igniting the fuel around it into a lake of ghostly blue fire.

And a centrifuge near the middle of the table rocked slightly.

It looked like an ice cream maker on steroids, a mass of brushed chrome about the size of a portable CD player. But once it began to rock it didn't stop, jerking spastically on the table like an extra out of *Ghostbusters*. Grinding sounds came from inside it. Seconds later it reached the edge of the table.

And fell.

The room filled with oily smoke from the spilled materials on the table. A piece of copper tubing had torn loose from the wall, and Pipedream could smell the hissing of gas. Propane fumes were heavier than air, and there was a fire on the floor. As soon as the fumes reached the flames, there'd be an explosion.

By now the centrifuge was hurtling through the air, banging off the walls like a hyperkinetic meteor. Slapshot's face was drawn and intent.

"Peyton—come on! Adam—now!" he shouted.

"Go, Cavaliers!" Rewind shrilled. The Kirtland Cavaliers were their football team, and for an instant Pipedream thought she'd lost her mind.

Then he found out what she meant.

The centrifuge slammed against the cable of Pipedream's cage where it entered the ceiling. The cage whipped around on the end of its tether—Pipedream felt as though he'd been sacked by the entire opposing line.

Then the centrifuge hit again—and again—settling quickly into a trip hammer beat.

Just like the go-cart back in Atlanta, Pipedream thought, clinging for his life to the sides of the cage. Once Slapshot had delivered it, all Rewind had to do was replay the moment of impact. The cage was swinging back and forth in a broad pendulum arc. Rewind didn't let up. Something would have to give.

Something did.

The cage dropped several feet as the cable unwound, and then things got worse. Slapshot grabbed it. Pipedream felt his prison fall *up*, descend with a yank, and then try to fly in every direction at once.

And then it did it again.

He thought he was going to be sick.

"Look out!" Charade squealed.

There was a huffing noise, a dull soft boom, and a wave of heat washed over Pipedream's skin.

And at the same time the outside door blew open.

Things were not going well, in Keithley's opinion. Unlike their last several encounters, this time the X-Men had a free hand and a clear field. Just minutes ago, Storm and Cyclops had taken out one of their major assets, Black Betty. Now Storm had disappeared, but Cyclops and Phoenix had destroyed—in short order—their employer's Absorption Wall and the Team's only remaining plasma cannon—wounding two members of the Team and nearly killing Keithley, a loss that he found personally unacceptable.

With the destruction of the cannon and the loss of the heavy machine gun, there wasn't much else in inventory here at the Retreat that could even part the X-Men's hair. The remaining machine gun could take out Gambit, maybe, if they could get a back shot, and they might be able to wound Wolverine if they used a chain-shot loaded bazooka, but the thought of a wounded Wolverine made even Keithley shudder.

Nothing was going right tonight. For another thing, what was wrong with the Retreat's defenses? There were several more layers of automatic defenses—each supposed to be triggered by the failure of the last. Keithley had signed off on the work himself eight months ago; the best anti-paranormal array that money could buy. Lasers, sonics, poisoned darts . . . it ought to stop half the heroes operating today and slow up anybody short of the Hulk.

So why wasn't it working?

He would haved liked to worry about that, he really would, but just now Keithley had other, even more pressing concerns. Like the fact that their employer's plot—something that had depended for its success on absolute secrecy until it had gone into effect—was about to be a front-page story in the *Washington Post*.

Of course, Sinister might still pull off his coup and gain his legislative fiat. The research was sound, the process had a high degree of success, and Sinister had engineered the death of Stewart Chisam's mistress at the hands of Psychostorm less than a year ago; the senator would push for his legislated revenge. Public opinion ran heavily against the X-Men at the best of times; survive this, and Sinister might be just in shape for a countercoup.

On the other hand, Keithley had just gotten word that the Team in Atlanta had suffered heavy losses today from an unknown source that had gotten in and trashed most of the manufacturing and testing complex. Between that, and the fact that the Team hadn't been able to find Crown Clarendon and sign off on him, it was pretty clear that any details Sinister might wish to have remain secret about his research would no longer be so.

In short, Project Level Playing Field was no longer an acceptable hazard of Black Team 51's resources.

It was time to withdraw.

There were no survivors.

Storm lost count of the victims, even as a picture of the violence that had been done here grew in her mind. The attacker had come on the plane. The corpse she had seen in the street was the first inhabitant of the village who had encountered him—or her. The villager had died quickly, but not without giving the alarm.

The attacker had moved quickly, searching for something as the village roused around him. Each time he had encountered someone he'd killed, using a weapon that slashed like a broadsword. Searching.

He'd found what he was searching for in the livery stable.

The small mountain town no longer kept horses in the building that still bore the painted legend DESPERATION LIVERY above its double doors. The livery stable had become a garage of sorts, with tools and a lift. There was a car in one of the bays, its hood open for repair.

The hood was spattered with buckshot, punched through here and there with rifle bullets. The windows had been shattered. Blood mixed with the broken glass.

And arcs of blood blanketed the walls like paint thrown by a fractious child. The people of Desperation thought they'd cornered their nightstalker here, but the hunters had been cornered instead. Three men and two women, armed and wary, had died here, their shattered bodies flung into the corner of the barn with a contemptuous gesture toward order. Storm found the murder weapons here, too, tossed upon the bodies like an afterthought: long, narrow sickle shapes, clotted with gore, shaped to be worn over the arms. The work of a professional somehow connected with CGI, but she already knew that.

The predator had been after transportation—Storm saw the bloody tire prints of a motorcycle heading in the direction of the street. There were boot prints along side the tire marks, outlined in red. Too small for a man.

A woman, then.

Run if you will, but I know where you have gone, Storm said to herself. *And your madness ends here.*

Rising into the sky, she headed for Sinister's lair.

Cyclops was worried. From long years as the X-Men's field leader, he knew the rhythm of battle as well as his own heartbeat; it had a tidal ebb and flow as the enemy assessed the threat you posed, and positioned his resources accordingly.

That was not the way this fight was going.

The seven of them—eight now that Rogue was back in the field—had faced Sinister before, and they knew his style. The rogue geneticist didn't rely on brute force—the power Sinister could wield was still an unknown quantity to the X-Men—but he was always well supplied with offensive mechanisms and powerful allies. He'd known he'd be facing them ever since he'd begun this mad plan, and certainly since he'd kidnapped Rogue earlier this evening.

So where was he? Even the hired help was nowhere to be seen at the moment—once Cyclops and Psylocke had destroyed the machine gun nest, they hadn't seen any of their ultra-stylish adversaries. In fact, with the paltry exception of a few floating mines, the opposition was minimal. The lights were even on, now that they'd gotten past the outer ring of defenses.

"I don't get it," Cyclops said, coming to a halt. The X-

Men had penetrated deep within Sinister's sanctuary by now, past the armored doors and blast shields intended to keep out intruders. "If we walk out of here with Rogue, Sinister loses big time. He's here; Rogue saw him. What's the point of luring us here if we just walk out again?"

"Perhaps," the Beast said, "we're not expected to walk out. 'Come into my parlor, said the spider to the fly'. . . ."

"A bomb?" Cyclops began, but the Beast held up one massive, taloned hand.

"Listen."

It was a sound like a berserk washing machine on spin, and it was coming from the other side of the wall. But no one was there: the other X-Men were free, and Storm was heading back from her sweep—upset about something, Phoenix had said, though what it was wasn't clear.

"There's someone trapped in there," Cyclops decided.

It might be a trap, but he could not take that chance. There was a door a few yards up the corridor; he ran to it and focused his optic beams on it. Here, at the heart of the complex, the door tore like paper—but as he blasted, he felt a pulling ache behind his eyes; the mutant equivalent of a low fuel dashboard light. He didn't expect his optic blast to cut out on him anytime soon, but it would be running weaker from now on.

The Beast bounded through the opening as soon as it was made, and a moment later Cyclops heard a strangled sound of dismay. A wave of foul air, reeking with the smell of propane, burning, and spilled chemicals, rolled out through the door. Her clenched fist glowing with the power of her psychic knife, Psylocke plunged after the Beast.

There was a crash as something fell.

Jean! Get here as soon as you can! Relay to Storm! Cyclops followed the other two in.

They'd reached Sinister's lab, but it looked like somebody'd already been here. Most of the apparatus atop the

long tables was smashed, and there were several large dents
along the walls as well.

The ceiling was hung with cages filled with kids—five
of them—the oldest of them looking to be no more than
seventeen or eighteen.

"Hey!" the black girl in the purple leotard whooped.
"It's the X-Men! We are outta here!"

"That's right," Cyclops called. *Nice to see somebody
happy to see us for a change.* "We'll have you down from
there in a jif."

"Be careful," the teen wearing powder blue warned. His
prison looked more battered than the rest. "There's a gas
leak."

"Oh, come *on*! It's the X-Men, Pipedream—they are too
cool," the girl in purple said.

"Well, could they be cool *later?*" the blonde in yellow
demanded. "Those other guys might come back."

"Don't worry, Rewind," the boy in the cage next to her
said. "We'll be out of here in a moment."

Rewind? Pipedream? Cyclops didn't recognize either the
costumes or the code names, but explanations could wait
until they were all out of here. Like Hank had said, this
entire base might be a booby trap ready to go off at any
moment.

Just the way these kids might be enemies in disguise.

"One at a time," Cyclops said aloud. He took aim at the
fraying cable holding Pipedream's cage aloft, and severed
it with a focused pulse of his optic beams. Pipedream
yelped in alarm, but the Beast was waiting below to catch
the falling prison. A moment later, Pipedream was free;
with the power source destroyed, the bars had shredded in
the Beast's massive fingers like licorice sticks.

"Not his best work," the Beast muttered, almost to himself.

"Thanks," Pipedream said shakily.

"Beast! I need you!" Cyclops barked.

"Allow me," Phoenix said. Another optic pulse, and Re-wind's cage drifted gently to the floor, caught in Phoenix's telekinetic grip.

Cyclops met her gaze and the Beast saw Phoenix shake her head slightly. He relaxed slightly—as far as Phoenix could tell, these wondertots were no threat.

"Get Jason down—he's our leader!" Rewind said ex-citedly. "Um, I mean Slapshot. Sorry, Jase."

"No problem," Slapshot said, grinning with relief. "But be careful with, um, Red Rover," he said, pointing. "He's hurt."

"I'll take care of him," Rogue said, bounding into the air. "Hel-lo, sugar. You in the mood for a li'l rescue?"

"M'ankle's bust," Red Rover said. His face was drawn with pain and exhaustion.

"Jus' don't touch the merchandise," Rogue warned, tak-ing hold of the cage. His body was covered, but his hands and face were bare—and she was without sleeves or gloves. A touch could transfer Red Rover's power to her, and leave him unconscious, crippled, or worse.

Holding the cage in one hand and the cable in the other as she hovered, Rogue pulled until they parted company, then gently lowered the cage to the ground.

Gentle as she was, however, Red Rover groaned as his ankle was jarred.

"Wolvie! I could use some help over here!"

"Sure thing, darlin'," Wolverine growled. Extending his claws with a ratcheting sound, he sheered away the top of the cage like the shell from the top a three-minute egg.

Red Rover looked up at Wolverine, his pale eyes flaring in the dimness. The repugnance on his face was plain, and Cyclops watched, stunned, as Red Rover bared his teeth at Wolverine.

"Hey there, easy, bub. We don't got nothin' t'fight over. I'm not after your pack." Wolverine raised his hands, palms out, and backed away.

"I . . . sorry," Red Rover said, flushing. "It's just . . ."

He doesn't like the way Wolverine smells, Cyclops realized in astonishment.

"Allow me, my young colleague in arms," the Beast said, plucking Red Rover out of the cage. The boy hissed in pain as the Beast lifted him upright.

"Mister, you smell like a wet dog," Red Rover gasped through gritted teeth, clinging to the Beast's fur.

"I shall accept that as the encomium it very nearly is, my dear colleague," the Beast said grandly.

By now the occupants of the other four cages were all on the ground as well.

"Now," Cyclops said to Slapshot. "Briefly—what's going on?"

The young Vietnamese hesitated, but only for a moment. "A genetic research lab—CGI—kidnapped us from Cleveland. They've got this program to turn mutants into human beings—and we're all mutants."

"Yeah," the girl in purple said. "And we're superheroes, too!"

"As if we haven't been, like, totally cured of the impulse," the blonde in yellow drawled.

"Charade, just—don't say anything, okay," Pipedream suggested weakly.

"Why don't we blow this joint and go home?" Red Rover said.

"Gambit secon's dat t'ought." An unlit cigarette dangled between the thief's lips, but he knew better than to either light up or charge an object in a room with an ruptured gas line.

"Um . . . hello?" Rewind said. She sounded frightened. "Does that mean anything?" She pointed.

00:22:59

On the opposite wall, a countdown still ran.

"Time to *go-o-o-o—!*" the Beast said, glancing toward Cyclops for confirmation. "My apologies in advance, *com-*

padre—but this is going to hurt.'' He lifted Red Rover, cradling the lad in his arms as he prepared to run.

"Oh, *gross*," Rewind moaned. "It's a bomb!"

"That's the way to bet," Wolverine shot back.

"Guys!" Slapshot snapped. The three members of the Ohio Mutant Conspiracy who were still on their feet—Rewind, Charade, and Pipedream—moved toward him.

"C'mon, people—let's move!" Cyclops said to the X-Men.

"Cyclops!" Phoenix cried. "Storm can't get in—the entrance is gone!"

"Well, dat put de icin' on de brass cupcake," Gambit said unhappily.

Storm battered the outside of the enormous bunker with icy gale-force winds, but she could find no access, nor any sign of the killer who had laid waste to the town of Desperation. The doors that Cyclops had destroyed to gain the X-Men entrance had vanished as if they had never been.

No entrance—and no exit for her teammates.

Riding the spiralling winds, Storm circled the bunker. There was another field half the size of the first one on the other side. The helicopter Storm had wrecked earlier was scattered across the area, and the space was alive with activity.

Black Team 51 seemed to be leaving.

A road of sorts led up to the stronghold on this side: the fence had already been dismantled, leaving a clear path of escape. There were half-a-dozen ATVs pulled up on the tarmac, and the area was swarming with men—carrying wounded on stretchers, dragging handcarts of salvaged weaponry.

There must be an entrance on this side, Storm thought—but to swoop down among them would only lead to a combat she did not have time for. If they were leaving, let them run. To trap them here would be to doom them when the bomb that Phoenix suspected had been left for them detonated. The important thing was to forge a path of escape for the X-Men and Sinister's other prisoners. She would find another entrance if she could.

While most of the bunker's levels were below the surface, the uppermost story was banded with windows. They were certainly designed to repel any possible assault from without.

But here—high in the Rocky Mountains—were they designed to withstand a tornado?

Storm intended to find out.

Summoning the whirlwind, the mutant elemental wrapped the upper tier of the bunker in a vortex that quickly escalated beyond the scope of the worst twister Earth had known since the days of its primordial infancy. The tempest sucked greedily at the panes of glass with the voracity of absolute vacuum, the relative pressure of the air inside increasing by the moment. Something had to give.

The windowpanes popped free, the glass lozenges—each weighing several hundred pounds—skimming the wind like demonic Frisbees. The contents of the rooms they had sheltered followed in their wake—papers, furniture, materials, doors—nothing that could be torn loose was immune.

Its purpose accomplished, Storm sent her vortex spiralling off to drop its tons of debris far from here in some safely desolate location. Then—on a wind that was a zephyr in comparison to the hurricane she had recently wielded—Storm lofted herself in through the opening she had created.

CHAPTER 15

"This way," Phoenix said.

Joined by Phoenix's psi-link, Cyclops and the others were already heading in the direction of the upper levels. He was glad to see that the kids seemed to be doing okay, though he could tell they were nervous. He doubted they'd been a "mutant superhero group" for more than a month, if that.

But everyone had to start somewhere, and the kid in the dark blue—Slapshot, their leader—appeared to be steady enough.

Cyclops waved the others on ahead, bringing up the rear himself. There'd be no stragglers, no one left behind. They had less than twenty minutes to get everyone on board the *Blackbird* and clear the blast area.

There was no time for a single misstep.

It had been a trap, a feint—and she'd fallen into it. The moment she'd stepped into the Auxiliary Control Room the exit had sealed and the air begun to grow foul. Mantrap pounded on the console with the pommel of her Bowie knife, but force couldn't change facts. Above the useless consoles, a scarlet LED clock was up and running, counting down to something unpleasant. An explosion strong enough to rock the complex in these subterranean levels plunged the decoy Auxiliary Control Room into darkness for a moment, and when the lights came back on, all the consoles were dead.

But there must be something here that communicated with the Master Control Room, or it would not have known to trap her. Mantrap pulled a K-bar from its sheath. Its edge was razor sharp, but that wasn't what she wanted it for. Using the heel of her hand as a hammer, she began to wedge the thin end of the blade into cracks in the housing. If she couldn't get out any other way, she'd take the entire place apart.

She wanted out of here. She wanted to find Bocklin, wherever he was.

And make him die.

"Storm!" Phoenix said in relief, catching sight of the wind-rider.

Storm's stern visage softened. "My friends!" she said, her voice husky with relief.

"Yeah, 'Ro, we're all here, so let's see about leavin' before the dawn comes up like thunder an' takes us with it," Wolverine growled. "We're on the clock."

Slapshot looked dubiously out the window, to the two-story drop onto bare concrete.

"Don't worry," Phoenix told him. "The X-Men are experts at this." Slapshot smiled back, but not as if convinced.

"Storm—Rogue—make sure nobody's gotten to the *Blackbird*."

The two women launched themselves through the opening where the window had been.

"And now, if you'd be so kind?" Cyclops said to Phoenix.

"Gladly," the redheaded telepath answered. "Beast, you'll go first. Don't want to jar the patient."

Carefully Phoenix lifted the Beast and Red Rover into the air, lowering them gently to the concrete.

"Thanks, Red, but I'll find my own way down," Wolverine muttered. He placed his hands on the sill and vaulted through.

"Same goes for me," Psylocke said, diving through in a forward roll.

"And—I think—I can manage this," Slapshot said. He climbed to the edge of the window and stepped off into space.

"Slapshot!" Charade squealed, bouncing to the edge and leaning precariously out.

Slapshot fell like a stone, and the Beast hurriedly set Red Rover down and moved to catch him. But it wasn't necessary. At the last moment, the young mutant's fall changed direction: he fell upward, the change of vector cancelling out his previous momentum, and bounced the last few feet to the ground.

"That's some trick, my dear companion," the Beast said.

"First time I ever did it," Slapshot confessed. "It worked!"

"Yeah, well, don't get cocky, kid," Wolverine snapped, stepping out of the shadows none the worse for a two-story fall. He looked up, to where Cyclops, Gambit, and Charade were floating to the ground, cushioned by a wave to telekinetic force. Phoenix stood in the window above. She spoke for a moment to Rewind, and the young blonde leaped into a handstand in the window, cartwheeling out into space.

Catch, Hank! Phoenix's voice said in his mind.

As the Beast bounded to catch her, Phoenix and Pipedream made their descent.

The *Blackbird*'s engines started, loud in the stillness. How long until the building blew? Cyclops wondered. If they could trust the timer, they'd had a little over twenty minutes, and at least seven of them had passed by now.

He waved the other X-Men forward. He didn't like the yards of open space they had to cross. Anything could happen.

"Wait," Wolverine said, turning back the way they'd come. "There's—"

A figure stepped out of the shadows.

Red Rover dragged himself to his feet, using Pipedream as a crutch. There was a faint grating sound as Wolverine popped his claws. ''Mantrap,'' he said bleakly.

She took a step toward him, hesitantly.

Storm settled to the ground beside Cyclops, staring at the intruder. ''In the town,'' Storm whispered. ''She killed them all.''

The scent of blood came off Mantrap's skin as if she'd bathed in it. The black suit was soaked in it; the strands of hair glued to her skin were outlined in red. Her feet left broken red prints on the concrete.

''Go . . . away,'' Mantrap said. Her voice was slurred, hoarse, nearly unintelligible, but the gesture she made with her bloodied knife was unmistakable. ''Want Bocklin. You go.''

Something was not right, Wolverine realized. From all he knew of her design imperatives, Mantrap should not be able to choose not to engage, even outmatched and gorged on slaughter as she obviously was.

''So this is what those so-called scientists have created of my work,'' a loathsomely familiar voice said from the opposite direction. ''How typical of a race mired in super-stition and wallowing in ignorance. As it has been truly said, 'the sleep of reason begets monsters.' ''

Suddenly the field was bathed in an actinic glare as floodlights surrounding the field woke into light. Beyond the transports, the radar-invisible skin of the *Blackbird* had a plum's dusty sheen in the unremitting glare.

Sinister and his two transports had appeared out of no-where, between the X-Men, the Ohio Mutant Conspiracy, and the *Blackbird*—making a crude but effective barrier between them and their only means of escape. The field was also ringed by tall gawky tripods with jointed legs—cybernetic machine gun platforms, waiting to slash the X-Men to ribbons at Sinister's command. Boots rattled on the concrete as the troopers in the transports debarked, and a whine of turbos on the still air heralded the sound of still more reinforcements.

Rogue and Storm launched themselves into the air.

He's outplayed us, Cyclops thought with a sinking heart. *He meant to meet us here all along—keep us from leaving. And we've got too many hostages to fortune to risk an all-out fight.*

Mantrap growled, circling wide around the X-Men to approach Sinister.

For the moment he ignored her.

"I have a few last adjustments to make on my process, before it is quite suitable for use on the large scale. No doubt my unsound young associate will have informed you of the complexity of the retro-mutagen's delivery system. I believe I have addressed these problems with this new version."

Sinister held a bulky fragile weapon against his chest. It looked like a cross between a laser rifle and a Gatling gun, and had an ammo-belt feeding it that contained long rows of transparent vials filled with milky blue liquid.

"If'n it works as well as the old one, Sinister, we haven't got a thing to worry about," Rogue crowed, landing between Cyclops and Sinister. "Because you tried it on me—an' it didn't work!"

Sinister smiled. "On the contrary, child, it works superbly—some of the time. Perhaps you were lucky once—do you care to try the odds again?" He lifted the rifle into firing position. "Submit to my experiment, and all of you are free to go. Except you, Cyclops—and you Gambit—but each of you has always known this, have you not?"

He was going to use it anyway, Cyclops realized. Sinister could hit most of them with a single sweep. He could see more footsoldiers lining up behind the transports. The moment any of the X-Men moved against Sinister, the kids would be cut to pieces.

And if they didn't move, the children would be sacrificed as well.

Trapped.

"No," Mantrap said. When she spoke her voice was clear, and for a moment she sounded nearly human again. "I won't let you use that, you . . . fraud."

Sinister recoiled, as if he'd been mortally insulted. The man's arrogance was Luciferian. That weakness might be the only card the X-Men had left to play.

"This device, genetic barbarian, holds the power to unmake you, to return you to the primordial ylem from which I raised you. Kneel to me if you wish to live."

Mantrap charged.

Sinister fired.

The rifle's payload hit her just below the collarbone, stitching her chest with the blue vials of retrovirus that discharged their cargo before she batted them away. She staggered back, dropping the knife she held.

The mercenaries flanking Sinister raised their rifles.

"I don' t'ink so," Gambit said. "I t'ink it is payback time, me."

A flurry of charged cards flew from Gambit's fingers like a shower of meteors. Most of them missed, but one of them struck the barrel of Sinister's rifle, knocking it from his hands.

The X-Men and the young mutants scattered. Storm filled the air with flashes of light. Mantrap lunged, but not for Sinister. Instead, she grabbed his rifle by the barrel and swung it like a club. He grappled with her for it, but Mantrap would not release her hold. For a moment they stood poised—Mantrap was Sinister's dark mirror: all appetite, passion without restraint. As perfect a betrayal of all that was noble in the human psyche as Sinister's merciless intellect was.

Then Sinister and Mantrap vanished.

And in that instant his commandoes opened fire, and the

empty stretch of concrete was transformed into a war zone.

"Get the kids to the plane!" Cyclops bawled over the sound of the guns. "Psylocke! Make sure it stays flight-ready!"

The British ninja saluted and vanished into the smoke of battle.

For an instant it was still possible to separate the good guys from the bad. Cyclops swept the opposition back, using his optic beams like a giant broom. Sinister had retreated. They'd make it out of this one more time.

They had to.

For an instant Slapshot was paralyzed by the sounds of gunfire, his mutant senses overloading with information about the vector and speed of a thousand moving objects.

Time to go. "Charade—Rewind!" he yelled, his voice cracking with the force of his shout. "Go!" He waved them left—toward the fence, away from the battle—and then onward toward the plane. He knew enough to realize that none of them could be much help in a fight—Charade and Pipedream's powers were useless, Red Rover was hurt, and Rewind was already tapped from short-circuiting their cages back in the lab.

As for him, he'd be lucky if his slapshot power was enough to cover their retreat.

Rewind grabbed Charade and started running.

"Pipedream!" Slapshot turned on him. "Hit Red Rover up—now!"

"What?" Pipedream's face went blank.

"He can't run on a broken ankle—unless he doesn't know it's broken." Did all leaders think their plans were this ridiculous?

"Yeah!" Pipedream said, getting the idea.

"Do it," Red Rover said, his voice ragged with pain.

Slapshot saw Pipedream falter—of all of them, Adam was the least confident of his mutant powers—then suddenly the air between him and Red Rover seemed to shimmer, and all trace of pain vanished from Red Rover's face. The two of them began to run.

That leaves me to cover them. The night air was icy, the bone-chilling wind intermittently accelerating to a gale that could knock a man flat. It was so noisy he couldn't hear himself think: the roar of explosions, the dazzling flash of energy beams, everyone shouting at once. He wondered how the X-Men could hear themselves think, let alone hear orders in this din.

Not my problem. Not this year.

A bullet spatted into the ground just in front of him. Slapshot stared at the bright smear of lead for a transfixed instant but there was no time to react. He reached out, touching each of the hurtling projectiles, moving it just enough to miss. Almost there. Red Rover was running as though his foot had never been hurt, Pipedream holding him by the arm.

Chessman was not happy. First Black Team 51 was ordered to pull out, then ordered to support the employer, who'd decided that the top of a ticking bomb was a great place to rehearse *Dies Irae*. Well, he didn't know what Keithley's opinion was—or, for that matter, *where* Keithley was—but he knew he was pulling his Team out of here in no more than five minutes despite anything the client might have to say and heading east as fast as the hovercraft could take them.

Then he saw the hard target.

The kid was wearing a dark blue leotard and standing as though he were admiring the weather. Chessman lifted his rifle and looked through the telescopic sight. Jason Gerber, one of the loose ends. Definitely.

Time to say goodnight, slinky-boy. This time I won't miss.

Chessman squeezed the trigger.

• • •

The others were almost there. Slapshot forced himself to run after them. Bullets whined around him, but he was concentrating on the others, keeping the fire away from them. And each time he grabbed for one he was a little slower.

Then he tripped over something, the impact sending him sprawling full-length to smack into the concrete. His concentration faltered, and suddenly he had no control over the flying bullets.

He reached back, touching his thigh. And felt the blood.

Far below, Storm saw the young mutants scattered across the concrete, but there was nothing she could do to help them. Sinister's forces were trying to cut off their retreat by destroying the *Blackbird*, and Storm was stretched to her limits deflecting the missiles being launched at it. Psylocke was in the cockpit, bringing the engines online as fast as she could—she could use the *Blackbird*'s defensive systems to save it, but not without power.

Jean! The children need help!

The stink of cordite and blood almost overwhelmed Wolverine's sense of smell, making it hard for him to sort out the players on the battlefield. There was one thing he was sure of, though, and that was that Sinister was playing least in sight.

This was going sour, Wolverine could feel it. Too many liabilities, not enough assets, and laser towers surrounding them that were doing a good job of cutting them to pieces. The *Blackbird* had already taken a couple of hits—she couldn't take many more and get them out of here.

That was something he could deal with.

Four down, two to go. Phoenix bore down on the fifth tower, running a mental assessment of the X-Men's soundness.

Wolverine was badly hurt, Gambit less so. Rogue was battered—nothing more—and Psylocke was safe inside the plane. Hank's agility and the fact that his fur was perfect camouflage had saved him so far, and she'd been shielding Scott as much as she could. She and Ororo were unhurt, though Ororo had relayed that one of the kids had been shot, she didn't know how badly.

Phoenix wished she could break off to protect them, but if she didn't take out the cybernetic towers, nobody was going to be leaving. And Black Team 51 was staging a fighting retreat. This battle could probably be seen and heard in Atlanta.

A web of lasers locked on her as Phoenix flew close enough to the tower to be perceived as the primary threat. She strengthened her psychic shield to take the strain, but they'd been fighting against every diversion Sinister could hurl at them for almost an hour, and the strain was beginning to tell.

Phoenix knew she had to stay sharp. Any lapse of attention could kill her.

She reached out through her own shield, and gripped the inner mechanism of the war machine with intangible fingers. And—slowly, her teeth gritted with the effort—Phoenix tore the gun platform apart. In the last moment, the strain forced her to drop her shield, and the lasers—now running at half-strength and flailing wildly—raked her across the legs.

The shock was enough to send her crashing to earth.

She did not hear Storm's cry.

Blood and chips of bone flew from Pipedream's chest. He staggered back from the force of the bullet as though he'd been punched, pushing Red Rover away from him in reaction. He stared down in incredulity as too many things happened at once. Then he began to fall.

· · ·

One second . . . five seconds . . . ten. . . .

They were almost there. Rewind turned back to see how far the others were behind them.

She saw Pipedream fall.

Bullets sprayed around them. Rewind shoved Charade to the ground.

I've never seen everything so clearly, Rewind thought through the gathering chill.

Fifteen . . . twenty . . . half a minute. The floodlights made everything sharp. Pipedream's blood was bright red against the light blue fabric, horribly real. He wasn't moving.

"*No!*" she cried aloud. Rewind turned back, away from the plane, *reaching* for Pipedream as she ran to him.

Forty-five seconds. . . . She fell to her knees beside him. The blood was warm, and she recoiled in revulsion. But she didn't quit.

Rewind pulled at the fabric of time, her heart hammering like a mad drummer's solo. Dragging Pipedream back to a time before the bullet.

Sixty seconds. One minute.

And Pipedream was on his feet, staring down at Rewind with jumbled memories fading. He stood staring down at himself, whole and alive and clean, and the place where the wound should be . . . wasn't.

Rewind collapsed.

She rolled to her back, clawing at the yellow leotard across her chest. Her mouth was open in surprise. It felt as if someone had hit her in the chest with a hammer. She gasped for air, but there wasn't any. It had all been driven from her lungs by the crushing pain of a heart that had suffered a mortal insult. Her legs splayed out awkwardly, and she began to thrash, her body fighting its death for a few seconds more.

• • •

"Peyton! *Pey!*" Pipedream screamed.

Nothing else mattered; Pipedream knelt and cradled her body in his arms, but she was gone, her body cooling and stopping even as he held her.

So nice, we'll do it twice, Chessman thought. Everybody was down but the other blue-boy. He squeezed the trigger again.

Storm had seen the shots fired, seen the children fall. She flung the last of the missiles from the air with a wild gesture. She saw the blood, bright against the concrete, and a fury that seemed to grasp her from without like a crushing hand took possession of her.

The sky swarmed with clouds that were blacker than the night, churning with flashes of eerie blue flame. An instant later lightning roared down out of heaven in a cascade so awesome that its strikes melded into one column of sheer power.

She pointed her finger at Chessman.

"Homeboys finally gettin' some smarts," Rogue muttered to herself. She could see Psylocke in the cockpit of the *Blackbird,* and the shimmer of the defense screens. *Time to go*—if the lot of them weren't lifting off within five minutes, nobody was going home.

The other side knew it, too; they were pulling back, concentrating the last of their efforts not on the X-Men, but on the *Blackbird.*

Which was where Rogue came in. She saw a mortar round lofting overhead and rose to it like a Major League outfielder. Her hand tingled as it slapped home, and she flung it back with the killer overhand pitch she'd learned playing softball. Bullets sprayed off her skin, and she anxiously searched the firefight below for her comrades. Everyone wasn't blessed with invulnerability as she was.

Suddenly there was a deafening explosion—a whipcrack

of sundered air—and a light as bright as a hundred suns appeared in the middle of the compound. Charade screamed like a rabbit in a snare, the high keening sound blending with the shrill howl of incoming shells. She'd seen Pipedream shot, and Rewind had shoved her to the ground as she'd turned. It had saved her life, but the unfriendly fire was coming closer. And she was no longer sure which way to go.

Wolverine had heard Storm's shout. He turned and headed in the direction of the kids, only to be slammed to the concrete by a hail of bullets across his chest. He felt his lungs fill with blood, as they were crushed inside him, and concentrated on surviving the next few minutes until his healing factor could work the bullets back out through his skin and close the wounds.

He heard a frying sound, and brilliant light burned through his eyelids. Storm, playing to the gallery. He wondered what had set her off—'Ro usually liked to hold back and use minimum force.

She missed a lot of fun, Wolverine thought fuzzily as his senses dimmed. *Live hard, play hard. . . .*

Leave a beautiful corpse.

This was no place for an honest thief, Gambit thought as he twirled his bo-stick in his left hand. His right arm was almost useless; nicked by the stray bullet that had sheared through leather and battle-suit and flesh. His fingers were numb; he'd used his left hand to tuck the right into a pocket to provide some support. There was a medical kit aboard the *Blackbird*—Gambit had a feeling he wasn't going to be the only one needing it.

He slapped the length of his stick down on one armored head and prodded another chest. Each time, the glowing metal rod discharged its kinetic potential as an explosion that effectively silenced the opposition.

He glanced over his shoulder, and saw Rogue running

interference for their ticket home. Despite the gravity of the situation, Gambit grinned. Rogue was safe, and that made Gambit a very happy man. He stole one more glance in the direction of the *Blackbird*, and began working his way in that direction.

Time to go.

The pipedream had shattered as Lloyd fell to the ground, and for a moment the pain was so extreme that he could barely breathe. Tears blinded him as he gasped for air; whatever he'd done to the ankle while he'd been wrapped up in Pipedream's fantasy, he didn't think he was going to be able to walk on it any time soon.

Then he heard Charade screaming. Her arms were wrapped over her head, and in the few minutes his mind had been fuddled, the tide of the battle had shifted.

Now it was heading right toward her.

Red Rover began to crawl toward his teammate.

"Jean!" In the midst of his own battle, Cyclops saw his wife fall. There was no way to judge how badly she was hurt, or to reach her across the inferno of battle. Cyclops gritted his teeth and fought on. Keeping the *Blackbird* in one piece long enough for them to retreat to it was the important thing now.

The good news: Black Team 51 knew about the bomb and had no intention of being caught in the blast. The bad news: the closer they came to disengaging, the heavier the weapons they deployed. Fortunately, Cyclops thought he'd destroyed their last plasma cannon—and Sinister and his drug-delivery system were gone. Without those two hole-cards arrayed against them, it was only a matter of time before the X-Men carried the field.

The trouble was, they didn't have time.

• • •

Red Rover reached Charade. He could feel her trembling, too frightened to speak. They couldn't stay here.

"Charade! Davetta! *Vette!*" He slapped her, shook her, anything to get her attention, and finally Charade opened her eyes.

"The plane!" Red Rover shouted, shoving her to her knees. "Get to the plane!"

"I can't!" Charade wailed. "Peyton—Adam—"

"This was all your idea, girl," Red Rover said desperately, not listening to what he said as long as it made her move. "You were the one who wanted to be a superhero! You can't punk out now—you want to get us all killed? Move it—*go!*"

With a startled sob, Charade staggered to her feet. She looked around wildly for a moment and then began to run for the boarding ramp of the plane.

It began to rain.

Red Rover curled on the tarmac, hugging his pain to himself.

Storm swept their foes backward with her wind-blasts, almost not caring if she hurt them. Intellectually, she had accepted long ago that to don an X-Men uniform was to choose to become a target for all the violence the madmen of the world could provide. But these young mutants—by their own words—had not chosen this life. She glanced down at them, just as the storm she had called broke into rain, feeding on its own fury.

One last task to perform.

His leg had gone numb and he was freezing. Slapshot huddled against the side of the wall, looking back at the trail of blood he'd left getting here. The blood wouldn't stop.

He had to do something about this, but he wasn't sure what. He was freezing to death, and everything seemed eerily fuzzy.

A *tourniquet.* Slapshot began fumbling for his belt. Making his hands do what his mind said was weirdly difficult, and it was only as he looked down that he realized he was wearing some kind of blue jumpsuit, and not his own clothes at all.

Oh, yeah. They took our clothes away from us. And put us in these insulated suits. So if I'm wearing something insulated, why am I freezing?

The blood had soaked through the entire leg of his leotard. He could see the exit wound welling scarlet; it felt cold running over his skin, hot when he touched the skin around it. He'd only been here a few minutes, and he was already sitting in a spreading pool of blood.

It isn't like this in the movies, a faint part of himself insisted plaintively. *You didn't die of being shot in the leg.*

But he was. He was dying. That was probably why he felt so cold, too. It gave him a weirdly exalted feeling to lay here and know it didn't matter how the battle came out, because he'd never see it. To know with supreme clarity that he was dying, and know he could do nothing about it.

He looked toward the plane, and saw Charade run up the ramp. One safe, but where were Pipedream and Rewind? And . . . oh, what's his name. Lloyd. Wonder Dog. Something.

The Conspiracy could have been good. Slapshot's mind skittered over random things as the darkness closed in, but he clung to that thought. *We could have been good.*

Suddenly he saw one of the X-Men flash down—the redhead in the blue and yellow—and pluck Red Rover up off the tarmac. He flailed weakly in her arms. Alive.

Two safe. Slapshot felt a faint spark of pride.

If you had asked him who he was in those last moments, he would have told you his name was Slapshot. In that moment he was what all five of them had aspired to be.

Hero. Leader.

And now Jason Gerber was leading his fallen teammates to one last sanctuary.

•   •   •

Wolverine opened his eyes, feeling himself being dragged along. The furry blue arm of the Beast circled his back, dragging him upright.

"S'alright, Fuzzy. I c'n walk," Wolverine growled. The pain in his chest was a faint constricting sensation now, and the bullets had worked to the surface.

"Excellent, my ferocious friend," the Beast snapped with unwonted asperity, "But at the moment we need to run."

"Phoenix!" Rogue's voice was frantic.

Phoenix looked in the direction of Rogue's voice. She was still on her feet—no thanks to the fifth watchtower—but she was striped with laser burns from hips to knees, and the pain made it difficult to concentrate.

"It's Gambit!" Rogue pointed.

The reason for Rogue's agitation became clear. Gambit had been cornered—backed against one of the transports—and there was nothing Rogue could do to save him. The assault hadn't harmed Rogue physically, but laser fire had torn her costume almost to shreds in spots. Too much flesh had been exposed for her to risk getting near Gambit, or anyone else.

"Allez-oop, Gambit!" Phoenix called. She telekinetically whisked the Cajun into the air, ignoring Gambit's startled curse. Weariness dragged at her very bones—she'd been battling since early this evening in Washington—but she would not let her teammates down.

"Rogue! Take care of that last tower for me, would you?"

"With pleasure, Phoenix!" Rogue sang out. She flashed through the air like a green-and-gold missile, intent on her prey.

There was no time to be gentle. Phoenix slung Gambit through the open hatchway and hoped he landed safely. The Beast crossed the open ground in enormous leaps, carrying

Wolverine under one arm like a loaf of bread. He dropped his cargo—none too gently—at the foot of the ramp and bounded inside.

Overhead, Storm was fighting to dissipate the tempest she had raised. Rogue was hunting for Cyclops, and for a heart-stopping moment Phoenix could not locate him, but at last his brain-pattern shone out clear and alive.

The Beast came back down the ramp.

"The kids! Only Charade made it! Jean, where are they?"

"I'll find them!" Phoenix cried, frantically. Before either of her teammates could stop her, she took to the air, searching.

Rogue arrived, bouncing a little with the force of her landing. "Hey, folks—we gotta be goin'," she jittered, her gesture taking in the now-deserted battlefield and the bomb only instants away from detonation.

"Kids're missin'," Wolverine said laconically.

"I've got one!" Phoenix said, landing again with Red Rover's body in her arms.

"One?" the Beast asked, before he could stop himself.

Phoenix's agonized glance was all the answer he needed.

"Lord—no," the Beast said in a soft stricken voice.

"Back there," Phoenix said in a dull, drained voice.

"We ain't leavin' 'em," Wolverine said flatly.

The moment he saw Rogue cradling Slapshot in her bare arms, Cyclops knew.

His jaw tightened, but he said nothing. Now wasn't the time for words. The *Blackbird*'s engines were revving, seconds away from lift, but they'd need every second they could steal to escape the blast.

And Sinister had slipped away again. For what he'd done here tonight, Cyclops would gladly have killed him without a second thought.

Next time you don't walk away, Sinister. I swear it.

"Go on," he said to Rogue, waving her up the ramp.

"One last thing, X-Men," Chessman said from behind him.

Cyclops turned.

Chessman was still here.

He was battered and bleeding, his white shirt soaked with blood. In one hand he held a machine gun, its muzzle pointing toward the ground. He must have stayed behind when the others had evacuated, for reasons of his own.

He was ten yards away. After the beating Cyclops had taken tonight, the X-Men's leader wasn't sure he had enough reserve power to take Chessman down, and Storm was busy clearing the sky of the remains of her own vortex. The others were inside, and before Cyclops could summon any of them, Chessman could empty his entire clip through the hatchway into the *Blackbird*'s interior, smashing it beyond use.

Then Mantrap stepped out from beneath the fuselage and walked toward Chessman. Her footprints were liquid with fresh blood and her skin was coated with red. One hand was pressed against her stomach, and Cyclops could see the glitter of fresh blood welling through her fingers.

"One last thing," she said, her tone an echo of Chessman's own.

"Genejoke," Chessman snarled.

Mantrap bared her teeth in a bloody smile.

"Not anymore." She drew a breath that pulled and rasped in her throat.

"The only thing a totalitarian regime needs in order to triumph is the sanction of its victims. Go, X-Men. Save yourselves."

"We—" Cyclops began. *We can't just leave you here.*

Appearing behind him, Wolverine put a hand on Cyclops's arm, silencing the X-Men's field leader. Silently he pointed back toward the interior of the *Blackbird*.

Risk the many on a chance of saving the one? She was

already dying. And Cyclops didn't have that option. He never had. He stepped back.

The boarding ramp of the *Blackbird* rose behind him.

As it began to move, Chessman swung his weapon up.

Mantrap crouched and flung herself at him. Chessman fired.

When the bullets hit her, Mantrap simply leaned into them, slowed but not stopped. Fresh blood welled from every wound, mixing with the blood of her victims.

But this time, the wounds did not heal.

The *Blackbird* rose straight up on a cloud of frost and dust, the howl of its turbines blanketing even the sound of the gunfire. Mantrap fell at Chessman's feet.

"Stupid—" he began, drawing back his foot to kick her.

Mantrap reared back, the bright needle-thin blade flashing in her hand.

Chessman's scream was the last sound the battlefield heard.

The fire welled up from deep below the surface of the earth, carrying the installation upon its shoulders for a brief moment before it began to consume them. As the surface cracked, the smaller pieces flew outward in a meteoric hail of destruction.

Storm did what she could to contain it. The *Blackbird* rode upon a tailwind of her creation, and sleet, ice, and hurricane fought to slow the explosion's destructive spread.

In the pilot's seat, Cyclops stared sightlessly eastward, riding the buffeting wind of the blast-front with unconscious ease. Had they won? It didn't feel that way.

Psylocke got to her feet and walked to the back of the jet. Wolverine slid into the copilot's seat. His uniform was shredded, but the flesh beneath was hale and whole.

"It's better we left her," Wolverine said shortly, as though they were continuing some previous conversation.

"D'ya think she coulda lived with what she did if Charley coulda put her head ta rights?"

Cyclops had no answers.

Suddenly, out of the darkness ahead, a pale image coalesced, shimmering like a candle flame.

"Sinister!" Cyclops exclaimed.

The radio woke into life, in response to a transmission of unknown origin.

"Farewell, X-Men," the hated voice said. "The battle is yours, but the game—as always—is mine."

The hologram rippled and vanished as the *Blackbird* passed through it. The X-Men flew due east, away from the birth of a star.

CHAPTER 16

t was Monday morning in the nation's capital, the day of the final vote on HR-485, the Emergency Intervention Bill. And preceding that vote, an event unprecedented in the history of Capitol Hill—a nationally televised open hearing on not the legality, but the morality of the new compulsory medical treatment legislation.

"—this is Trish Trilby, live from Washington, D.C. In just a few hours, the fate of mutant Americans across the nation will be decided by a joint vote of the House and Senate on the controversial bill that will make it illegal to be a mutant. The candlelight vigil here on the Mall continues, as it has since Saturday night—folks, I wish you could see everything that I'm seeing from my helicopter—Billy, can you take us down closer?—this is surely the world's largest-ever gathering of mutants, and—well, I guess you'd have to call them superheroes, though there's a lot of costumes down there I don't recognize, Ivan. What does it look like to you? Let's go to Ivan Gale, down on the ground—"

"Well, Trish, I'd have to say heroes and villains; I recognize several very famous faces from the FBI's Most Wanted List here, but I have to say there are a lot of ordinary folks, too. It's the most peaceful gathering I've ever seen, and—"

Crown Clarendon tuned the reporters out, and fidgeted in his new suit. He'd been cooling his heels here in this anonymous Capitol Building Green Room all morning, and once he went through that door into the hearing chamber, he'd be facing wall-to-wall politicians armed with nothing more than a laser pointer and a box of slides. The television that was *not* showing Trish, Ivan, and the crowd on the Mall was tuned to C-SPAN4 and showed the hearing chamber on a split screen—alternating between shots of the podium and scans around the chamber. The Hearing Chamber was jammed to overflowing—Crown had lost count of the witnesses who had already spoken, but Henry Peter Gyrich of the NSA and the former Avenger Dr. Henry McCoy had been among them. Someone else was speaking now, answering questions from the committee in charge of the hearing. Soon it would be his turn.

Crown dragged at his collar.

"I think I'm going to be sick," he muttered.

"You'll be fine," Roberta Everett said briskly. She'd already spoken, reporting the FDA's conclusions about CGI's treatment, but all the witnesses were being held until the end of the hearing to prevent a media feeding frenzy. "Just go and tell them exactly what you know about the production and testing of the retro-mutagen. That's what you're here for."

He also might be the last person standing who had any understanding of Bocklin's work, Crown reflected. He'd spent the weekend locked up in a hotel room with a bunch of Secret Service agents determined not to let him hear anything, but when Professor Xavier and Laura Severn— and several agents of SAFE, the very same nascent government organization that offered him a job way back when—had come to get him this morning, he'd gotten a quick update filled with some not-very-nice news.

Like the fact that somebody'd trashed CGI sometime Thursday—for which he fortunately had an alibi. Like the fact that his supervisor, Arnold Bocklin, not only didn't exist, he'd been a cover identity for some immortal super-villain.

Like the fact that of the five kids he'd helped rescue Tuesday night, three were dead and one was in a hospital somewhere.

Crown glanced away from Bobs, toward Charade. She was wearing a white blouse with a black sweater and skirt, and was sitting hunched over in a chair next to one of their other protectors. Crown couldn't even begin to imagine what kind of strings had been pulled to let the X-Men be here, but they were all over the place, including standing as silent guards on the ends of the podium. Somebody had told Crown that the guy over there in the corner behind Charade was named Bishop—personally, Crown thought he looked more like the Terminator . . . in a really, *really* bad mood.

"Mr. Clarendon?"

One of the SAFE agents touched his arm, and Crown jumped.

"You're on."

Half an hour later, he was back. Crown had no idea how his presentation had gone, only that he hadn't left anything out. Senator Chisam had asked most of the questions, and that part had been no fun at all. By the time the day was over, he'd probably be facing murder charges.

He came back into the green room followed by the X-Man called Phoenix—a babe redhead with eyes as cold as ice—who went over and knelt beside Charade's chair. Crown couldn't hear what she said.

Charade was only here to make a statement; there would be no questions afterward. Four X-Men—Phoenix, Storm, Cyclops, and Archangel—stood behind her on the stage, along with six armed SAFE agents.

The room was absolutely silent.

"Everybody else here today has said about how this stuff they're going to use on us is bad, like it would be okay if it just worked," Davetta Mantlo began, her voice wavery but true. She stood beside the podium in the hearing chamber, not behind it.

"But my friends are dead—and they died of your legislation, not from any treatment."

She clenched her hands in front of her, looking very small.

"We all went to Kirtland High School, in Cleveland, Ohio, and we're all mutants. I could make you believe me, but I'm not going to. You could go to the cemetery and count the tombstones." Her voice cracked, and she stopped. There was total silence as the audience waited for her to go on.

"The Center for Genetic Improvement in Atlanta kidnapped us to turn us into human beings. But we're *already* human beings. We're just different. You aren't supposed to lock up people and kill them just because they're different. But if you make this a law, that's what you're going to be doing. Your law says that people who are different don't have the right to choose what happens to them. It doesn't matter if they're sick—you say it's okay to kill people you don't like. Like Jason, and Pey, and Adam."

Her composure crumbled, and tears began to spill down her face. "So don't vote for it, okay?" Davetta whispered.

Phoenix came back to the microphone to lead her off the stage, but the mike was still live, and everyone in America heard her next words:

"We were just kids. That was all we were."

Charade was crying as she came back inside, her hands over her face. Crown got up to go to her, but Bishop shot a look at him and he sat back down. The monitor showed that the people in the hearing chamber were getting to their feet and leaving for their voting chambers.

It was over. They'd all—humans, mutants, superheroes—taken their best shot.

Now all that was left was to call the vote.

ELUKI BES SHAHAR also writes as Rosemary Edghill and is the author of over fifteen books, like eluki's "Hellflower" series and Rosemary's Bast novels, plus the occasional short story in places like *The Ultimate X-Men* (where she introduced Black Team 51) and *Alien Pregnant by Elvis*. From earliest infancy she has suspected mutagenic influences in her environment, and bought *Uncanny X-Men* #1 off the stands, thereby changing the entire course of her life. She thinks Scott and Jean should have gotten married *years* ago and has always thought the green costume with the skirt was silly. She is presently working on the third volume in the upcoming *X-Men and Spider-Man: Time's Arrow* trilogy, in collaboration with Tom DeFalco.

Born in Sao Paulo, Brazil, in 1976, **ROGER CRUZ** started out as a letterer for the Brazilian translations of Marvel Comics. His big break as an artist came when he was assigned to ink *The Executioner* for Innovation Comics, and also pencilled *Armor* for Continuity Comics and *Hyperkind* for Marvel. He joined the X-Men family of artists with *Uncanny X-Men* #315 and *X-Men: Alpha*, and currently is the regular penciller of the monthly title *X-Man*. He also provided the illustration for the Magneto story in *The Ultimate Super-Villains*.